The Girl on the Beach

MARY NICHOLS

First published in Great Britain in 2012 by
Allison & Busby Limited
13 Charlotte Mews
London W1T 4EJ
www.allisonandbusby.com

10 9 8 7 6 5 4 3 2 1

ISBN 978-0-7490-1106-2

Typeset in 11/15.5 pt Sabon by
Allison & Busby Ltd.

Paper used in this publication is from sustainably managed sources.
All of the wood used is procured from legal sources and is fully traceable.
The producing mill uses schemes such as ISO 14001
to monitor environmental impact.

Printed and bound by
CPI Group (UK) Ltd, Croydon, CR0 4YY

*To my husband, Bryn, whose D-Day adventures
I have 'borrowed'*

Prologue

Summer 1926

'Where is that dratted girl? Julie Monday, come here at once or we shall go without you.'

The last thing Julie wanted was to be left behind. The Foundling Hospital's outings were few and far between and this one promised to be the best yet. They were going to the seaside for a whole day and the weather was glorious. Breaking all the rules, she dashed down the stairs and ran pell-mell along the corridor to join her excited peers who were standing in line to board the fleet of motor charabancs that were to take them to Southend, girls and boys separately of course, each bus being looked after by a member of staff.

'Sorry, Miss Paterson.'

Grace Paterson, thin and stiff as a rake and with a back to match, had scraped-back grey hair and a severe expression, but all the children knew she was soft as butter inside and loved her, in as far as they were capable of understanding what love was. Few of them had known such a thing outside the orphanage or had any idea what a family home was like, although, to give them their due, the administrators, teachers and household staff did their best. The children all knew, because it was hammered into them every day of their lives, that they were the objects of charity and needed to be suitably grateful.

Julie, being eight years old, was aware of this but it could not subdue her natural exuberance. How someone who had been in the institution since birth had come to have such an independent spirit and capacity for mischief, neither Miss Paterson nor any of the other members of staff understood. According to the meticulous notes made on her admission, she had been found on the doorstep by one of the kitchen staff arriving for work at six o'clock one morning in July 1918. Wrapped in a thin blanket she was very underweight even for a newborn baby, and this one, according to the doctor who examined her, was about a week old. There had been a note pinned to the blanket. 'Husband killed in France. Can't cope no more.' A woman, who had recently given birth, had been pulled from the Thames that night and it had been conjectured that this had been Julie's mother, though there was no proof.

And so she had become one of hundreds of orphan children, the majority of them born of unmarried mothers, looked after by the home. Discipline was strict and punishment harsh, but the children were adequately clothed and fed and given the rudiments of an education. Besides the three Rs and religious instruction, they learnt a little of history and geography and, as they progressed, the boys learnt a trade and the girls learnt to be domestic servants. As soon as they were big enough to understand what was expected of them, they were given their allotted tasks: making their own beds, dusting, sweeping the floor, polishing, laundry work and helping in the kitchen. The bigger ones helped look after the smaller ones and so they became self-reliant at an early age, but at the same time remaining ignorant of matters the ordinary slum child grew up knowing: about having babies and learning to survive.

Julie was constantly being made to stand in the corner of the classroom or being sent to the governor for some misdemeanour or other, where she was either caned or locked in a cupboard for a few hours. Even though it hurt, she preferred the cane; the darkness and silence of the cupboard terrified her – she would do anything not to have to endure that punishment but somehow never managed to escape it. Ever since the news of the outing had broken two weeks before, she had been a model of rectitude, determined nothing would stop her from going. She had so nearly spoilt it all at the last minute by going to the sickroom to see her friend, Elsie, who was too ill to make the trip. 'I'll tell you all about it when I come back,' she had promised.

Miss Paterson ushered her onto the last coach, where the girls were crammed three to a seat intended for two, found her own seat near the driver, and the vehicle rolled away through the gates and onto the road. It was really happening. They were really going to the seaside. Some began to eat the small packet of sandwiches they had been given for their dinner, others were sick into the brown paper bags thoughtfully provided for them. Julie looked out of the window at the busy streets. There were shoppers hurrying along with baskets on their arms, children skipping, a dog tied to a lamp post, a gentleman alighting from a cab. A black cat sunned itself on a window ledge, which she took to be a sign of good luck. After a time the streets were left behind and they were in the open country.

Trees, fields, farm buildings, villages, cows, pigs and horses passed before her enchanted gaze, and then they were in a town again and there was the sea. A huge cheer went up from the occupants of the bus as it drew to a stop behind the rest of the fleet.

Julie had never seen the sea before. Grey and greeny-blue in patches, it was vast, stretching away in the distance to join up with the sky. There was a ship on the horizon, its two funnels belching smoke. It hardly seemed to be moving but she supposed it was going somewhere. It was not until she tumbled out with everyone else and was herded along the road that she saw the beach. Here was golden sand and hundreds of people enjoying themselves. There were donkeys being trotted up and down with children on their backs and kiosks selling ice cream. There were pools of water in which tiny children paddled. Bigger children were playing cricket or simply throwing a ball from hand to hand. Adults and children alike walked along the water's edge, laughing as it whooshed up to cover their feet and then was sucked back again. Further out heads bobbed up and down.

Julie stood and gaped, while those about her argued about what they wanted to do first. The older ones were all for going on the pier, where they hoped the threepenny piece they had been given to spend could be changed into pennies which would be multiplied in the slot machines. Miss Paterson remonstrated that this was gambling and wicked and she could not allow it, much to their disappointment. Others wanted an ice cream cornet and hurried to buy one from a man standing beside a tricycle with a large container on the front of which was written 'Stop me and buy one' in flowery script. Nearby was a tall, narrow, tent-like structure surrounded by an audience of children all agape at the antics of a puppet show. 'It's Punch and Judy,' Johnny Easter said. He had not been in the orphanage long and knew these things. Julie's group settled down on the sand to watch it.

She was soon bored with that and the sea was inviting her, so she wandered off on her own, right down to the water's edge. The first thing she did was to take off the starched white cap she wore and stuff it into her skirt pocket, the second was to sit down and remove her black button shoes and stockings. She carried them with her as she gingerly stepped into the water and felt the wet sand oozing between her toes. It tickled and she laughed aloud. A larger-than-usual wave rolled up and she had to run backwards to keep her dress dry. Other girls had tucked their skirts into their knickers and were venturing in up to their knees, and, greatly daring, Julie did the same with her brown cotton uniform. The water struck cold but she soon became used to it and turned to paddle along the shoreline, dodging the bigger waves as she went. So absorbed was she, she did not notice she had left the crowded part of the beach behind and was almost alone. Alone except for a boy who came up out of the sea like Neptune, dripping water, although she was sure Neptune was never dressed in a blue-and-white-striped bathing costume that clung ever so closely to his body.

'Hallo,' he said.

'Hallo,' she answered.

'Are you lost?'

'No. Just walking.'

'Where to?' He had dark auburn hair and soft amber eyes. She guessed he was about the same age as Johnny Easter and that was twelve, and though he was by no means fat, he had more flesh on him than Johnny.

'Nowhere. I just felt like it. The sea's lovely, isn't it?'

'Grand.' He walked up the beach a little way to where he had left a towel and a pile of clothes and sat down to rub his hair which sprang into little curls as it dried. She went and stood over him.

'What's over there?' She nodded across the water.

'Belgium and Holland, I should think.' He was vigorously towelling himself.

'Oh.'

'Haven't you got a towel to dry your feet?'

'No.'

'You can borrow mine if you like.'

'Thank you kindly.' She sat down beside him and took the towel he offered.

'What's your name?'

'Julie Monday.'

He laughed. 'Monday. You mean like the day of the week?'

'Yes.'

'That's a strange name.'

'It's on account of I was taken in at the hospital on a Monday in July, so I'm Julie Monday.'

'What hospital?'

'The Coram Foundling Hospital.'

'Never heard of it. Where is it?'

'In Bloomsbury, but we're going to move to the country soon.'

'Will you like that?'

She shrugged. 'Dunno, do I? It'll still be the Foundling Hospital, still an orphanage.'

'Are you an orphan?'

'I think so.'

'You only think so. Don't you know for sure?'

'I was left on the doorstep when I was a baby. They told me my father died in the war and my mother threw herself in the river and was drowned.'

The information had been imparted to her in a matter-of-fact way one day when she had had the temerity to ask why she didn't have a mother and father and she had accepted it philosophically. None of the other children had mothers and fathers, or if they did, they had no contact with them.

'How old are you now?'

'Eight.'

'My sister's eight but she's bigger than you.'

'What's your name?'

'Harold Walker – most people call me Harry.'

'Do you live here by the sea?'

'No, we're down for the week, staying in a boarding house. We live in Islington.'

'Who's "we"?'

'Me, my dad and mum, my brother Roland, who's ten, and my little sister, Mildred.'

'It must be nice to have a mother and father,' she said a little wistfully.

'Yes, I suppose it is. I never thought of it before.'

'And a brother and a sister.'

He laughed. 'Sometimes it is, but sometimes they are a pest, particularly Millie, that's why I like to come down here and swim by myself.' He paused. 'How about you? What brought you here?'

'We came in a lot of charabancs with our teachers. They were paid for by Sir Bertram Chalfont. We had thruppence to spend too.'

'Sir Bertram!' he exclaimed. 'I know him. My father is production manager at his factory in Southwark.'

'I saw him once, when he came to inspect us. He had bushy ginger whiskers and grey hair. He smiled a lot.'

'That's him.' He was putting a shirt and trousers on over his costume as he spoke.

'I suppose I had better be going back,' she said, standing up and pulling her skirt out of her drawers and shaking it out. It was sadly crumpled and, in spite of her care, stained with seawater.

He picked up his shoes and socks. 'I'll walk with you.'

They strolled along the water's edge in no hurry. He stopped and picked up a round flat stone and skimmed it over the water, making it bounce several times before it disappeared.

'That's clever,' she said. 'How do you do it?'

'It's a knack.' He selected another pebble and handed it to her. 'Here, you try. Keep the angle low.'

Her missile failed completely and disappeared under the waves. He showed her again, with the same result, and thus they proceeded back towards the town, skimming pebbles as they went. She was happy as a sandboy and did not notice the beach was emptying until they returned to where the Punch and Judy had been. The little tent had gone and so had her classmates.

'Where is everyone?' she asked, looking about her in dismay.

'I expect they've gone for their tea.'

'Nobody said anything about having tea.' She crammed her cap back on her head and scrambled into her stockings and shoes, though her feet were covered with sand, and began running up and down looking for someone she knew, growing more and more panicky. He followed and stopped her by taking hold of her arm.

'Don't go off half-cock. Stand still and think. Were you told where to meet if you became separated?'

'No. We weren't supposed to be separated. They've been and gone home without me. Oh, what am I to do?' She was very frightened but determined not to cry in front of him. Crying was frowned on by her teachers and, according to them, was a sign of weakness and achieved nothing. 'I can't walk all that way.'

'Don't be silly, of course you can't. Can you remember where the coaches were parked?'

'Up there somewhere.' She pointed to the promenade. 'They were in a long line.'

'I don't think they are allowed to stay there all day. I've seen coaches parked on a field on the edge of town. That's where they'll be. Come on.' He took her hand and obediently she went.

He was right. The field was full of charabancs, both motorised and horse-drawn, some of them crowded with noisy children. He led her from one to the next until she spotted Miss Paterson standing by the vehicle in which they had arrived and looking about her with a mixture of worry and exasperation. When she saw Julie the exasperation took over from the worry. 'Where have you been, Julie Monday?' she demanded, grabbing her by the shoulder and propelling her towards the coach. 'I was about to report you missing to the police and what a to-do that would have caused. Get in your seat and let us be off.'

Half in, half out, Julie screwed herself round to look back at Harry. 'Goodbye,' she called. 'Thank you.'

He lifted his hand in salute and turned away. Julie was

found a seat right next to Miss Paterson. The bus lurched and bumped over the uneven field and they were on their way, back to the city and the routine of life in the orphanage. And as far as Julie was concerned, back to her punishment.

'Who was that boy?' Miss Paterson demanded.

'He said his name was Harry. I forget his other name.'

'Where and how did you meet him?'

'Down on the beach. He was swimming. I couldn't find you. He helped me.'

'You foolish girl. Don't you know better than to talk to strange boys?'

'Why not?'

'Anything could have happened. You do not know him. He could be wicked, degenerate . . .'

'What does that mean?'

'Someone who knows nothing of decency and proper behaviour, an evil person.'

'He's not evil. He was kind to me and helped me when I was lost. He lent me his towel to dry my feet.'

'Merciful heaven! What have you been up to?'

'Nothing, Miss Paterson. I went paddling and my feet were wet and there was sand between my toes.'

'Do you mean to tell me you removed your stockings?'

'I wanted to paddle and I couldn't do that with my stockings on, could I?'

'Don't be cheeky, miserable rebellious girl. You were expressly told not to wander off. Have you learnt nothing of obedience? You will have to be punished. What a sorry end to what could have been a lovely day.'

'It was a lovely day,' she said, aware that everyone else on the coach was looking at her, goggle-eyed at her temerity. 'I made a new friend.'

'Don't be ridiculous. I don't suppose you will ever see that boy again. And a good thing too.'

'I know,' was said with a resigned sigh.

'I shall have to report your disgraceful behaviour to Mr Carruthers.'

'Oh no, please, Miss Paterson. He'll make me go in the cupboard . . .'

'You should have thought of that before. Now be silent. I have had enough of you for one day.'

Julie lapsed into silence, but it was not a silence of shame or remorse, it was a silence of happy recollections. Nothing they could do to her could stifle those.

'I met a girl on the beach today,' Harry said, after the waitress had served them all with roast chicken, stuffing and several dishes of vegetables, and left them to their meal.

'Don't you think you are a little young to be picking up girls, son?' his father queried with a smile, one eyebrow raised.

'She was lost.'

'Oh, you mean a little girl,' he said with relief. 'What did you do?'

'I helped her find her party. She'd come down in a charabanc from the Coram Foundling Hospital. I thought hospitals were for ill people.'

'So they are, but originally the word had a wider meaning and the Foundling Hospital is a very old institution.'

'She said she had been left on the doorstep when she was a baby. They told her that her father was killed in the war and her mother threw herself into the river. The hospital called her Julie Monday because she arrived on a Monday in July.'

'Poor child,' his mother murmured. 'How dreadful for her.'

17

'She didn't seem unhappy.'

'No, I believe the children are well looked after and she would not have known any other kind of life, would she?' his father said, frowning at Roly and Millie who had paused with mouths agape to look from one to the other in curiosity.

'No, I suppose not. The funny thing was she said the outing had been paid for by Sir Bertram.'

'I am not surprised. Sir Bertram is a good man. I believe he has recently been appointed to the Board of Governors of the hospital. It is a testing time for the institution. The present building has been sold and they are looking for new premises.'

'She said they were going to move to the country.'

'You seem to have had quite a long conversation with her,' his mother said. 'I am surprised a little girl like that was so articulate.'

'She wasn't that little. She said she was eight. She had walked the whole length of the beach and could not find her way back.' That was stretching the truth, he knew, but it sounded better than saying he had simply offered to walk with her. And he had helped her to find her charabanc.

'Your good deed for the day, eh?' his father said.

Harry grinned and attacked his roast chicken with gusto. Swimming always gave him a good appetite and their landlady was an exceptionally good cook. He found himself wondering what Julie was having for her supper and if she had been punished. The teacher, or whatever she was, had grabbed her a bit roughly and almost lifted her off the ground when she pushed her into the charabanc. She was a lively girl, full of curiosity, and not a bit sorry for herself; he had no doubt she would survive.

Chapter One

Summer 1936

How Julie had come to be chosen to work in Sir Bertram's grand Maida Vale home, she never knew, but at the age of fourteen, when the orphanage decided her education was complete, she had been packed off to take up a position as a chambermaid, for which she received her board and lodging, her uniform and the sum of twenty-four pounds a year, paid monthly. Her job was to strip and make beds, empty chamber pots and wash them out, clean the bathroom, sweep and dust the bedrooms and the upper landings, shake out the mats and, in the winter, clean out and relight the fire in Her Ladyship's boudoir, carrying the coal up from the cellar in a large scuttle, which had to be replenished during the day. There were fireplaces in the bedrooms but fires were only lit in them if someone was ill. When that was done, she was expected to help with the laundry.

It had taken her a long time to settle down. It was not that the work was too onerous, she had been schooled to expect that, but she missed the regimented atmosphere of the home and her friends. From sleeping in a crowded dormitory, she found herself, for the first time in her life, sleeping in a tiny attic room alone. There were no whispered secrets after lights out, no one to confide in, no opportunity to play. And the other servants, a cook, a kitchen maid and a parlour maid, looked down on her because of where she had come from. Coram orphans were almost always bastards, so they said.

She had been there two years when the nursery maid left and she was promoted to the domain of Bernard, who was four, and the new baby, Emily. They were Sir Bertram's second family; he had two grown-up sons by his first wife who had died some years before. The children had a nurse, Miss Thomas, who was far superior to a nursery maid, a distinction Julie soon learnt. The nurse's job was to look after the children, Julie's was to keep the nursery suite clean and tidy, washing up after their meals and doing the laundry.

It was the laundry that occupied her one Friday in the summer of 1936. It was a fine sunny day with a stiff breeze. She finished the washing, mangled it and took it out to hang on the line at the bottom of the garden, well out of sight of the house. She was struggling with a sheet in the wind when it was taken out of her hands and thrown over the line. She looked round to see Ted Austen grinning at her. He was the family chauffeur and full of his own importance because he could drive a motor car and wore jodhpurs and a peaked cap when on duty. She did not like him. He thought he was God's gift to the opposite sex and was always trying to touch her. She tried ignoring him but he grabbed her round the waist and waltzed her behind the sheet, where he put his arms about her and tried to kiss her.

'Leave off, Ted,' she said, struggling to free herself.

'Leave off? You don't mean that. You've been making sheep's eyes at me for weeks, don't think I haven't noticed.'

'I have not.' She was not quite sure what 'sheep's eyes' meant, but she could guess. 'Why on earth would I do that?'

'Because you'd like a bit of slap and tickle, and as you aren't half bad-looking, I thought I'd oblige. Like this, see.' He brought his mouth down to hers at the same time as he fumbled for her skirt in an effort to lift it. She tried to beat him off, and though he was obliged to lift his head to take a firmer hold of her, she was no match for him. She felt his warm hand on her thigh above her stockings and screamed and kept on screaming until he dropped her skirt and clapped his hand over her mouth. 'Shut up, can't you? Do you want the whole household down on us?' This had been her intention, but she realised how useless that would be when he added, 'They won't believe you, you know, not when I tell them you came onto me. You're from the orphanage and that means you're up for anything—'

He was suddenly hauled off her and she found herself free and Ted struggling with a strange man who had come in the back gate from the mews. Before her horrified gaze, the stranger delivered a blow that sent Ted reeling to the ground with blood pouring from his nose. 'You'll be sorry for that, Julie Monday,' he muttered, scrambling to his feet. 'No one ever messes with me and gets away with it, and I mean no one. You'll pay for it, see if you don't.' And, clapping his handkerchief to his nose, he disappeared through the gate to the mews garage where the car was kept.

The stranger turned to her. 'Julie Monday,' he said, laughing. 'It *is* you.'

She was mystified. 'Yes, but—'

'You don't remember me, do you? I'm Harry Walker. We met at the seaside. Goodness, how many years ago was that? It must be ten at least.'

'Harry!' She stared up at the young man who faced her. He was tall, well built and well dressed. His auburn hair was ruffled and his tie askew, but when she looked closer, she recognised the amber eyes and the cheerful smile and her own eyes shone with delight. 'I never thought I'd see you again.'

'Nor I you. How have you been? Are you working here?'

'Yes, in the nursery. This is Sir Bertram Chalfont's house.'

'I know. Do you like it?'

'It's all right, I suppose. What do you do?'

'I work in Chalfont's factory with my father, but I'm studying for an engineering qualification at night school.'

'How did you come to be here?'

'I was passing on my way home from a football match and heard your cries for help. I'm jolly glad I did. Are you all right?'

'Yes, I am now.'

'Will you report him?'

'There'd be no point. They wouldn't believe me, especially Lady Chalfont wouldn't. Ted Austen is one of her favourites on account of he kowtows to her, and I daren't go to Sir Bertram. I shall just have to keep out of his way.'

'Mind you do. Fellows like him are a menace.'

She didn't want to talk about Ted Austen. 'I can't believe it's you.'

'I can't take it in either.' He stood looking at her. The

coltish child, all arms and legs, had become a handsome young woman with a superb figure, due no doubt to the better diet she received under Sir Bertram's roof. Her wispy blond hair had grown and thickened and was now confined under a white cap similar to the one she had worn as an eight-year-old. He was curious about her. What had her life been like since he last saw her? How had she come to be working for Sir Bertram? 'I say, we ought to meet again. I'd like to hear what you've been doing. Catch up, you know. Do you have any time off?'

'I have a day off a week.'

'What do you do then?'

'If the weather is fine, I usually go for a walk, sometimes in Regent's Park, sometimes Hyde Park.'

'And if it's wet?'

She shrugged. 'If it's a Sunday, I stay in my room or find a café. If it's a weekday, I go to the library or wander round a museum, usually the Victoria and Albert. Sometimes, if I've got a few pence, I go to a matinee at the pictures – anywhere out of the rain.'

'I can't meet you in the week but what about a weekend? That's if you want to.'

'Oh, yes, I'd like that. I'm off this Sunday.'

'Good. I'll meet you at two o'clock by Speakers' Corner in Hyde Park.' He combed his fingers through his hair and straightened his tie. 'If you're sure you'll be all right, I'll be off. See you Sunday.'

As soon as he had gone she felt vulnerable again and hurriedly pegged out the washing, keeping a watch out in case Ted returned. Once safely back in the nursery suite, she collapsed onto her bed. Miss Thomas had taken the children for a walk in the park and, for a moment, she could relax, though there was a pile of ironing to do. Unlike the hospital, where she had to use flat irons heated on a stove, Sir Bertram's house boasted an electric iron.

Ted Austen's assault had shaken her up and she was worried about his threats and wondered what he would do, but that was soon set aside in dreaming about Harry Walker. He was grown-up now and really handsome, but underneath she sensed he was still the same boy who had befriended her so long ago. Fancy him remembering her! It was the name, of course. Everyone remembered that.

She hoped Sunday would be fine, she was looking forward to meeting and talking to him. She wouldn't tell anyone about it; she was sure it would be forbidden. She remembered a homily she had received from Lady Chalfont when she first arrived, something about not having followers. She had not understood what a follower was and had not dared to ask, but since then she had discovered her predecessor had been dismissed for having a follower, which she learnt had been a boyfriend who took her out on her day off and got her in the family way. Harry wasn't a boyfriend, he was simply an acquaintance, but he was meeting her on her day off, so it had to be kept a secret. But she was glowing with it and went about her work with renewed vigour.

Her prayers for good weather were answered. Dressed in the only non-uniform dress she possessed – a calf-length blue cotton printed with tiny white flowers – a woollen cardigan and a tiny felt hat perched on the side of her head and held by a hatpin, she set off for Hyde Park. The park was crowded with people enjoying their Sunday afternoon, strolling about, playing ball, swimming in the Serpentine, riding horses along Rotten Row or listening to the soapbox speakers who vied with each other to see who could shout the loudest for their particular hobby horse. She hardly noticed them as she hurried to the rendezvous, searching out the young man she looked upon as her saviour. And there he was, dressed in a brown suit and a bowler hat, which he doffed as she approached. The gesture made her laugh; people weren't usually that polite to her. 'You came, then,' he said.

'Why wouldn't I?'

'You might have thought I was as bad as that fellow who attacked you.'

'I know you are not. He's a nasty piece of work and you're . . . you're nice.'

He laughed aloud. This young lady, pert though she was, had no idea of the rules of flirtation, of saying one thing and meaning another, of playing hard to get. He must be careful not to spoil her simple faith. 'Nice, am I? How do you know that?'

'Because I do. You're Harry.' As if that answered his question.

'What would you like to do now?'

'Anything. Let's walk and talk. I want to hear all about your life. Do you still live with you parents and brother and sister?'

They turned to walk side by side, though neither seemed to bother about the direction in which they were going. 'You remembered that?'

'Yes, I remember everything. You see, that was a grand day, the day we met, and I've never forgotten it.'

'Me neither. Were you punished when you got back?'

'I had to go in the cupboard for a whole day. It was dark

25

and full of spiders and I could hear the mice in the skirting. I was frightened but I kept telling myself it didn't matter because they couldn't take the day away from me, could they? Not once I'd had it.'

'No.' She was a strange mixture of naivety and wisdom, half woman, half child, which appealed to him. 'Did you often have to go in the cupboard?'

'Not often. Only for very bad deeds.'

'What was so bad about paddling in the sea?'

'It wasn't the paddling, it was talking to you and letting you see me with my legs all bare.'

He laughed. 'Did they know you also had your skirt in your bloomers?'

'No, thank goodness, but it's not fair of you to remind me of that. I didn't know any better.'

'You do now?'

'Oh, yes, I had it drummed into me about behaving with decorum.' She laughed. 'I think I am not behaving with decorum now.'

'Who cares?'

Julie certainly did not. She took his arm and quizzed him about himself. She learnt that he had passed a scholarship to go to grammar school and could have gone on to college but decided he wanted to learn on the job and go to night school, so he had been given a position at the Chalfont Engineering Works. 'We make radios,' he said. 'When I get my qualifications, I'll be promoted.'

'You will be a great man.'

'Nice of you to say so.'

They carried on walking and talking. She learnt his brother Roland was at Cambridge University and learning to fly, which he fully expected to come in useful in the event of war. Already there was a civil war in Spain and he was convinced, like many others, that it would happen to the rest of Europe before long, what with Herr Hitler striding about making speeches and promising the German people the earth. Millie was walking out with a young man she had met at a ball and would no doubt soon be announcing her engagement. His mother was already getting very excited about it.

Julie responded with tales of her life in the Foundling Hospital which had taken over a convent in Surrey soon after they met. 'Then last year they went to a new place in Berkhamsted,' she said. 'I used to meet some of the girls sometimes, but I've lost touch with all of them now.'

'Have you been at Sir Bertram's long?'

'Four years. Ever since I left the Coram.'

'Do you like it?'

She shrugged. 'It's all right, I suppose, though what I'll do when the children no longer need a nursery, I don't know. Bernard is going to be sent away to boarding school but Emily will be educated at home, so I've been told. She is to have a governess.'

'I expect you will easily find another position. Sir Bertram will give you a good reference, I am sure.'

'If I don't blot my copybook.'

It was easy to talk to him. He listened with grave attention and broke in now and again with a question or a comment and the afternoon flew by. He escorted her home but she stopped him at the end of the street. 'Leave me here. They mustn't see me with you.'

'Why not? Can't you do what you like on your day off?'

'I'm not allowed followers.'

He laughed. 'I'm not following you, I'm right beside you.'

27

'Yes, but the girl before me was dismissed for it. He got her in the family way.'

'I wouldn't do that, Julie, I promise you.'

'I know, but they wouldn't understand.'

They arranged to meet again the following Sunday and she hurried back to her mundane routine, wondering if Harry constituted a follower. She had better be careful.

She was careful, so was he, and they continued to see each other week after week, through summer and into winter, when she appeared in a brown tweed coat she had bought from a second-hand stall on the market. They would walk in Hyde Park or visit the zoo in Regent's Park. Sometimes they sheltered from the elements in museums and picture galleries which contributed to her further education, as did the arrival of the Jarrow marchers in the capital, one pouring wet Sunday in October. The Jarrow shipbuilding yard had been closed down the year before, throwing thousands of men out of work and causing real hardship. They had marched nearly three hundred miles, singing to the accompaniment of a mouth organ band and staying with sympathisers on the way. It was the feat of the walk by hungry ill-dressed men that attracted the attention of the populace, not the cause for which they marched, and they achieved little. It made Julie realise how lucky she was to have a job – however hard and ill paid – and a comfortable home.

Once they went into Westminster Abbey out of the rain and she stood looking down at the grave of the unknown soldier. 'That could have been my father,' she said thoughtfully. 'I think I'll pretend it was.'

He smiled and squeezed her arm. 'Why not?'

They discussed the death of King George the previous

28

January and the succession of Edward VIII, wondering what sort of king he would make. In the event, he was not king for long because he abdicated in December in order to marry the twice-divorced Wallis Simpson, who was not acceptable to most of the British public, certainly not to its religious leaders. He became the Duke of Windsor and his brother became George VI and, in the summer of 1937, there was a coronation. Harry and Julie stood in the street with everyone else to watch the King and Queen pass in the great golden state coach, followed by the little princesses in another coach and a whole string of cars containing the great and the good. Everyone was cheering and waving little flags.

Very occasionally she was allowed an evening off and they went to the cinema to laugh at Charlie Chaplin and the Keystone Cops and saw newsreels of happenings in Europe. The Spanish Civil War still raged, Hitler had tested his muscles by occupying the demilitarised area of the Rhineland and no one had tried to stop him, and Mussolini was becoming a force to be reckoned with in Italy – all very worrying to the politicians, but such distant happenings did not encroach on Julie's life and Harry did not want to spoil her happiness by telling her of his own misgivings.

Life, for Julie, took on a new dimension; her horizons widened. She was vibrantly alive and instead of feeling isolated she felt part of it all, especially when she was with Harry, whom she idolised. She didn't want it to end and neither did he, but end it did. And it was all the fault of Ted Austen.

She always did her best to avoid him, but sometimes they met in the kitchen or the garden and he would grin at her and tell her he had not forgotten the beating he had endured on her behalf and that it had to be paid for. She would be sorry. 'Not as sorry as you if you touch me again,' she retorted on one occasion.

'Oh, and who is to stop me?'

'The same person who stopped you before.' She knew as soon as she spoke she had made a grave mistake. He did not say anything, but he was grinning like a Cheshire cat.

The next Sunday, returning from her meeting with Harry, she was summoned to Lady Chalfont's sitting room. She went with some trepidation, but with no idea what was to come.

'I believe you have been meeting a young man on your afternoon off,' Her Ladyship said. 'You know it is expressly forbidden for the servants to have followers, especially servants like you whose family background no one can know. I was always sceptical about employing you but Sir Bertram said we should give a Foundling inmate an opportunity to make good. And this is the sorry outcome.'

Julie stood and stared. It was so unexpected she didn't know what to say. 'Well, miss, what have you to say for yourself? Do you deny it?'

'No, My Lady.' Julie had been taught always to be truthful, and in any case, denying Harry would be like a betrayal.

'I cannot have you contaminating my innocent children and setting a bad example to the rest of the staff. Go to your room and pack your bags. You may stay there for the rest of today and tonight. You will not see the children or do anything for them, do you understand? You will leave first thing in the morning and take nothing you did not bring with you when you first came here or buy with your own money. I am prepared to pay the wages owed to you and that is being generous.'

'But where am I to go?'

'That is not my concern. You should have thought about that before you embarked on this affair. Go to your young man, seeing as you put him before your job here. You will probably discover he has feet of clay, just as you have.'

Julie turned away. She did not think Lady Chalfont knew Harry's name and she would not divulge it. Harry was employed by Sir Bertram, as was his father. Going to Harry would put them at risk.

She trudged up to her room at the top of the house and shut herself in. It was here, where no one could see or hear her, she gave way to despair and howled with misery, frustration and anger, mostly anger. She had no doubt who had betrayed her and wondered how anyone could be so vindictive.

When she had no more tears left, she stopped crying and scrubbed at her eyes. It was done now, but where could she go? She dragged her carpet bag down from the top of the wardrobe and began stuffing her things in it. They did not amount to much: some underclothes, a few toiletries, a hairbrush and comb, a pair of slippers and two nightdresses she had bought to replace those the hospital had provided her with when she left them. There was her Sunday dress but she would have to wear that because her two uniform dresses, aprons and caps would have to be left behind. There was a book of poems Harry had given her for her birthday, which the Foundling Hospital had decreed was exactly a week before she arrived there, and a scarf and gloves he had given her for Christmas. Everything was soon stowed in the bag and, as she had nothing else to do, she went to bed. But not to sleep.

Next morning, bleary-eyed, she collected two weeks' wages from the housekeeper; Lady Chalfont declined to see her again and would not allow her to say goodbye to the children. She picked up her bag and left by the mews gate. Ted Austen was lounging against the garage door smoking a cigarette. She turned and hurried away in the opposite direction, half afraid he would follow her. But then she told herself not to be so silly; he had to drive Sir Bertram to the factory, as he did every weekday morning, returning to take Lady Chalfont to the shops or to her various social engagements, and he would not dare absent himself. But she was aware of his triumphant grin.

She took a train to Berkhamsted and the Foundling Hospital, the only other home she had ever known.

Harry stood by the bandstand for two hours the following Sunday before giving up and going home. He did not think for a minute that Julie would stand him up on purpose, so something must have prevented her from coming. He did the same thing the following week and by then he was becoming very worried. She had become important to him; he missed her infectious laugh, her serious moments, her naivety mixed with a kind of age-old wisdom which made her uniquely Julie. At work, he tried to find out if anything catastrophic had happened at the Chalfont residence which might have prevented her from meeting him, but no one knew anything and Sir Bertram arrived at the factory each morning as he always did and seemed his usual smiling self.

The third Sunday it was raining and he toured their indoor haunts but there was no sign of her. On subsequent Sundays, he took to standing at the end of her street in the hope of catching a glimpse of her, and when that proved futile, he wandered down the mews and peeped in the back gate. It was here, one Sunday, he saw Ted Austen who took a malicious delight in telling him Julie had been dismissed.

'What for? Where's she gone?'

'What for? On account of you. As for where she's gone, how should I know? Good riddance say I. She was a tease.'

'She is not a tease. What you mean is you couldn't have your way with her. I know who to blame for this . . .' He was clenching his fists down his sides and holding himself rigid to prevent himself lashing out. It was more important to find out where Julie had gone. 'Where is she?'

'How should I know? Didn't she come running to you? Now, there's a surprise. No doubt she's found a new protector.'

Harry raised his fist, changed his mind and strode away. He had to find Julie. But how? She could be anywhere in the whole of London, might even have gone further afield. It seemed hopeless. Why hadn't she come straight to him? She must have known he would look after her.

He went home and sought out his father who was reading the Sunday paper in the sitting room. They lived in a large semi-detached house in Islington. It was close enough to get to the factory easily, but far enough from it and the rest of the docklands to be considered above it in the social hierarchy.

Harry flung himself down in the chair opposite his father. 'Pa, how do you go about finding someone who's disappeared?'

Donald set aside the newspaper to answer his son. 'It depends. Who's disappeared?'

'A girl I know.'

His father grinned. 'I thought there was something different about you. Putting all that stuff on your hair and dressing up of a Sunday afternoon. Who is she?'

'Julie Monday. You remember when we went to Southend, I said I'd met this girl who was lost?'

'No, when was that?'

'The year I went to grammar school. She was down there with a crowd from the Foundling Hospital and I took her back to her charabanc.'

'I seem to remember something about it. What about her?'

'I met her again last year. She was working in Sir Bertram's household. I heard her screaming for help and found this fellow molesting her in the garden, so I waded in and saw him off with his tail between his legs. We've been seeing each other off and on ever since. Now she's been dismissed because Her Ladyship found out about it. I don't reckon that's fair, do you?'

'No, perhaps not, but Her Ladyship is one of the old school.'

'It isn't as if we were doing anything wrong, simply going for walks and talking. Now she's gone and I don't know where. I've been going round all our old haunts but there's no sign of her. She's such a little innocent, I'm afraid she'll get into trouble.'

'I don't see it's any of your business, son.'

'Of course it's my business. She lost her job because of me and I don't think she'll have been given a reference either. I can't understand Sir Bertram. What's so bad about seeing me?'

'Nothing if you have been behaving yourselves.'

'Of course we have. I wouldn't—'

'Glad to hear it.'

'I've got to find her, Pa. She means the world to me.'

'Oh, come on, son, she's only a little orphan you've befriended. Don't take it to heart.'

'She is not only a little orphan. She's Julie. There isn't another like her in the whole world.'

His father sighed. 'Oh dear, you have got it bad, but I should try and forget her if I were you. She'll survive on her own.'

Harry could not forget her. He had remembered her for ten years and he would remember her for another ten, and it would not change how he felt about her nor his growing anxiety that she had come to grief. That bounder, Ted Austen, might know and he had a good mind to beat it out of him.

Seeing his obdurate expression, his father added, 'Don't do anything rash, Harry. Remember she was working for our boss and you don't want to make trouble, do you?'

Harry didn't, but it didn't stop him seeking Ted Austen out and giving him a hiding. It didn't do any good. Ted didn't know where Julie had gone and he cared even less.

What Ted did care about was the fact that he had a black eye and Sir Bertram would be bound to ask how he got it. He went to the kitchen and told the astonished staff he had caught a tramp snooping in the garden and seen him off. They were all for reporting the matter to the police, but he said the fellow had gone now and wouldn't be back, he had seen to that. But he promised himself that wasn't the last of it. He had endured regular beatings from his drunken father as a child and been unable to fight back, but after one particularly vicious punishment when he was twelve years old he had run away from home, vowing no one, no one at all, would ever lay a finger on him again. His life from then on had been one of begging and stealing and dodging the police, not always successfully. It was borstal that found him a job cleaning cars at a garage and it was there he had learnt to drive. When he saw the advertisement for a chauffeur for Sir Bertram, he invented a past that would be acceptable, forged a reference and found himself with a well-paid job, a smart uniform and comfortable home. But more importantly, there were no more beatings, until that fellow turned up and hurled him back into his childhood and the pain and suffering he had endured, and that he could not forgive or forget.

'The hospital cannot take you back in once you've left,' Miss Paterson had told Julie when she arrived on the doorstep of the brand-new Coram home, tired and hungry, and related her sorry tale. 'And I'm afraid they would be disinclined to help you after getting yourself dismissed.'

'It wasn't my fault. We weren't doing any harm.'

'You broke the rules. Goodness me, after all the years with us, you must have realised the importance of obeying rules.'

In spite of the scolding, Miss Paterson, who was very near retirement and had found herself a small first-floor flat in Shoreditch in preparation for that day, had taken pity on her and allowed her to move into the flat and helped her to find a job washing up and scrubbing floors in a boarding house on City Road, run by a Mrs Thornby.

Julie was lonelier than ever and she missed seeing Harry. She wondered if he missed her. While her hands became red and rough from the soda in the scrubbing water, she mourned the days they had spent together and dreamt of meeting him again one day.

It came about one Friday in January 1938. It was very early in the morning and she was on her knees stoning the front step when she became aware that someone had stopped behind her. Thinking he wanted to come up the steps, she got off her knees and stood aside to let him pass. And then she gasped. 'Harry!'

He stared. 'Julie! I can't believe it. I searched all over for you. Tell me what happened. How did you come to be here?'

Julie looked fearfully towards the door of the boarding house. 'I can't talk now. I'll get the sack.'

'When do you finish work?'

'When it's all done and I go home to bed.'

'Oh, come, you must have some time off.'

'I have a half day a week and a Sunday once a month. It changes about according to what the other staff are doing. Now and again Saturday half day is followed by Sunday and that makes a lovely weekend.'

'When is your next half day?'

'Tomorrow.'

'That's marvellous. I'm off tomorrow too. I'll wait at the end of the road for you. What time?'

'Julie!' someone shrieked from inside the house. 'I don't pay you to gossip.'

'Go away, Harry, please.'

'Very well. Just tell me a time.'

'Half past two. But I'm not promising.'

He grinned and strode away.

She watched him go. He was so handsome, so smart and, wonder of wonders, he had been looking for her. He had not forgotten her. Somehow or other she must make it to the rendezvous.

The next day was bitterly cold and threatening snow, but that in no way deterred her. She wore her brown tweed coat, the scarf and gloves Harry had given her, a beret she had knitted for herself and a pair of black button shoes. It was not the weather that filled her with nervous apprehension as she hurried down the street that Saturday afternoon, but wondering if Harry might feel too ashamed to be seen out with someone as shabby as she was. Perhaps he would not be there, perhaps he would decide it was too cold.

To her delight he was waiting for her, well wrapped up in a warm wool coat with a fur collar, a trilby hat and leather gloves. He took her hand and tucked it under his elbow. 'Shall we find somewhere warm? A hot cup of tea and a bun, don't you think?'

'Lovely.'

He took her to Lyons Corner House and they sat over tea and cakes, talking, talking, talking. 'I nearly went mad wondering what had happened to you,' he told her. 'That fellow, the one who assaulted you, took great delight in telling me you had been sacked.'

'He snitched to Lady Chalfont that I'd been seeing you. I don't know what's so bad about that. Her Ladyship was really nasty to me over it. I didn't tell her who you were, though.'

'Why not?'

'I didn't want to get you into trouble too.'

'Bless you. Is that why you didn't meet me as we arranged?'

'I couldn't. I'd just started working for Mrs Thornby

38

and I daren't ask for time off as soon as I got there. I didn't want to lose another job.'

'Scrubbing steps.'

'Among other things.'

'Do you live in?'

'No, I live with Miss Paterson. She was one of the teachers at the Coram.'

'The one I saw that day at Southend?'

'Yes. She's just retired and we live in a flat in Shoreditch.'

'Poor you, having to live with that dragon.'

'She's not a dragon, she's kind-hearted and generous and if it hadn't been for her, I'd have ended up in the workhouse.'

'How loyal you are. You shield me and defend her and in the process ruin your pretty hands scrubbing.'

'We all have to work.'

'Not all. People like Lady Chalfont don't do a hand's turn and many women do nothing but look after husband and house.'

'That's work,' she retorted.

'But it's work most of them choose to do. Wouldn't you like to be free to make that choice?'

'Pigs might fly.'

'I mean it. Did you tell Miss Paterson why you were sacked by Lady Chalfont?'

'Of course I did.'

'And have you told her you were meeting me today?'

'No, but I will. I didn't want to say anything in case you didn't turn up and I'd have looked a fool.'

He laughed. 'Don't you know me better than that?'

'I hoped I did. Now you are here, what have you been doing? Are you still working at Chalfont's?'

'Yes. We've turned part of the production over to radios for aeroplanes. They will be needed if there's a war.'

'You think there'll be a war, then?'

'It looks more and more like it. Everyone at the factory thinks there will be and we're working two shifts a day and my father spends all hours there. Mother worries about him and about Roly, who's in the RAF now.'

'Mrs Thornby is full of gloom. She lost her husband in the last war and keeps telling everyone how awful it was. All those thousands of men killed. My father might have been one of them. I shall never know for sure. It must be terrible for the fighting men and just as bad for those at home waiting for news. I know I should be worried to death if it were you.'

'Would you?' He reached out and took her hand and appeared to be studying it.

'Of course.' She looked down at their joined hands, one strong and beautifully manicured, the other red and angry with broken nails. How different they were, how indicative of the different lives they led.

'Julie,' he began. 'I don't know if this is the right time to say this, but I'm going to say it anyway. I love you very much and I couldn't bear to lose you again, and the only way I can be sure is to ask you to marry me.'

She stared into his face in disbelief. 'What did you say?'

He laughed and repeated it. 'So what do you say? Will you marry me?'

'Do you mean it? Really, really mean it?'

'Of course I mean it, silly. I think we were meant for each other, right from the beginning when we met on the beach. Why else was I on hand when Ted Austen attacked you? Why else did I find you again after I thought I'd lost

40

you for good? I was on my way to work when I spotted you yesterday. I usually go on the Tube but for some reason I decided to walk. It is fate, our destiny, whatever you like to call it. Don't you feel it too?'

'Yes, oh, yes.' Her eyes were shining and she was very near to tears.

He lifted her work-worn hand, opened the palm and put it to his lips. 'Then I shall tell my family, and next week I shall take you home to meet them and we can arrange a wedding.'

'I shouldn't have said yes,' she told Miss Paterson, when she went home that evening and related what had happened over supper. 'I didn't stop to think. He's posh and I bet his family will look down on me and I shall feel such an idiot.'

'Julie Monday, I despair of you. You've been pining for that young man for months, don't think I haven't noticed, so why the sudden doubts?'

'I never thought he would ask me to marry him. It's such a big step and I don't know anything about being married. I shall get it all wrong, I know I will.'

Grace Paterson laughed. 'No doubt he will set you right.'

'Did anyone ever ask you to marry him?'

'Yes. I was engaged once but he was killed in the last war, so I don't know anything about being married either. I took to teaching instead.'

'I didn't know that.'

'Of course you didn't. It's not something I'd teach in class, is it?'

'Do you think there'll be another war?'

'I don't know. I pray not.'

'If there's a war, Harry might have to fight.'

41

'He might. Does that make a difference to how you feel about him?'

'No, nothing could make a difference to that. I was wondering what it would be like for those left at home.'

'Hell,' Grace said. 'But I cannot think it will be as bad as last time. Lessons have surely been learnt.'

'It's all very worrying. Harry said the Chalfont Works were making radios for aeroplanes and working double shifts.'

'Julie, if you are asking my advice, I'd say seize your happiness while you can, make the most of every day and every night you are together. You can't know how long it will last.'

Julie jumped up and kissed Miss Paterson on the cheek. 'That's just what I wanted to hear.' She sat down again, her exuberance suddenly evaporating. 'But what about his family? What if they don't like me?'

'You are not marrying his family, Julie.'

All the same, the visit to meet Harry's parents was a terrifying prospect, but Harry had assured her they would all welcome her with open arms. He was somewhat over-optimistic; his mother welcomed her, not with open arms but with cool politeness.

Chapter Two

Hilda Walker was very correct, dressed impeccably in a dark-grey calf-length skirt, a white high-necked blouse and a rope of pearls. Her hair was precisely coiffured and her fingernails long and buffed to a shine. Julie tried hiding her hands in the folds of her skirt but had to bring one out to shake hands.

'Do sit down, Miss Monday,' Mrs Walker said.

Harry laughed and pulled Julie down on the sofa beside him. 'Oh, Mum, this is Julie, not Miss Monday.'

'Yes, I understand it is a made-up name.'

'It's the name I was registered with,' Julie said. 'No one knows my real name.'

'It will soon be Walker,' Harry put in. 'And that will be real enough.'

Mrs Walker did not respond to that as her husband entered the room and Julie jumped up to be introduced to him. He was an older version of Harry, silver-haired, very upright and a little portly. His amber eyes were so like

Harry's she would have taken to him even if he had not been smiling a welcome. 'I am glad to meet you at last,' he said. 'Do sit down again and tell us all about yourself.'

She obeyed hesitantly, but there wasn't much to tell and she realised how feeble she sounded and her voice faded to a stop.

'No doubt we will learn more as we go along,' he said. 'Harry tells me he has asked you to marry him.'

'Yes, but—'

'But?' Harry repeated in surprise. 'You didn't have any buts last week.'

She turned to him. 'I know. I was bowled over and pleased as punch, but when I stopped to think—'

'Stop that, this minute, Julie Monday,' he interrupted, reaching for her hand. 'I won't listen. We love each other and we are both old enough to know our own minds. You can't back out on me now, I won't allow it. You do love me, don't you?'

'You know I do. How could I not? You're Harry.'

'Then it is a done deed. You are engaged to me. We are here to talk about wedding arrangements and where we'll live afterwards. We can do that over tea.'

It was all going too fast for her and she played with her food and only half listened as dates and churches were suggested and decided upon and they moved on to discussing the reception. 'I assume you have no one to arrange that for you,' Mrs Walker said, still tight-lipped.

'No. Do we need a reception?'

'Of course we do. It will look odd if we don't. If we are going to do it, we will do it properly. I'll take over. We can hire a hotel room and they can do the catering. What about your wedding dress?'

That was too much for Julie. Her spirit returned. 'I can provide my own wedding dress, thank you,' she said.

This seemed to silence the lady, but not for long. She was soon talking about wedding cakes and flowers and whom to invite. Apart from Grace Paterson, Julie had no one to ask. Any friends she had had at the orphanage had gone their separate ways and none of the staff at Sir Bertram's or those at the boarding house could be called friends.

'Never mind,' Mrs Walker said. 'Some of our relations can sit on your side of the church.'

'Can't we go to a register office, then it won't matter?'

'No, certainly not, that's ungodly. You must make your vows in church. They are more binding that way.'

'I do not need vows to bind me to Harry. And wherever I make them, they will be kept, I promise you that.' She had spoken sharply and felt Harry reach for her hand under the table and squeeze it.

'And where will you live?'

'I'll find a house to rent,' Harry said. 'Not too far from Chalfont's – Southwark, Bermondsey, Lambeth, somewhere like that.'

'But they're nothing but factories and slums,' his mother said.

'Not all. A lot of the old unfit houses have been pulled down and there are some decent ones there now. And we need to go carefully to start with, until I make my way up.'

'I don't know if you'll do that at Chalfont's. You are marrying one of Sir Bertram's servants, after all.'

'I am no longer one of his servants,' Julie reminded them.

'We know that.' Again that repressive tightening of the lips.

'It wasn't Julie's fault,' Harry put in. 'And my choice of wife has nothing to do with Sir Bertram.'

The tense meeting came to an end at last and Harry walked her home. 'There, that wasn't so bad, was it?' he said.

'It was awful. Harry, I can't go through with all that, I really can't. Your mother made it very clear you were marrying beneath you. And the sort of wedding she's talking about will make that plain to all your friends and relations.'

He laughed. 'Don't be silly, sweetheart. Dad climbed his way up from being a delivery boy with a horse and cart and Mum was a shop assistant. We can do the same. I'll make my way up in the world and you will be with me every step of the way. You have to believe that.'

'I will, if we can be married quietly somewhere, just you and me and a couple of witnesses.'

'They won't like it.'

'Then we won't tell them until it's over.'

'I don't think I can do that.'

'Then you must love pomp and ceremony more than you love me.'

'Oh, Julie, how can you say that? You're not being fair.'

'It's you not being fair.' They had reached her door and she stopped to turn and face him. 'You don't seem to understand.'

'I'm trying.'

'Try harder.' She turned and let herself in the flat, leaving him staring at the green door with a number seven painted on its centre panel.

He walked away, deep in thought. Was Julie being unreasonable? Was his mother intent on humiliating her?

46

He did not think so, but in Julie's shoes he might. She was extremely sensitive about her origins, or lack of them, and putting her into a crowd of his relations and friends might make her feel put down. All he wanted to do was put her on a pedestal and tell the world how wonderful she was.

'It's all off,' she told Grace. 'They are snobs and I'm not good enough for their precious son.'

Grace put a cup of cocoa in front of her. 'What happened?'

'Harry was on their side,' she said after she had told the tale. 'I thought he would understand but he didn't.'

'He'll be back.'

'Not if his mother has her way.'

'If she does, he's not the man I thought he was and you've had a lucky escape.'

Julie gave her a rueful smile. It was strange to think how close they had become, the anonymous orphan and the spinster teacher. When she had been at Coram's, Grace Paterson had not shown her any favouritism, quite the contrary, but when she had gone to her in trouble, she had turned out to be a brick. Besides giving her a home, Grace had taught her how to speak properly and how to behave in company. It wasn't that which was her downfall, but the fact she had no past, no family – 'breeding', the upper classes called it.

'The Walkers aren't upper class, nowhere near it,' Grace said when she voiced this thought. 'Mrs Walker might aspire to be something she is not but that's her problem, nothing for you to worry about. For all you know, you might be the daughter of an earl and can be amused by her pretentiousness.'

Julie laughed. 'Oh, you have cheered me up.'

'Good.'

Grace was right. Harry was outside the following evening when she left work to go home. He fell into step beside her. 'I can't bear to be at odds with you,' he said. 'So I told my parents we are going to be married in a register office with a handful of witnesses and have a meal in a hotel afterwards and that's all.'

'And did they agree?'

'I didn't give them the chance to agree or disagree. I said that's what we were going to do. They have accepted it. Has that put your fears at rest?' He stopped walking and twisted her round to face him. 'So, will you marry me now?'

'Yes, Harry. And I love you all the more for being so understanding.'

He kissed her, there in the street, to the wolf whistles of those passing by. He grinned back at them. 'She's going to marry me.'

'Lucky dog!'

Harry found a house to rent in Bermondsey, after the previous occupants had decided to leave London for somewhere safer in the event of war. It was at the end of a terrace and had a patch of garden at the back, reached by a narrow alley which ran down the backs of all the houses. Downstairs there was a sitting room and a kitchen which contained a sink, a cold tap and a bath covered with a plywood top when it was not in use. Water was heated in a boiler beside the kitchen range. The lavatory was outside but at least it flushed. Upstairs were two bedrooms. Julie was thrilled with it.

Here was her very own home, one she could decorate and furnish just as she pleased. They bought kitchen equipment, a table and chairs, a three-piece suite, a bedroom suite and a few rugs for the floor, helped by Harry's parents, because, as his mother said, 'I don't want my son to have to live in squalor.' Julie would have liked to refuse the largesse but she was realist enough to know that would be cutting off her nose to spite her face and hurt Harry. She would do nothing to hurt him, however much it dented her pride. She borrowed Miss Paterson's sewing machine and made curtains and runners and cushion covers and then set about making her wedding dress.

There was some consternation when it was discovered that, as she was not yet twenty-one, she needed parental permission to marry. Grace Paterson saved the day by asking the governor of the orphanage to sign as her guardian. For Harry's sake she relented over the register office wedding and they were married in church in March 1938, witnessed by Harry's parents, his brother, his sister and brother-in-law and Grace Paterson. It was the first time Julie had met Roland and Mildred. Roland, who arrived in the uniform of a pilot officer, was like his brother in looks and gestures. Mildred was a younger and prettier version of her mother and heavily pregnant with her first child. Her husband, Ian Graham-Mellcott, was several years older than Millie, tall and thin and descended from some titled family, which Mrs Walker took great pains in informing Julie when they were introduced, though the man himself made little of it.

The simple ceremony was intensely moving and Julie, standing beside Harry in her white taffeta dress and a little headdress of orange blossom and lace, was glad she had changed her mind about a church service. Saying her vows before an altar made the day more special, if that were possible. The three-course meal they had in the hotel afterwards was no grander than the everyday luncheon at the Chalfonts' mansion, but everyone was jolly and smiling and toasted the newly married couple in sparkling wine.

Afterwards, glowing with happiness, Harry and Julie took a train to Southend. It was here they had met and it held special memories for both of them. The seaside holiday had grown in popularity in the intervening years, but it was essentially the same. The donkeys still plodded up and down with children on their backs, Punch still beat Judy about the head, children still paddled, built sandcastles, played bat and ball and poked about in rock pools for living creatures. Harry had booked them into the boarding house that his family had always frequented and here they spent the first night of married life.

They were both virgins, but Harry had a little more idea of what was expected of him than Julie had. They undressed shyly and scrambled into bed and lay there in each other's arms. He put his arm beneath her shoulders and pulled her round so that he could kiss her. He was gentle, she was responsive, and then nature and instinct took over and their marriage was consummated in the most joyful satisfying way. Exhausted and happy, they slept.

The week flew by – they paddled and swam and walked along the beach, skimming pebbles; they strolled along the pier and tried out the slot machines with pennies; they played bowls on the green, went to the theatre and the cinema, and at night they made love, discovering new pleasures along the way. It seemed nothing and no one could spoil their delight in each other. And the following Saturday they went home, taking with them a garden gnome which had taken Julie's fancy because of his round red cheeks and beaming smile. 'He's one of Snow White's dwarves,' she told Harry, hanging onto his arm. 'He's Happy. Just like me.' He had bought it for her and found a spot for it in the garden and they settled down to married life in their new home. It would have been idyllic if the fear of war had not been hanging over everyone.

Harry went to work at the factory every day, working twelve-hour shifts. Radios were needed for the new aircraft coming off the production line, for communications in the army and navy, and for the ordinary household who needed the wireless to listen to the BBC and keep abreast of the news. The Great Depression of earlier in the decade was put behind them as the populace found employment in the preparations for war.

'Too little, too late,' Donald Walker said gloomily as he stood beside his son's workbench one day in October. Everyone in the factory was working flat out and most were doing overtime every evening. 'We should have been doing this years ago.'

Hitler had annexed Austria earlier in the year with hardly a murmur of dissent and now his attention was turning to Czechoslovakia, a country created by the Versailles Treaty after the Great War and which contained, in Sudetenland, three million German-speaking people. In an effort to avoid war Neville Chamberlain had flown to Munich to meet Hitler and come back with a document they had both signed. It was not a treaty but an agreement not to go to war so long as Germany was allowed to take over Sudetenland. The whole country gave a huge sigh of relief, but it did not stop the preparations. Only the foolhardy believed it meant peace was assured.

'I think you had better get that wife of yours out of London,' Donald added. 'We're right on the docks here and a prime target for the bombers.'

'I've told her all that, but she won't have it. She won't leave me and she won't leave her home, especially after Mr Chamberlain came back from Germany waving that scrap of paper and saying it meant peace in our time.'

'Do you believe that?' his father asked him.

'No, I'm afraid I don't, but Julie has been brought up to believe implicitly whatever those in authority tell her and she is convinced there will be no war. I don't want to worry her by shattering her faith, especially now.'

'She ought to have more faith in you, if only for the baby's sake.'

Julie, like many another, chose to put her head in the sand and get on with her life, a life entirely wrapped up in Harry, her cosy little home and her coming baby, which was due in December, nine months after their idyllic honeymoon. She could not have been happier and she did not want to hear talk of war.

George Harold Walker was born on 7th December 1938 weighing just over seven pounds. Because Julie was so small it was a difficult birth and she was in labour a whole day and night, while the midwife sat and knitted and Harry paced the living room, drinking endless cups of tea. When the little one finally arrived, Julie forgot all that in her delight. He was perfect in every way and, according to both Julie and Hilda Walker, who arrived within hours, was the image of his father. He certainly had Harry's amber eyes, though Julie's very fair hair. It was an unusual colour combination which, so his mother said, meant he was going to be a very unusual man.

Harry doted on him. He watched Julie breastfeed him with a grin on his face and his eyes shining. He even learnt to change the baby's nappy and would sing him to sleep if he was at home at his bedtime. Their lives revolved around George and neither wanted to think of anything else, certainly not the clouds gathering on the horizon as 1938 became 1939.

The trouble was that they could not avoid it because the subject was on everyone's lips. There were those who, like Julie, believed war had been averted, and those who were convinced it had only been postponed.

'It will come, you see,' Mrs Golding said. She and her husband were their next-door neighbours and had come to England from Austria ten years before and considered themselves English. Even so, they were hugely unpopular in the neighbourhood because of their origins and the fact that they were Jewish. Julie, who knew what it was like to be an outcast, felt sorry for them and always spoke to Mrs Golding when they were both in their back gardens hanging out washing, or met in the queue at the grocer's.

'The bombers will come,' Mrs Golding said, as they both took advantage of a good blow to hang out sheets. 'They're building shelters in the Old Kent Road. I saw piles of bricks and men mixing cement and they told me that was what they were doing. And the council is offering everyone a shelter for their garden.'

'I haven't heard anything about garden shelters.'

She asked Harry about them when he arrived home. 'Mrs Golding says the council are issuing everyone who wants one with an air-raid shelter,' she said, dishing up his evening meal. He was very late home and she had been keeping it hot over a pan of boiling water. 'Is that true?'

'Anderson shelters – yes, I believe so.'

'Why? The prime minister said there would be no war.'

'He's playing for time.'

'Oh, no, Harry, surely not? Hitler got his way over Sudetenland, what more does he want?' Like many another she had never heard of Sudetenland until it filled the front pages of the newspapers.

'The whole world,' he said, attacking his food while she sat at the table opposite him watching him eat. She loved cooking for him and he always appreciated her efforts, but it was a pity she never knew what time he was coming home so that she did not have to keep it hot, letting it spoil. He never complained. Nor did he complain when the week's housekeeping money ran out before the end of the week. 'I'm not used to managing money,' she said when she had to ask for more. 'When you give it to me I think it will last easily and then it seems to disappear all of a sudden. I don't know why.'

'You must learn to budget, sweetheart. We mustn't get into debt.'

So he sat down and went over what she spent the money on and it was usually something frivolous for George, like a new toy because she saw it in the shop window and thought he would like it, or a treat for Harry's tea, so that when it came to buying the basics, she found herself short. 'Let's get some jars and put some in each for the essentials, like rent and groceries and insurance, and when they are all paid for, you can spend the rest on whatever you like. But don't dig into the jars unless it's a real emergency.'

'I'm stupid, aren't I?'

'No, of course you're not stupid,' he said, giving her a

54

hug. 'It's just that you never had to handle money in the orphanage, did you? And when you were in service your board and lodging was found and your wages were your own to spend as you liked. Don't worry about it, I'm sure you will soon learn.'

'You are so patient with me.'

'Why wouldn't I be? I love you.'

'And I love you, more than I can possibly explain. You and George are my whole world. I don't want it ever to change.'

'Unfortunately, my darling, times are changing. We can't avoid that.'

'War, you mean.'

'Yes, war.'

'Oh, Harry, what have we done to deserve it?'

'We won the last war, that's what, and we made the Germans pay heavily for it and they won't forgive us. Hitler is stirring them up to hatred and blaming us and the Jews for all his country's ills.' He pushed his empty plate away from him. She took it to the kitchen and brought back a bowl of rice pudding, sweet and creamy and topped with ground nutmeg. 'Julie, I really think you should think of moving to the country,' he went on, digging his spoon into the pudding.

'And leave you here? No, Harry, I will not. We stick together, come what may.'

'And the baby?'

'The same for George. Besides, where would I go? I know no one in the country and I should be lonely and miserable. At least here, I've got neighbours I know. Don't ask me again, please.'

'But you don't know what it will be like.'

'I don't want to know. Suffice unto the day is the evil thereof.'

'What do you mean by that?'

'We'll take it as it comes, Harry. Do you want to get rid of me?' This last was said tearfully and he jumped up to put his arms round her.

'Darling, how could you even think that? You are the whole world to me. I just want you safe.'

'I am safe with you to look after me.'

Her faith in him worried him. He could never live up to it, but for the sake of harmony he dropped the subject. He did not even renew his plea when council workmen delivered fourteen sheets of corrugated iron, six girders, some nuts and bolts and a spanner, together with instructions for constructing the shelter and a bill for six pounds fourteen shillings, which they could pay by instalments if they chose. He simply set about digging a hole in the back lawn, five feet by seven and four feet deep. It took the whole of one Saturday afternoon, and the following day he assembled the shelter in the hole and covered it with all the earth he had excavated and topped it with the turf he had removed. He cut three steps down to it and then called to Julie. 'Come and try it out.'

She went reluctantly and ventured down the steps. It was pitch dark because she was standing in the doorway blocking out the only source of light. It smelt dank and the earth beneath her feet was oozy mud. She screamed and scrambled out again. 'I'm not going in there again. It's just like the cupboard at the Coram, only worse. At least that was dry.'

'I'll put some duckboards in and some seats and a lantern. It won't be so bad.'

'It's dreadful.'

'It's that or go to the country,' he told her. 'I want you and our son safe.'

'Oh, well, I don't suppose it will ever be needed,' she said.

Harry came home from work one Saturday lunchtime to find her standing over George's cot in tears. Lying beside him was a strange contraption made of rubber, canvas and Perspex. 'I can't put him in that,' she wept. 'It will frighten him. Why can't he have a little gas mask like the ones we've got?' They had gone to the council offices some time before to pick up their gas masks and had practised putting them on and sitting in them for several minutes to get used to them. Julie hated being enclosed like that and ripped hers off the minute Harry indicated they had practised long enough. Never had she imagined her baby would have his whole body enclosed in one and she would have to pump air into it for him to breathe.

'He might pull an ordinary mask off,' he said. 'And perhaps they can't make them small enough.'

She flung herself into his arms. 'Harry, I'm frightened. What's going to happen to us?'

'I don't know, I really don't. Pray God we never have to use them.' He dried her tears with his handkerchief. 'Come on, cheer up. We're not dead yet. Let's have our dinner and go for a walk.'

Her laugh was a mite watery. 'Harry, it's raining cats and dogs.'

'So it is. Then we'll do that jigsaw puzzle Miss Paterson gave you for Christmas.'

'I haven't seen Miss Paterson since she came to visit when Harry was born. I should think she's worried too.'

'We all are, sweetheart. Tomorrow, if it's fine, we'll take the bus and see how she is.'

The winter was wet and miserable and did not help to lighten anyone's mood, and in March German troops invaded Czechoslovakia, breaking Hitler's agreement to stick to Sudetenland. The following month men aged twenty were called up for military training; aircraft production was stepped up and Chalfont's Engineering were making radios twenty-four hours a day. On 21st August Hitler announced he had made a non-aggression pact with the Soviet Union, the strangest bedfellows you could imagine. When, on 1st September, he invaded Poland, not even the most diehard ostrich could ignore the fact that Britain had pledged to come to Poland's aid and the time for keeping that promise had come. Burying one's head in the sand was no longer an option.

That same day, the Territorial Army was mobilised and the evacuation of Britain's schoolchildren began. Julie, pushing George in his second-hand cream and navy-blue pram, watched them lining up outside the school to be taken to Waterloo Station in charabancs, each carrying a small attaché case and a gas mask in a cardboard box, with a luggage label attached somewhere on their clothing, as if they themselves were pieces of luggage. Some looked bewildered, some excited by the prospect of adventure, some terrified to be leaving their mothers. And the mothers stood by in tears as their children were taken away to heaven knew where. Julie had been told she and George could be included and had received written instructions about what to take and where to meet, and Harry had renewed his pleas for her to go, but she was adamant. In his distress he shouted at her and she shouted back until George began to cry and they stopped to soothe him.

'Harry, we mustn't quarrel about it,' she said, rocking the baby in her arms. 'It upsets George.'

He smiled and kissed her. In one way he was glad she was so obdurate. Being parted from her and the baby would be terrible and there would be time enough to do something about it when the bombers actually came over.

Sunday, 3rd September was a lovely day of almost unbroken sunshine, unusually warm for the time of the year, and many people were in church, or working in their gardens, or taking a walk along the Embankment. Hearing there was to be an announcement they hurried home to switch on the wireless. At eleven o'clock Prime Minister Neville Chamberlain broadcast to the nation. The country was at war with Germany. Almost immediately the air-raid warning sounded, a terrible wail that froze Julie's bones, so that she couldn't move, couldn't think clearly. Being Sunday Harry was at home and ushered her and George down into the dreaded Anderson shelter. He had been as good as his word and installed a wooden floor and put two deckchairs in it, together with a couple of orange boxes standing on end and a storm lantern. He had made a rockery round the door and stood the happy gnome at the entrance. It was slightly better than her first view of it, but only slightly. Harry's presence soothed her, but she wondered if she would have the courage to go down there if the siren went when he was not at home.

After a few minutes the all-clear went and they emerged into the bright sunshine to the realisation that it was a false alarm. Nothing had happened.

It was all happening elsewhere. A British Expeditionary

Force was sent to France; the RAF dropped leaflets, not bombs, on Germany; a U-boat torpedoed the aircraft carrier *Courageous*, and another managed to breech the defences in Scapa Flow and sink the *Royal Oak*; and in November Russia attacked Finland. At home Winston Churchill was back in the Cabinet and being characteristically pugnacious.

Everyone had to black out their windows when darkness fell so that not a chink of light escaped to guide the bombers to their targets, as if the broad ribbon of the Thames were not guide enough, and vehicle lights were covered leaving only a small slit for the drivers to see where they were going. There were no street lights. Everyone was supposed to carry their gas masks and identity cards everywhere they went. It all seemed a waste of time and trouble. No bombers came and many of the evacuees drifted back. Julie relaxed and began to make plans for George's first birthday.

It was time he came out of gowns and into proper boy's clothing and she searched the shops for little shorts with button-on braces and little shirts to tuck into them. She bought his first soft leather shoes to replace bootees. He was no longer a baby but a little boy, sitting up and giggling when she played with him, reaching out for anything he could put in his mouth to test out his new teeth.

'Mum wants us to take him over there for a birthday tea on Sunday,' Harry told Julie. 'Millie's bringing Dorothy.' Dorothy was eight months older than George. 'She's baking a special cake. I've said we'll go. That's all right, isn't it?'

'Yes, of course.' Julie's relationship with her mother-in-law was one of guarded neutrality. They were polite to each other, though not exactly warm. They both doted on George, which made a big difference.

Julie wouldn't travel by Underground when she was

60

alone, it always brought back memories of being shut in the dark even though it was well lit, but with Harry beside her carrying George in his new warm wool coat and a knitted pixie hat, she endured it. She had spent more on the clothes than she should have done, but as far as she was concerned nothing was too good for her son. And Hilda Walker echoed that. The cake which stood in the centre of the tea table was a work of art: a sponge filled with jam and cream and thickly iced. It had 'Happy Birthday, George' inscribed in yellow icing on its surface alongside a yellow sugar rose. There were also sandwiches filled with all sorts of good things, a whipped cream trifle covered in hundreds and thousands, and chocolate iced buns.

Hilda took George from Harry as soon as they arrived and hugged him. 'My, you are growing into a big boy. We shall soon have you running around and getting into mischief.'

'He can already pull himself onto his feet and shuffle round the furniture,' Julie said. 'Harry is going to make a gate for the stairs.'

Dorothy did not like this attention given to her cousin and began grabbing at her grandmother's skirt demanding her share. Harry picked her up and made a fuss of her and they all sat down to enjoy their tea: Donald and Hilda, Millie and Ian, Harry and Julie and the two children.

'Looking at this you would never believe there was a war on,' Julie said, surveying the table. 'However did you manage it?'

'You can always get things if you know where to go,' Hilda said. 'And we must make the most of it before everything is rationed.'

Everyone had been issued with ration books when they

collected their identity cards the previous September, but so far they had not been used. They had been told they would have to register at a grocer's for all their rationed goods and Julie had dutifully registered with a small shop in the Old Kent Road, where she did most of her food shopping.

They were halfway through tea when they heard someone come in the back door. Before Hilda could go and investigate, the dining room door opened and Roland put his head round it. 'Is this a party and can anyone join in?'

'Roly!' Hilda flew across the room to hug him and drag him into the room. 'You're just in time for tea. Are you on leave?'

'Forty-eight hours. Hallo, everyone.' He kissed his sister and Julie and stood looking at his nephew and niece. 'My, they've grown.' He delved in his kitbag and produced a little aeroplane carved in wood, which he presented to George. 'There, little fellow, happy birthday.' Then he went to his kitbag again. 'Can't leave the other little monster out, even if it's not her birthday.' This time he produced a rag doll for Dorothy.

'Sit down and have some tea,' Hilda said. 'Tell us what you've been doing.'

He pulled up another chair while his mother fetched out more crockery and cutlery. 'Flying about the countryside, patrolling the Channel looking for enemy shipping, whizzing over to France – nothing very exciting.'

'That won't last,' his father said.

'No, I don't suppose it will, but all this waiting about is making everyone jittery.'

'We're not hanging about,' Harry said. 'The factory is working round the clock.'

'Yes, well, there's some catching up to do.' He paused. 'What are your plans? Going to stay at home and wait to be called or are you going to enlist?'

'He's in a reserved occupation,' Julie put in. 'Radios are needed urgently.'

'So they are, but I reckon women can make them as easily as men. That right, Pa?'

'Yes,' his father agreed. 'Chalfont's has already taken on a lot of women as the men leave for the forces. Harry knows that.'

'Well, one of you in uniform is more than enough,' Hilda said. 'So let's drop the subject.'

They dutifully obeyed but the conversation left Harry musing. Was it cowardly of him to want to stay at home and look after his wife and child? After all, he was doing a useful job, and how did he know he would be able to do any good in the forces? He'd probably get called up anyway and then he wouldn't have a choice. Wait or go? He looked at his wife, laughing and wiping chocolate icing from George's face, and his heart almost burst with pride and joy, mixed with a feeling of helplessness that he did not know how to keep them safe.

It was after tea was over and he and Roly wandered out into the garden that the subject was brought up again. 'Do you think I should enlist?' he asked his brother, as he flicked the wheel of his lighter and held it out for Roly to light his cigarette and then lit his own.

'It's up to you, old man, but if you wait until you're conscripted you probably won't get your choice of service.'

'Does that matter?'

'Of course it matters. Just think about it. The poor bloody infantry get the worst of it and if it's anything like the last lot it will be hell. As for the navy, they are at the mercy of the U-boats. Being blown up at sea, perhaps floating about on a bit of wreckage for days and dying of exposure, is not a nice way to go.'

'How cheerful you are! You can get blown up in an aeroplane.'

'Yes, but at least it's quick. And if you survive you do get to come back to base every night, and if you're lucky and near enough, you can get home more often. There's something about flying, being up among the clouds, swooping about like a bird, that gets to you. You can't beat it.'

'Mum will climb the wall if we're both in uniform, you heard what she said. As for Julie, I dread to think what she'd say . . .'

'Your decision, old man.'

'Yes.'

Ian strolled out to join them. 'The women are washing up and your father is listening to the news, keeping an eye on the babies at the same time.' He accepted the cigarette Roly offered him. 'Do you think those things will do any good?' He nodded towards the Anderson shelter a little further down the garden.

'They are supposed to withstand everything but a direct hit,' Harry said, offering his lighter. 'Haven't you got one?'

'What, in a flat with no garden? Where would we put it?'

'Never thought of that.'

'The basement has been designated our shelter. At least it's warm down there right next to the boiler. The landlord has installed bunks and a lavatory and some heavy steel doors to withstand shock waves.'

'You're not sending Millie and Dorothy to the country, then?'

'She won't go.'

'It's the same with Julie.'

They fell silent, contemplating a future they could only imagine. They looked towards the house as Julie came to the door and called them in. 'It will soon be blackout time.'

'Let's make the most of Christmas, shall we?' Harry said as they trooped indoors, shut the door behind them and drew the blackout curtains.

Making the most of Christmas meant ignoring the news, stocking up on tinned foods, flour and sugar, candles and oil for lamps to be used in the shelter and in the event of the electricity being cut off. The trouble was that everyone seemed to be doing the same thing and already the price of foodstuffs was rising and some things were becoming hard to find, especially those that had to be brought into the country by sea. Bananas had disappeared and oranges were like gold dust. Julie had to pay a shilling for a single orange to put in George's stocking and it turned out to be sour. He pulled a face and spat it out.

'You shouldn't have bought it,' Harry said. 'George isn't old enough to know the difference, is he?'

'No, but I so wanted him to have one,' she said, sprinkling it thickly with sugar and offering it to him again. 'The only time we had an orange at the Coram was on Christmas Day.'

Her life in the orphanage had left an indelible mark on Julie. She was scarred because of it; her claustrophobia, her obsession with cleanliness and routine and her fear of doing wrong in the eyes of those in authority were ingrained in her. But she could be extraordinarily stubborn when she chose, and when she dug her heels in, nothing and nobody could budge her. Coram had not taught her that; it was

65

something inbred in her, a throwback to one or other of her parents – probably her father, because her mother had given up on her. That rankled; she did not know what she could have done as a tiny baby to be abandoned in that way. She had tried to talk to Harry about how she felt, not only about her background but how much his loving her meant to her, but the inmates had never been encouraged to speak of their emotions in the home, and she found it difficult to express herself. But she swore to herself that whatever it took she would make sure George did not go short, either of affection or food.

Chapter Three

The shortage of oranges was the least of their problems as 1940 was ushered in with bitterly cold weather. In the countryside, snow blocked the roads and piled into drifts, rivers froze over and potatoes could not be dug out of the ground. The railways were almost at a standstill, which meant any produce that could be gathered could not be transported to the cities. In London the roads were cleared one day, only to be covered again the next; water pipes froze and milk went solid on doorsteps and even the Thames froze. The greengrocer's shop in the Old Kent Road had very little on its shelves and the coalman ran out of coal. Julie was at her wits' end, trying to keep the house warm and her little family fed.

She was in the queue at the greengrocer's one day, gazing at the empty shelves, wondering how she was going to manage to cook a dinner without vegetables, when someone behind her said, 'It's awful, isn't it?'

She turned to see who had spoken. She was a young

woman, about the same age as Julie, warmly wrapped up in a tweed coat and a headscarf from which a few blond curls peeped. She had a pleasant smile. 'Yes, it is,' Julie agreed. 'It's bad enough with the war and all, but this weather is making it a hundred times worse.'

'Did you hear the news this morning? Rationing is starting on Monday.' She laughed. 'I don't know what good that will do, there's nothing to buy.'

'I heard the beginning of it but the baby woke up and started to cry, so I missed most of it.'

'It's butter, sugar, bacon and ham. Why those in particular, I don't know. I've given my book to my landlady and she's going to register me.' She paused. 'Fancy a cup of coffee or tea?'

'Not coffee, that imitation stuff tastes awful, but a cup of tea will go down a treat.'

They went to a café just down the road. Julie picked George out of his pram and left it outside while they went in and settled themselves at a table near the window where they could see the pram.

'He's a darling,' the woman said. 'What's his name?'

'George.'

'It suits him. I'm Rosemary Summers, by the way.' She pulled off her glove and held out her right hand. 'Rosie to my friends.'

Julie took the hand. 'Julie Walker.'

'Walker? My boss at Chalfont Engineering is Mr Walker. Any relation?'

'He's my father-in-law.'

'Really? Then you must be Harry's wife.'

'Yes, I am.'

'He's a lovely man. You're so lucky.' She turned to the

waitress who stood over them, pencil poised. 'Two teas, please.'

'Yes, I know it. How long have you been working at Chalfont's?'

'Only three weeks. I came down from Scotland. I was going to join up, but I failed the medical on account of childhood asthma. They said I'd do more good working in a factory on essential war work, and sent me to Chalfont's.'

'Do you like it?'

'It gets a bit boring doing the same thing on the same machine day after day.' She laughed again. 'And night after night. I'm on nights this week which is why I was exploring. You can't sleep all day.'

'Exploring Bermondsey, that's a laugh.'

'Well, I thought I'd need to know my way about, where the shops and shelters are, things like that.'

'Where do you live?'

'I've rented a room on the Waterloo Road. It was the first place I came to when I got off the train. It's handy for the factory. Where do you live?'

'Just round the corner. We've got a nice little house with a garden.' She laughed. 'And an Anderson shelter. I hate it.'

'Perhaps you'll never have to use it.'

'I hope not.'

They finished their tea and would have gone on talking all afternoon, if George had not reminded them of his presence and begun to grizzle. 'I must take him home to give him his feed and put him down for his afternoon nap,' Julie said, standing up.

They left the café and walked together along the busy road to Julie's turn. 'That's our house,' she said, pointing. 'Come and see me, when you've got time off.'

'I will, thank you. I haven't made any friends here yet, and working such odd hours, it's difficult to get to know people.'

'Well, you know *me* now. Any time you're passing.'

Rosie took her at her word and arrived two afternoons later bearing gifts: a tin of golden syrup, a bag of potatoes and two onions. 'I thought these might help,' she said.

'Goodness, yes. Wherever did you find them?' She busied herself putting a kettle on the gas stove.

'There's a chap I've met at work who seems to be able to get almost anything for a price . . .'

'How much?'

'Oh, it's a gift from me to you, for taking pity on me.'

'Taking pity. I don't pity you, why should I?'

'I meant being friendly when I was feeling lonely. I'd never been out of Scotland before, except for childhood holidays with my parents, and it was all rather nerve-racking.'

'Yes, I felt like that when I left the Coram and went to work. It was such an enormous change.'

'The Coram?'

'An orphanage. I was left on the doorstep when I was a tiny baby.'

'Poor you! Don't you know who your parents were?'

'Not a clue. The authorities were my parents. When I was old enough I went to work for Sir Bertram Chalfont as a domestic.'

'Sir Bertram who owns the factory?'

'Yes.' The kettle boiled and she made tea and they settled down at the kitchen table to drink tea and talk while George slept in his pram.

'Is that how you met your husband?'

'No, I met him before that.' Julie went on to recount how she had first met Harry and how she had met him again later. 'We've been married two years in March.'

'How romantic!' Rosie said. 'And now you have a home of your own and a darling baby.'

'What about you? Have you left a boyfriend back in Scotland?'

'No. Perhaps I'll meet someone like your Harry down here.'

By the time Rosie left they were firm friends and promised to meet as often as they could. Julie never knew quite when she would turn up because of the shift system at the factory and she almost always brought supplies with her: a tin of condensed milk, a bag of sugar, a bar of chocolate. Sweets weren't rationed, but the shortage of ingredients meant many of the factories had been turned over to producing more important things. At first she refused to take money for them but on Julie's insistence she allowed her to pay for the items. They were more expensive than anything bought through normal channels, but if it meant she could feed Harry and George better than by sticking to the letter of the law, she was prepared to pay. She did not tell Harry about this because she had a feeling he would disapprove. It was the first time she had ever kept anything from him, and she salved her conscience by telling herself it was in a good cause.

Harry was battling with his own conscience, as more and more men left the factory bench to join up and their places were taken by women. How could he sit at home when others, including his brother and brother-in-law, were in uniform? His only uniform was an armband and a tin hat with ARP painted on it in white, which he put on to report to the warden's post every evening when he was not at the factory, and to patrol the streets around his home, looking out for telltale chinks of light from ill-fitting blackout curtains and shouting at anyone having the temerity to light a cigarette in the street after dark. He had to know the names of everyone on his patch and where they lived so that the dead and injured could be identified in bombed buildings. The siren had wailed several times making everyone rush to the shelters, but nothing much had happened, except road traffic accidents and people walking into lamp posts in the dark.

When he was at the factory he had to take his turn on the fire-watching on the roof. They were supposed to report if a raid was getting close and give warning, so that the workers could stay at their posts until the enemy aeroplanes were overhead, then they would troop to the shelters in orderly fashion. The fire-watcher's other task was to put out incendiaries with stirrup pumps. So far neither had occurred.

He decided to defer a decision until after their wedding anniversary, which they celebrated quietly at home. Julie managed to put on a celebration dinner, even though meat had been put on the ration that same week; he did not ask her how she did it. The dreadful winter had gone and daffodils were blooming in the garden beside the happy gnome. Looking at it through the kitchen window, he smiled, remembering their honeymoon and how perfect it had been. And now everything was being spoilt by the war and an uncertain future. He turned and sat down, taking her hand and pulling her onto his knee as she walked past him to the sink. They had just finished their evening meal and there was a pile of washing-up on the draining board.

'Julie, my love, I have something to tell you,' he began. 'And I want you to listen.'

'I'm listening.'

'I went to the recruiting office this afternoon.'

'You've been called up! Oh, no, Harry. Didn't you tell them you were in a reserved occupation?'

'I haven't been called up and my being at the factory is not making a jot of difference to the war. There are plenty of women who can make radios, your friend Rosie will tell you that. I enlisted.'

She jumped up from his knee and faced him. 'I don't believe you. You are making a joke to frighten me.'

'It's not a joke, sweetheart. I couldn't stand by and let others do the fighting for me, could I?'

'Didn't you think about me at all? And Georgie? It's not fair of you, Harry.'

'Nothing's fair in war, my love.' He tugged at her hand and brought her down onto his knee again and pulled her head against his chest. 'And I was thinking about you and George. My whole life is devoted to looking after you, and if I can best do that by getting into uniform and helping to win this war, then I must do it.'

'I don't want you to go. Can't you change your mind?'

'No, I can't. It's done now. I'm going into the RAF like Roly. It has one advantage over the army and the navy: you get to come back to base every night. I'll be able to come home on leave quite often. Please, Julie, don't cry.' He mopped her tears with his handkerchief. 'It's not the end of the world.'

'It feels like it. What happens if we get invaded? You won't be here.'

'Hitler will never invade England,' he said, far more confidently than he felt. 'He's got to cross the Channel and do you think we'll let him do that? He'll be bombed to smithereens before he gets halfway across. And I'll be one of those doing it. Now cheer up and let's get the washing-up done.'

'When do you go?' Her voice was still watery, as she stood up to put the kettle on for hot water to wash the dishes.

'When they send for me. In a week or two. I'll be sent somewhere for training, probably up north somewhere. After that I'll be posted somewhere south, closer to home.' He picked up the tea cloth to do the drying. 'We've all got to make sacrifices in this war, Julie. You heard Churchill's speech on the wireless about having nothing to offer but blood, toil, tears and sweat. The sooner we get stuck into it, the sooner it will be over and we can go back to normal.' Churchill had become prime minister after the resignation of Chamberlain. Those who had branded him a loose cannon were now wholeheartedly for him.

'I suppose so.'

He was relieved the confession was over and she appeared to have accepted it, but it had left him drained. And tomorrow he would have the arguments all over again when he told his mother of his decision. But on the other hand, he felt suddenly uplifted. Whether he could make a difference to the eventual outcome he had no idea, but if everyone pulled together they must surely win.

They made the most of the time left together and two weeks later he was summoned for a medical examination; the following week his papers arrived requiring him to report to the Recruiting Centre from where he was sent to Harrogate.

* * *

Left alone, Julie survived on Harry's letters and Rosie's friendship. Although they were of an age and of similar build and colouring, the girls could not have been more different in their backgrounds; Julie's family had been the other inmates at the orphanage and the adults who ran it, all very impersonal and regimented. Only Grace Paterson had shown any affection for her and that had only really been evident after she was sacked by Lady Chalfont.

Rosie, on the other hand, had been loved and cosseted by her parents and had everything a child might need: a good education, clothes, toys, books, music and tennis lessons. Coming to London had been a nerve-racking experience in one way, but a huge adventure in another. 'I'm glad I met you,' she told Julie, one day when they were walking in the park with George in his pushchair. The area in which he could play was sadly depleted because of a huge ack-ack gun, pointing skywards. They had heard it firing on one or two occasions when the siren went and it made them feel safer to know it was there. 'I might have been very lonely otherwise.'

'Haven't you made friends with anyone at the factory?'

'One or two, but it's difficult when you're on shift work.'

'I understand. Harry was always coming home at all sorts of strange times. I never knew quite when to expect him for his dinner.'

'Have you heard from him?'

'Yes, almost every day. He's somewhere up in the north of Scotland now but he can't tell me exactly where. When his training is done he'll get some leave, then I'll hear all about it and where he's going to be stationed.'

He had been gone six weeks and in that time Hitler had overrun the whole of Europe and thrown the British

Expeditionary Force out of France. The evacuation of three hundred thousand troops from the beaches of Dunkirk had been a truly heroic episode, but it could not disguise the fact that German troops were poised on the other side of the Channel, ready to strike. Julie couldn't believe she was the only one terrified of the prospect, yet everyone else seemed to be going about their business, pretending everything was normal. She felt she had to do the same and hide her fear.

'Do you think Hitler will invade?' Rosie asked. 'Everyone at the factory is talking about it and a lot of the men have joined the Local Defence Volunteers. I don't know which is more frightening, the prospect of air raids or of being overrun by German troops.'

'Harry is convinced they won't come, the air force will stop them.'

Rosie laughed. 'And as far as you are concerned Harry is always right.'

'He has been up to now.' They turned round and started back. 'What time do you have to be back at work?'

'Eight o'clock. I'm on nights.'

'Then you have time for a bite of supper with me before you go.'

'I don't want to take your rations.'

'Don't be silly, you provide me with a lot of it. I don't know how I'd manage without your contribution. I owe you for the last lot anyway. I'll pay you when we get home.'

Paying Rosie was becoming a bit of a problem because the cost had gone up so much, but she didn't know how she could manage on her rations and non-rationed goods were so hard to come by she had come to rely on what Rosie brought. Even the price of rationed goods had rocketed. Milk had doubled to fourpence a pint, though George's was half price; butter and sugar and syrup were half as much again as they had been when war started. As for bacon, that had shot up to two shillings a pound and many poor families could not afford to buy their rations.

Her worry about this was temporarily set aside when they approached the house. There was a police van outside the Goldings' gate and both husband and wife were being escorted none too gently towards it. Each was carrying a small suitcase. She left Rosie with the pushchair and ran to them. 'What's happened? What have you done?'

'We are Austrian and we're Jews,' Mrs Golding said. 'That's enough.'

Julie turned to the policeman who had hold of the woman's arm, as if he feared she would try and escape. 'There must be some mistake. These people are doing no harm. They've lived in England for years.'

'So they say,' he said. 'But we have orders to round up all enemy aliens.'

'What will happen to them?'

He shrugged. 'It's up to the tribunal.'

She watched the van drive away. 'I can't believe that,' she told Rosie as they went indoors. 'She's a harmless old woman.'

'Maybe, but you can never tell, can you? There's been a lot of talk about fifth columnists and reds, lately. People saying they should all be interned. If they were left free and we were invaded, they might find it safer to be on the side of the invaders and help them all they could.' She paused, dismissing the subject. 'Shall I peel these potatoes for you?'

'Yes, please. I'll cook those sausages you brought me. And there's a cabbage in the larder. And we can have a tin of peaches.' The peaches were also provided by Rosie. 'This supplier of yours seems to be able to get almost anything. Do you know how he does it?'

'No, and I don't ask.'

'What's his name?' She shredded the cabbage and put it in another saucepan.

'I don't think I should tell you that. He might not like it.'

'OK. I was curious, that's all.' Julie laughed. 'You haven't got a thing about him, have you?'

'No, course not.'

'You're blushing.'

'No, I'm not. It's the heat from the stove.'

'If you say so.' The frying pan went on and a tiny knob of lard was put in it to cook the sausages. 'But you can thank him from me.'

'What are you doing with all that stuff I'm giving you, Rosie, my love?' Ted asked. 'I can't believe you're using it all yourself.'

'I pass some of it on.'

They were talking in undertones in the Chalfont factory canteen in their lunch hour. The canteen was not geared up for the influx of all the extra workers and they had had to queue for half an hour for their meal, leaving barely half an hour to eat it.

'And make a tidy profit, I've no doubt,' he said. He had once been Sir Bertram Chalfont's chauffeur, he had told her, but now there was so little petrol Sir Bertram was coming to work on the Underground and he had been given a job in the factory. He hated it, telling her it was a great comedown from what he was used to, and if it hadn't been for his little sideline, he'd have been bored to tears.

'Only a little. A girl has to live.'

'And do these customers of yours know where you get it from?'

'No. I thought it best not to say.'

'Very wise of you. How many customers have you got?'

'Only two. My landlady and my friend, Julie Walker.'

He laughed. 'Julie Walker, eh?'

'Yes, do you know her?'

'If it's the one-time nursery maid at the Chalfont residence who married Harry Walker, yes, I do.' Since working at the factory he had come to realise who his assailant had been and he still bore a grudge. If it were not for the fact that Donald Walker was the production manager and his immediate boss, he would have taken his revenge long before. When Harry had joined up he thought he'd lost his chance. Now he'd been handed new opportunities on a plate.

'Yes, I'd forgotten she said she used to work for Lady Chalfont.'

'She likes what you take her, does she?'

'Yes, wouldn't you?'

'We could make it more, you know. Can't let the little thing go short of anything, can we?'

'No, but I'm not so sure she can pay for more, she never seems to have much money in her purse. It'd be a bit risky, don't you think?'

'Everything is a risk these days.'

'Where do you get the stuff from anyway?'

He laughed. 'Do you think I'd tell you that? I wasn't born yesterday, you know.'

'No, and I suppose it's best not to know.'

'Attagirl! Fancy the flicks tonight?'

'Yes, if you like.'

*   *   *

Julie had put George to bed one warm evening in late June and was sitting in the kitchen over a cup of cocoa when the back door opened and a figure in an RAF uniform stood in its frame. 'Harry!' she squealed, jumping up and throwing herself into his arms. 'You're back.'

He hugged her and kissed her over and over again. 'God, I've missed you.'

'And I you. Sit down. I'll make you a cup of cocoa. Are you hungry?'

'What have you got?'

'Bacon and an egg do you?'

'Fine. And a slice of fried bread, if you've got it.'

She busied herself about the stove, glancing every now and again towards him, as if to make sure he was really there.

'How's George?'

'He's getting on a treat. Walking now, a bit wobbly and he sits down on his bottom every now and again, but if you hold your arms out he crosses the room to you. Go up and see him while I do this, but don't wake him. It might upset him to see a man bending over his cot.'

'I'm his dad.'

'All the same . . .'

He left the room and she heard him dash up the stairs two at a time and cross the floor in the bedroom above her. She finished the cooking and went to the foot of the stairs to call him down. 'It's on the table.'

He ate hungrily and helped her wash up and then she sat on his knee on the sofa in the front room to tell him all that had been happening to her, about Mr and Mrs Golding being taken away, the funny little things George did and his attempts to talk, and about Rosie's continuing friendship.

But she said nothing of the black market supplies Rosie brought her. She knew it was wrong but she stifled her conscience by telling herself it was for George's sake and telling Harry would only worry him. 'What about you?' she asked. 'How long are you home for?'

'Forty-eight hours.'

'Forty-eight hours! Is that all?'

'Yes, then I have to report to Manchester. We're off to Canada.'

She sat up and stared at him. 'Did you say Canada?'

'Yes, as in North America.'

'But Harry, why? Why so far?'

'It's all to do with the Empire Air Training Scheme. We go over there for training and when we come back we're fully operational.'

'How long will you be gone?'

'Not sure. Three or four months.'

'Oh, Harry, and I thought I'd got you back.'

'You never lost me.' Absent-mindedly he wound one of her blond curls round his finger. She had had it cut short to make it easier to look after. 'You've managed so far, haven't you?'

'Yes, but it's awful without you. I miss you so. Until now I've never had to be on my own and I'm not much good at it.'

'I miss you too, but you can go and see Mum and Dad, can't you?'

'I do sometimes, but I always feel awkward with them when you're not there.'

'Why?'

'Oh, I don't know. They think you married beneath you.'

'That's nonsense. You are not beneath me. You may not have known your parents but they bequeathed you some very good traits that you could not have learnt at the Coram.' He smiled and lifted her chin with his finger to look into her eyes. 'You are beautiful, bright and intelligent. You care about people and you are a wonderful wife and mother. What more could I ask?'

'Oh, Harry, you make me so happy.'

'I'm glad, because if you were not happy, I should be miserable too, so shall we cheer up and make the most of the time I've got?'

She stood up and pulled on his hand. 'Shall we go to bed?'

'What a good idea!'

Forty-eight hours went by in a flash. They visited his parents and Millie, whose husband had a desk job at the War Office, took George to Southwark Park and watched him toddling about and trying unsuccessfully to catch the sparrows that came for the crumbs they took them. And they made love. He had vouchers for his own rations while he was on leave and Julie took them to her grocer and came away with enough to make sure he had a good breakfast, some mince for dinner and an egg for supper. He was not au fait with exactly what the rations were, nor how to make them stretch, and he did not question the fact that his bacon ration was supplemented by sausages and the mince was cooked with an onion, which were almost unobtainable and changed hands, one at a time, for an exorbitant amount.

The morning he left to catch his train, her stoicism was called on as never before. She made sure his shirt and underclothes were clean and neatly ironed, packed his bag and made him some sandwiches to eat on the train, all the time chattering brightly about nothing in particular and gulping back tears. When the moment came for him to leave, she picked George up and took him to the door to say goodbye to his father.

Harry hugged them both. 'Be good. The time will fly by, you'll see, and we'll be together again.'

'Oh, Harry.' The tears spilt; she just could not hold them back.

He put his kitbag down to mop her eyes with his handkerchief. 'Don't cry, sweetheart. Let me have a smile to go away with.'

She sniffed and managed a watery smile.

'That's better. Now I must go. There'll be hell to pay if I'm not back on time.' Gently he put her from him, gave her one more searching look as if to imprint her features on his memory, then picked up his bag and strode away.

She watched until he stopped at the corner to turn and wave, then went back indoors and collapsed in a chair in a flood of tears, gripping George so tightly on her lap he wailed to be put down. She let him go and watched in a blur as he toddled over to pick up his woollen ball and throw it to her. George needed her to be strong. She mopped her eyes, played with him for a few minutes, then got on with the day's chores, and in the afternoon she took him to see Miss Paterson.

Grace was too old for war work, but she had joined the Women's Voluntary Service and put on the bottle-green uniform and the rather unbecoming hat in order to be useful. One of her first tasks had been to help organise the evacuation of the children in 1939 and to help provide the poorer children with clothes to take with them. The WVS were also to help the ARP when people were made homeless by air raids in her area, finding them food, clothing and shelter, though this had not yet become necessary. She did not doubt it would happen.

'I've got myself in a bit of a mess,' Julie told her as they sat over a cup of tea.

Grace looked at her over the rim of her cup with an eyebrow raised. 'What sort of mess?'

'I've been buying under-the-counter stuff and it's costing rather a lot of money.'

'Oh, Julie, Julie, don't you know better than that?'

'Yes, but I needed it for George. I can't let him be hungry, can I? And he loves syrup on his porridge.'

'Other people manage, my dear.'

'I don't think they do. Everyone buys black market stuff if they can get it.'

'Not everyone, Julie. It's unpatriotic.'

'I never thought of that. But it's only for George. It isn't as if I buy things for myself. I wouldn't.'

'And now you are in debt.'

'A bit.'

'It's a great pity they did not teach you how to manage your money in the Coram, but that wasn't considered necessary for girls.' She smiled. 'They were expected to go into service until they married and you do not need a degree in mathematics to manage a servant's wages, and if you married, your husband would deal with money matters. Times are changing and women must learn these things nowadays.'

'I don't see what I can do differently. We were comfortable and I coped all right until Harry joined up. I wish he hadn't done that. Now all I've got is my married and child allowance.'

'He did what he thought was right, Julie.'

'He's gone off to Canada now and I hate being alone.'

'You have friends.'

'Yes, there's Millie, though it's a bit of a trek across London to see her, and there's Rosie, she comes now and again, and the people across the road, but I don't have a lot to do with them. Their two children were evacuated but they came back and now they're getting into mischief because there's no school for them to go to. I was friendly with the Goldings, but they have been deported and their house is boarded up. It's creepy at night, knowing it's empty.'

'I doubt the landlord will let it stand empty for long. Count your blessings. Now, about these debts of yours.'

'It's mostly the rent and what I owe Rosie. I've been out the last two weeks when the rent man's called but I can't keep doing that.'

'No, you certainly cannot. I can let you have a little money, but that's not really the answer, is it?'

'No, and I can't take money from you.'

'It would be a loan.'

Julie listened to Grace's advice, which mirrored the advice Harry had given her before he left, promised to put it into practice and came away with five pounds, which would pay Rosie and the rent and then she must try and manage on her allowance and what she could buy legally. At the same time she must save up to repay Miss Paterson. She did not expect Rosie to have other ideas.

'Why don't you want any more?' she demanded when Julie handed over the money she owed. 'It's not doing anyone any harm and you really need things. Look at Georgie, how plump and happy he is. It's more than can be said for the other children round here. That lot across the road are in rags and skinny as skeletons. Do you want your son to look like that?'

'No, of course not. But they were skinny and in rags before the war started. It's nothing new for them. In fact, I gave Mrs Jenkins a tin of syrup the other day. She was ever so grateful.'

'Did she pay you?'

'She offered but I couldn't take it.'

Rosie laughed. 'You're a fool, Julie – a generous fool, but a fool all the same. I'll get you more to make up for it. And I can get you some silk stockings.'

'Silk stockings!' Julie echoed. 'Oh, Rosie, can you? I'm so fed up with ankle socks.'

'Next time I see you, you shall have them.'

But when Rosie brought the stockings she told her to take them away again. She could not afford the enormous amount being asked for them. 'Five shillings!' she exclaimed. 'I can't afford that or anything like it.'

'You can owe me. I don't mind.'

'No.' She was adamant. 'I'll take things for George, but not for my own vanity.'

'OK.' The stockings went back into Rosie's bag. 'Do you need anything else?'

Julie was beginning to realise that her friend was running a nice little business and wondered again where everything was coming from. 'No.'

'You're being silly, Julie. Everyone's out for what they can get. We'd all starve otherwise. If the shops didn't put everything under the counter for their favourites, it wouldn't be necessary. Here.' She delved into her bag and brought out two tomatoes, an onion and two small tins of condensed milk. 'Have these for your dinner.'

'All right, but it's the last.' She dug into her purse and handed over some coins, knowing she was being weak. The trouble was she was afraid Rosie would take umbrage if she refused and wouldn't come again. Then she really would be lonely.

'Don't you want me to come again?' Rosie asked.

'Of course I do. I value your friendship, you know I do. And George is very fond of you. His little face always lights up when he sees you.'

Rosie laughed. 'That's because he knows I'm the one who brings chocolate.'

'All the same, we both love you. Please don't stop coming.'

'Good. I start day shift again next week, so I've got the weekend off. I'll come over on Saturday if you like, air raids permitting, of course.'

If there was one good thing about Harry's absence, apart from the fact that he did not know the muddle she had got herself into, it was that he was a long way away when the Luftwaffe began bombing airfields all over the south and east. It reminded Julie of his assertion that the air force would prevent an invasion. Hitler obviously thought the same thing and was determined to destroy it first. The air-raid siren was going off at more and more frequent intervals, with bombs falling on airfields and ports, though only a few had so far dropped on London.

Julie delayed going to the Anderson shelter until she could hear the planes going over and left it the minute the all-clear sounded. If it hadn't been for keeping George safe she would not have gone anywhere near it. With the door shut it was more like the prison cupboard of her childhood than a place of refuge. But the raids were getting nearer. Croydon, Dulwich, Richmond and Kensington had been hit. She had heard the drone of aeroplanes, the distant crump of explosions and the boom of the ack-ack guns as she crouched in the bottom of the shelter, holding George close to her chest and uttering soothing noises so that he wouldn't be frightened and also to help herself overcome her claustrophobia. Coming out after the all-clear, she was relieved to find her house still standing. There were fires in the distance but most of them seemed to be north of the river, and during the day she heard tales of how people had been killed or had lucky escapes, or had been bombed out and were camping out in reception centres waiting to be found somewhere to live. She knew it could not be long before Southwark and Bermondsey had a visit from the Luftwaffe.

As soon as Rosie had gone, Julie tipped all her money out on the table and counted it carefully. Where had it all gone? There was not enough there to pay the rent and nothing at all in the jar reserved for repaying Miss Paterson's loan. She could not go back to her for more. She sat looking at the little pile for a long time, but nothing could make it bigger. Putting it all back in the rent jar, she fetched George from his cot where he had been having his afternoon nap, put him in his pushchair and set off to visit her parents-in-law.

As usual, Hilda made a great fuss of George and found a custard cream for him. 'How is it over your way?' she asked Julie, referring to the bombing.

'Nothing too near, so far.'

'It won't last.' She filled a kettle and put it on the stove, lit the gas under it and set out a teapot, cups and saucers and milk in a jug.

'No, probably not.'

'Chalfont's is moving the factory.'

'Moving it? How can you move a factory?'

Hilda laughed. 'The same way you move a house. They're taking over a pram factory in Hertfordshire. Production must be kept up and it won't be if the place is bombed. We're going to rent a house nearby.'

'You mean you're leaving London?' In spite of her wariness of her mother-in-law, this piece of news dismayed Julie.

'Yes, lock, stock, and barrel. I suggest you and George come too. You can live with us.'

Julie's dismay deepened. 'But I can't leave my home.'

'Don't be so stubborn, Julie. It's better to lose your home than your life and it's not fair on George to put him through it. I'm sure that's what Harry would want you to do.'

'Has he asked you to persuade me?' Harry had been urging her in almost every letter to go to the country.

Hilda hesitated. 'Well, he did mention it. I'm sure he's said the same thing to you, hasn't he?'

'Yes,' she admitted. 'But I want to have his home there when he comes back.'

'That's all very well, but suppose there's no home. And no wife and son either.'

'Don't say things like that, please.'

'Then come to Letchworth with us. Millie and Dorothy are coming.'

'What about Ian?'

'He has to stay in London, naturally, but he'll come down to see them whenever he can.' She paused, as Julie hesitated. 'Think about it, Julie, and let us know. We'll help you with the move.'

'All right, I'll think about it.'

All the way back from Islington to Bermondsey she turned over in her mind the pros and cons of a move. It would mean she would not have to go into the dreaded Anderson shelter, a great plus as far as she was concerned. Could she and Hilda get on in the same house and would Hilda take over her life and dictate how George was looked after? When Harry came home, they would have no privacy. And she would miss Rosie, but on the other hand, if the factory was moving, Rosie would go too. It began to look very much as if she were going to say yes.

One thing she could not do was ask her in-laws for money, and Miss Paterson would have to be paid. She had to pass a pawnbroker's shop on the way home and decided to turn in there. She had nothing to pawn but her wedding ring, but as soon as her next allowance was due she could get it back. No one need ever know what she had done. She came out of the shop feeling naked without the ring, though it had not been on her finger long enough to make a lasting impression. She felt dreadful about it and almost went back into the shop to redeem it straight away but the five pounds she had in her purse was needed urgently. 'Forgive me, Harry,' she murmured. 'It doesn't mean I don't love you and don't want to be married to you anymore. I'll get it back, I promise.'

Chapter Four

Harry was off duty, sitting on his bed writing to Julie, when Tim Harrison strolled in to the barracks. He was grinning from ear to ear. 'We're off home,' he said.

Harry looked up from telling Julie how much he missed her and stared at his friend. 'Home?'

'Yes, back to Blighty.'

'Are you sure?'

'I saw the order. We entrain tomorrow after the passing-out parade and sail on the seventh.'

'That's less than a week away.'

'So it is. Now, at last, we might see some action.'

'I don't know about action, I can't wait to see my wife and son again. Presumably we'll get some leave.'

'There'll be hell to pay if we don't.'

Harry dashed off the rest of his letter, telling Julie he would see her soon, then sealed it and took it to the postbox, which was in the HQ building right next to the orders board. There it was in black and white: instructions to fall in with all kit on 3rd September at 0800 hours. He was going home!

He had enjoyed his sojourn in Canada, where everyone was so friendly and treated them all like heroes, though they hadn't seen any action yet, except a few minor scrapes and damage in the course of training. Now he was a fully fledged wireless operator. It hadn't been his first choice, because he wanted to be a fighter pilot, but there were always more volunteers for that than any other and he had been told, because of his peacetime work with radio, he would do more good in that capacity. He knew it was no good arguing, so he had acquiesced and was passing out with top grades.

Now, at last, he was going home to a war-torn country and his beloved wife and child. In twelve days' time – four on a train, seven on board ship and one to get leave and go home – he would see them both again. George would have grown a lot. He wondered if he would remember him or if he would have to get to know the little chap all over again. As for Julie, he could not wait to hold her in his arms again and tell her how much he loved her and wanted her safe. He would be able to persuade her himself that she must leave London and go with Chalfont's to Letchworth. His mother had told him about the proposed move in her last letter and offered to have Julie and George to live with them. Knowing Julie, he thought she might baulk at that, but perhaps while he was on leave he could find somewhere for her to live independently nearby. More than anything he wanted her and George safe.

London was experiencing a heatwave that first Saturday in September. George was uncomfortable, hot and grizzly.

After dinner, Julie stood his bath in the garden and filled it with cold water and, leaving nothing on him but a little pair of shorts, she sat him in it. Kneeling beside him she splashed the water over him. He was chuckling happily when Rosie arrived.

'I envy him,' she said, kneeling down on the other side of the bath to kiss him. 'He looks so cool and happy.'

'Yes, but I ought to take him out. I have to go and see Miss Paterson.'

'Why don't you leave him with me? I'll play with him a bit and take him out later and give him his tea. You'll be quicker on your own.'

This was certainly true. It would take a crisis of epic proportions to persuade her to manhandle a pushchair and a heavy toddler onto the Underground and so she always used the bus, which took a lot longer. 'I suppose I could,' she said slowly. 'Are you sure you can manage him?'

'Of course I can, silly. He loves his Auntie Rosie, don't you, my pet? And I've got some jam in my bag. He shall have bread and butter and jam for his tea. Go on. He'll come to no harm, I promise you.'

'OK. I'll be as quick as I can.'

She dashed indoors to put on a cardigan, grabbed her bag and gas mask and went back into the garden. Both George and Rosie were shrieking with laughter. She decided not to interrupt them to say goodbye, which might upset him, and crept away.

She was with Miss Paterson at four o'clock when the siren wailed. 'Drat it!' Grace said, putting down her teacup and standing up. 'I'll have to go on duty. You had better go in the shelter.'

'No, I must get back to George.' She rose and picked up her handbag and gas mask.

'Is that wise? You never know—'

'I'll be all right on the Underground.' Much as she hated the close atmosphere of the Underground, not only was it quicker, it was safer and there would be other people about, which would help her overcome her claustrophobia.

They parted at the door and Julie hurried to the Tube station. The streets were full of people hurrying to shelters or, like her, making for the Underground. There was no panic; some had become very blasé about that banshee wail and thought of it more of a nuisance than anything.

It was when she came above ground at the Elephant and Castle she realised this was something more than a nuisance raid. The sky was thick with aeroplanes and bombs were dropping everywhere, screaming earthwards, shaking the ground beneath her feet and shattering windows. Like most Londoners, she had come to recognise the different types of bomb: high explosives were fitted with fins and their dreadful screaming as they came down was terrifying, while the incendiaries started fires wherever they landed and were usually put out by fire-watchers using stirrup pumps.

Already there were buildings on fire near the docks, close enough for her to feel their warmth, and a shard of glass from a window just missed her as she ran along the pavement, praying that Rosie had taken George into the shelter and they were both safe.

'Hey, miss, where are you off to?'

She looked up to find herself confronted by a warden. 'Home. My friend is looking after my baby and I must get back to them.'

'They will have gone into a shelter. Best take shelter yourself. It's a bad one this one, not safe to be out in the open.'

'But my baby—'

'You won't be much good to a baby if you get yourself killed, will you?' He took her arm in a firm grip. 'Come along, I'll take you to the Linsey Street shelter.' He would brook no argument and hustled her along to the shelter constructed under the railway arch. 'You can go home when the all-clear goes.'

He saw her into the shelter and left her there. The place was crowded, noisy and stuffy. There were whole families obviously occupying their own particular seats, women sitting knitting, others breastfeeding babies, old men pretending they weren't afraid and children running about everywhere. One man was standing on a box trying to organise a sing-song, but the response was half-hearted and he gave up. Julie had to wend her way, stepping over legs, bags, boxes and bedding to find a seat on a bench. She sat on its edge wishing she had never let the warden persuade her into it. It was every bit as bad as the Anderson shelter, but added to her rising panic, which set her heart racing and made her want to scream to get out, was the desperate need to get home. She strained her ears for the all-clear, but all she could hear was the drone of aeroplanes, the high-pitched whistle of high explosives and the heavy crump as they hit the ground. She could feel the earth shaking and lumps of plaster came off the underside of the arch and rained down on everyone. Children were sobbing and screaming, people were being sick and the heat was stifling. She could see nothing, except those closest to her, and not even those when the electric lights suddenly went out. She was too terrified even to scream.

'Damn,' one of the women said in the sudden silence that followed. 'I've gone and dropped a stitch.'

'And I've dropped my false teeth,' said one of the men, which raised a half-hearted laugh. It was cut short by the terrifying scream of a high explosive which had every one of them holding their breath. They never heard it land.

'Damn those Huns,' Rosie said. She was in Julie's kitchen heating some milk for George's tea. He had been hauled reluctantly out of the water, been dried and dressed and compensated for the loss of his pool with bread and jam. 'I had better take you to the shelter.' She turned off the gas and carried him out to the Anderson shelter. The sky was thick with German planes and she could see the bombs as they left the aircraft, hurtling downwards one after the other. Already dockside buildings were on fire with flames shooting high into the sky. Fire engines were tearing along the road, bells ringing. 'It looks like a bad one. I hope your mum is not out in it.'

She went down the steps into the shelter and settled down in one of the deckchairs with George on her lap, where she began crooning to him, trying to drown out the frightening sound of explosions and the debris rattling on the corrugated iron of the roof. It was too close for comfort but she had to stick it out until the all-clear went, praying that Julie was safely sheltering somewhere.

Just before they left Canada, Harry and his colleagues had heard news on the Canadian wireless of severe raids on the London Docks and that there had been substantial damage and loss of life, but the report gave no details. It would not do to let the enemy know the extent of the damage, nor deflate the public's morale. That didn't stop the rumours of dreadful carnage as half of London burnt and its citizens fled in terror to the surrounding countryside. He hoped the tales were exaggerated but it didn't stop him worrying. Where had Julie been at the time? Had she left London with his parents as he had urged her to do? Or was she still in Bermondsey? If there was a letter in the post telling him she had moved, he had left before he could receive it, which resulted in a miserable seven-day crossing, every minute of which was torture. He could not eat and could not sleep for thinking of her in the Anderson shelter she hated so much.

Looking about him as they docked in Liverpool on the afternoon of Friday the thirteenth, he saw evidence of raids, ruined buildings, glassless windows, craters in the road. If London was anything like Liverpool, it was bad. His thoughts were with Julie and not on where he would be taken on leaving the ship. Harrogate, he had heard, and after that a posting to an operational squadron.

'Anyone here got folks in London?' their group captain asked them as they assembled ready to disembark. Several men put up their hands. 'Right, you can fall out and go home. Report to Harrogate seven days from now.'

They did not need telling twice. They collected their passes, ran down the gangplank, grabbed a taxi and were taken at speed to the station where they boarded the first train going south.

It was packed with troops and civilians, many of whom had horror tales to tell about the raids, which might or might not have been true, of bits of bodies being found in strange places like roofs and people being burnt out of all recognition, which did not make him feel any easier, though there were also stories of miraculous escapes when people had been brought out alive from seemingly impossible situations. He tried to block the conversation out and listened instead to the wheels repeating 'Julie, George, Julie, George' over and over again. His comrades were in the same state as he was and they had little to say.

The train seemed to be going at the pace of a snail and spent hours in sidings while armaments trains rattled by and it did not arrive in Euston until the following morning. He was out before it had come to a stop and running for the barrier.

The devastation in Southwark and Bermondsey was unbelievable. There were huge craters where once houses had stood and they were half full of water. A whole side of one road had collapsed. The railway arch over Linsey Road had gone; factories had been destroyed and wisps of smoke drifted up from the ruins. There was an acrid smell of burning tar, leather, fermenting beer and glue from the bombed factories which caught in his throat. Nearer home, two adjacent houses had lost their whole front walls, revealing the interiors: beds perched precariously on the edge of upper floors, dressing tables with smashed mirrors, curtains snagged on broken window frames, and downstairs the crushed furniture was covered in rubble from above. Harry wondered if the occupants had survived as he rushed on towards his own home.

At the corner, he came to a sudden stop. Where his house and garden had been was a gaping hole. He stood staring at it, unable to take in what his eyes were telling him. The home which he and Julie had cared for and loved was gone; there was nothing there but a hole in the ground and a heap of rubble and broken glass. Numb with shock, it was a moment before he could ask himself what had happened to his wife and son. He clambered over the debris, some of which he recognised as their broken furniture. The gas cooker lay on its side, its door lying open. A battered saucepan lay beside it. The Anderson shelter was no more than a twist of metal and the rockery he had so painstakingly built was under a heap of rubble. He bent to move some of it. It was almost as if he were searching for his loved ones in the ruins, and yet if he had stopped to think he would have known they could not be there. His foot struck the garden gnome lying on its side; the tip of its pointed hat was broken off and one of its arms was missing but, covered in dust as it was, it was still grinning happily. He picked it up.

'Looking for someone, Sergeant?'

He whipped round to see a warden approaching him. 'Yes, my wife and baby son. They lived here. Do you know where they've gone?'

'Would you be meaning Mrs Walker?'

'Yes.'

'I'm sorry, sir.'

'Sorry?' he queried, not quite understanding.

'Yes. The house took a direct hit. They wouldn't have known a thing about it. I'm very sorry, sir. If there's anything I can do . . .'

'Do?' he repeated dully, clambering back onto the road. 'No, there's nothing you can do. Where were they taken?'

'I don't know. Go to the ARP post, they'll have records.'

His feet took him there, but his mind was on another plane altogether. He did not even notice he was still carrying the gnome.

He sat on a hard chair in the warden's office, drinking

tea and smoking while the man on duty searched the records. 'There were so many and we could not identify them all, so most of them were cremated,' he said, flicking through files.

This brought Harry out of his stupor long enough to ask, 'You mean they haven't got a proper resting place? I can't go and see where they're buried?'

'Ah, here we are. Mrs Julie Walker and son, George Walker. Their bodies were taken by Mr Donald Walker for burial. Is that your father, Sergeant?'

'Yes.' Why couldn't he wake up, why couldn't he be decisive? All he felt was guilt that he had left his wife to cope on her own, red-hot fury with the Luftwaffe for what they were doing and a burning desire for revenge. It bubbled inside him with no way out.

'I should go and find him, Sergeant.'

'Yes.' He put the tin mug which had contained the tea on a desk already stained with rings, and stood up. 'Did he say where he was taking them?'

'He gave his address as Islington, but as for where your wife and son are buried, I couldn't say.'

They hadn't moved yet. His parents, and presumably Millie too, had been in the thick of the raids themselves. He thanked the man, hoisted his kitbag on his shoulder and went to the door.

'Do you want this, sir?' the man said, holding out the gnome. Absent-mindedly, he took it and set off for Islington, wondering what he would find when he got there. If anyone on the Underground wondered why an airman in uniform was clutching a broken garden gnome, they did not comment. People were doing all sorts of strange things nowadays, hanging onto bits of a past life.

The Islington house was still standing, though several of the windows were broken and covered with plywood. He went in by the kitchen door to find his mother wrapping crockery in newspaper and packing it in a tea chest. She looked up when he entered and flew to him to hug him fiercely, saying his name over and over again.

He was so exhausted, both mentally and physically, he could hardly stand. He disengaged himself from her embrace and almost fell into one of the kitchen chairs, dropping his kitbag on the floor. 'I didn't know where you were,' he said, putting the broken gnome on the table. 'I hoped you'd all made it to the country.'

'No, there was a snag about getting the electricity laid on. We're going this weekend.' She put the kettle on the stove. 'Have you been home?'

'Yes.'

'Then you know the worst. I'm sorry, son.'

'They said they wouldn't have known what hit them.'

'No, there is that.'

'Where are they?'

'We buried them together in Highgate Cemetery two days ago. There weren't many people at the service, just the family. There were so many burials and cremations after that dreadful night, we were lucky to get it in. Couldn't wait for you to come home because we didn't know when that would be, but we knew you would want her to have a proper send-off. We wrote but I suppose you were already on your way home.'

'Yes, you can't rely on the post. I often used to get no letters for days and then a whole bundle would arrive at once.' He paused and tried to pull himself together. 'What . . . how . . . did she look?'

'Julie? I didn't see her. The coffin was already nailed down. Your father saw her and said she looked peaceful. George too.'

'That's a relief. You hear such dreadful tales . . .'

'I know. Don't think about it.'

'What about you and Dad and Millie and Dorothy? Are you all OK?'

'Yes, thank God. The factory's a mess but all the machinery was moved a few days earlier, which was a blessing, and no one was hurt. Your pa's there now, seeing everything's secure before we leave. He'll be home later.'

'That's something anyway.' His response was automatic, made without thinking because his thoughts were in such a muddle. Julie, his beloved Julie, and his precious son were dead. He would never see them again, never hear them laughing, never praise, never scold, never again cuddle up in bed with her and feel her soft body in his arms. He just could not take it in.

'How long are you here for?' his mother asked.

'Seven days. Can you put me up?'

'Of course. You can help with the move. Did you bring your ration card?'

'Yes.' He bent to his kitbag and extracted the card to give to her, then he stood up. 'I'm going up to the cemetery.'

'If you must, but if the siren goes, you take shelter. The raid that took Julie was only the beginning. We've had one – more than one – every day and night since. It's terrifying. I shall be glad to get out of it. Losing Julie and George was bad enough, I don't know what I'd do if anything happened to you or to Roly.'

'He's all right, is he?'

'So far. He rings when he can but he doesn't say much. The telephone lines were down but they're back now, thank goodness.'

'I'll be back in time for supper.' He picked up the gnome and let himself out of the house.

There were several new graves in the cemetery, some with flowers on them, some with nothing except a simple wooden cross with a name on it. Julie and George had been buried together and there was one wreath on it from all the family. He had paid an exorbitant amount for a bunch of colourful flowers at the station and knelt to lay them on the mound of freshly turned earth beside the wreath. Then he stood the gnome in front of them. 'Goodbye, sweetheart,' he murmured on a choking sob. 'You're safe now in heaven. God keep you both.'

It was some time before he could bring himself to get up off his knees, but it was other people walking along the path behind him, talking loudly to each other, that roused him. He could not stay there, he had to leave her. He murmured goodbye again and blundered along the path and out of the gate.

The siren went when he was nearly home. He looked up at the sky. It was growing dusk and he could see no aircraft, though a drone in the distance told him they were on their way. Already the searchlights were criss-crossing the sky. He shook his fist upwards in a futile gesture of fury and went indoors to see his mother preparing to go into the Anderson shelter. She was carrying a large bag containing goodness knows what, a blanket, a pillow and a lantern. He took them from her and accompanied her into the shelter. Safe in Canada he had had no real idea of what his family were enduring, but he learnt some of it that night, as

103

he sat drinking tea from a flask and listening to the noise. It was then, lying on a bunk usually occupied by his father, the tears finally flowed.

That bitch, Rosie Summers, had scarpered owing him money and Ted did not like that at all. It had all been going so swimmingly too. He had a nice little business with more and more customers wanting what he supplied. At first he had bought the stuff, but that seemed a daft thing to do when the blackout and the air raids which drove everyone into shelters made it easy to filch things from bombed and abandoned houses, shops and warehouses. He had hired a garage to store it all and had left Chalfont's to concentrate on what had now become his main business. Looting was considered a heinous crime and earned dire penalties, but he felt safe enough because Rosie was doing all the front-running. She didn't know how he acquired the stuff and he often spoke of its cost and the need to make a bit of profit to put her off the scent. Now she had disappeared.

He did not doubt that if he could get into her lodgings, he would find some of the last consignment of goods he had given her, and maybe the cash too, but her landlady had refused to let him into her room, though he cajoled and pleaded and offered her money and half a dozen eggs. 'It's more than my life's worth,' she had told him. 'She's likely staying with her friend, Julie. She does sometimes.'

Julie Walker's house, he had discovered when he went there, had received a direct hit and she had been killed outright with her baby, so he couldn't question her. 'Was Mrs Walker the only one in the house?' he asked the warden.

'She wasn't in the house, she was in the Anderson shelter

and there was only her and her baby.' Another dead end and his scheme to get Julie in so deep he would have her at his mercy had been foiled by the Luftwaffe.

Chalfont's was moving to Hertfordshire and some of the staff had already gone, but when he went to the factory and asked Donald Walker if Rosie was one of them, he was told she had been expected to go, but hadn't reported for work since the raid on the seventh. 'She had a weekend off and should have returned to work the following Monday,' he was told. 'We have reported her missing.'

And so was his money. 'When I catch up with you, I'll have you for this, Rosie Summers,' he told himself.

Ted wasn't the only one searching for Rosie. Her parents were sick with worry. Rosie usually telephoned them every Sunday afternoon just to let them know she was all right, but two Sundays had passed with no call and no letter. They had rung the factory but the phone had been cut off, which worried them even more. They had tried all the hospitals in and around Southwark but no one by the name of Rosemary Summers had been admitted to any of them. 'We have several patients too ill to tell us their names,' Stuart was told by someone at St Olave's Hospital, which was one of the receiving hospitals for local casualties. 'But they've usually got their identity cards or ration books on them, so we know who they are.'

'Could they have cards and books belonging to someone else?'

'Anything's possible with the way things are at the moment.'

He had rung off and turned to his white-faced wife.

'They weren't very helpful. There's nothing for it, I'll have to go down and find out what's going on.'

'Then I'm coming too.'

'Better not. It's too dangerous. There are air raids all the time.'

'I don't care. If you think you are going to leave me here to worry, you've got another think coming, Stuart Summers. If you go, I go.'

The young lady in the hospital bed was finally coming out of her comatose state and the nurse designated to watch over her called the ward sister. 'She's stirring, Sister. I saw her eyes flicker.'

'Good. Now perhaps we'll find out who she is.'

The patient had been dug out of the ruins of the Linsey Street shelter with a broken left arm and left leg, abrasions to her face and a bump on the head. The broken limbs had been plastered and would heal and so would the grazes, but the head injury was worrying. They did not know what to expect when she regained consciousness, if she ever did. She might be living the rest of her life as a cabbage. She had no means of identity on her when she had been brought in, but that was hardly surprising, since almost everything and everyone about her had been blown to smithereens. Bags and papers had been scattered everywhere and there was no way of telling which body they belonged to, even supposing you could piece together the bodies. In any case the chaos as the ambulance crews dashed back and forth ferrying casualties meant possessions frequently became separated from their owners.

Sister stood and looked down at the still form in the bed, watching the flickering of the eyelids, waiting with a fixed smile of reassurance until the eyes opened fully. They were forget-me-not blue. 'Hallo,' she said.

'Where am I?'

'In St Olave's Hospital, Bermondsey. You were in a shelter that was bombed. Can you tell us your name?'

'It's . . .' She stopped suddenly and tried again. 'It's gone. My name has gone.' Tears filled her eyes. 'How can I forget my own name?'

'Easily, my dear. You have sustained a nasty bump on the head, as well as the other injuries, and temporary loss of memory under those circumstances is not uncommon. It will come back.'

'Do you know who I am?'

'Unfortunately, no. You were pulled out of the rubble of the shelter on Linsey Street after it was destroyed by a bomb. There was nothing on you; certainly nothing arrived here with you.'

'Bomb?'

'Yes. There's a war on and we're being bombed. Do you remember that?'

'I remember being very frightened. And noise, a lot of noise and darkness.'

'That's something, I suppose.'

'How long ago was that?'

'Over three weeks now.'

'Hasn't anyone been looking for me?'

'There have been several people looking for lost relatives who came and saw you, but unfortunately you did not belong to any of them.'

'What about other people in the shelter? Didn't any of those know me?'

'There weren't many survivors and those that did get

out said you were a stranger and not one of the people who usually used that shelter. You may have just been visiting the area when the siren went. Do you remember anything about yourself?'

'I'm trying, I really am. I suppose I must have had parents, brothers and sisters, a husband even . . .'

'You are not wearing a wedding ring.'

She felt her wedding ring finger which was sticking out of the plaster that encased her broken arm. 'Oh, no husband, then.'

'But you have given birth, though not recently.'

'I've had a child? What happened to it?'

'We don't know. There were no unidentified children in the shelter. It may have been stillborn some time ago, or it might have been adopted or put into a home, since you're not married.'

'A home?' She was silent, struggling to recall something, anything that might help. 'That rings a bell. I seem to remember something about a home and lots of children. And the seaside. Was the home at the seaside? Oh, why can't I remember? Surely I must have loved the child. I would not have put it in a home unless there was no alternative.'

'Sometimes it's the only thing you can do, especially if the father won't face up to his responsibilities and your parents were not prepared to help.'

'That would have been cruel.'

'Yes, but some people are strict like that. Of course, you may not have had parents alive. It would have been a struggle to manage in that case.'

'But I must have tried. Are you sure my memory will return?'

'Pretty sure.'

108

'When?'

'That I cannot tell you. In a day or two, a week, maybe longer. The brain is a funny thing and we don't altogether understand how it works.'

'What have you been calling me?'

The sister smiled. 'C10. It's the number above your bed.'

'What will happen to me now? Where will I go? I can't even remember where I live.' The blankness of her mind was worrying, but it wasn't exactly blank; her brain was going round and round trying to grasp at something, anything, to tell her who she was and where she came from.

'You will have to stay in hospital until your plaster comes off and then you will need exercises to get your muscles working again. If you still cannot remember after that, you will be rehoused, but until then we are moving you to another hospital away from the bombing. We need the beds here for new casualties. With every raid there are more and more. We are rushed off our feet.'

'When will I go?'

'Tomorrow, by ambulance.'

'What's the date?'

'Friday the twenty-seventh of September.'

'I shall have to remember that.'

'Oh, I think you will. It's only your past you have lost.'

Only my past, she thought as the sister left her. Her past was what made her who she was; without it she was nothing, a number. C10. What sort of person was she? How had she come to have a child and not be married? Did that mean she was wicked? Had she loved the child's father? Why hadn't they married? Was it a boy or a girl? How old would he or she be? Come to think of it, how old was she? Had she got a job, employers who might wonder why she had not reported for work? Why had no one come forward to claim her? If only someone would come she might not feel so isolated and frightened. She nagged and nagged at her memory until she was exhausted and fell asleep.

The next day she was put in an ambulance with three other patients and driven to the King Edward VII Hospital at Windsor, and C10 had become Seaton. She had been asked to choose a Christian name and tossed a few about in her head to see if they jogged her memory, but when that failed, decided on Eve. After all, Eve was the first woman and she had had no past. The name Eve Seaton was written at the head of her notes and it was as Eve Seaton she was admitted.

The couple who faced the matron at St Olave's were distraught with anxiety. They had come all the way from Scotland searching for their missing daughter. He was silver-haired, with a neat grey moustache; her hair had a blue rinse. Both were more smartly dressed than most of the people who came and went into the hospital. What with the high price of clothes and the dirt and dust which seemed to cover everything these days, the population of the bombed areas was looking decidedly shabby.

'Small build, fair hair, blue eyes, age twenty-four,' Matron repeated, taking the snapshot of Rosie she had been offered and squinting at it in the feeble light of her office. It had been taken on their last holiday before the war and Rosie was in a bathing costume and laughing into the camera. 'It could be her, but it's a different hairstyle.'

'You mean she's here?' Angela asked eagerly. 'She's here and you don't know her name?'

'She didn't know it herself.'

'Didn't?' Stuart seized on the past tense, dreading to hear the worst. 'You mean she's not here now? You don't mean she's . . . she's dead?'

'No, she's alive but badly injured. We transferred her to Windsor for safety.'

'Badly injured,' Angela repeated. 'How badly?'

'She has a broken leg, a broken arm, cuts and abrasions, but more troubling is her loss of memory. She doesn't know who she is.'

'Oh, Rosie.' Angela was trembling. 'We must go to her at once.'

'We cannot be sure it is our Rosie,' Stuart said, as they left in a taxi. 'Don't get your hopes up too much.'

'It *must* be Rosie. The description fits and Matron looked at the photo.'

'It's not a very good one, you must admit.'

'It was the most recent and her landlady recognised her easily.'

'That's another thing I can't understand. All that stuff in the cupboard in her room. Where did she get it and what was she going to do with it?'

'I have no idea. She probably bought it in case things got short. I did myself at the start of the war.'

'True.'

They fell silent and looked out of the taxi window at the devastation around them. 'It's awful,' she said. 'If I had known how bad it was, I'd have insisted on her coming home at once.'

'She had to do war work.'

'Yes, but not in London. We'll have her taken to a hospital near home, then we can see she's looked after properly.' Already in her mind the unknown girl was her daughter.

'That might not be easy. I doubt they'd spare an ambulance to go that distance.'

'Then we'll arrange one ourselves. I don't care how much it costs. In any case, we'll need transport to take all her things out of that room too.'

'You are assuming it is Rosie.'

'I pray to God it is.'

But the patient known as Eve Seaton was not their daughter. They stood and looked down at the young woman and slowly shook their heads, then Angela burst into tears and stumbled out of the ward, followed by her husband.

Eve Seaton was as disappointed as her visitors. Several people had been to see her, some of whom she liked, some of whom she could not take to at all, none of whom she had recognised, not even the young soldier searching for his wife. He had been a nice man and she had even been sorry in a way that she was not his wife. Mr and Mrs Summers had been her best hope; they had been so sure she was their daughter. She had meant to ask what had happened to her baby, but being strangers, of course they would not know.

Her memory was as blank as ever. The only things she had been able to call to mind were trivial things that did not help to identify her. She sometimes dreamt up pictures. There was a vast building with shiny corridors which might have been a hospital or an institution; there was a beach with sea lapping over her feet. That one made her feel happy. There were two small children who ran about a garden shrieking. Were they hers? She could not recall their faces. And there was darkness and a terrifying noise which she had been told was probably the bomb that hit the shelter. The more she tried to pull at the memories, the more they refused to solidify. Somewhere, out there beyond the four walls of the hospital, were people she knew, people who knew her. She must have had some family, neighbours, friends, workmates; they could not all have died. If it were not for the plaster of Paris on her leg, she might go out and wander about the streets near the shelter where she had been found and wait for someone to smile in recognition and ask her where she had been hiding herself. She might try that when she was well enough to leave hospital.

And if no one recognised her, then what? She had no money, no clothes, no ration book, no identity card, nowhere to live. What had she done for a living? What could she do? Was she skilled or unskilled?

She read newspapers, studying every word, even the advertisements, in the hope that something would jog her memory. In that way she learnt about what was happening in the world about her, or as much as the government were prepared to divulge, and she knew that London was being bombed every night, sometimes more than once, and that everyone was trying to go about their business notwithstanding. She read about great heroism, as well as crime and looting, rationing, new regulations and the black market, but she did not learn who she was. Eve Seaton was an enigma.

Chapter Five

Added to Harry's misery over the loss of Julie and George was the frustration of not yet being assigned to an operational squadron. He was itching to get into action, but all that happened was that he was sent to Cosford where there was a radio training school. As one of the best wireless operators to be turned out in his group he found himself as an instructor, passing on his knowledge to others. It wasn't what he joined up for, though if Julie had still been alive she would have been pleased to know he wasn't in the front line. He felt a bit of a fraud because it was the population of London and other cities who were truly in the firing line and they were suffering unbelievable hardship. He was glad his parents had moved. Three-quarters of the workforce at Chalfont's were women now and, according to his father, doing a great job.

Sometimes, when he had leave, he went to stay with them. Letchworth was a purpose-built garden city and an oasis of calm. The air-raid siren went off now and again, but the bombers were on their way to or from somewhere else and left them alone. He would spend his leave wandering about the countryside and often found himself thinking, *Julie would like to see this*, or *I must tell Julie about that*. And then he would remember and be thrown into gloom. He visited Millie, who was renting a house near his parents, but the sight of Dorothy running about and talking in her own baby language reduced him to tears. He found the companionship of his fellow airmen easier to cope with than the cloying sympathy of his family and often he did not leave the station when on leave.

He would go to the pictures and for a little while lose himself in the story on the screen, or watch a football match, but more often than not he would join a crowd of his fellows going to the nearest pub, where they drank too much and the jollity was forced.

Once, when he had a whole week's leave just before Christmas, he took a train to London and went to Highgate Cemetery to stand over Julie's grave and contemplate what might have been if there had been no war. There was a stone cross at its head with the names of Julie and George engraved on it, which he had ordered before he returned from leave. The grave was kept tidy and there were flowers in a vase beneath the cross. He was wondering who had put them there when he saw Miss Paterson coming along the path towards him carrying a holly wreath. She seemed thinner and frailer than when he had last seen her and her hair was almost white, reminding him that time never stood still however much you might wish it could.

'Sergeant Walker,' she said. 'How are you?'

'I'm well, thank you. I had a day or two's leave and thought I'd come down. Have you been looking after the grave?'

'Yes, you don't mind, do you?'

'No, I'm grateful.'

She bent and took away the spent flowers and replaced them with the wreath, picking up the fallen petals and putting all the rubbish in a bag she carried. 'I'll leave you, shall I?'

'No, don't go. Tell me about Julie. Did you see her often?'

'Not all that often, but strangely enough she came to see me that day. The siren went while she was with me. She would not take shelter and insisted on going home because she had left George with a friend. It was a hot day and he had been having fun sitting in a bath of cool water and she didn't want to drag him out. She didn't intend to be gone long. In a way I'm glad she got back to be with him in the end, though I don't suppose it's any consolation to you.'

'Yes and no. What happened to her friend?'

'I suppose she went home when Julie returned. Foolish of her to risk being out in a raid, but as it happened it probably saved her life.'

'Was she all right? Julie, I mean. Was she well?'

'Yes, but she missed you. She talked a lot about what you would do when you came home. And of course, she doted on George. She would risk anything for him.'

'I know.' He bent and propped the gnome against the wreath.

'I didn't know whether to leave that there,' she said.

'Yes, Julie loved it. She said he was happy and that was how she was. Whenever she looked at him, she would smile. I hope he's keeping her smiling now.'

'I am sure he is, but Harry, you must not grieve too long, you know. You have your whole life ahead of you and you mustn't waste it. Save the good memories and make a new life for yourself.'

'If Herr Hitler lets me.'

'Amen to that.'

They parted at the cemetery gate and he went back to Harrogate feeling cleansed. The visit had eased his pain a little and brought some sort of finality to Julie's death, something he had been finding it hard to come to terms with. He stiffened his back and decided, come hell or high water, he would get himself into an operational squadron and do something about winning this war. Let someone else teach the others how to operate wireless sets.

It was March 1941 before Julie was discharged from the convalescent home she had been sent to after being several weeks in hospital. Now she was fit and well in body if not in mind, but her past remained as elusive as ever. She had accepted her new name, together with a new identity card and ration book, a little money which came out of a government fund for people who had been bombed out, and clothing and toiletries provided by the WVS. She was now, to all intents and purposes, Eve Seaton, aged twenty-two, so they guessed, birthdate and birthplace unknown, next of kin none.

The first thing she did, even before finding lodgings, was to go to Southwark and wander round the streets to see if anything jogged her memory. The bomb damage was extensive and all she could see were ruined buildings: houses, shops and factories. Even the sight of the railway bridge, now repaired, did nothing to stir anything in her mind but a feeling of terror. Some of the factories were still functioning and she watched the workforce making their way inside. No one gave any sign of recognising her. A few shops, their windows boarded up, were open for business and one grocer even had a notice stuck to the door: 'Assistant wanted'.

She went inside. 'I believe you need an assistant,' she said to the elderly man who came from behind a blackout curtain at the back of the shop to serve her.

'Yes. My wife's ill upstairs and I need to look after her. I want someone to take over down here. Have you done this kind of work before?'

'No, but I'll do anything.'

'Can you add up?'

Julie was fairly sure she could. 'Yes.'

'What's your name?'

'Eve Seaton.'

'Mine's Doug Green. You don't come from round here.'

'How do you know?'

'The way you talk. More West End than East End.'

'Do you think so?'

'Yes. Can you start tomorrow?'

'Yes.'

'Then be here by eight o'clock. I like to catch the factory workers before they clock on. They buy snacks and cigarettes usually.'

Julie thanked him and left to find lodgings. Very little had escaped the bombing, but there were still buildings standing, some hardly touched, and she wandered about the rest of the day trying to drag her memory back, but the harder she tried the more it eluded her. Mr Green had said she sounded more West End than East End, so perhaps she didn't come from about here at all. Giving up, she found a room in a lodging house and sat down to contemplate a future which was as unknown to her as her past.

Working for Mr Green was hard work and the hours long, and by the time she had finished and returned to her lodgings each night, all she wanted to do was eat her evening meal and fall into bed. She was lonely and the only human contact she had was with her landlady and Mr Green and his regular customers, none of whom gave any sign of recognising her. But with a shifting population – people being bombed out and moving away, men away in the forces, children evacuated and new people coming in to work in the factories – it was hardly surprising. She was lonely, so lonely that she wondered if she had been used to having a lot of people around her. A big family perhaps? But if that were so, why had no one come looking for her? Was she in the wrong area altogether?

When the siren went, she refused to go into a shelter; not for anything would she venture into one of those again. Her landlady gave up trying to persuade her and left her in her room. She would switch off the light and pull back the curtains so that she could lie in bed and see the sky and its criss-cross of searchlights. She would lie there sleepless and listen to the planes coming in, the noise of the guns and the heavy crump of explosions, with her heart beating uncomfortably fast. It only slowed down when the all-clear sounded.

After one particularly bad raid in early May, she thought the whole city must be on fire. From her window she could see the flames reaching skywards in whichever direction she looked. She could hear the drone of aircraft, wave after wave of them, and occasionally one was caught in a searchlight beam, and then the guns opened fire, but she never saw one brought down. She went to work the following morning to find the grocer's shop was no more than a pile of rubble.

'What happened to Mr and Mrs Green?' she asked an ARP warden who was surrounding the ruin with a barrier and a notice: 'Danger. Keep Out.'

'You a relative?'

'No, I work for Mr Green. Or I did.'

'They are safe. They were in the shelter down the road and were taken to the school. They'll be looked after there.'

She thanked him and went to find them. They were sitting on mattresses on the floor of the school hall, shaken but otherwise resigned. She talked to them for a few moments and learnt they would be rehoused and given whatever was necessary to make a new start somewhere away from the bombing. There was nothing she could do for them and she returned to her lodgings. 'Now what?' she asked herself, sitting on her bed and surveying the dingy room, made worse because plaster had fallen off the ceiling during the raid, and there was a huge crack in the window.

Her landlady knocked on her door. 'Miss Seaton, I heard you come back,' she said when Julie answered it. 'I wanted to tell you I've had enough of this and I'm moving out. I'm off to stay with my sister in the country and shutting up the house.'

'You want me to move?'

'Yes, I'm afraid so.'

Julie gathered up her few belongings and left. She was homeless and jobless again. Trying to live in the community in the hope it would jog her memory had failed, so she might as well do something entirely different. Since the beginning of April unmarried women between twenty and thirty had been required to register at their nearest employment exchange in order to be directed to war work, but Julie had still been convalescing at the time and was deemed unfit, but nearly two months working for Mr Green and being on her feet all day had strengthened her muscles and she decided to give it a try.

Allowed to choose between the Women's Royal Naval Service, Women's Auxiliary Air Force, the Auxiliary Territorial Service, the Land Army or essential factory work, she decided on the Women's Auxiliary Air Force – why, she did not know, unless it was the blue uniform which she thought looked more feminine than the khaki of the ATS or the navy of the WRNS. She filled in some forms and then returned to find new lodgings and wait for her call-up.

A week later she was ordered to report to Adastral House on the corner of Kingsway. Here she was directed to a room where she found a crowd of other young women, all waiting to join up. Some were noisy and excited, some, like Julie, quiet and wondering what they had let themselves in for. An RAF sergeant called them to order and herded them like a flock of sheep out to a lorry and told them to climb in the back. Julie, being so small, struggled to get up, but someone put a hand under her bottom and heaved her up where she lay in a heap on the floor. She scrambled up and found a seat on one of the benches. They were taken to Euston Station and boarded a train, bound, so they were told, for Bridgnorth in Shropshire.

'I'm Florrie, Florrie Kilby.' The girl sitting next to Julie held out her right hand. About Julie's age, she was taller and broader, with the tanned complexion of someone who was accustomed to spending a lot of time out of doors. She had hazel eyes and an infectious smile.

Julie shook the hand. 'I'm Eve Seaton.'

'Where are you from?'

This was what she had been dreading, but she had been rehearsing in her mind a past that they would accept and one she could remember; it would never do to slip up and contradict herself later. 'Southwark,' she said, only because that was where she had been rescued from the bombed shelter, and, in a way, where she had been reborn.

'Gosh, that took a pounding in the Blitz, didn't it?'

'Yes.'

'Were you bombed?'

'Yes.' She couldn't just keep saying yes and so she added, 'We were bombed out. I was injured and had a long stay in hospital.'

'Poor you. Are you well now?'

'Yes, I think so. I hope so because I don't want to be rejected on account of being unfit.'

'No, but I expect it might please your folks.'

'All gone. I was the only one who survived.'

'Oh, how awful. I'm sorry, I shouldn't have asked you.'

'You weren't to know. I just don't like talking about it.' Why she didn't tell her new friend the truth she did not know. Perhaps because she knew everyone would be curious and bombard her with questions she could not answer. Perhaps it was a feeling that there might be something murky in her past she didn't want anyone to know and she was better off not remembering. Why else would she have shut it all out as if she were ashamed of it? She must make the most of her new life, embrace it, learn to live without a memory further back than 7th September 1940. That, she had decided, would be her birthday.

'Then I won't. We'll talk about something else.'

Florrie was as good as her word and took it upon herself to make introductions to the rest of the girls in the carriage.

Sylvia Burrows, who was sitting on the other side of Julie, was a Londoner – a little plump, brown-haired, rosy-cheeked. She was engaged to a fighter pilot. 'Thank God he came through the worst of the bombing, but I still worry about him,' she said. 'He's stationed at Duxford and I want to wangle a posting there if I can.'

Connie Braithwaite, sitting opposite, was older and had been twice married: once divorced, once widowed. She came from Yorkshire and had joined up because she thought it might be an adventure and she might meet a new man in her life. 'Some hope,' she said. 'If that Sergeant What's-his-name is anything to go by, I'll stay single.'

'Sergeant Parrish, you mean,' Florrie said, referring to the sergeant who had taken their details at Adastral House and shepherded them onto the lorry. 'It can't be easy for him, looking after a lot of women. We don't come in standard packs.'

'No, thank goodness. Where do you come from?'

'Harston in Wiltshire. It's near Andover.'

'What about you, Eve?' Connie asked, turning to Julie. 'Where do you hail from?'

'Southwark.'

'Eve was bombed out,' Florrie said. 'She was the only one of her family to survive.'

'My God! How awful!' This from Sylvia. 'We get raids in Edgware but nothing like the East End.'

'Eve spent months in hospital,' Florrie put in. 'Then she joined up straight away. I'm going to be her family from now on.'

'We'll all be your family,' Sylvia said, putting her arm round Julie's shoulder and giving her a hug. 'You're not alone.'

Julie was near to tears. Kindness seemed to hit her like that, which made her wonder if she had not been used to kindness in the past. Everything set her wondering, every new sight, every new voice, every new situation.

'May I join you?' They looked up to see a dark-haired girl hovering in the doorway.

'Of course,' Julie said, hitching along to make room for her. 'We're just getting to know each other. I'm Eve. This is Florrie, Connie and Sylvia.'

'I'm Meg, short for Megan.'

'We can tell where you come from,' Florrie said. 'You've got Welsh written all over you.'

Megan looked down at herself and laughed. 'Does it say Llangollen?'

'Is that where you live? It's a beautiful part of the country,' Connie said. 'I was there on my first honeymoon. Nothing to do but walk and climb hills, but we didn't care. Pity it didn't last.' She didn't sound particularly unhappy about it.

To Julie's relief the conversation became general, much of it speculation about what lay ahead of them, and she did not feel she had to contribute, except for a comment here and there, and the rest of the journey passed pleasantly.

They arrived at Bridgnorth Station in the dark and were met by another lorry which took them to the camp, a few minutes drive up a very steep hill. 'I'm starving,' Florrie said. 'I wonder what we'll have for supper?'

Supper had to wait until they had been taken to their hut, which held beds for thirty-two recruits and a tiny private room for their corporal, who was there to greet them. There was a stove in the middle of the room, whose metal chimney disappeared through the roof, and a table with a few upright chairs round it.

'Find yourself beds,' Corporal Wiggin told them as they milled around. 'Then I'll show you the ablution block and toilets.'

124

The scramble for beds next to friends was noisy but good-natured as everyone claimed a bed and put what little luggage they had in the lockers beside them. The beds were iron-framed and the mattresses each consisted of three square biscuits which, laid on end, covered the steel springs. Now they were piled on top of each other at the head of each bed, topped with two blankets and a pillow. Sheets there were none. After visiting the severely basic washroom and toilet huts, they were herded to the canteen where they were given cutlery and a tin mug and lined up for sausages and mash, stewed apples and custard and a mug of strong tea. After that, tired and bemused, they stumbled in the dark back to their billet to make up their beds and fall into them.

Julie sat on the end of her bed and watched the others undressing. Some were so shy they scrambled into their nightclothes under the blankets, some knelt to say their prayers before getting into bed. Others were brazen and stripped off flimsy underwear before donning pyjamas. Their accents ranged from the London of Sylvia Burrows to the aristocratic accent of Joan Parson-Ford, the Welsh of Megan Jones to the Yorkshire of Connie Braithwaite, and everything in between. It was obvious that the population of the hut came from many backgrounds and levels of society. It would be interesting to see how they all got on. Strangely, she didn't feel uncomfortable in the crowd, nor did the spartan conditions worry her, so had she known communal living before? At school perhaps?

'Hi, Eve, what are you sitting there dreaming about?' Florrie called out from the next bed. 'Get undressed, for goodness' sake. It'll be time to get up again before you know it.'

Julie turned and smiled at her friend. 'Just thinking.'

'Well, don't. Brooding on the past won't help you know. We've just got to get on with it.'

'I know.' No good saying she wasn't dwelling on the past, that she had no past to dwell on; no one would understand how it felt not even to know the name she was born with. She undressed, put on the winceyette pyjamas given to her by the WVS and climbed into bed. 'See you tomorrow,' she murmured, already half asleep.

They were woken at six next morning by Corporal Wiggin's strident voice telling them to 'Rise and shine'. Reluctantly they stirred and ambled over to the wash house in dressing gowns, then returned to dress, after which they were taught how to make their beds, with biscuits stacked and blankets precisely folded on top, followed by the tick pillow. It was obvious that no one was to be allowed to lounge on their beds during the day. That done, and the spaces around the bed swept to the corporal's satisfaction, they went for their breakfast.

It was daylight now and they could see that the camp was a collection of wooden huts and a parade ground. Their corporal pointed out the admin office, the cook house, the sickbay and the stores. The rest were accommodation huts for new recruits and the permanent staff. Aeroplanes there were none; there wasn't even a runway. Breakfast was substantial and they did it justice before being taken for a medical. Julie held her breath as the medical officer paid particular attention to how well her leg and arm had healed, but he expressed himself satisfied and she rejoined the others.

The next stop was another hut. 'Right, you lot.' The voice was loud and belonged to a WAAF sergeant who was standing beside a long table piled high with clothing. Behind each pile stood a WAAF. 'Get in line and collect your kit.'

They shuffled into line and passed along the table and were handed items from each pile. Because they were all different shapes and sizes, this took some time, but they eventually ended up at the other end of the table with a mountain of clothes: skirts, shirts, tunics, a cap with a badge, an overcoat, black lace-up shoes and lisle stockings, and four pairs of enormous bloomers, two in blue and two in white, big enough to cover them from bust to knees.

'We aren't meant to wear these, are we?' Florrie asked the sergeant, holding them up for everyone to see.

'Yes; now move along, you're keeping everyone waiting.' This was said with only the faintest glimmer of a smile.

'No wonder they're called "passion killers",' came from Connie, raising a nervous laugh.

They continued along the line. Overalls, two pairs of striped pyjamas, shoes, laces, spare buttons, a button stick and a sewing repair kit joined the growing pile, together with a haversack and kitbag to put it all in. At the end of the line they were handed a sheet of strong brown paper and some string. 'Pack your civilian clothes up ready to be sent home,' the sergeant told them. 'You won't be needing them again for the duration.'

'I haven't got a home address,' Julie said to Florrie as they walked back to the barracks laden like donkeys. 'I went straight from hospital into digs.'

'You can send your stuff to my home if you like. Mum and Dad won't mind.'

'Are you sure?'

'Course. We'll stick together, shall we?'

'Yes, if we're allowed to.'

They took everything over to their billet where they changed into uniform and stowed everything else away in their lockers. They had been told their hair must not touch their collars and that involved pins and combs for those with longer hair. Julie's had been cut while she was in hospital in a kind of boyish cut that suited her pixie face and she had no trouble conforming. Florrie's was a rich brown, thick and long, and the only way she could get it off her collar was to plait it and wind the plaits round her head. Megan rolled her dark tresses round a thin silk scarf and secured it with pins, a style adopted by others with long hair. Now they began to look and feel more like members of the armed services. 'You look nice in your uniform,' Florrie told Julie.

'Thank you, so do you.'

Their civilian clothes parcelled up and left to be collected, they were taken to the Astra Cinema where the occupants of several other huts joined them to learn the hierarchy of the service and the various ranks, and the rules and regulations, which seemed unending, together with a frightening film about venereal diseases and another about the birth of a baby. It set Julie wondering about the baby she was supposed to have had and had forgotten. How could you forget something like that?

After that they had lunch and then assembled on the parade ground, there to be greeted by an RAF sergeant who proceeded to tell them in no uncertain terms what was expected of them as new recruits and what was in store for them, which on the first day and many subsequent days meant assembling on the parade ground and learning to march. Up and down they went, back and forth, falling in, falling out, wheeling and turning. There was no quarter given on account of their sex and it was no good complaining their feet hurt in their new shoes; they were quickly silenced.

Released from that at the end of the day they went to the canteen for their evening meal which was substantial but uninspiring. By that time the thirty-two had formed into smaller groups. Julie and Florrie were joined by Sylvia, Connie and Megan.

'There are walks and hills, hereabouts,' Julie said. 'When we get time off I intend to explore.'

'If we get time off,' Sylvia put in.

'What work did you do before you joined up?' Connie asked her.

'I was a shop assistant at John Lewis in Oxford Street.'

'And I worked in a hotel looking after tourists,' Megan said.

'What about you?' Connie asked Julie.

She couldn't say anything that needed qualifications or special training because she would undoubtedly be caught out. 'I was in service.'

Connie laughed. 'Out of the frying pan into the fire, then. I was a typist before I married. Haven't done much since – a job here, another there.'

'You'll find this a bit of a shock, then,' Florrie said. 'I'm used to hard work. My father has a farm and I was always expected to do my share.'

'Surely farming's a reserved occupation?'

'Yes, but I wanted to spread my wings, learn something new. I've been told there are opportunities galore in the services.'

'What, to learn square-bashing?'

'I heard you can choose to do what you like within

reason,' Julie ventured. 'You can be almost anything: cook, telephonist, typist, clerk, driver, wireless operator, medical orderly, plotter, parachute packer . . .'

'I'm going to ask to be a driver,' Florrie said.

'Can you drive?' Julie asked.

'I can drive a tractor and I drove my brother's Austin Seven before I pranged it. He was furious, but then the war came and petrol was rationed so he couldn't use it anyway. Can you drive?'

This was another of those questions to which she did not know the answer. 'No,' she said, to be on the safe side. 'We never had a car.'

'If you want to do it, the WAAF will teach you, providing there's room on a course.'

'I'm not really fussy what I do.'

'Don't be like that, you'll get the worst job going if you say that, cleaning out latrines, washing dishes. You're too intelligent for that.'

'How do you know I'm intelligent?'

'I can tell by the way you speak, the things you say and how you hold yourself, head up and eyes shining. I bet you went to a good school.'

Having no idea whether this was true or not, Julie laughed. 'Thank you for that. I'll see what they offer me.'

'When the time comes, say you want to be a driver and we'll stay together.'

'What's so special about being a driver?' Sylvia said.

'You get to move about a bit and meet all sorts, better than being stuck in one place all the time. You might get to drive a wing commander or a group captain, preferably an unmarried one.'

'I'll have some of that,' Connie said, making them laugh.

They laughed a lot; everything was found to be funny, incidents that would previously hardly raise a smile had them giggling uncontrollably. Their NCOs and officers all seemed to have character traits that caused hilarity. Laughing at them counteracted the severity of their commands and the rules and regulations one or other of them was always breaking. Joan Parson-Ford was always in trouble. She had led a privileged life with servants to do her bidding and she did not like being ordered about or criticised, nor did she take to communal living, making Julie wonder why she had joined up in the first place. It did not surprise them when, one Saturday, she packed her bags and disappeared. 'What d'you know,' Connie said, joining everyone in the barracks after lunch. 'Lady Muck's been posted for officer training.'

'Then I hope I don't come up against her,' Florrie said. 'There's transport going into Bridgnorth this afternoon. Anyone coming?'

It was their first Saturday afternoon off and they had been debating how to spend it. Exploring Bridgnorth seemed a good idea and Julie, Connie, Sylvia and Meg elected to go with her.

Bridgnorth, divided by the River Severn, had a High Town and a Low Town, which had once been a thriving port. On either bank the houses, shops and pubs climbed upwards. The girls climbed the narrow cartway, which had once been the route that donkeys and mules took bringing goods up from the river, a walk which, in spite of their being fit, made them breathless. It was only after they had made the ascent they realised there was a funicular railway which took passengers up and down the steep hill. 'We'll know another time,' Julie said, as they set off along the

Castle Walk to the ruins of a castle, one wall of which was so far out of perpendicular it looked in danger of falling over. According to Megan, who knew the town, it had suffered at the hands of Cromwell's troops who had tried and failed to bring it down. Here they leant over the railings to admire the extensive view. Below them the river wound its placid way, and on the far side the hills climbed again. 'I never realised England was so beautiful,' Julie murmured, eyes shining as she looked about her at the rolling green countryside.

'Didn't you ever go away on holiday?' Sylvia asked.

'No, we couldn't afford holidays. A day at the sea sometimes.' A day at the sea; that rang a bell in her head, but though she worried away at the thought, she could not place where or when she had been to the coast. It was connected with a child, she thought, but she couldn't be sure.

'You must have seen pictures,' Connie said.

She pulled herself together. 'Yes, but it's not the same, is it?'

'When we get leave, you can come home with me,' Florrie said. 'It's beautiful where I live too.'

'Won't your parents mind?'

'No, course not. We've got a telephone – Dad had it installed just before the war. I can always ring them and warn them we're on our way.'

They turned and went into the town where, after wandering about looking at the shops and buying a pot of tea in a café, they decided to go to the Majestic and see *Gone with the Wind*, a very long film about the American Civil War, starring Clark Gable and a new English actress called Vivien Leigh. It was so late when they emerged, they missed the transport back to camp and had to walk, which they did, linking arms and singing 'It's a Long Way to Tipperary' as they went. They just managed to get in by 11.59, which was the latest they were allowed out.

Julie, who was still a little reticent on account of having to invent answers to questions about herself, slowly learnt to relax and became one of the crowd, perhaps not as noisy as the others, but ready to take part in anything that was going. Her niggling over her unknown past slowly began to fade as she built up a new life. They got to know some of the men in the camp, but none made any lasting friendships when the future was so uncertain and anyone could be posted at a moment's notice.

Training continued until, one day in July, they were issued with passes and travel warrants and told they could have a week's leave, after which they would be posted for more training in whatever job they had been allocated. Florrie and Julie headed for Wiltshire and Hillside Farm.

The warm welcome Julie received made up for the dismally long journey by several different trains, all going at the pace of a snail. 'Come along in, make yourself at home,' Mrs Kilby told Julie. 'I'm Maggie, by the way.' She was a big woman, wearing an apron over a dark skirt and a flowered blouse, sleeves rolled up to the elbows, a wisp of flour on her nose and lustrous brown hair pulled untidily into a bun on top of her head. 'You don't mind sharing a room with Florrie, do you? Only I've got two little evacuee girls in the spare room.'

'Mum, we've been sharing a room with twenty-eight others for six weeks now,' Florrie said. 'Come on, Julie, I'll show you where to go.' She conducted her upstairs and into a spacious bedroom.

'It's quite a big house,' Julie said, standing to look out of the window at the front lawn and a paddock where a couple of horses grazed.

'Mum and Dad inherited it from my grandfather along with the farm. I'll show you round later. Let's get out of uniform into civvies and then go down for supper. I can smell something good.'

They were soon seated round a big kitchen table enjoying roast pork and apple sauce and plenty of fresh vegetables; rationing seemed not to bother them. There was Mr Kilby, whom she was told to address as Walter, Maggie, Florrie's brother Alec, Julie and two little girls, Liz and Alice, who had been evacuated from Plymouth. Both were very shy. Stretched on the hearthrug before the kitchen range was a black Labrador, twitching in his sleep, and on a cushion on a rocking chair by the hearth a ginger cat snoozed. It was so cosy and welcoming, Julie had to blink back tears.

Alec was a younger version of his father, in that he was well built and tanned from spending most of his time out of doors, but his hair was fair and he had Florrie's hazel eyes and winning smile. 'Fancy coming to the Three Bells for a quick one after dinner?' he asked his sister.

'I don't mind, it's up to Eve.'

'I'll go along with whatever you decide,' she said.

They walked there, with Julie in between them. Florrie and Alec kept up a lively conversation and all Julie had to do was listen. She liked Florrie's family. They all seemed so cheerful and concerned for each others' welfare and happiness. That, she decided enviously, was what family life was all about; she had a strange feeling, listening to their banter, that she had not had a family like that. Maybe she had been an only child. On this warm starlit night, with her arm through those of her companions, she was really content for the first time since she had woken up in hospital.

The week went by in a blur of eating, sleeping, going into Andover to shop – where Julie used some of her pay and clothing coupons to enlarge her tiny wardrobe with a cotton dress, a skirt, a couple of blouses and some stockings – exploring the countryside on foot, watching Alec milking the cows, and learning to ride a small docile pony, which took all her courage. Whatever had been in her past, it did not include farm animals, she decided. No one questioned her too closely on her past, perhaps because they had been warned by Florrie that being reminded of the loss of her family would upset her. Instead they brought her into the family circle, just as they had the two little evacuees, cracking jokes and suggesting things to do. Alec was particularly good with the evacuees and they adored him, scrambling onto his back and being taken for piggyback rides, telling him to 'Gee up' and giggling when he collapsed in a heap on the floor. Julie thought he would make a wonderful father, though she had seen no sign of a girlfriend.

'I'm so grateful to you,' Julie told Maggie when the week came to an end and they were preparing to leave. 'I've had a lovely time.'

'Good. Now, you come again. Even if Florrie can't come, you come. Think of this as home.'

At which Julie burst into tears and was enveloped in brawny arms. 'There, I didn't mean to make you cry. Don't be sad.'

'I'm not sad,' she sniffed. 'I'm happy.'

Maggie laughed and held her at arm's length. 'It's a funny way to show happiness. But there, I understand. I think you're so brave, after what you've been through. Now smile. Here comes Florrie. Alec will take you to the station.'

Alec bundled their kitbags into the boot of the family Ford, held the door for Julie to sit beside him and Florrie climbed in the back.

'Have you enjoyed your leave?' he asked Julie as he swung out of the farm gate and along the lane to the main road.

'Oh, yes, very much.'

'You'll come again, I hope.'

'Course she will,' Florrie put in from behind them. 'You haven't seen the last of her.'

'Good,' he said.

'There,' Florrie said, tapping Julie on the shoulder. 'You've got yourself a new brother.'

'Brother be damned,' he muttered.

They had no sooner arrived back in Bridgnorth than they were on the move again. The others were scattered but Florrie and Julie managed to stay together and were posted to Morecambe to learn to be drivers. Here, they were billeted in a boarding house taken over for the purpose and spent most of their time up to their elbows in oil and grease, learning basic mechanics. There were lectures on theory, rules and regulations and the Highway Code, all before they ever found themselves behind the wheel, but when they did, it was not long before they graduated from cars to all manner of vehicles, from trucks and lorries to tea wagons and ambulances. Florrie took to it like a duck to water and was soon driving heavy lorries with ease. Julie struggled. She was too small to reach the pedals comfortably and in the end it was decided between her and her instructors that driving wasn't for her. She found herself working in the stores, which was safe and boring.

'I think I'll apply for a posting,' she told Florrie one day when they had some time off together and were walking along Morecambe sands with their shoes and stockings in their hands.

'Why? Aren't you happy here?'

'Yes and no. I don't feel as though I'm contributing much towards the war effort. I need something to get my teeth into.'

'What do you want to do?'

'I don't know, that's half the trouble.' Another reason was the proximity of the seashore, which niggled away at her memory until she thought it would drive her mad. She had walked along sand like this before and it had been significant, or why did it awaken a feeling of things past, of matters left undone, of children? At least, one child. She could not grasp more than that, not even to decide on the sex of the child. But perhaps the child had been her? Was it her own childhood that was slowly coming back to her? In one way she welcomed it and in another dreaded it. Just when she thought it was coming back, it slipped away again. 'Something to keep me busy.'

'But you are busy.'

'Not my head. My head wanders.'

'You are a little silly. Tell you what. Hang fire until I'm given my posting and see if you can come to the same place. I don't want to lose you.'

'You won't lose me. We'll keep in touch.'

'Of course we will. You're going home to the farm on your next leave, you promised Mum, but that's not the point. You're such a dreamer, you need me to keep your

137

feet on the ground. How you ever got by before you met me, I don't know.'

Julie laughed. 'I'm not that helpless.'

'I didn't mean you were helpless – far from it – simply that you often seem to have your head in the clouds.'

It was the perfect opportunity and she nearly told her then, nearly said, 'You might have your head in the clouds if you couldn't remember your own name or where you come from,' but still she hesitated. Supposing whatever it was she could not remember was so dreadful that no one would want to know her and she lost Florrie's friendship? She dare not risk it.

'OK,' she said. 'I'll wait until you know where you're going and see if there's a vacancy there too. Will that satisfy you?'

'Yes. Come on, we'd better turn back. Have you brought anything to dry your feet?'

'No, I didn't think.' More echoes, more nudges of her memory. Was it coming back, bit by bit?

'Good job *I* did.'

They left the sand and sat on a bench to dry their feet with the small towel Florrie had with her and replace stockings and shoes, before returning to their billet and their daily routine which left Julie no time to brood about the past. It was hard enough dealing with the present. The war was not going well. Apart from the air raids which went on almost without let-up, food was short owing to heavy losses at sea, and rationing was extended. The Allied armies, fighting in North Africa, were having a hard time of it and the German army had overrun Poland, captured Kiev in Ukraine and were driving towards Moscow. Julie's problems were insignificant by comparison.

138

Chapter Six

Stuart and Angela Summers were back in London. They seemed unable to stay away. They had no sooner eliminated one lead in their search for Rosie and returned to Scotland than they felt compelled to return and try another. The Salvation Army and the Red Cross were helping them but so far there had been no luck. They had advertised in every newspaper, even including a snapshot and offering a reward. All in vain. Stuart was slowly coming to the conclusion that his daughter had perished in one of the many bombing raids on London, but Angela would not believe it. Ashen-faced and losing weight, she clung to hope like a drowning man clinging to a straw.

'There's something not quite right about her disappearance,' she said over and over again. 'All that stuff in her room and then the break-in when it was all stolen is decidedly suspicious. She's got herself into trouble, that's what, and is ashamed to tell us.'

'I don't believe that.'

'What other explanation is there? Her landlady said there was a shifty-looking character came asking after her.'

'Angela, you must stop this,' he told her as often as she brought the subject up. 'Our Rosie was lost in the Blitz. They couldn't identify all the casualties.'

'Well, I don't believe people can just disappear like that, wartime or no wartime. Perhaps she's been injured and is lying in hospital somewhere, lost her memory or something. It does happen . . .'

'We've been to all the hospitals and convalescent homes.'

'So you are just going to give up, are you, Stuart Summers?'

'No,' he said wearily. 'I can't give up any more than you can, but I don't know where we go from here.'

'We could try tracing the man that went to her lodgings. I'm sure it was him broke in and stole those supplies from her room.'

'We don't know his name or what he looks like.'

'Perhaps she met him at work. We could try Chalfont's again.'

He had sighed and given in. It was easier than arguing, and to tell the truth, he was as unsettled about Rosie's disappearance as his wife was. Even to have her death confirmed might give them a little peace.

Chalfont's had evacuated to Letchworth, and to Letchworth they went and asked to speak to the manager.

Donald Walker recognised the couple because they had gone to him in Southwark when their daughter had first gone missing. He shook their hands and offered them seats in his office. 'Have you any news?' he asked, pulling his chair round so that he was not sitting behind his desk.

'No, we hoped you might have.'

'Nothing, I'm afraid.'

'I gather from her landlady that she had a man friend,' Angela said. 'Could she have met him at work?'

'I cannot say, but I'll make enquiries if you like. She was friendly with my daughter-in-law . . .'

Angela sat forward eagerly. 'Can we speak to her?'

'I'm sorry, no; she was killed at the start of the Blitz. The same weekend your daughter went missing. It was a dreadful night and there were so many casualties, our little grandson among them.'

'Oh, I am dreadfully sorry for your loss,' she said, but even then she could not let go a lead, any sort of lead. 'What about your son?'

'He was in Canada at the time. In the RAF. He came back to find them dead and buried.'

'Oh.' She was suddenly deflated. Another blind alley, each one more disappointing than the last. She could hardly hold back her tears.

'I am sorry we troubled you,' Stuart said, standing up.

Donald rose too. 'If it helps, I'll see if anyone in the factory remembers your daughter and who her friends were, but it's a long shot – we have so few of our old workers with us now.'

'Thank you. It's very kind of you.'

'Not at all. When I write to my son, I'll ask him if Julie ever mentioned Rosie or any other friends.'

'Please don't upset him,' Stuart said. 'He must be grieving for his loss.'

'Yes he is, but putting a brave face on it, as we all must.'

Stuart gave Donald his card. 'That's where you'll find us, if you have any news.'

Donald watched them go, feeling very sorry for them.

If he were asked for his opinion he would say Rosemary Summers was dead, had died that same dreadful night as Julie. There had been so many bodies, so many bits of bodies that it had sometimes been difficult to piece them together and make a whole. He had told Harry Julie looked peaceful and unmarked, which had been a blatant lie. She had been unrecognisable, and it was only her slight build and the colour and texture of her hair, and the fact that she had been cradling the baby against her bosom for protection, that allowed him to identify her. Poor Harry. He had taken it badly, but who could blame him for that? Since then he had changed. His softness had gone; the young lad who had befriended a little waif and married her had matured, had become a hard man who had little time for sentiment. In a way that was to be regretted, but it made it easier for him to function. That was what this war was all about: functioning to the best of one's ability in the face of adversity.

He put the card in the top drawer of his desk and then drafted out a request to put on the noticeboard in the factory, asking if anyone remembered Rosemary Summers. He did not see what more he could do.

'You're the quiet one.'

Harry looked up to see the barmaid standing beside him, her hands full of glasses she had gathered up from the tables. She was about his own age, well built but not fat, with light-brown hair and greeny-grey eyes. 'Sorry?'

She smiled. She had a lovely smile, he noticed. It lit her whole face. 'I said you're the quiet one.'

'Am I? Well, we can't all be like that lot.' He indicated his fellow airmen with a jerk of his head. They were letting their hair down after returning from a successful bombing raid. It was a kind of release of tension and thankfulness that they had survived to fight another day.

'Were you with them?'

He knew what she meant. 'Yes.'

She nodded towards his empty glass. 'Do you want another?'

'Yes, please.'

She disappeared with the empty glasses and returned with a full one which she put down in front of him, then sat opposite him. 'What's your name?' she asked.

'Harry Walker. What's yours?'

'Pam. Pamela Godwin. Why don't you want to join in with the others?'

'Dunno. Didn't feel like it.'

'Pretty awful, was it?'

'Yes.' That was an understatement. The target had been Berlin, about as far as they could go on their fuel. The flak had been worse than usual and the enemy fighters buzzed round them like wasps, waiting to sting. Harry's job, when not operating the wireless, was to drop bundles containing thin strips of silver paper, called 'window', out of the aeroplane to confuse the enemy radar. The Germans counteracted this by concentrating their searchlights on the cloud layer above which the bombers were flying, silhouetting them clearly. Tim had thrown the Boston all over the sky in an effort to evade them, which made it doubly difficult for the navigator and bomb aimer. Luckily the target had been well lit by earlier fires and they had dropped their bombs and turned for home. He was never more glad to see the coast of England and then drop down on Swanton Morley, mission accomplished.

'Where do you come from?' she asked, bringing him back from his reverie. 'Originally, I mean.'

'London. Bermondsey.'

'That's right on the docks, isn't it? Didn't it get a pasting in the Blitz?'

'Yes. I lost my wife and son in that first big raid.'

'Oh, I'm so sorry. I shouldn't have mentioned it.'

'You weren't to know.'

'I lost my brother at Dunkirk.'

'I'm sorry. This damned war has a lot to answer for.'

'Yes.'

They sat in silence for a minute but she made no move to leave him. He drank some of his beer and set the glass back on the table. 'Do you live in Swanton Morley?' he asked.

'Yes, just down the road, with my mum and dad. He's the local baker. You've probably had some of his bread. He supplies the station.'

'And very good it is too.'

'It was better before we had the National Loaf. He hates that.'

'It's not that bad, and it's supposed to be healthier than a white loaf.'

'Can I get you a sandwich?' she asked, then chuckled. 'Dad's bread.'

'Yes, please.' He wasn't particularly hungry but he didn't like to hurt her feelings by saying no.

'Cheese and pickle do you?'

'Fine.'

He watched her go and continued to drink his beer. His companions were becoming noisily drunk and he wondered if they would make it safely back to base without falling into a ditch. They were great lads, some of them very young, and they had to let off steam now and again. Sometimes he joined them, sometimes, like tonight, he preferred to sit quietly. Not that he brooded; he had got past that, but sometimes he reflected on his life as it was now compared with what it had been. It seemed a lifetime ago since he had come back from Canada to stand over Julie's grave with that broken garden gnome in his hand and felt so lost, guilty and angry.

After pestering the powers that be at Cosford he had been posted to 226 Squadron who were stationed at Wattisham in Suffolk where they flew Blenheim bombers, mostly on coastal patrol against German shipping. It was while he was there he was sent for officer training and returned a flight lieutenant. Just before Christmas 1941 the whole squadron had moved to Swanton Morley in Norfolk. Its runway had a grass surface covered with steel mesh, but there was some new hardstanding and a tarmac perimeter track, plus a couple of new hangars and the usual conglomeration of huts. From here, he found himself making bombing raids on coastal shipping and targets in occupied Europe, dodging enemy fighters and flak. He had been lucky so far, but many of his new-found friends had not returned. It was something you had to accept or you'd go mad.

'There you are, one cheese and pickle sandwich.' She put the plate in front of him and sat down again, putting her elbows on the table and her chin in her hands. 'Tell me about yourself.'

So he did and she listened attentively and at the end she said, 'What will you do after the war?'

'I dunno. I haven't thought that far ahead. Go back to

work in the factory, I suppose. We've got to win the war first.'

'We will,' she said. 'We've got to.'

'Yes, of course.' It was easier to agree than point out how bad things were. Singapore had fallen to the Japanese and thousands of Allied troops had been taken prisoner; the Germans were almost at the gates of Moscow and were advancing in Libya. Malta was under constant siege and shipping sent to relieve it suffered horrendous casualties; three German battleships had made a sudden dash from Brest where they had been holed up and made it through the Channel to the safety of German waters in spite of the efforts of the Royal Navy and the RAF, some from Swanton Morley, to stop them. The future looked bleak and it was only the RAF bombing of German cities that gave anyone anything to cheer about. Even that had its downside: losses were heavy, and after a huge raid on Cologne, Hitler decided on reprisals and sent his bombers to Britain's historic cities. Canterbury, Bath, Exeter, York and – near enough to worry the inhabitants of Norfolk – Norwich were all bombed.

'It'll make a difference now the Americans are in with us.'

Japan had attacked the American fleet at Pearl Harbor the previous December, taking the Americans by surprise, and there had been a lot of casualties, not to mention ships sunk, but as a result the war had become truly global.

'Unless they come and help us in Europe, it won't make a lot of difference,' he said.

'Oh, you are down in the dumps, aren't you?'

'Sorry, I'm a bit tired.' He made an effort to cheer himself up. Civilians on the ground could have little idea what the

146

aircrews were going through, night after night. 'How long have you been working here?'

'In The Papermakers? Not long. I used to work for my father at the bakery all day but he really only needed me in the mornings, so when Greg Powter – he's the landlord – said he was short-staffed, owing to all you RAF bods coming in wanting to be served, I thought, *Why not?* Now I do both jobs.'

'That must be hard work.'

'There are plenty of people working a lot harder than me and not even able to live at home, so I'm lucky.'

'You've got a boyfriend?'

'Not so's you'd notice.'

'Go on, pull the other one. You're one pretty girl surrounded by a crowd of handsome men. Don't tell me you haven't had offers.'

'Offers galore, but it doesn't mean anything. It's just a bit of fun. I don't take them seriously.'

'Very wise of you.'

'I'll probably get directed into war work before long. I've only escaped this long because my father needed me.'

'If you do, what will you choose to do?'

'Land Army, I think. I'm hoping to get taken on locally, then I might be allowed to stay living at home. Norfolk is good farming country.' She laughed. 'Or it was before it became one vast airfield.'

'I expect it will revert back after the war.'

'Are you on duty again tonight?'

'No, we've been stood down for twenty-four hours. Weather's not good enough, hence the noisy party.' He finished his sandwich, swallowed the last of his beer and stood up. 'I'd better see that lot back to their beds or they'll be in trouble. How much was the beer and sandwich?'

'Have it on me.'

'Go on, you can't treat every lonely airman who comes in.'

'Not every lonely airman, just one who seemed as though he could do with some company. Don't insult me by insisting on paying.'

'Then I won't. Thanks.' He picked up his cap and put it on. 'I'll be seeing you.' Then he strode over to the crowd of airmen, as the landlord called, 'Time, gentlemen, please.' They rolled out of the pub and set their feet towards the airfield, weaving erratically along the country road, singing as they went.

'You looked very cosy in the corner,' Tim Harrison said. Unusually, they had stayed together throughout their service so far. Tim was his pilot and now a squadron leader. Harry was wireless operator-gunner and the crew of four was completed by Ken Moreson, the navigator, and Bill Repton, the bomb aimer, who were walking ahead of them. Tim was not quite as drunk as the others, feeling a kind of paternal interest in their welfare.

'Oh, you mean Pam.'

'Yes, the delectable Pam. I should say you've made a hit there, Harry my lad.'

'Rot. She was only being friendly.'

'Very friendly, I should say. She was hanging on your every word. Shooting her a line were you?'

'No, just talking.'

Tim laughed. 'That's how it usually begins. What do you think, Ken?'

'I think she's a bit of all right,' Ken called over his shoulder. 'I should make hay while you can, old boy.'

Harry laughed at their banter. He had enjoyed a little respite talking to Pam. It even helped to talk about Julie and George; she was a good listener, perhaps because she, too, understood about loss. That didn't mean he was ready to fall into bed with her. He had a feeling she wouldn't have it anyway.

Harry's gloomy forecast that the Americans would not help in Europe proved to be wrong when nine bomber crews arrived in Swanton Morley to begin training with the RAF. They caused quite a stir in the village. Thirty-six men, plus their support staff, in a different uniform, talking in an accent only previously heard in the cinema, chewing gum and calling the women 'ma'am', as if they were royalty, and driving too fast on the winding country lanes, often on the wrong side, so that others on the road had to take evasive action. They were noisy and brash when together, but taken one by one were often shy and polite. They had very little idea of what the people of Britain had been through in the previous three years and were often tactless about the general war-weariness and shabbiness which afflicted its inhabitants. They appeared to have an endless supply of cigarettes, chewing gum, chocolates, beer and nylon stockings, things which were unobtainable in Britain, or in such short supply it made the villagers resentful. It was only when they appeared ready to share their bounty, especially with the children, attitudes softened. They were invited into the people's homes for meals and came gratefully, bearing gifts of tinned fruit or canned meat, sometimes oranges, which hadn't been seen since the beginning of the war. In return their hosts and hostesses listened to tales of family left back home.

Harry, together with the rest of the squadron, had problems of a different sort. The American discipline was easier-going than that of their British counterparts and the flight procedures, though the same in essence, differed in the detail. It was important that they learn to work together because they were aiming for combined operations. RAF personnel, like Harry and Tim, who had trained in Canada, found it easier to understand them, and the pair often found themselves breaking up an argument and even stepping in between fist fights. 'We're supposed to be on the same side,' Tim would say. 'So pack it in.' But both had the same aim, to defeat the enemy, and with a willingness on both their parts to try to get along, they were soon making practice flights and gelling into a fighting force.

They knew something was up at the beginning of July, when Winston Churchill and General Eisenhower appeared on the station and walked round inspecting everything: the living quarters, the new hangars and hardstanding. They were in the briefing room in Bylaugh Hall, joint headquarters, when six RAF crews and six American crews were briefed for a combined bombing raid on targets in occupied France. It did not take Harry and his crew long to realise they were going to be guinea pigs for this kind of operation.

It was the Americans' first taste of being over enemy territory and having to dodge flak and be on the lookout for enemy fighters. Harry could tell by their voices over the intercom that they were nervous, and their reaction to the German fighters' latest tactic was to exclaim 'Jeez!' It was understandable; the enemy fighters had managed to get above them and were dropping flares so that the night sky was lit up like day, making them sitting ducks for the guns below.

Tim reminded them of the drill they had been practising, and told them to dodge about a bit, which they did. They dropped their bombs and turned for home, though their vigilance had to continue until they were safely back over the English coast. Not all landed safely: one of the RAF Bostons was lost and one American crash-landed on the airfield. The debriefing over, they fell into their beds and slept the sleep of the exhausted for several hours, until woken by hunger and the feeling it must be near dinnertime. Afterwards they set off for The Papermakers, to celebrate and drown their sorrows at the same time.

Pam always sought Harry out when he went into the pub and when they weren't busy. They would sit and talk together about what had been happening while they had been apart – on his part a guarded résumé of what he had been doing, and a cheerful report of village life on hers. She understood if he wanted to be quiet and did not try to make him talk, and if he felt like joining in with his fellows and getting tipsy and noisy, she did not trouble about that either, knowing he would come to her and have a few minutes with her before he left.

One day in early September she asked him if he would like to have tea with her and her parents the next time he was off duty on a Sunday afternoon. For a moment the invitation took him by surprise. Had things really progressed that far? He hadn't meant them to. For a start he still thought a lot about Julie, although it was two years since she had died and the raw misery had faded to a gentle nostalgia and a realisation that life had moved on. For another thing the life he led was not conducive

151

to long-term relationships; the squadron was taking heavy casualties and every sortie might be his last.

'You don't have to,' she added, sensing his hesitation. 'It was only an idea. I talk about you to Mum and Dad and they said they'd like to meet you.'

'Of course I'll come,' he said quickly. 'I'd love to.'

Two Sundays later, with some trepidation, he left the station and walked into the village and across the green to the house which stood next to the mill and bakery. Pam answered his knock and, taking his hand, led him into a room off the hall. It was an untidy room, a room with a lived-in feel about it. It had a large plain table in its centre, a sideboard along one wall and a sofa and easy chairs before the hearth. A magazine rack was full to overflowing and two newspapers, untidily folded, lay on a side table beside the radio. Beside it was a framed photograph of a young man in army uniform. Pam's brother, he surmised.

'Mum, Dad, this is Flight Lieutenant Harry Walker. Harry, my mum and dad.'

The couple who rose to shake his hand were like Jack Sprat and his wife. He was tall and lean and she was short and plump, but both had ready smiles.

'You are very welcome, Flight Lieutenant,' Mrs Godwin said.

'Please call me Harry,' he said, taking the offered hand.

'Very well, Harry, I'm Jane and this is Albert, known to one and all as Bert.'

Bert shook his hand. 'Come you on in, bor; sit down and mek yarself at home.'

Harry sat on the edge of the sofa, wondering what Pam had told them about him. He felt awkward, as if he were being sized up, but Pam made up for it, plonking herself down beside him and telling her parents what she knew about Harry, which resulted in them asking him about London, which neither of them had visited, and before long the tension eased, and by the time they went into the dining room for tea, they were chatting amicably.

After salad, sandwiches and cake and several cups of tea, Pam suggested they went for a walk, and so they strolled hand in hand past All Saints Church and along a footpath by a tributary of the Wensum to Penny Spot, a favourite area of courting couples, children playing and people walking their dogs. It was a warm day, with a blue sky interspersed with an odd fluffy cloud or two, and for once there was no drone of aircraft coming and going; for the first time in ages Harry felt at peace with himself. When the talk ran out he didn't feel the need to resurrect it, but simply enjoyed her company in companionable silence.

Without either of them suggesting it, they found a quiet spot and sat down on the grass. He flung off his cap and lay back, his hands behind his head, contemplating the blueness of the sky. 'You'd never know there was a war on, would you?' he said.

'Not today. I'll bet you will tonight. They're bound to take off again.'

'Probably, but not me, not tonight. I'm stood down.'

'Good. You can forget about it, then.'

'Hard to forget,' he said. 'Even when you're not on duty. It's always in the back of your mind. Your last op, your next one. Life's one mad rush. You rush to get into the sky and have a go at the Hun, you rush back to celebrate your little victories, you rush to drown your sorrows, you rush to take advantage of stand-down and get off the base before the powers that be change their minds. In between, there's hours of being bored to death, waiting for the next call.'

'I listen for the planes and count them going over the house,' she said. 'And then I count them coming back. I think of all you boys, wondering if you've made it back safely.'

'Sometimes we don't.'

'I know. It makes me sad to think I'd been serving them beer the night before and now they won't come into the pub any more.'

'It's a fact of life, Pam.'

She began idly picking daisies and stringing them together to make a chain. 'You do take care, don't you? You don't do anything foolish, do you?'

'No, feet on the ground, that's me.'

She laughed. 'Even when you're flying?'

'You know what I mean.'

'Yes, I know what you mean. When I hear the planes taking off I wonder if you are among them and I pray for your safety.'

'Do you? That must be why I keep bouncing back.' It was said with a light embarrassed laugh.

She had a long daisy chain now and set about joining it into a ring, then put it on her head. 'How's that?'

He grinned up at her. 'Lovely. Queen of the May.'

'It's September.'

'So it is.'

She lay down beside him and he put his arm about her so that she could snuggle up against his chest. It was the first time he had held a woman in his arms since the time he kissed Julie goodbye before going to Canada, if you didn't count those he had met at last year's noisy Christmas and

New Year parties; he couldn't even remember their names. Pam felt good. She was soothing to be with and didn't ask anything of him, though he had an idea she was just being patient. Her hair was tickling his chin and he used his other hand to brush it back, and in so doing knocked off the daisy crown. He picked it up and went to replace it. She took it from him and threw it behind her, before taking his hand and guiding it round her. 'Hold me tight,' she murmured. 'Don't do anything, just hold me.'

He obliged and kissed the top of her head; her hair was soft and smelt of the lavender shampoo she used. She moved her head to look up at him. He bent and found her lips with his own, very gently, a butterfly of a kiss. Neither spoke, certainly not to reveal their feelings. It was too soon for that and he still had a vague notion he should not be doing it.

She jumped up suddenly. 'Time we were going back. Mum and Dad will think we've got lost.'

The moment was gone but not forgotten by either of them. They walked back to the bakery hand in hand in silence.

Pam didn't know what had come over her. She had always said falling in love in wartime was a stupid thing to do and she didn't want the heartache, but you couldn't govern your feelings, could you? She had known Harry was the man for her as soon as she set eyes on him, but at first, lost in his own little world, he had hardly noticed her. She had had to take the initiative. She had been surprised and pleased when he responded so positively. But now she had joined the ranks of all those sweethearts, wives and mothers who lived in constant fear. Counting the bombers leaving and coming back became even more important. If anything happened to Harry she did not know what she would do; her world would fall apart. When he walked into the pub of an evening her whole body would lighten, and when he knocked on the door of her home to take her out, she would fling herself into his arms, fighting tears of sheer relief and joy that he was safely back from wherever he had been. Their time together was precious.

Her call-up came and she chose to serve in the Women's Land Army, for which she received eighteen shillings a week, all found. She was posted to Chepstow for several weeks of training and she missed seeing Harry. She wrote him long letters and he wrote back, at first a little diffidently, but more and more lovingly as time passed. She was not to worry about him; the thought of her waiting for him kept him safe. She would have been a fool to believe that and always listened to the BBC Home Service from which the news was broadcast, or as much as the powers that be were prepared to make public. When the announcers said so many of our aircraft failed to return, she was on tenterhooks until she heard from him again. If only she could be posted near to home, she might see him more often, might count the bombers out and back as she used to do and know when he was safe.

She was a sturdy well-built girl and the hard work did not bother her; brought up in the country, looking after animals did not terrify her as it did some of the girls. Some were city girls, some were hard-working girls from the industrial north, some came from wealthy backgrounds and hadn't done a hand's turn in their lives. Why they chose the Land Army Pam didn't know, except perhaps a belief that it was safer than the other services. It was certainly not the uniform; the khaki jodhpurs and thick knitted socks, the green pullover, the dungarees and wellington boots for working in, were far from glamorous.

She learnt to drive a tractor and milk cows, harness the big shire horses, clean out the byres and the stables, hoe between rows of potatoes, help with the harvest, standing on the rick with a pitchfork as the threshing machine rattled and shook, separating the grain from the chaff, and taking the straw on a pitchfork as it was thrown up to her. She sweated and choked on the dust, and all the time she was thinking of Harry, taking off at night, returning in the early hours of the next morning, perhaps with a holed bomber, always exhausted and glad to be back. She wanted to be with him then, to help him relax and talk about the future, a future they would share.

By dint of much lobbying that her elderly parents needed her to help at home, she was finally sent to work on a farm between Swanton Morley and East Dereham and came home to sleep each night. It meant getting up before dawn to cycle to work, and as the days shortened, it was dark when she left and, in spite of double summer time, dark again by the time she returned home, but she preferred that to living in a hostel and she did get a living-out allowance. She was back where she wanted to be, although even then it was not easy for her and Harry to be off duty at the same time, but they made the most of any opportunities. She knew he sometimes thought about his wife; she was a little jealous, she was prepared to admit, but in time she would make him forget, simply by loving and caring and being there when he needed someone. He would forget his first wife and come to realise the present

157

and the future were all that mattered, and when this dreadful war was over, there was a whole new life to be lived. Together.

'We're off on leave on Monday,' Florrie told Julie, on the day the news of the victory at El Alamein was announced. The tide of war seemed to be turning at last. The Russians had managed to lift the siege of Stalingrad and launched a counter-attack. The Americans and Australians were having some success in the Pacific and the Germans were in retreat in North Africa. After the miserable three years which had gone before, the change of fortune was received with great pleasure.

'Monday?' echoed Julie, as a memory flitted into her brain and out again before she could grasp it. Had something significant happened to her on a Monday?

'Yes, you know, the day after Sunday,' Florrie said, laughing.

How they had managed to stay together so long, no one knew, except that it was generally accepted that they were joined at the hip and separating them would require major surgery. From Morecambe they had gone to Wales and from Wales to Coningsby in Lincolnshire where they were now, Florrie as a sergeant driver and Julie working in the stores. They were certainly seeing parts of the country they never would have done but for the war. Coningsby was a bomber station and they were close to the aircraft and could watch them take off and return. The first time it had given them a great thrill, but when two of the Sterlings had failed to return it put a damper on their spirits. They had learnt to harden themselves and not become too close to any of the airmen, though they were friendly and often went dancing and to the pictures with them.

Julie had matured a lot in the two years since she had become Eve Seaton. She had lost her diffidence and had more confidence. She knew her job and did it efficiently, and in spite of her small stature had learnt to stand up for herself. She sometimes wondered if she had been like that before the bomb took away her past or whether it was something she had learnt since. War changed people. It hadn't changed Florrie, though; she was the same good friend – more than a good friend, more like a sister, as she was fond of saying. And she looked forward more and more to spending time with Alec.

He was fun; he had a quirky way of making everything less daunting and he smiled a lot. He had taught her to stifle her nervousness of horses and learn to ride and they would go trekking across the countryside for hours, enjoying the clean air and each other's company. They went to the pictures in Andover occasionally, sometimes to a dance, and they wrote to each other frequently. It amused Florrie no end and she teased Julie about it. 'I was wrong,' she said more than once. 'He's not your brother.'

'Of course he isn't.'

'Do you like him? Really like him, I mean?'

'You know I do, he's a good friend, but if you think there's more to it than that, you are way off the mark.'

Florrie's answer to that was to laugh and tap her nose.

Julie did like Alec, she liked him a lot. He was sometimes funny, sometimes serious, but always caring and he didn't press her about her past, possibly because he had heard her story of being an only survivor and didn't want to make her sad. He did not know about her loss of memory and the fact that at some time in the past she had borne a child;

no one knew that, not even Florrie. It was a huge barrier which could not be overcome, and the longer she kept her secret the harder it was to tell. Sometimes she didn't think of it for days on end until something jogged her into a faint memory, like the mention of Monday. If the raid that buried her under tons of rubble had been a Monday, she might have understood it, but it had been a Saturday. She could hear and say the word 'Saturday' with no qualms at all.

She didn't like deceiving anyone but at the same time she was sure her past must hold something of which she was ashamed. Having a child out of wedlock might be the reason, but supposing it was something else, something so dreadful she had to bury it deep inside her where no one could get at it, not even herself. Why did she feel so guilty, especially when anyone was being kind to her, feeling she didn't deserve it? Could she have done away with her child? The mere thought of that gave her nightmares.

They arrived at Hillside Farm on the late afternoon of 9th November. The farmhouse was warm and cosy after the long cold journey and all they wanted to do was curl up by the fire. Alec had other ideas. 'What are you two planning to do this week?' he asked, when he came in after seeing to the animals.

'Nothing much,' Florrie said. 'It's not the weather for outdoors, is it?'

'It's all right if you're well wrapped up and keep moving.'

'You're up to something.'

'Well, sort of. You can join in if you want to. We're going to have a Guy Fawkes bonfire for the kids in the village. You can come and help with that if you like.'

'Surely we're not allowed to light bonfires,' Julie said. 'What with the blackout and everything.'

'It'll be all right if we do it on Saturday afternoon and make sure it's out before dark. It will cheer all the children up, not just our two. And we do have something to celebrate, after all, what with the victory at El Alamein. If they're going to let us ring the church bells to mark it, surely we can have a bonfire?'

'Where?'

'On the field behind the pub. What d'you say?'

'Might as well,' Florrie said. 'If Eve wants to.'

'If you're sure it'll be all right,' she said.

'Course it will,' Alec said, grinning.

The pub was the obvious place to set the ball rolling for any social event in the village, and Alec, Florrie and Julie strolled down to the Three Bells after dinner to find others there already discussing the idea. Saturday wouldn't be the fifth, which was Thursday, but it couldn't be done on a working day, especially as the fire would have to be extinguished by dark. Suggestions and offers of help came from all round. Potatoes baked in the embers were no problem, though other food might need a little ingenuity. Joe Salhouse said he'd do what he could to provide at least one pint of beer for the men and lemonade for the children, which had to be paid for, of course. He couldn't afford to give it away, not when he didn't know when he'd get his next delivery from the brewery.

'We can get the children collecting the wood,' Alec said. 'Pity we can't have fireworks.'

'We haven't had any of those since before the war,' Mrs Green, who kept the village shop and post office, told them.

'Don't suppose you have,' he said. 'Factories won't have been making kids' fireworks, more likely high explosives, bombs and shells and things like that.' He laughed suddenly.

161

'They go off bang too.' But it had given him an idea. 'I think I can get some.'

His sister turned to him. 'You're joking.'

'No, I'm not.' He tapped his nose. 'Wait and see.'

Joe called time, they drained the last from their glasses and set off home, arms linked.

'Do you really think you can get some fireworks?' Florrie asked, as they walked.

'No, but I can find something to make a bang. It's easy enough, a few detonators, a little gunpowder and a longish fuse.'

'You mean you're going to make them?'

'Yes, why not? If everyone stands well back and the fuse is long enough, they'll be safe enough.'

'You're mad.' She leant across him to address Julie. 'You know he's mad, don't you, Eve? Better not have anything to do with him.'

'I'll remember that,' she said, laughing.

When they were not in school, the children dragged branches from the woods and down the lanes. On the Saturday morning, dressed in green cord trousers tucked into wellington boots, and a thick hand-knitted jumper, Alec helped to construct the pile so that it would stay in one piece as it burnt, aided by Florrie and Julie, also in slacks and warm jumpers, and a whole crowd of excited children, including Liz and Alice, who were plump and rosy-cheeked and pining less and less for the home they had left behind. When the heap was twice the height of a man, they made a guy to go on it. It was hardly surprising that it had a black moustache, black hair and a swastika on an armband. They were going to burn Hitler and enjoy doing it. An added bonus was that it brought the village children and the evacuees together in a joint project.

'Can't do anything more now,' Alec said. 'We'll go home for something to eat and come straight back.'

The bonfire was a huge success and blazed merrily in the damp November afternoon. Everyone in the village was there; it was as if they had unanimously decided to forget the war for a few hours and enjoy themselves. Potatoes were pushed into the embers and everyone brought something to cook – a couple of sausages, a bit of bacon, bread to toast – for which they had to improvise very long toasting forks out of sticks. The children ran round and round, taunting the effigy of Hitler, and had to be stopped from singing a bawdy song about the dictator's lack of testicles. 'Where do they learn such things?' Maggie asked Walter, trying not to laugh. When the guy had been consumed by the fire, Alec turned to Joe. 'Come and give us a hand with the fireworks, will you?'

'You mean you actually got some?'

'Well, no, they're home-made. I got hold of some detonators and fuses and emptied the powder out of a few cartridge cases and put it in toilet roll tubes—'

'God, that's lethal!'

'Not really, not if the kids are kept well back. They'll make a nice bang for 'em. Can't make pretty coloured fountains and things like that, but they'll have to be satisfied.'

'Where are you going to set them off?'

'On the other side of the field.'

Alec went and told his father, who helped them set everything up so that one bang led to the next and they were angled away from the crowd round the bonfire. 'Don't say anything to the ladies about how it's being done,' Walter told Alec. 'Just make sure they all keep well back. We can't have anyone getting hurt. And you'd better have a few buckets of sand handy. We don't want to start any other fires. Thank God the grass is still wet.'

The men who were in on the secret were like schoolboys themselves, gleefully rushing round and arranging everything. It was left to the ladies to organise the children behind a screen of the hotel's picnic tables turned on their sides. A sizzling line of fire was the first sign that something was happening and then there was a terrific bang which made many of them scream. It was followed by more bangs, one after the other. The bigger children were bright-eyed and jumping up and down in excitement, but the noise made one or two of the smaller children cling to their mothers in fear, and a couple of recently arrived evacuees, thinking they were being bombed again, screamed. 'It's all right,' their foster-mother said, gathering them into her arms to comfort them. 'They're not bombs. No one's going to hurt you. You're quite safe.'

Julie stood beside Florrie and Maggie, apparently calm, but she was listening to a voice inside her head, a male voice saying, 'All right, miss, we can see you. We'll soon have you out of there. Don't move or you'll have everything down on top of you.' Standing with her friends as the last of the bangs died away and the end of the field was obscured by smoke, she remembered screaming – was it her or someone else? – choking on dust, unable to breathe, and how sweet the cup of water tasted when it was handed to her through a tiny aperture. That was a true memory, not one of her fantasies, but that had been after the bomb. What had gone before? And why, as they were digging her out, had she not shown more concern for family and friends? She

164

remembered being in pain. Had she passed out? She looked about her at the crowd of villagers, the excited children, Florrie laughing beside her, and Alec, looking pleased with himself, and the recollection faded like a bad nightmare with the coming of dawn. She didn't even try to drag it back; it was too frightening.

Alec, who had only been thinking of amusing the children with a few innocuous fireworks, had been dismayed by the size of the explosions. He was even more embarrassed when a platoon of local Home Guard, who had been on a training exercise nearby, turned up with rifles at the ready to repel invaders. It took all Walter's diplomacy to persuade the platoon commander that the war hadn't come to Harston and they had only been amusing the children with a few Guy Fawkes fireworks.

'Fireworks?' the lieutenant queried. 'I'm sure there's a law about not letting off fireworks in wartime.'

'If there is, I haven't heard of it,' Alec said.

'Where d'you get them anyway?'

'They were stock left over from before the war,' Joe lied. 'We thought we'd give the kids a treat.'

'I hope he doesn't decide to go and inspect the evidence,' Alec whispered to his father. Aloud he said, 'They're all gone now, Lieutenant, and I think we'd better get that fire doused before blackout, don't you?'

The lieutenant, his attention diverted from explosives, turned to look at the glowing embers and agreed. 'Get on with it, then,' he said, and marched his men away.

Alec, turning to do so, noticed Julie's pallor. 'Eve, what's the matter? You look as if you'd seen a ghost.'

'That's what it felt like. I've heard explosions before and guns going off and not been bothered by them, but this time, for some reason, it sent me back and I suddenly remembered being buried in rubble and choking on dust while the ARP dug me out. It might have been the children screaming that triggered it.'

He came and put his arms about her shoulders and pulled her to him. 'Oh, God, I'm so sorry, I wouldn't have had you upset for worlds. I didn't think it would be as noisy as that.'

'It's all right. I'm over it now.' She smiled to prove it.

'Go home with Mum and Florrie and have a good stiff drink. I'll help clear up here.'

Florrie took her arm. 'Come on, Eve, try not to dwell on it. You've got us now.'

'Yes, I know. I'm very lucky.' She felt a terrible fraud, keeping her secret from them, and that made her quiet for the rest of the evening. Tactfully, no one commented on it, for which she was grateful, and the next morning she and Florrie came down to breakfast ready to go back to Coningsby. Doing her job, surrounded by others doing theirs, her past did not matter. She could tuck it away out of mind.

'I'll be joining you in uniform soon,' Alec said, as they went out to the car. There was no such thing as petrol for private mileage now, but as a farmer Walter was allowed a certain amount, and as usual Alec was going to drive them to the station. 'I'm joining up.'

Florrie stared at him. 'You can't mean it.'

'Yes, I do.'

'What on earth for? You're in a reserved occupation and Dad needs you.'

'No, he doesn't. He's got a couple of Land Army girls to help him and I can't let you girls strut around in uniform while all I'm doing is milking cows.'

'I'm sure you do more than that,' Julie put in.

'Not much. Anyway, I've been feeling guilty for a long time about not doing my bit.'

'What do Mum and Dad say about it?'

He shrugged. 'Mum wasn't too happy, but Dad understood.'

'When are you going?'

'Dunno. I'm waiting to hear.'

'I told you he was mad, didn't I?' Florrie said, addressing Julie.

Four days later, on 11th November, the day of the Armistice of the Great War, the church bells rang out for the first time since 1939 and Churchill was reported saying: 'This is not the end. It is not even the beginning of the end. But it is, perhaps, the end of the beginning.'

Julie wondered if that could be true of her too. Was it the end of her beginning to accept that her memory would never come back, except in tiny incoherent fits and starts?

Chapter Seven

'Do you think we'll stay together this time?' Julie asked a few weeks after they returned. Christmas had come and gone and 1943 had begun on a note of optimism, though men were still dying in their thousands, planes still took off and were shot down, ships were still being sunk, and those at home still struggled with air raids – fewer now – and rationing, which was becoming more and more restrictive. Those in the forces were lucky in that respect: they were well fed and clothed, albeit in uniform.

They had just heard they were to be posted and were discussing it while they dressed to go to a Saturday night dance in Sleaford with a crowd from the station. They couldn't dress up because they had to wear uniform, but they could give themselves a shampoo and set and take extra care with their make-up.

'No idea. We'll have to wait and see.' Someone was sitting with his hand on a horn outside their barrack room; it could be heard all over the camp. 'Come on, let's go before he has the whole station down on him.'

They picked up handbags and gas masks and dashed out to the truck which was to take them into Sleaford, and scrambled aboard to join two more girls and four airmen.

'Last time for this,' Florrie said. 'Eve and I are being posted.'

'Where to?' Matt Cotton asked. He was driving and didn't seem bothered about the truck's springs or his passengers' comfort as they bounced along the uneven ground to the main gate.

'Don't know yet. I only heard through the grapevine.'

'We'll miss you and your cheeky voice.' He paused and laughed. 'Among other things.'

'Yeah, and we'll miss you, you crazy idiot. Why don't you slow down a bit before we're all thrown out?'

'Florrie, you shouldn't call him names,' Julie said, though she was hanging onto her seat.

Florrie laughed. 'He knows I don't mean it. He knows I love him to bits, don't you, Matt?'

'It's the first I've heard of it,' the young man said laconically.

They continued to tease each other all the way into Sleaford, but Julie noticed when they arrived at the dance hall that Florrie danced with Matt most of the time, while she and the other girls shared their favours with the other three. Was Florrie serious about him? After all they had said about not falling in love, had she done just that? It left Julie wondering how it might affect their friendship and then scolded herself for begrudging Florrie a little happiness. It wasn't Florrie's fault that she couldn't follow suit. Had she ever been in love? Had she loved her child's father? Was he dead or alive? Would she still love him if her memory returned? Perhaps she hadn't loved him in the first place, perhaps they had simply been ships that passed in the night. She did not want to believe she was really as flighty as that. Her self-questioning led her nowhere, which just went to prove she would never be able to let it rest.

The notice went up on Sunday evening and it was the parting of the ways. Florrie was going to Manston in Kent and Julie, now promoted to corporal, to Ringway near Manchester. Their parting was mournful but they promised to write often and try and get home together sometimes. Alec had been as good as his word and joined the army and was stationed at Bulford. It was unlikely all three would be together for some time, but it could not be helped and she looked forward to his long chatty letters.

Ringway, Julie discovered almost as soon as she arrived, was a parachute training school and many of the men were in khaki and not air force blue. They were supremely fit. She would see them running round the station perimeter with big packs on their backs, or practising their jumps from the tower in one of the hangars, or they might be marching out to the Whitleys and taking off. Later the aircraft would return without them and they would come back in trucks. As soon as one group had completed their training and their requisite eight jumps and left, another lot appeared. Some who failed the stringent tests for one reason or another were returned to their units. They came and they went and she didn't get to know any of them, though their RAF instructors remained. She would chat to them when they came into the stores with a chit for this or that or to collect parachutes. Packing the parachutes was done in a hangar by WAAF personnel. It was meticulous work, every stage of which was inspected and passed before going on to the next.

Occasionally a parachute failed to open, resulting in a fatality, and though no one blamed the packers, they felt the loss keenly and were miserable for hours afterwards, but then they pulled themselves together and went back to work. You had to do that, you had to put the horrors behind you, whether it be an unopened parachute, a bomber not returning from a raid, or being bombed yourself. You had to become hardened, at least on the outside.

The news that Florrie was going to marry Matt did not come as a complete surprise, though what was surprising was that the wedding was going to be so soon. 'You must try and get leave,' she wrote to Julie. 'I'm being married from home and I want you to be a bridesmaid.'

Dates were bandied back and forth in increasing panic, but at last one was chosen which everyone could make and Julie travelled down to Wiltshire by train the day before. It was a damp windy day in March, but Alec was waiting for her at Andover Station with his father's car. He kissed her cheek and took her small case from her. 'Glad you could make it.'

'So am I. I should have been miserable if I'd had to miss it.'

'It's pandemonium at home, what with all the preparations. Mum's determined it's going to be a grand day, war or no war.'

This proved to be true. The farmhouse was warm, made even warmer by the kitchen range, which had been on the go all day, making sausage rolls and cakes, cooking chicken and pork. 'Goodness,' Julie said after she had been kissed and hugged by everyone, including Liz and

Alice. 'You'd never believe there was rationing.'

'You don't know what you can do until you try,' Maggie said. 'We killed a pig a week or two ago and the chickens yesterday.'

'Come upstairs,' Florrie said, dragging Julie behind her. 'I want to make sure your dress fits.'

Julie sat on her bed and watched as Florrie brought out a rose-coloured pink silk dress. 'I was going to have blue,' she said. 'But you're in blue every day so I thought pink would be more feminine.'

'Yes, it is, and it's beautiful.'

'Try it on. Mum made it. She took the measurements from that flowered dress you left behind in the wardrobe.'

'Where on earth did she get the material?'

Florrie laughed. 'Don't you recognise it? It's parachute silk. Best not to ask where she got it from. She dyed it in the copper. It's come up all right, hasn't it?'

'Yes, beautiful.' She stripped off her uniform and slid the dress over her head. 'It's grand,' she said, smoothing it down over her hips. 'I must pay you for it.'

'You will not. Whatever next. You're family, Eve.'

Whenever Florrie said something like that, it made her want to cry with love and gratitude. She could not even begin to imagine what life would be like without the Kilbys. It made that great void in her life bearable. She was slowly coming to the conclusion that her memory was not going to come back and she had better settle down living the life she had. She had so much to be thankful for: her good health, her work which she enjoyed, her dear friends, what more could she ask?

She took the dress off and replaced it on its hanger. 'Show me your dress.'

Florrie took it from another wardrobe. It was in shimmering white satin. 'It's a make-over from Mum's,' she said. 'What do you think?'

'Put it on.' She watched as Florrie did as she was asked. 'It's gorgeous. Matt will be bowled over.'

'He'd better be.'

'Where is he?'

'Staying with his best man at the Three Bells. Can't have him here the night before the wedding, can we? I think Dad and Alec are going to meet them there later tonight for a stag party. I hope they don't get too drunk.'

'Your dad will see that they don't.' Julie paused. 'Are you sure about this, Florrie? We always said we wouldn't fall in love while there's a war on.'

'I know what we said, but that was a silly thing to say. Falling in love is not something you can control, is it? I want to be with Matt 'til death us do part, however long or short that is, and I can't wait.'

'But you won't be with him, will you? He has to go back to Coningsby and you back to Manston. The war won't stop just because you've got married.'

'I know, but we'll try and wangle leave together, and you never know, we might end up on the same station.'

Florrie was so exuberant and optimistic, Julie let that go. 'Then let's hope you do.' She had dressed in a civilian skirt and jumper while they had been talking. 'We'd better go down. I heard your mother call she was dishing up.'

Supper was a noisy affair with everyone competing to be heard, and afterwards, while the women washed up, Walter and Alec set off for the pub. 'We'll have a little drink ourselves,' Maggie said as they finished, stacking the crockery away. 'And then it's an early night for you two.'

'Mum, I'm too excited to sleep,' Florrie said.

'Never mind, you'll be resting.'

A watery sun was shining next morning, which everyone said was a favourable sign. Neither Florrie nor Julie could eat any breakfast, and after drinking innumerable cups of tea, Julie had a bath and then dressed while Florrie had hers. Maggie was busy dressing Liz and Alice who were also to be bridesmaids. She sat them in the front parlour to do a jigsaw puzzle and stay out of mischief while she went to help Florrie dress.

'I feel a bit sick,' Florrie said as she was helped into her dress. 'I keep wondering if Matt will be there.'

'Of course he'll be there. Don't be so silly.'

Florrie was a bag of nerves by the time she was dressed and her headdress and veil put on her curls; it took a glass of sherry to calm her. The bridal car arrived for Maggie, Julie and the two girls and they set off for the church, leaving Walter and Florrie to follow in the pony and trap. The pony had been groomed within an inch of its life and the trap was bedecked with white ribbons.

The Kilbys were popular in the village and the church was full of well-wishers, friends, neighbours, relations, farm workers, including the two land girls. Matt and his best man, both in uniform, stood at the altar as the bridal procession entered the church. Florrie gave a huge smile of relief and was rewarded with a broad smile from her bridegroom.

Julie, standing behind Florrie, was happy for her friend, but it was tinged with a little personal sadness at the fact that this meant her relationship with Florrie would inevitably change. They would still be good friends, but Matt would be first in Florrie's life from now on, which was as it should be. If only she did not have that cloud hanging over her, she might find someone to love and who loved her. While she was busy on the station, she could put the problem of her memory to one side, but now it niggled in her head again. The same unanswerable questions over and over again. She thrust them from her, determined to enjoy the party, toast Matt and Florrie in home-made elderberry wine and watch them cut the cake. Icing was forbidden, so it was a sponge cake filled with jam and cream – eggs and cream being easier to come by on the farm than dried fruit. Afterwards she waved the couple off on their five-day honeymoon with a big smile on her face.

After the guests had gone home, leaving a sense of anticlimax in the farmhouse, Julie helped Maggie and Alec clear up while Walter went out to see to the animals. 'I hope things go well for them,' Maggie said. 'Life is so uncertain nowadays.'

'All the more reason to seize what happiness you can, while you can,' Alec told her. 'Don't you agree, Eve?'

Julie came out of her brown study to answer him. 'You may be right.'

'I don't have to be back until midnight tomorrow, how about you?'

'The same.'

'Then let's have a good long ride tomorrow morning. The horses could do with some exercise. Now I'm not living at home, they're getting fat and lazy.'

'You're on,' she said.

Alec knew, without a shadow of doubt, that Eve was the girl for him, had known it almost from her first visit to the farm, but he was finding it difficult to get close to her. Her pale good looks, her slight figure, her quietness all attracted him. She had a kind of feyness, an other-worldliness which intrigued him. Florrie had told him about her being bombed out in the Blitz and being the only survivor in her family and she didn't like to talk about it. Even Florrie did not know how many of her family had perished, whether she had had brothers and sisters, parents and grandparents. All she knew was that Eve was alone in the world and putting a brave face on it. He wanted more than anything to try and repair the damage, to make her see that she was not alone, that there were people who cared for her and loved her.

It wasn't that she was miserable, far from it; she enjoyed a joke with the best of them, loved dancing, and cried when the film they went to see was sad, laughed when it was funny. She let him kiss her chastely on the cheek but had not encouraged any closer intimacy. He wondered why; she could not be unaware of how he felt for her. Tomorrow, while they were out, he would try to draw her out, get her to talk. Talking might lay the ghosts.

In that he failed. She would not be drawn. They had been riding for two hours when they stopped to dismount and rest the horses. He took her hand; she allowed that. He kissed her cheek; she allowed that. Encouraged, he took her in his arms. 'Eve,' he said. 'You do know how I feel about you, don't you?'

'No, Alec, please.' She struggled away from him.

'No you don't know, or you don't want me to talk about it?'

'I don't want you to talk about it. You'll spoil everything if you do.'

'Why?'

'We're all right as we are, good friends.'

'Friends be damned. I want more than that. I love you. I knew it the moment I saw you. It was like being struck by lightning.'

She managed a smile. 'Have you ever been struck by lightning?'

'No, but I know what it can do. I hoped you might feel the same.'

'I don't know what I feel. It's too soon.'

'Too soon, how can you say that? We've known each other over two years. You've come to the house, called it home . . .'

'Perhaps that was presumptuous of me. Your mother said—'

'Oh, for goodness' sake, Eve, I didn't mean that. We love having you, all of us, me particularly. I just thought it meant you might return my feelings.'

She stood up. 'Alec, leave it please. You'll spoil everything if you keep on.'

'Very well.' Disappointed, dismayed and hurt, he helped her mount, remounted himself and they rode back to the farm in silence, and that afternoon they caught separate trains and went their separate ways.

'God I'm nervous. This is worse than going on an op.'

'Remind me not to do it, then,' Tim said, watching his friend fiddling with his tie. He tied that tie every day of his life, so what was so difficult about fixing it today? It wasn't going to be a silk-cravat-and-morning-suit sort of do; most of the men would be in uniform. 'Anyway, you've done it before.'

'I know, but that was different.'

'How different?'

'We weren't much more than kids, Julie in particular. She had been brought up in an orphanage and that made her kind of young and old at the same time, an innocent in some ways, wise beyond her years in others, but it made her vulnerable. And there was this chap who was pestering her . . .'

'You mean you just felt sorry for her?'

'No, I don't. There was more to it than that. We were happy as sandboys. It was a great adventure, getting married and having our own home and a baby. He was a grand little chap . . .'

'Hey, this is your wedding day. Don't dwell on it.'

'I'm not. You asked and I was only pointing out that this time it's different. Pam is more mature; she knows what she wants . . .'

'And that's you.'

'Yes, and I want her too. I wouldn't be marrying her otherwise.' After six months of courtship, in which their love had grown stronger and more enduring, they had decided not to wait until the war was over to get married. Life was so uncertain and Pam wanted to seize what happiness was theirs while they could and, though he doubted the wisdom of it, he felt the same. Being married again was a statement of optimism in the future.

'Good. Now we've got that out of the way, put your jacket on, it's time we were on the way to church. You can't have the bride turning up before we do.'

Harry followed Tim out to the car, an open-top two-seater, though the hood was up against the cold March wind. Where his friend had found it, and how he had managed to get petrol for it, he did not know and thought it better not to ask, but it was Harry's and Pam's for the next five days. Tim drove him to the church.

They were met at the door by Jane Godwin with a tray of buttonholes: a carnation and a spray of fern wrapped round with silver paper. 'You're in good time,' she said. 'Pam won't be long. Last minute nerves, you know . . .'

'She's not changed her mind, has she?' Harry asked in alarm.

'Good Lord, no. She had you marked out from the first, Harry me lad, the last thing she'll do is back out. She just wants to look her best for you.' She paused to look into his face. 'You aren't having second thoughts, are you?'

'Definitely not.'

'Good.'

Tim took one of the flowers and fastened it on Harry's uniform jacket, did the same for himself, then they made their way into the church and down the aisle to the pew at the front.

Harry was conscious that the church was full on both sides. 'I didn't think there'd be so many here,' he whispered to Tim.

'Why not? Very popular couple, you are. There's Pam's relatives and yours and as many as could make it from the station, including some of the Yanks we've got to know, half the Women's Land Army, all the pub regulars, not to mention anyone who has ever bought Godwin's bread.'

Harry turned to look behind him. His mother and father, Roly and Millie and her husband in a captain's khaki uniform were all there. He grinned at them.

'Good luck, son.' his father said.

'Are you nervous?' Millie asked.

179

'A bit.'

'I'm on tenterhooks. I hope Dotty behaves herself.'

So did Harry. His niece was well named Dotty. She was somewhat spoilt, and as her father was so rarely to be seen, was hardly ever chastised. He really hadn't wanted Dorothy to be a bridesmaid because she reminded him of George and, today of all days, he did not want that reminder, but when Millie had suggested it, Pam had agreed at once. This, he realised, was to be the big occasion his first marriage had not been, even though it was wartime and it had taken a great deal of organising to get everyone together on the day. Pam's mother and his own ought to be in charge of the conduct of the war, he thought ruefully – they'd have it won in no time.

He looked back towards the church door as the organist, who had been quietly playing 'Sheep May Safely Graze', struck up the wedding march. He rose and moved out into the aisle, not once taking his eye off the bridal procession as it made its way towards him. Pam looked stunning in a flowing white dress and veil, lent to her by a friend who had married just before the war. She carried a bouquet of red roses. Her cheeks were blooming and her eyes shining and at that moment he knew he wanted this marriage more than anything. Behind her were two of her friends in short burgundy dresses that matched the bride's flowers, ushering Dorothy ahead of them, in a velvet dress the same colour, trimmed with white lace. She had a little basket of tiny white rosebuds in her hand and looked very solemn.

Pam reached him, smiled happily and took his arm. He smiled back and together they turned towards the rector. A little shiver ran down his spine as he heard him say: 'If any of you know cause or just impediment why these two persons should not be joined in matrimony, ye are to declare it.' No one had, of course, and the service continued without interruption.

It was a moving service, but a happy one; both spoke their vows clearly and then Harry slipped the ring on Pam's finger and it was done. They signed the register and went back down the aisle, her hand tucked into his arm, smiling at everyone. Rose petals were used for confetti and both mothers fetched out box cameras and took pictures outside the church and again when they arrived back at the bakery, where everyone enjoyed a feast that had taken all the ingenuity of Jane Goodman, Hilda Walker and the landlord of The Papermakers to bring about, not to mention generous contributions from Harry's American friends. The celebrations went on all afternoon, but Harry and Pam did not stay to the end. Once the speeches were over, Pam changed into a going-away costume and they climbed into the little sports car and drove away with tin cans rattling behind them.

Harry stopped the car as soon as they were clear of the village and got out to untie the cans. He flung them in the back, got in the car and turned towards her. 'I haven't kissed you yet, Mrs Walker.' And he proceeded to do just that.

'Mrs Walker,' she said and giggled. 'It sounds funny.'

'You had better get used to it. You've got it for life.'

'I know. Oh, Harry, I couldn't be happier, not if you were to offer me the Crown Jewels.'

'I'm not likely to do that. Not that I wouldn't, of course, if I had them to offer. You'll just have to make do with a plain gold band and five days on the Broads. We can't go far; the petrol won't last out.' He had decided not to go to the coast; for one thing the beaches were mined and

181

they wouldn't be able to go on the sand, and for another it would remind him too much of Julie.

'That'll do me. We'll laze about, take out a rowing boat, go for long walks and we won't talk about the war at all.'

'That suits me.'

They did their best to do just that and, at the end of it, returned to Swanton Morley where he had rented a small house close to the end of the runway. It was called Honeysuckle Cottage because there was a vigorous specimen of that plant climbing all over a tiny wooden porch at the front door. Harry was convinced it was the clinging honeysuckle that prevented the porch from disintegrating. Everything about the place was small. It was no more than four rooms, a kitchen and sitting room downstairs and two bedrooms upstairs, each with a tiny window which was easy to blackout. There was no running water, no gas or electricity, no main drains or sewerage, nothing but four walls and a roof. There was a well which provided water, oil lamps and candles for light when it became too dark to see, and the lavatory was a bucket under a bench in a tiny hut at the bottom of the garden, which had to be emptied but which made good manure for the garden. It was decidedly primitive, but it was home, and they furnished it with help from Pam's parents and a special chit for furniture given by the Government to people who had been bombed out or were newly married.

Harry could sleep at home every night when he was not on standby. Pam was blissfully happy with her airman husband and he with her. They began to make plans for what they would do when the war was won – a proper home, a good job and a family were high on the list.

* * *

Julie settled back at Ringway, watching the men come and go for parachute training, being cheerful, friendly and efficient without getting close to any of them. She wrote frequently to Florrie, who was now driving bigwigs all over the place, and to Alec, though her letters to him were a little constrained. She had half suspected he was becoming fond of her and that last leave had filled her with alarm. She was in no position to commit herself to anyone, but she could not bear to cut him off altogether. He was a kind of lifeline to normality and she longed for normality. Time and time again she thought about telling him about her loss of memory, that she had no idea of her real name or if she had a family who might be thinking her dead, worst of all that she had been a mother. So much had happened since, it seemed unreal, a distant dream and sometimes she had to pinch herself to prove she was alive and awake. What would he make of such a confession?

At other times she was tempted to tell him she reciprocated his feelings and say nothing of her past, but how could she do that to him? He was too obviously sincere, much too nice a person to deceive. In a way she was glad they were apart; if they were together, within talking and touching distance, she would not be able to hold out. She still had odd snatches of memory, at least that's what she thought these fleeting visions were. Unless she was psychic. One such twinge came in late May when she was at the cinema watching a newsreel about the raid on the German dams. The destruction had been caused by bouncing bombs, so it was explained, which were dropped at low level and skimmed along the surface bouncing off the waves. 'Like skimming pebbles into the sea,' the commentator said. This was followed by a demonstration of someone doing it and

Julie sat bolt upright. She had done that, some time in the past she had done that and she had not been alone. She groped and groped at her memory, but nothing more came to her. Too unsettled to sit still, she left the cinema and caught a bus back to Ringway, where there were friends and colleagues to take her mind off it.

'I don't know where she is,' Ted Austen told the couple who faced him. The woman might once have been a big woman, but she appeared frail, with hollow cheeks and a haunted look in her eyes. The man looked as though he could handle himself, and though he must have been in his late forties, Ted did not want to tangle with him. He could beat him all right in a scrap but it would draw attention to himself and that he most definitely did not want.

He led a semi-nomadic life, trying to avoid the police, not only because of his black market activities, but because he knew he should have registered for call-up and he hadn't done so. He changed his lodgings often and at first kept his illicit stores in his various wardrobes, but he didn't trust his landladies not to snoop and latterly there had been too much to hide successfully. He had taken to concealing it in bombed-out factories and warehouses, moving it regularly, until the council had started demolishing the buildings as unsafe and flattening the ground. So he had hired two adjoining lock-up garages. He kept his stores in one, where his favourite customers knew they could contact him on certain days. Usually he met them in different pubs, going round in a battered van using black market petrol. The van was dressed up to look like an ambulance, which had been a stroke of genius on his part. He had only to wear a white coat and set the bell ringing and he whizzed through

184

roadblocks and cordons and no one questioned him. He kept it in the second of the two garages.

Someone had ratted and sent these two to him and he'd have his guts for garters if he ever found out who it was. He was thankful the garage doors were shut and there was nothing for them to see. 'I haven't seen her for goodness knows how long – it must be nearly three years, when we both worked at Chalfont's.'

'But you knew her quite well?' the woman asked.

'Not well,' he said guardedly. 'Sometimes we sat together in the canteen, sometimes when the siren went we'd go to the shelter together. I took her to the pictures once or twice, that's all.'

'But it's not all, is it?' the man said. 'You got her into some dodgy business with the black market.'

'Not me,' he said. 'You've got the wrong man there. If she was into the black market it wasn't anything to do with me.'

'If not you, who then?'

'How should I know? I didn't ask her business and she didn't ask mine.'

'Did you know any of her friends?'

'Only Julie Walker and she's dead.'

'We know that.'

'Then you know as much as I do. If your daughter didn't die on the same day as Julie, she might have left London for somewhere safer, or she might have died in any of the raids afterwards. I never saw her again.'

Stuart handed him his calling card. 'If you do get news of her, will you be good enough to contact me at this address? Even if it's only something very tiny. There'll be a reward.'

'OK.' Ted took the card and stuffed it into his pocket

without bothering to look at it. They thanked him and left. He breathed a huge sigh of relief but their arrival worried him. Had they been to the police? Perhaps he ought to lie low for a bit, or go somewhere else, perhaps north of the river. He waited until they had gone, then set off in the ambulance to reconnoitre a new patch.

'He's lying, isn't he?' Angela said as a taxi carried them away.

'Yes, I'm pretty sure he is.' It had taken a long time to trace the man and that had only been done through Mr Walker who had found someone at the factory who remembered Rosie being friendly with him. Mr Walker had given them Austen's last known address but he no longer lived there. His landlady had had a forwarding address for his mail, but she couldn't remember it. 'I wrote it down on a piece of paper but I don't know what happened to it. It was a long time ago. If I find it I'll send it to you.' They had given her their address and gone back home to the endless waiting and uncertainty which was taking its toll on Angela's health.

They had decided the woman had forgotten all about them, when almost a year later she wrote saying she had found the address while redecorating after having some bomb damage repaired, so the next weekend off they went again, enduring hours on unreliable trains. Ted Austen hadn't been at that address either, but they had been told he frequented a pub not far away.

Stuart had taken Angela back to their hotel and left her there while he went to investigate. He was glad he had; it had been a sleazy kind of place, where he imagined all sorts of shady deals going on, and that reminded him of the store of cached goods in Rosie's digs. He had hung around and pretended to want petrol. Someone heard him ask. 'Ted Austen's the man you want to see,' he had told him.

'Where can I find him?'

He had been told the whereabouts of the garages, gave the man a fiver and returned to the hotel to tell Angela, who had insisted on accompanying him. 'Do you think he does know where Rosie is?' she asked him now.

'That's another matter. I'm not sure. We'll have to keep an eye on him.'

'Do you think we should report him to the police?'

'What for? We've got no proof. And if he's arrested, we'll never know what happened, will we?' He had long ago stopped talking about finding their daughter alive.

She sighed. 'I sometimes wonder if we'll ever know that.'

'Perhaps it's time to let go.'

'I don't want to, not yet. Let's go and see Miss Paterson. You never know . . .'

Donald Walker had given them Miss Paterson's address at his son's suggestion, but they didn't expect to learn any more from her than they had from Rosie's landlady and that dreadful man they had just left.

In that they were wrong. Miss Paterson had not met Rosemary, but she did know that she and Julie Walker were good friends. 'Your daughter would go and visit Julie quite frequently,' she told them. 'I'm not sure, but I think she was looking after George the day Julie was killed. Julie wanted to see me about something important and Rosemary had offered to stay with the baby, so she could be quicker. Julie got back home to George and they died when the Anderson shelter had a direct hit, but as Rosemary was not also in the shelter she must have decided to risk going home. I didn't know she had disappeared.'

'She never arrived back at her lodgings.'

'Oh, I am so sorry. She must have been caught out.'

'Caught out?' Angela queried, startled. 'What do you mean?'

'I'm sorry, I meant caught out in the open when a bomb dropped.'

'Then why did no one find her body?'

'It was all very confused that night. It was the first really big raid and things weren't as organised as they might have been and have been since. I'm dreadfully sorry I can't help you any further.'

'There is one thing,' Stuart said, after some hesitation. 'Do you know anything about any black market dealings?'

'Oh dear.'

'You do?' Angela seized on the note of regret in Miss Paterson's voice.

'Well, Julie did say something.'

'Then tell us, please. We must know.'

They listened as she recounted what she knew. 'I'm sure it wasn't anything really dreadful,' she said. 'Rosemary had this friend who could get things and Julie was always anxious about George and wanting to have everything she thought he needed, so she accepted what was offered. It got a bit out of hand and Julie owed Rosemary money. I lent her a little so that she could pay her, but last time I saw her, she said she wouldn't do it anymore.'

'I knew that man was lying,' Angela said.

'What man?'

Stuart told Grace Paterson about Ted Austen. 'He denies all knowledge of Rosie,' he said.

'Maybe he's telling the truth,' Miss Paterson said. 'If he

knew where she was, he wouldn't have broken into her lodgings to retrieve his goods, would he? Always assuming that's what did happen.'

They conceded she might be right, and though they had learnt a little more, they were no nearer finding their daughter, or, as looked most likely, her remains.

'Angela,' Stuart said carefully as the taxi took them back to Liverpool Street Station for the journey north. 'I think we have to accept that Rosie died in that raid. If, as Miss Paterson says, she was caught outside . . .' He dare not put his thoughts into words: that she had been blown into little pieces too small to identify.

She was in tears. Her fierce conviction that her daughter was alive somewhere, perhaps injured or frightened, was fading. She could not make the evidence fit. In a way she was glad they had pursued the search, in a way she was sorry because then there had been hope; now there was none. 'If only we could have had a body to bury,' she said, mopping her face.

He put his arm about her and drew her to him. 'I know, love, I know. Perhaps we should have a service – not a burial but a remembrance, and a little plaque to put in the wall in the kirk. We could lay her to rest that way.'

'Yes,' she said, but she still wasn't sure.

Chapter Eight

Everyone was talking about the second front that summer – when it would happen and where – but it was largely conjecture. Those in the know realised there was a great deal of work to be done before that happened: planning, raising the troops, gathering the equipment, arms and ammunition, and training, a great deal of training. Alec heard that volunteers were needed for a new parachute division and put himself forward. He liked the idea; it had a certain glamour attached to it and there was a shilling a day extra pay once you passed out. Not only that, he knew Eve was stationed at Ringway where the training was done. He had no intention of giving up on her.

He found himself in the newly formed 13th Battalion and stationed at Larkhill on Salisbury Plain, with no idea what was in store for him. Being in the south it was a long way from Ringway, but they were not there long before they were sent to Hardwick Hall in Derbyshire. He did not tell Eve what he was doing; he was determined to make her see that he would not accept defeat and the element of surprise might help.

Hardwick Hall was one of the most historically important stately homes in the country and they weren't allowed anywhere near the house. Their quarters were huts on the estate. The training here was meant to toughen them up and weed out any who were not up to the physical aspect of the job. Alec found himself on assault courses set up in the woods, where they clambered about like monkeys in the treetops and wallowed in mud, and undertook route marches in full kit, carrying arms and ammunition. These started at ten miles, which had to be done in two hours, then twenty miles in three hours, and ended up with fifty miles to be done in twenty-four hours. Alec, used to working all day on the farm, considered himself fit, but this was something else altogether. The disgrace of being sent back to their units as unfit was a spur to most, but Alec had the extra one of being determined to go to Ringway. He arrived there in July 1943.

He had no time to make enquiries or go looking for Eve, the training was so intense. Apart from the continuing physical exertions – they were up at the crack of dawn for PT – he soon found himself in one of the hangars, where they learnt to fall, jumping out of an old fuselage onto matting, keeping knees and feet together and learning to roll, both forwards and backwards. They did it over and over again until it became second nature.

'When are we going up in a bloody plane?' someone muttered under his breath as they toiled to the top of the tower, a contraption from which they jumped, their rate of descent being controlled by a fan. It was much higher than a fuselage and the landing harder.

His words were heard by the RAF instructor. 'Not yet, you don't,' he said. 'Not until I'm satisfied you won't break your ruddy neck on landing.' He held out a helmet on the top of which were painted the words 'Dig here', which produced a laugh from the fledgling parachutists. Though they were all keen to make their first jump, they were also nervous. So much could go wrong. The instructor's job was to minimise that.

At the end of the week they were told they could have the weekend off, which was received with a cheer and a general exodus into Manchester. Alec went looking for Eve.

She was on duty in the stores, looking forward to going off at lunchtime and having the rest of the day to herself, not that she could go until the queue of men with chits to draw stores had been dealt with. Head down, concentrating on the paperwork, she did not notice Alec until she heard his quiet voice say, 'Hallo, Eve.'

Her head shot up. 'Alec! What are you doing here?'

'Looking for you.'

'How did you get here?'

'By train and truck, as if that mattered. I'm here.'

'On leave?'

'No, silly, posted here to do parachute training.'

'Oh, Alec, why didn't you warn me?'

'I wanted to surprise you.'

'You certainly did that.'

'When are you off duty?'

She looked up at the clock on the wall. 'In about half an hour.'

'Come on, Corporal, we can't stand here all day while you chat,' the man next in the queue grumbled.

'Go away,' she told Alec.

'OK, I'll wait outside.'

She was in a blue funk. Alec was here and he was wonderfully vibrantly alive; he was not at the end of a letter, subject to the vagaries of the postal service. Feelings she had been manfully suppressing had suddenly shot to the surface on seeing him. She had wanted to throw herself into his arms at the same time as she was dismayed by her reaction. Now what to do? She toyed with the idea of slipping out of the back door and avoiding him, until she could sort herself out, but told herself that would be cowardly. She worked for the next half-hour in a daze, then walked out to meet him.

'Where to?' he asked, kissing her cheek.

'Wherever you like. We could take a bus into Manchester, go to a dance, or the pictures.' Anywhere public where they would not be alone, she thought, admitting to herself that, after all, she was a coward.

They went to see *Mrs Miniver*, which was not a good choice, Julie realised, when she found tears running down her face, and not all to be laid at the door of the film. She mopped them up, hoping Alec had not noticed. Afterwards, walking through the darkened streets to catch a bus back to the station, he put his arm about her shoulders. 'You're not as tough as you'd have us believe, are you?' he said.

She laughed. 'No, I'm a big softie.'

'Could you not spare some of that softness for me?'

'Oh, Alec, you know I do.'

'Then why turn away from me?'

'I haven't turned away.'

'Yes, you have. On that last leave at home, you pushed me off.'

'I'm sorry, it's just that . . .' She was floundering and

stopped to calm herself. 'It's just that life is so uncertain. You never know from one day to the next what's going to happen, do you?'

'And after losing all your family, you are afraid of losing me, is that it?'

It was a way out. 'Partly, I suppose.'

'Isn't that all the more reason to make the most of the time we might have together, however long or short. That's what Florrie and Matt decided and I think they were right.'

'But you don't know much about me, do you?'

'I know all I want to know. The past is gone. You can't bring it back.'

She sighed. 'I wish I could.'

'Oh, Eve, I wish I could take away the hurt. Please, let me try.'

'You'll hate me then.'

'I could never hate you. I love you. Don't you understand what that means? It means that I want to marry you, to call you mine, to be joined with you, body, mind and spirit for always. We could be happy together and I could make you forget the horrors.'

'Forget,' she murmured. 'I wish I could and I wish I didn't.'

'That's an enigmatic statement if ever there was one.' There was a bench at the bus stop and, instead of going to stand in the queue, he pulled her down beside him onto it. 'Are you going to tell me what's troubling you?'

She looked about her; there were people coming and going, not the time or place to unburden herself, but she knew she would have to, sooner or later. She could not go on stringing him along. 'Not now, it'll take too long. Tomorrow. I'm off duty.'

'Is that a promise?'

'Yes.'

He hugged her to him and kissed her cheek. The bus drew up and they climbed aboard behind the queue. He was cheerful; she was withdrawn. Already she was rehearsing in her mind what she was going to say. And after it was all over and he had left her, angry and disappointed, she would have to write to Florrie and repeat it all. And that would be the end of their friendship, the end of her visits to the farm and the dear people there who had been so good to her. She would be alone again.

'Good God!'

They had taken a bus into the countryside and walked for miles. He had tried light conversation, but she was unresponsive until he had almost lost patience with her and pulled her down onto the grass beside the track. The sun was shining, the heather was in bloom and the skylarks soaring, but she noticed none of it. He put his arm about her shoulders. 'Eve, we can't go on like this.'

'I know.'

'Then what's bugging you?'

She had taken a deep breath and launched into her story, the words tumbling over each other in her effort to get them out, and at the end of it his reaction had been, 'Good God!'

'They told me I'd had a child. Whether it's alive or dead, I've no idea. Whether I wanted it or not, I've no idea. Whether I loved its father, I have no idea. How can you want to marry someone like that, someone who does not exist?'

'Of course you exist. You are sitting here beside me. The problem is, what do we do about it?'

'There's nothing we can do. I've tried everything.'

'Do you think you will remember in time?'

'At first I thought I would, the doctors thought so, but it's been so long now I think it's gone for good.'

'I can't imagine what it must be like, not to remember a childhood, not to remember mother, father, sister, going to school, taking that first job. Can't you recall any of that?'

'No. Sometimes I have odd flashes of what I think might be memories, but they're never substantial enough to grasp and say, 'Yes, I remember that.'

'What sort of flashes?'

She told him about the long corridor in what she assumed was an institution where she might have left her baby, the feeling that it was at the seaside, reinforced by the most recent one about the bouncing bombs, which had left her unsettled for days, and her fear of being shut in the dark, which she assumed was on account of being buried under rubble during the air raid. 'As far as I am concerned that was when my life began,' she said, relaxing a little now the story had been told. 'The seventh of September 1940.' She gave a troubled laugh. 'Eve Seaton came into this world already an adult.'

'Oh, my love,' he said, hugging her to him. 'I wish I could help, but if you can't remember, you can't, and that's it.'

'I'm sorry I've been such a disappointment to you, but you'll soon find someone else.'

'Find someone else! What are you talking about? I don't want anyone else. I want you. Why, if you were to marry me, you would have a new name, a real one.'

His words echoed for a second, as if she were being nudged, but the feeling left her as had so often happened in the past. 'But would such a marriage be legal?'

'I don't see why not. In any case, I don't care. The past's gone, water under the bridge.'

'No, it's not. It's a whirlpool, going round and round, going nowhere, dragging me down and everyone I love with me.'

'Eve Seaton, you are talking nonsense. Either you put the lost life behind you and get on with the one you have, or we make a concerted effort to find out the truth and all that entails, good or bad. There must be something that can be done. Somewhere or other there must be lists of people missing in air raids. At least you know the place and the date, so that's a starting point.'

'I've done all that.'

'Then we'll do it again. Together.'

'And if we don't succeed?'

'Then I want you to promise me you'll put it behind you and become Mrs Alec Kilby.'

'Can you put it behind you?'

'Yes.' He was firm on that score.

'I don't think you realise how difficult it will be. Every day something or someone will remind you that you've only got half a wife, the other half will be gone into some void, a ghost to haunt you. I might even be a criminal. Who's to tell?'

'I don't believe that for a moment. Losing your memory does not change you fundamentally. You're still the same person inside, still the sweet, compassionate, brave Eve Seaton I know and love, and I reckon you always were.'

'Oh, Alec.' She was in tears. He mopped them up.

'Don't cry, sweetheart, I was trying to cheer you up.'

She gave him a watery smile. 'You have.'

'Good.'

'What about Florrie and your parents? I'll have to tell them now I've told you.'

'Of course, but they know how I feel about you and will go along with whatever we decide. All I need to know is if you love me. That's all that matters.' He turned towards her and took both her hands in his, looking earnestly into her eyes, such very blue troubled eyes. 'Do you? Yes or no?'

'Yes.'

'Thank heavens for that.' He gathered her into his arms and kissed her good and long, but he was careful not to let his feelings run away with him. This love was too precious to spoil and he had to take it very slowly. He was also aware that nothing else had been resolved. It was all very well to say they would find out the truth, but how could they do anything about it while they were subject to the vagaries of the War Office? Sleuthing would have to wait while he went back to helping win the war.

For the next few weeks he saw Julie as often as he could, but the training was even more intense as they progressed. They had to do eight jumps to qualify, three from a cage suspended from a barrage balloon, one of which was done at night, and five from an aircraft. He was a bundle of nerves before that first balloon jump, as they all were, but once in the air with the parachute open above him it was a wonderful sensation. They had been told how to control their descent by manipulating the harness straps, but that was not easy as they swung to and fro while an instructor on the ground yelled up at them through a loudspeaker. They all landed safely, if not elegantly, rolled up their parachutes and carried them to the trucks to be taken back to Ringway, where WAAF parachute packers would repack them.

'It's the most exhilarating feeling,' he told Julie, later that day when they both had a few hours off duty. 'You feel so free and the world's spread out below you. The landing was a bit hard and one or two hurt themselves . . .'

She knew that happened quite often and had seen the ambulance careering out of the gate towards Tatton Park where the men were dropped. Broken femurs and ankles and dislocated shoulders were fairly common. Now and again there was a fatality when a parachute failed to open 'But you were OK?'

'Yes, fine. Don't worry about me.'

'What does your mother think about you doing this?'

'Oh, she's all right about it. She thinks it's keeping me out of harm's way.'

'Oh, Alec, what sort of yarn have you spun her?'

He laughed. 'Parachuting is great fun and miles away from any action. I could be on active service in Italy instead of safely in England, which I pointed out to her. And don't you dare tell her any different.'

They were a couple now, everyone knew it, and Julie had accepted it, though she still had enormous doubts. It was a good thing, she decided, that they couldn't think about marriage or she would have to make decisions she wasn't ready to make. Not that she didn't love Alec; she loved him heart and soul and knew he was 'the one', as Florrie would have said, but they were no nearer a solution to her dilemma. She had told Florrie about it in a very long letter and been forgiven for keeping her in the dark for so long, and Florrie had told her that if Alec wanted to marry her, then what was she waiting for? Speaking for herself, she had never been happier and would not have forfeited her time with Matt for anything, even though it took a lot of organising and switching of duties and leaves to bring it about.

Julie knew about that because she and Alec were doing the same thing as far as they were able to, but even being on the same station did not help when he was being kept at it night and day. There was a purpose to it all, and everyone appreciated that.

The balloon jumps out of the way, Alec found himself lining up with his 'stick' of ten men to climb aboard a Whitley to make his first descent from an aircraft. They had to clear the aeroplane in the shortest possible time after reaching the dropping zone. It was important that they land close together because the jump was really only the beginning; they had to assemble and turn themselves into ground troops ready for battle. When the red light came on in the fuselage, they stood up and hooked themselves onto the static line which would automatically release their parachutes, and shuffled into line. The exit was through the floor and they had practised it many times, because if you didn't jump clear the pack on your back hit the back of the opening and sent you spiralling, but jump too enthusiastically and your nose hit the front – the 'Whitley kiss' they called it. The first man sat on the edge. Red light changed to green and the RAF dispatcher shouted 'Go!' and they went out one after the other with no hesitation. A refusal to jump meant being sent back to your original unit and was the ultimate shame. 'Go!' was the command that governed all their training and was ingrained into their brains, so that obedience became an instinct.

'I've done it,' he told Julie after his eighth jump. 'Passing-out parade tomorrow and I get my wings and my red beret.'

'Congratulations.'

'And you know what? It's ten days' leave before we're posted.'

Julie suddenly felt miserable; she had known it had to end, this being on the same station, but now it was close she realised how much she would miss him. 'Where are you being sent?'

'Back to Salisbury Plain, I expect.'

'Nearer home, then.' It was said flatly to cover her dismay.

'Yes, but that's not the point. The point is ten days' leave. Can you get some leave, so we can have time together before I go?'

'I don't know.'

'But you'll try, won't you? It'll be the last time we'll be able to see each other for ages. I reckon the invasion's not too far away and all leave will be cancelled. I want to have some happy memories to take with me.'

Happy memories. Why did remembrance feature so strongly in everyone's lives, especially her own? He wanted happy memories and so did she.

'You do want to be with me, don't you?' he queried, sensing her hesitation.

'Yes, yes, of course I do. I'll ask.'

'You'll do more than ask, you'll beg.'

She laughed. 'OK, I'll beg.'

If she had expected their leave to be spent at the farm she was mistaken. Florrie had told him what a wonderful time she and Matt had had on the shores of Lake Windermere and he had booked a week at the same holiday cottage. He did not tell her until they were well on their way, and she

201

realised with a sudden jolt that when he said he wanted them to spend their leave together, he had meant night and day. It sent her into a panic. Had he taken her agreement for granted?

Her first reaction was to tell him to turn round and go back, but that was quickly followed by 'Why?' Why go back? What had she to lose? Not her virginity, that had already gone, but she might lose the man she had come to love. Life was too uncertain to be prudish. She settled back in her seat and closed her eyes, letting the cool wind flow over her face and relax her. She was lucky, so very lucky, and she must make sure he knew how she felt. Her loss of memory seemed suddenly less important, not really important at all.

Slowly and surely as the year progressed, the tide of war began to turn in the Allies' favour. The Russians had turned defeat into victory at Stalingrad and were on the offensive. They were difficult allies, in spite of the help being sent to them in Arctic convoys which braved the U-boats and the terrible weather conditions to reach them. They wanted a second front in the west to take the pressure off them. They didn't want it any more than the British people, who were war-weary and longed for peace. An invasion of Europe would surely be the beginning of the end, but it could not be done in a hurry, and Italy had to be dealt with first.

The North Africa campaign ended in total victory, leaving the troops to turn their attention to Sicily and then to Italy. News of the invasion came on 3rd September, exactly four years after the declaration of war. Five days later the Italian government surrendered and changed sides and Italy became one of the occupied countries. The

Germans still held out and the Allies' slow progress up the boot of Italy was frustrating for those who had been anticipating a second front that year.

It was the main topic of conversation in The Papermakers. It was always full, even when there was a shortage of beer. Half a pint could last all evening if it was larded with conversation and a game of darts or shove-halfpenny, which amused the Americans. They hadn't taken over the airfield at Swanton Morley as they had done in other places, but since that first draft, they had arrived in huge numbers and spread themselves all over the country. There was no ignoring them and even those who hadn't a good word to say for them realised they had come to be part of the invasion of mainland Europe, and if they had to invade Britain first, then so be it. There were still some in Swanton flying combined ops with the RAF. The villagers had become used to seeing them around. There had even been a couple of weddings, though the more sceptical among the population wondered what the new wives were letting themselves in for. 'A strange country, strange customs, and how do they know their new in-laws will welcome them?' Jane had said.

'It's too late this year,' someone said gloomily, staring into his almost-empty glass, swilling the dregs round as if it would suddenly fill again. 'Another bloody year of this.'

'It can't get any worse,' Pam said. Harry was on duty, which was why she had come into the pub with her parents. She had a weak lemonade shandy on the table in front of her. She would not allow herself anything stronger because a baby was due in April the following year. 'Perhaps the war will be over by then,' she had said, so happy and optimistic no one had the heart to argue with her. Harry had expressed himself 'pleased as punch'.

'Wanna bet?' the landlord said. 'Did you hear on the news there's been more air raids on London. Don't look like they're ready to give up yet. At this rate there'll be nothing left standing.'

'There i'n't nothin' left standing of Hamburg,' Bert put in. 'We're givin' them hell. You ask Harry.'

Harry, along with all the other airmen, was flying almost every other night, pounding away at targets in Germany and the Low Countries, softening them up for the invasion which was sure to come. Germany was being repaid several times over for the Blitz on London and other British cities. He had told Pam the euphoria he had felt at the beginning was wearing thin, and when he looked down at the burning cities, he found himself wondering about the people down below, not only the troops which he said were legitimate targets, but the women, old men and children – women like Pam expecting new life and instead having it snuffed out. He said it was making him feel like a murderer.

Leave was in short supply that Christmas, but Julie managed a seventy-two-hour pass for the New Year and travelled down to Hillside Farm on New Year's Eve, which was a Friday. The Kilbys made her as welcome as they always had even though they now knew her secret. As far as they were concerned she was Eve Seaton, their son's chosen bride. If they had misgivings they certainly did not voice them.

Maggie and Julie were toasting their toes by the kitchen range after washing up the lunch things, when the door was opened. Thinking it was Walter, Julie did not look up from contemplating the flames, but Maggie did. She jumped up . . . 'Alec!' . . . and flew to embrace him.

Julie was on her feet as soon as she heard his name and he crossed the room and hugged her to him, kissing her soundly before she could even utter a word. It was Maggie who did all the talking. 'Why didn't you let us know you were coming? We'd have delayed lunch. Have you eaten? Are you hungry? How long have you got?'

He released Julie and turned to his mother, laughing. 'I didn't know myself, so I couldn't let you know, and I'm due back on Sunday night. And I could eat a horse. Any more questions?'

'Not now, later perhaps. Take Eve into the sitting room, there's a fire in there, while I rustle up some food.'

Julie followed him into the next room and they sat down side by side on the sofa where he kissed her again, this time more thoroughly. 'God, I've missed you,' he said.

'And I've missed you.' She nestled in his arms, no longer afraid. She had seen men come and go, listened to the news and followed the conduct of the war, or as much of it as was made public, and had decided the past did not matter – especially her own past, which had no bearing on the momentous events unfolding about her – that the future was as unknown as the past, and it would be better to concentrate on the present.

'It will be over soon and then we can think of getting married.'

'The war, you mean.'

'Of course the war. I reckon the invasion's not far off and that will put paid to Hitler and all he stands for. The world will be at peace.'

'When d'you think it will be?'

'Your guess is as good as mine, but judging by all the training we've been doing, it can't be that far away. We've been on so many night exercises I feel like an owl. We've criss-crossed Salisbury Plain with maps so many times I'm beginning to think I know every rock and pool. Salisbury Plain in midwinter is perishing cold and we've been soaked to the skin many a time. We've dug defensive positions and been on exercises, when we've jumped into supposed hostile forces and practised capturing and holding bridges, and then we've taken our turn to be defenders on the ground. On one occasion we were dropped up in Scotland with nothing on us – no money, no identity, nothing – and told to make our own way back to camp in twenty-four hours, and if the police or MPs picked us up, we'd have failed. All good fun but none of it gave any hint as to where we're going and when.'

'Did you manage it?'

'To get back? Yes, hitched a lift to start with and got as far as Manchester. I'd have stopped by to see you, but I didn't have time. Then I got on a freight train when no one was looking, which landed me in the middle of nowhere, but there was a little country station with no one checking tickets, so I nipped on a train, dodged the ticket collector when he came round and jumped out just before it rolled into Salisbury Station. I pinched a bike for the last few miles.'

'That was naughty of you.'

'All's fair in love and war. I reckon the owner got it back. The road to the camp was littered with stolen bicycles, cars and motorbikes. There was even a light aircraft. They couldn't pin the crimes on anyone and in any case we had been told to use our initiative and a blind eye was turned. But it was made known that anyone who had had a vehicle stolen on the particular day could come and pick it up.'

'And how could they do that if you'd taken their only means of transport?'

'I've no doubt a bit of initiative was called for,' he told her wryly. 'Anyway, they were paid compensation. Enough of me – what have you been up to?'

'The usual. Minding the stores. We're not getting so many training courses at Ringway now so perhaps you're up to strength. I might get moved.'

'Any idea where?'

'No.'

Maggie called them back to the kitchen, where she had cooked bacon, eggs and fried bread for Alec. He sat down and attacked it with gusto. 'Anyone would think you were starving,' she said, watching him eat.

'I am.'

Julie laughed. 'You're lucky your people live on a farm. You should see what townspeople have to manage on. Even tea is rationed now and the cheese ration's reduced again. There's a lot of scrounging and dodgy dealing going on.'

'You'll always get that, town or country,' Maggie pointed out.

He put down his knife and fork with a satisfied sigh and turned to Julie. 'What do you fancy doing tonight, sweetheart?'

'I don't mind. You choose.'

'There's a New Year's Eve dance in Andover,' his mother suggested.

'Fancy that?' he asked Julie.

'Yes, why not?'

Walter had come in while Alec was eating, and having greeted his son, he sat down to remove his boots and put on his slippers, warming on the fender. 'You can take the car if you like,' he said. 'There's petrol in it.'

The weather was cold; Julie changed out of uniform into a green woollen dress with a matching bolero which could be removed if it became too warm in the dance hall, brushed out her short hair, applied a little make-up and donned high-heeled shoes. It was lovely to be in civvies again and even lovelier to be with Alec. That had been a surprise, but a very welcome one.

The dance hall was crowded with civilians and service people of both sexes in khaki, navy and air force blue, with a fair proportion of Americans. Everyone was determined to have a good time and the band played all the latest dances, from traditional waltzes and foxtrots to boogie-woogie and swing, from rumba and tango to the hokey-cokey and hands, knees and bumps-a-daisy and the conga, when everyone grabbed the person in front of them and paraded round the floor in a long crocodile. Just before midnight the last waltz was announced and Alec took Julie into his arms for that.

'Had a good time?' he asked her.

'Yes, lovely, and so unexpected.'

'I love giving you surprises.'

'So I noticed.'

'There's one more to come.'

'Oh, what?'

'It wouldn't be a surprise if I told you, would it? Wait and see.'

The music stopped and started up again to play 'Auld Lang Syne' and they linked hands with their neighbours for the traditional ushering in of the new year. 'Happy New Year, my love,' Alec said as someone switched on a wireless and they heard the strokes of Big Ben chiming midnight.

'And to you.'

He kissed her chastely and they stood for the national anthem and then went out to find the car. Halfway home he stopped in a lay-by and turned towards her. 'I haven't kissed you properly for ages.'

She laughed. 'It was only a few hours ago in your parents' sitting room.'

'That was ages ago.' He proceeded to remedy the situation. 'Pity we can't go to bed,' he said ruefully. 'But I don't think Ma would stand for it.'

'No, I don't think she would.'

'It was good, though, wasn't it, that last time?'

He was referring to that leave they had spent in the Lake District and what he laughingly called their honeymoon without a wedding. 'Yes,' she said, remembering again the wonderful feeling of being loved and wanted, and wanting him with every fibre of her body and soul, and how they had explored each other's bodies and achieved something she could only call profound and unmatched ecstasy.

'It'll happen again, over and over when you become Mrs Kilby.'

'I haven't exactly said I will,' she reminded him.

'But you're going to, aren't you? You're going to say yes, and you're going to say it now.' He pulled a small box from his pocket, took off the lid and picked out the ring that lay there. It sparkled in the moonlight. 'Eve Seaton, I love you very much. Will you consent to marry me and make me the happiest man in the world?'

She looked from the ring in his fingers to his pleading face. How could she deny him when it was so much what she wanted herself? 'Yes, Alec, I'll marry you.'

'Whoopee!' he shouted and kissed her and in the process

dropped the ring on the floor of the car. They spent several seconds laughing and scrabbling round in the dark trying to find it, and as soon as they did and were once more seated side by side, he slipped it on her finger. 'There it is and there it stays until the day you take it off to have the wedding ring put on,' he said.

'You know we're not allowed to wear jewellery in uniform except a wedding ring.'

'Then put it on a ribbon round your neck. Let's go home and tell Ma and Pa.'

'They'll have gone to bed.'

He grinned. 'Want to bet on it?'

'You told them?'

'Yes, while you were changing. They'll be waiting with the wine uncorked.'

He was right. They toasted each other with Maggie's home-made wine and laughed a lot and talked about getting married and dates and times for the wedding and the reception, until Julie was quite squiffy. She had to be helped to bed. Alec would have stayed with her but she was sober enough to send him away with a passionate kiss and no more.

She woke next morning with a raging headache. Alec, who was more used to his mother's wine than she was, seemed not to be suffering and after breakfast suggested a long walk to clear her head. This they did and on returning home found the house empty and a note on the kitchen table. 'Gone into Andover to shop. Dad's helping with the hunt. Make yourselves some lunch.'

'She thinks she's being tactful,' Alec said, laughing, and taking Julie's hand, he led her upstairs.

* * *

Harry was tired; he was more than tired, he was exhausted. He had lost count of the number of times he had flown to Berlin in the last three months, and more recently against railways, bridges and other important targets in France, and it was taking its toll, not only of everyone's nerves, but of men and machines. He was now one of the oldest and most experienced members of his squadron and it was his bounden duty to remain calm under pressure and set a good example. As soon as they landed he went to debriefing and then raced across the airfield to home, where Pam was there to soothe him and feed him and let him sleep. She was a roly-poly now, the time for her to give birth approaching, and he worried it would happen one night when he was flying, not that anything could be done about that. The local midwife had been alerted and her mother was near at hand, and they wouldn't want an agitated man dancing round them when the time came.

The trouble was that he couldn't help thinking about George – plump, happy George whose life had been so cruelly cut short. He could not bear the thought of something like that happening again. It was a good thing there hadn't been so many air raids lately. Hitler had other things to worry him; when and where the invasion was going to take place for one thing. No one, except those at the very top, knew that but it couldn't be long now; all the signs pointed to it. A ten-mile strip of the coastline from the Wash to Land's End had been banned to civilians, more and more troops went on manoeuvres, more and more strange vehicles clogged the country roads. Guns and ammunition trains whooshed past wayside stations, holding up passenger trains. Southern England, and that included East Anglia, was becoming one vast army camp, but still there was no announcement. No doubt he would have a role to play, but he was glad he wasn't in khaki.

He didn't know whether to be pleased or furious when the group captain sent for him and told him he was to be grounded and given a job in the ops room. 'You've done your bit, Flight Lieutenant,' he said. 'Let some of the others take over . . .'

'But, sir, I can't sit on my arse, twiddling my thumbs while the rest of the crew go off night after night.'

'You won't be twiddling your thumbs, you can be sure of that. The job is a vital one and will be even more important when the balloon goes up. You've done more that your stint of operations. The MO tells me you're tired . . .'

'He's an old woman.'

'Flight Lieutenant, you will not refer to our medical officer in those terms,' he said sharply. 'Captain Marison is responsible for the fitness of everyone to do the job required of them and he says you need a rest. It's non-negotiable. Take fourteen days' leave and come back refreshed. You are soon to be a father, concentrate on that.'

Harry saluted and walked out of the office but underneath his annoyance was a sense of relief he would not admit to. He went to find Tim and tell him the 'bad' news, only to discover that Tim had also been taken off the flight and was being posted somewhere down south where he was to take on a training role. 'I reckon it's something to do with the invasion,' he said. 'They need extra pilots.'

'They need wireless operators too. I don't see why they have to break us up.'

'Don't tell me you want to move, with the delectable Pam about to drop her sprog any minute. Count your blessings, man.'

'I'll miss you.'

'I'll miss you too. We'll have a good knees-up at the pub to see me on my way.'

'You're on.'

Pam, of course, was delighted by the news that Harry was grounded. She was tired too and felt lumpy and ungainly and longed to be slim again. She was looking forward to being a mother, and though she did not mind whether she had a boy or a girl, for Harry's sake she would like to give him a son to make up for the one he had lost. He was a loving husband, caring, considerate and always cheerful, but she sensed he was under a lot of strain, and the only way she could help him was to be especially calm and not bother him with trifles. She knew he was disappointed at being grounded and would badger the powers that be to let him fly again. She hoped they would not listen to him, though she did not say so. They were extremely lucky to have been allowed to live together in the village and have something approaching a home life, if you discounted the times when he went off in the evenings and didn't return until dawn, or when he was required to stay on the station in case he were needed. He'd have to do some nights in the ops room, but at least he'd be on the ground, and when she heard the planes take off and zoom over the housetops she would know he was not in one of them and she would not be sick with worry until he came back.

'When's Tim having this party, then?' They had finished supper and she was sitting on his lap on the sofa, her head nestling in his shoulder, the big bump of her coming child sticking out under his hand where he could feel the baby kicking.

'Saturday night. You don't mind me going, do you?'

'No, of course I don't, silly. You enjoy yourself.'

He looked at her with his head on one side. 'I love you, Pam Walker. Without you I'd fall apart.'

'Oh, go on with you.'

'I mean it. You hold me together, and when the little one comes and this war is over, we'll have a grand life together, you and I and our children. I'd like more than one.'

'So would I. Two little Harry Walkers as handsome as you and two little girls to match.'

He laughed. 'We'll need a bigger house.'

'So, we get a bigger house. The Government has promised homes for everyone after the war. It was on the news.'

'Believe that if you like. They'll have to be paid for and there's a lot of other things need rebuilding as well.'

'You're just a natural-born pessimist.' She kissed him fondly and scrambled to her feet. 'I'm going to make some cocoa, d'you want some?'

'Yes, please, and then I'm for bed.' He laughed suddenly. 'And I don't have to get up in the morning. Fourteen days, fourteen glorious days. If it weren't for the baby we could go away somewhere.'

'Do you want to go away?'

'Not without you, I don't. No, I'll be content just to laze around here and watch you getting bigger and bigger.'

'I'm not going to get much bigger. Very soon, I'll be a lot smaller, perhaps while you're on leave. That would be perfect.'

She had her wish. Colin Harold Walker was born at four o'clock on the morning of March 1st 1944 and his sister, Louise Jane, ten minutes later. Twins had not been expected and caused a little consternation at first, but when everyone had recovered from the surprise they were delighted. 'We've got half of our four at one go,' Pam said, looking fondly at her tiny babies, lying head to toe in the cot they had prepared for one. Colin was the bigger of the two by half a pound, but they both had dark-brown hair and dark eyes and equally loud voices.

Harry, sitting on the edge of her bed, holding her hand, kept looking from her to his children and almost burst with pride and happiness. He knew he would have to go back to the war in a couple of days and there were some difficult times ahead, but he did not doubt that victory was within grasp and then there would be peace. Peace. How good it sounded.

Chapter Nine

Julie had been right when she told Alec she expected to be posted. She was given a seventy-two-hour pass at Easter, when she went to Hillside Farm and spent the time amusing Liz and Alice, riding and walking. And on Easter Sunday she went to church with Walter and Maggie, where apart from celebrating the Resurrection, they prayed for the success of the coming second front. At the end of her leave, now promoted to sergeant, she reported for duty at RAF Manston. She couldn't have been more pleased because Florrie was still stationed there, driving RAF bigwigs all over the place.

At the gate she was told to report to Section Officer Murray, officer in charge of the WAAFs, before she did anything else. Looking for Florrie would have to wait.

'Welcome to Manston, Sergeant Seaton,' the OC said, as Julie stood at ease in front of her desk. 'You have been in the service long enough to know how things are done, so there's no need for me to repeat it.' She paused and looked closely into Julie's face. 'Nor do you need telling that we are going to be very busy in the next few weeks and some of the things you will be dealing with will seem very strange indeed. You are not to speak of them to anyone, do you understand?'

'Perfectly, ma'am.'

'Good. Report for duty at 0800 tomorrow and good luck to you.'

Julie saluted and turned about. She had the rest of the evening to find her way about and be reunited with Florrie, always supposing her friend was on the station and not away driving somewhere. She went outside, picked up her kitbag and haversack from where she had left them and asked to be directed to her billet. She was soon unpacking her kit beside her bed.

'Where is she? Where is my soon-to-be sister-in-law? Let me get at her.'

Julie, in the act of hanging a skirt in her locker, spun round as Florrie came through the door. 'Florrie.'

They hugged each other. 'It's good to see you,' they said together and laughed.

'I was going to see if I could find you as soon as I'd unpacked,' Julie said.

'Oh, I couldn't wait for you to find me. Let me take a look at you.' Florrie stood back and surveyed Julie with her head on one side. 'You look good, really good; being in love must suit you.'

Julie laughed. 'It does. I could say the same for you.'

Florrie sat on the end of Julie's bed to watch her finish her unpacking. 'We're lucky, aren't we?'

'Yes, me in particular.'

'Why you in particular?'

'You know why. I thought my past, or lack of it, would put everyone off me, but it hasn't, has it?'

'No, of course not. It doesn't change who you are, the person you are now, never mind what happened in the past. Anyway, you really were bombed out, so who's to know that the rest of your story isn't true? It easily could be.'

'That's what Alec said. He said the name I go by is unimportant.'

'There you are, then.'

The last of her kit was stowed away. 'Are you on duty?'

'Not 'til the morning. We've got a lot of catching up to do. Let's take a stroll and I'll show you round. We can talk as we go.'

Manston, being so close to the coast and on the flight path of bombers returning from raids, had become an emergency landing field and was equipped with one of the longest and widest runways in the country. 'When it's foggy, they light flares all down both sides,' Florrie told her. 'It dispels the fog and guides the aircraft in.'

'Doesn't that attract German bombers too?'

'It did, but there aren't many raids now. One of ours came down only last week. It had been badly shot up and burst into flames and then it exploded.' She shuddered. 'The crew were all killed. I saw them being taken away in ambulances. I wish I hadn't, it made me think of Matt . . .'

'Don't dwell on it,' Julie said quickly, putting her hand on her friend's arm.

'No, let's go and look at the sea. We can't go on the beach, but sometimes I like to stand and look at the waves. There's something timeless about the ocean, don't you think? It's so vast it puts our little lives into perspective and yet it's part of us, especially in these islands. I like to remember times before the war when Alec and I were children and we used to go on seaside holidays.' She laughed. 'I had a knitted costume that covered me from head to foot and drooped when it was wet. Alec had one of those striped costumes with legs in them and straps to hold the top up. He was always a bit of a daredevil and would frighten my mother by swimming out too far.'

'He told me he likes to stretch himself to see what he's capable of,' Julie said. 'Perhaps that's why he joined the paras.'

'Possibly.' Florrie laughed. 'But I think it also had something to do with the fact that you were at Ringway.'

From where they stood, the coastline went round in a wide curve. Every inlet seemed to be filled with landing craft. 'They're not real,' Florrie said. 'They're just empty drums and canvas. I reckon they're there to fool the Germans.'

Julie wasn't really taking in what Florrie was saying because she was looking at the beach. A faint memory stirred, as it had once before, of a crowded beach and a boy – not a toddler, too old for him to be her own child – and he wore a striped costume just as Florrie described Alec's. There was music too and a Punch and Judy show. When and where had that happened? She strained at it, trying to make it stay and enlarge, but instead it faded, as so many memories had faded in the past, and left her wondering if they were real memories or only products of her imagination.

'It can't be long now.' Florrie broke in on her thoughts and the vision faded and all she could see was the deserted beach dotted with seaweed and the odd tussock of marram grass.

'What can't?'

'The invasion. What else would I be talking about?'

'Sorry. I wasn't really paying attention. I was remembering a beach . . .'

Florrie whipped round to face her. 'Your memory's come back?'

'No, it's gone again. Sometimes I get pictures, but they don't connect up and then they go again.'

'Oh, you poor dear. It must be dreadfully frustrating.'

'Yes, it is. I feel as though I'm living a lie.'

'Well, you're not. No one could be more honest and straightforward than you.'

Honest and straightforward? Had that always been true? What was her loss of memory hiding? 'Let's go back,' she said, inexplicably ill at ease. 'I don't know about you, but I'm starving.'

They went to the canteen for something to eat and drink. Florrie introduced Julie to one or two of the airmen, but they did not join them, preferring to continue chatting, reminiscing about previous postings, talking about their plans.

'When this war is over, Matt and I are going to look for a house in the country,' Florrie said. 'All mod cons and three bedrooms for the children. You and Alec could live nearby and we could see lots of each other. Do you realise our children will be cousins?'

'Of course I do, silly.'

A home of one's own; how many people longed for that, Julie asked herself? People who had been bombed out, people who had been evacuated, people newly married, all praying that the invasion of France would signal the beginning of the end that Churchill had spoken about. She could not remember a time when there had been no war, but she could imagine it. Peace. The sky would be full of birds and butterflies and maybe the odd leisure aircraft, not the roar of warplanes. There would be no air-raid sirens, no bombs exploding, no great guns going off, and the children – all children – would be able to play in safety. It was a long time since she had asked herself what had become of the child she had given birth to, but now she found herself wondering what had happened to it all over again.

Maybe it was triggered by Florrie talking about children, or the fact that she was going to marry Alec and they had talked of having a family; maybe it was the brief stirring of something that might have been a memory earlier in the day. Whatever it was it made her feel uneasy. 'I'm for bed,' she said, standing up. 'It's been a long day.'

The strange things Flight Officer Murray had talked about turned out to be inflatable rubber tanks, lorries, guns and gliders, which arrived deflated on the backs of lorries and were taken out to sites dotted round the countryside and inflated. Even from a short distance it was difficult to tell them from the real thing; from the air it would have been nigh on impossible. An attempt was made to camouflage them – not too well, but well enough for enemy aircraft to believe there was something to hide. Tails of gliders stuck out from under trees and the undergrowth round them trodden down and wheel marks of heavy vehicles made in the grass to make it look more realistic. The contraptions were left *in situ* for a few days and then moved somewhere else, giving the effect of one vast army gathering, ready to invade the Pas de Calais. What it did for those on the ground was to tell them that Calais was not going to be the real invasion site, though when and where it would be Julie had no more idea than anyone else, but she knew, without being told, that Alec would be involved in it; all that training was not for nothing.

She longed to be able to talk to him, to compare notes, to tell him he went with her prayers for his safe return and she could not wait for them to be together again and the war over. She was not such a fool as to think everything was going to be plain sailing. There would be difficult times ahead, but she would not let herself dwell on the possibility of tragedy.

Security was tight, and towards the end of May everyone, except those who had official business outside like Florrie, who had been detailed to drive truckloads of airmen from stations in the north and east to the West Country, was confined to barracks until further notice. No telephone calls were allowed, except in the line of duty, and all letters were more heavily censored than usual. Sitting outside her billet in the warm May sunshine, Julie wrote to Alec, a loving letter of hope and optimism, but a little melancholy too. *'I miss you, darling. I miss not being able to talk to you or write to you properly. I wonder where you are and if you are as nervous as I am. Pray God, all this waiting will soon be over and we can be together again. Be sure you are in my thoughts all the time, especially when I hear aircraft overhead. Take care of yourself because I want you safely back, to feel your arms once more about me . . .'*

She couldn't say half of what she wanted to, but he would know what she was thinking and feeling.

Alec was at Brize Norton where his training had continued, day in, day out, without let-up. They had practised jumping with kitbags, which they carried on their legs and released on the end of a line once they were in the air with the parachute opened. At first they had jumped from a single aircraft, and then been put through their paces in a mass drop at battalion strength. It was nerve-racking and at the same time extraordinarily impressive the way the sky appeared to be full of parachutes and aircraft dropping more and more, until the sky seemed full of them. How they didn't get tangled up with each other was a minor miracle. There were one or two incidents but little was made of them for fear of deflating morale.

From battalion strength they graduated to brigade strength and were flown in Dakotas with American crews. The Dakotas carried a stick of twenty and the exit was through a port door and not the floor, as in the Whitley. After flying out over the Channel to give them an idea of what it would be like, they turned for home. Below them the sea was packed with shipping, line upon line of it of all shapes and sizes, filling all the ports and every inlet. It was an awesome sight. They couldn't admire it for long because they were approaching the dropping zone and the usual drill began: hook up, red light, shuffle to the door, green light, 'Go!'

The next day they began ground exercises in which they were to seize a bridge against Home Guard opposition. They soon discovered that if they surrendered they were taken to the Home Guard headquarters and entertained with tea and biscuits and took no further part in the exercise, a ploy which did not go down at all well with those in command and they had to do it again, but this time there were dire penalties for surrendering. Knowing the real thing could only be days away, they decided to be more cooperative.

All they were waiting for was the time and place, and that was as closely guarded as ever.

Alec dearly wanted to see Eve, to share his experiences with her, tell her how much he loved her and that he had every intention of coming safely back to begin their new life together and she was to start planning their wedding. But he couldn't do any of that. The south of England was sealed off from all communication with the outside world: the local population and all evacuees had been sent away, telephone lines to call boxes cut off, postboxes sealed and the perimeter patrolled to make sure no one chanced his luck on creeping out.

Tension was building alongside the boredom of waiting, even though they were kept busy with last-minute training and checks, topped off with a night drop from Sterling aircraft. Towards the end of May they were told there would be a full rehearsal and half the battalion were sent to a tented transit camp at Broadwell while the other half stayed at Brize Norton. No one was fooled by this tale of a rehearsal; they knew it was going to be the real thing and spirits were high.

They were allowed to write one letter, which they were warned would be heavily censored for any clue about what they had been doing, where they thought they were going and any guesses about the timing. '"Love and kisses and hope to see you before long" is about it,' they were told. Torn between writing to his mother and writing to Eve, Alec decided to send it to his mother but expect it to be shared with everyone in the family, including Eve. If he wrote to Eve it would be one she would not want to share and he could not leave his parents out. Consequently it was a difficult letter to write. *I'm fighting fit, so don't worry about me,'* he wrote. *'I don't suppose there'll be any leave for a little while but when I do come home, we'll have a party. Tell Eve it's to be a proper engagement party and I can't wait to hold her in my arms again. So Mum, get making the wine, and Pa, fatten up the porker. Give my love to Florrie and Matt and keep some for yourselves. And to Eve, my continuing and everlasting devotion. See you again soon, Alec.'*

It seemed a stilted and inadequate description of how he felt for her, but he was mindful that it would be read by all the family and acutely aware of the censor's eyes scanning it. He would tell her properly to her face when he saw her again, show her too in as many different ways as he could think of. The letters were collected by their platoon officer and taken to be vetted before being sent on, and the waiting continued.

The last Monday in May was Whitsun Bank Holiday and the weather was glorious, but for those waiting for the call, confined to their various transit camps, not one they could enjoy. The officers had been briefed and had briefed their men; now they knew where they were going and what was expected of them. Alec would be one of those parachuting into Normandy on the night of 4th June, ahead of the seaborne invasion of British, American and Canadian troops. C Company's task was to clear the landing ground of the forest of upright poles put there to deter gliders, and when that was done to join the assault on Ranville, one of the villages on the Cotentin Peninsula. The weather held right up to 3rd June, then, just when they needed it to be good, it broke with squally rain and wind, which meant a postponement and had everyone feeling despondent.

Alec, already tense, felt sick and disinclined to eat the meal prepared for them. They should have been in the air by now and here they were still on the ground and kicking their heels in frustration. The weather showed no sign of abating but they were still on full alert. He spent the time reading Eve's last letter over again and looking at the snapshot he had brought back with him after that last leave together. She was standing under a sprig of mistletoe in the hall of the farmhouse and laughing, her head thrown back and that lovely dress she had been wearing for the New Year dance straining across her bosom. He ran his fingers over it, wishing he could be with her, but on the other hand not wishing to be anywhere but where he was at that moment.

The weather abated sufficiently for them to take off the next night, twenty-four hours later than planned, although it was still windier than those who were going in by air would have liked. Alec, in charge of his stick of twenty, led the way to the Dakota. 'What d'you reckon it'll get postponed again?' Trooper Langford said, as they numbered off and climbed in to sit down on either side of the fuselage ready for take-off. Keyed up as they were it seemed to take for ever. The engines had been running as they embarked, but now one of them coughed and stopped.

'Sorry, folks.' This was the American pilot. 'We're having trouble with the engines. We'll have to transfer to a standby aircraft.'

'That's all we need,' someone said as they scrambled out of the stricken plane and marched across the tarmac to another one. Everyone else was silent, wondering if it was a bad omen and not daring to say so.

They went through the drill again and this time they

did take off. After a few minutes' tense silence while they realised they were in the air and really were on their way, someone started to sing. Everyone followed suit and the strains of 'Onward Christian Soldiers' competed with the noise of the engines. Below them in the Channel a huge armada was steadily making its way towards the coast of Normandy. A lot depended on the airborne troops doing their job before the troops landed.

'French coast ahead,' the pilot called back to them. They flew on through the flak which was spitting at them from the coastal guns, some of it rattling on the fuselage like pebbles. They hooked themselves up ready to jump and waited for the red light, but it remained stubbornly unlit. Alec unhooked himself and made his way to the cockpit. 'It's only supposed to be about a minute from the coast to the DZ,' he told the pilot.

'We've been blown off course. Don't know where we are.'

'Well, we've obviously overshot, so go back and try again.'

'Not so easy, we'll come up against the incoming aircraft and paratroopers, if we manage to find them.'

'You mean you're lost?' He couldn't keep the annoyance from his voice.

'That's about it. We're going back to England.'

'Not with us on board, you're not. We're jumping.'

'Where?'

'Here. Now. We'll find our own way.'

'If you say so.' It was obvious the pilot thought he was mad.

Alec returned to his place. 'We've overshot and the pilot doesn't know exactly where we are, but I don't reckon you want to go home, do you?'

'Not on your life,' was the answer from Corporal Glover, his number two, and this was echoed by everyone else. 'We've come this far, we're not going home with our tail between our legs. You tell him that from us.'

'I already have.' As he spoke the aircraft levelled out, the red light came on, the door was opened and they went through the drill in silence.

Green light. 'Go!' Alec heard the dispatcher's voice at the same moment he flung himself out.

As he drifted down, with his kitbag dangling on its line below him, he looked about him. He was alone in the sky. He was joined by the rest of the stick and the canisters containing their weapons, which had been carried under the fuselage and were released by the dispatcher in the middle of the stick, but he knew, even before he hit the ground, that they would be well scattered, and what was more, they were some way behind enemy lines.

Harry was back in the air. Every available aircraft and aircrew were needed and he wasn't going to be left behind if he could help it. He had had a few qualms about Pam and the babies, but they had been overcome; these were momentous times and he was determined to be part of it all. Best of all, Tim had returned and they would be flying a Mitchell, a sturdy aircraft that could take a good deal of punishment but whose twin engines were the noisiest they had ever experienced. They had spent the last few weeks bombing the northern coast of France, targeting bridges, railway yards and factories, anything to disrupt Germany's ability to hit back at the invasion forces, and doing exercises with the army because one of their roles would be to support the ground troops. He had not known any more than anyone else where the invasion was to take place, nor its exact timing, but the area around Calais and the Normandy Peninsula featured strongly. Every time he came back safely, he sent up a little prayer of thanksgiving and at the first opportunity raced across the field to Pam and his children. His family was everything to him; they were what kept him going. He parted from them reluctantly and at the end of each raid returned to them joyfully.

Tonight was no different and yet it was very different. The tension and feeling of expectancy were palpable as they kept the usual lookout for enemy fighters.

'Look at that,' Tim shouted above the noise of the Mitchell's engines, though the rest of the crew hardly needed to be told. Through a break in the clouds the Channel appeared to be thick with shipping making for Calais, but they knew, because they had been told at their briefing, that it was a diversionary tactic, the barges were not full of troops; the real invasion was well to the west. Their job was to continue the deception by bombing installations in the Calais area. They left the make-believe armada behind and flew on to their target, all grinning from ear to ear, elated that it was happening at last.

They were going back to France to avenge Dunkirk and all those who had died then and since, Harry thought, and that included those many thousands of civilians, like Julie and George, who had perished as a result of Hitler's bombs. Now he could think of Julie with a kind of affectionate nostalgia; someone he had once known but who had faded into history. It was difficult to recall her face now, and he could hardly remember what George looked like. That did not mean they didn't have a place in his heart, but the memories were tucked away in a corner where they no longer tormented him.

The babies often disturbed Pam's sleep, but it wasn't the babies that woke her that night; it was the noise of aircraft. Out of habit she sat up in bed and began counting, but soon realised how futile that was. Leaving her bed, she went to the window. The night was cloudy and blustery, but even so, she could tell the air was black with aircraft, not just those from Swanton Morley, but hundreds, no thousands of them, droning on and on. This was it, this was what they had been building up to, ever since Dunkirk. Some of those aeroplanes would never return. She stood at the window and prayed, as hard as she had ever prayed in her life, that Harry would come safely back to her.

Everyone had the wireless on the following morning and all work stopped as they listened to the news. 'This is the news and this is John Snagge reading it,' came over the airwaves. 'D-Day has come. Early this morning the Allies began the assault on the north-western face of Hitler's European fortress, Paratroopers have landed in northern France . . .' Julie and Florrie had been stood down and were listening to it in the mess, along with a crowd of off-duty airmen. The headlines were followed by a short account of the landing and the tremendous organisation which had been involved to bring it about. It had gone according to plan, so they were told, although the weather had not been favourable. It had been cold and cloudy and the sea rough.

'Well, we know that,' Florrie said to Julie. 'Why don't

they tell us about the airborne troops? I know Matt shouldn't have told me, but he's towing gliders, and there's Alec. He's bound to be involved. I shall be like a cat on hot bricks until I know they're both safe.'

'Me too,' Julie said. 'How long do you think it will be before we know?'

'Dunno. Probably days, if at all.'

Julie jumped to her feet. 'I can't sit here doing nothing. We won't learn anything more for ages. Let's go for a walk.'

'It's going to rain again.'

'We can wear waterproofs. Come on. We can't do any good here.'

And so they went. It was blustery but the rain held off.

It was strange how deserted the countryside was. The day before it had been bristling with troop movements. Now they had gone. The tented camps were deserted, the sea empty of craft, the inflatable equipment gone. And there were few aircraft on the ground.

'It's creepy, don't you think?' Julie said.

'Yes, but it's only a lull. Not everyone has gone, they will be assembling reinforcements and you can bet your life we'll be as busy as ever tomorrow.'

'You mean because people will have been killed and wounded. The news didn't say much about casualties.'

'Well, they wouldn't, would they? I'm going to try and ring Matt tomorrow.'

They heard the drone of an aircraft flying very low and then a Mitchell broke through the clouds, coming down very fast, one propeller idle. 'It's going to crash,' Julie said and started running back towards the airfield, with Florrie behind her.

*   *   *

231

'We can come down at Manston, Skipper,' Harry said, turning from the radio. 'The runway's clear to land.'

'Right.' The enemy, believing the invasion was going to be at Calais, had subjected the bombers to even more flak than usual, and they had been hit in the port engine and the undercarriage, which had affected the landing gear. 'I can't get the wheels down, it'll have to be a belly flop, so hold on to your hats.'

The ground seemed to come up at an incredible speed and then they were sliding down the runway, bumping and jolting, making a terrible scraping noise along the tarmac as bits of the undercarriage sheered off, and then one wing tip hit the ground, the tail came up and they were all thrown towards the cockpit as the nose buried itself into the grass beside the runway. There was a second of complete and eerie silence.

Harry extricated himself from the tangle of arms and legs. He felt battered and bruised and his ribs ached. Tim was unconscious with blood pouring from a head wound. The gunner was moaning his legs were broken, the other two were swearing, so they were not so badly hurt. 'Out!' he said.

They didn't need telling; the fear of an explosion and fire was uppermost in their minds. Harry reached across Tim to try and release the canopy, but it wouldn't budge. The bomb aimer, ignoring his injured leg, crawled across to help. By this time they could hear vehicles arriving and then someone appeared on the other side of the canopy. He had an axe in his hand. 'Keep clear,' he mouthed.

Harry tried to shield Tim while the others hitched themselves up the splintered floor of the aircraft. It only took seconds to get them all out but it seemed like years.

They had barely got everyone clear than the remaining engine burst into flames, followed by a huge explosion. Debris flew everywhere.

Julie and Florrie came sprinting across the field just in time to see and feel the explosion. They stopped and watched in horrified dismay as the Mitchell was engulfed in flames. Only then did they see the five airmen in flying kit nearby, two standing, two sitting and one on a stretcher. They were being put into the ambulances which had raced up behind the fire engine. 'Did they all get out?' she asked one of the firemen who was playing a hose on the wreckage.

'Yes, all out, though we aren't sure the pilot will survive; he's badly hurt. The others will be all right once they get to hospital.'

'Thank God.'

'Come on, Eve, we can't do anything here,' Florrie said, pulling on her arm.

Julie was reluctant to leave. She had heard of casualties before, of aeroplanes who didn't return from an op, paratroopers whose parachutes hadn't opened, of road crashes in the blackout, of people dying in air raids, but since being bombed herself she had not been this close to a disaster and she felt she ought to be doing something to help.

'Your friend is right,' the fireman said. 'We'll deal with this and the medics will look after the men. Don't trouble yourself about them.'

'I can't help it,' Julie told Florrie as they moved away. 'I keep thinking of Alec and hoping that if he was hurt someone would help him.'

'I know. I think the same about Matt. Let's go back to the mess, there might be more news.'

* * *

233

'Pam, it's me.'

'Harry! Oh, thank you, God, thank you.' It had been the longest and most miserable twenty-four hours of her life, since the station commander and the padre had come up her garden path to tell her Harry had not returned and they feared he had been shot down. 'Of course, they could have come down somewhere miles from anywhere and unable to contact us,' the padre said in an effort to cheer her up.

'You mean in occupied France?'

'Perhaps.'

'He could have been taken prisoner?'

'It's possible,' the station commander said. 'He could have been picked up by the Resistance. We haven't had any contact since they turned for home. It may just be his radio malfunctioning and they've landed somewhere in England. If that's the case, we'll hear soon enough.'

They had no telephone at Honeysuckle Cottage but there was one at The Papermakers, and the landlord had sent her a message that a call had been booked for her at midday. Guessing it had something to do with Harry, she had been sitting beside the instrument, fearing the worst, for the last half-hour, and to hear his voice, sounding so normal, had filled her with unbounded relief and joy. 'Where are you?'

'I'm in Canterbury Hospital. We had to come down early, couldn't make it all the way home.'

'Hospital!' she squeaked. 'You mean you're hurt?'

'A few bumps and bruises, nothing serious. I'll come home by train just as soon as they let me out of here.'

'Thank God! What about the others?'

'Tim bought it.'

'Oh Harry, I'm so sorry.' She knew how close the two men had been and how it must be affecting Harry. He'd try

234

not to show it, of course. That's why he used that idiomatic phrase, prevalent among airmen.

'Yes. He was a damned good pilot besides being a good pal – but for him we none of us might have made it. I hope he gets a posthumous medal.'

'What about the others?'

'One broken leg, one gashed ear and broken ribs, one dislocated shoulder, nothing too serious but they'll be in hospital a bit longer.'

'Shall I get Mum to look after the twins and come down?'

'Good heavens no, I'll be on the way home in no time. I must go, my pennies have run out. I'll ring again when I leave here to tell you when to expect me.'

She put the receiver down and burst into tears.

'Bad news?' Greg was standing over her with a glass of whisky in his hand.

She took the drink and gulped it down. 'No, he's all right. Harry's safe. He's in hospital in Canterbury but coming home soon. I must go and tell Mum and Dad.' She handed the empty glass back to him and hurried out of the pub and down to the mill house.

'The Mitchell crew, Sergeant?' queried the sister on duty when Julie approached her. 'What do you want to know for? Do you know any of them?'

'No, but I was there when the plane came down. It was awful.' Florrie had advised her not to come, that it would only upset her, but Florrie had gone off to drive the group captain to London for a debriefing and was not around to stop her.

'It always is. I've lost count of the number of casualties

we get in here from Manston. It's right on the flight path of planes coming home and many's the one that's come down there in an emergency.'

'I know that, but what about the crew of that Mitchell? I've brought them some cigarettes and magazines. Can I give them to them?'

'Very well. You'll find three of them at the far end of the ward. Their injuries are not life-threatening, though I don't think they'll be flying again for a little while.'

'Three? I thought there were five.'

'The pilot died and one was well enough to be discharged; he's only just this minute gone off to catch a train.'

'He must have been the one who passed me coming in. I'll go and see the others.'

'Don't stay too long,' Sister called after her as she set off down the ward.

The crash must have affected him more that he realised, Harry thought, but the WAAF he had just seen was uncannily like Julie. Older, of course, and not so waif-like, smart in her uniform with her sergeant's stripes on her sleeve. He thought she had been on the airfield when the Mitchell blew up, but in the confused state he had been in at the time, he couldn't be sure. He had nearly stopped and spoken to her, but she had hurried past him into the hospital without sparing him a glance. The encounter left him feeling a little disturbed, as if he had seen a ghost. Oh, he knew airmen were a superstitious lot and often claimed to have been aware of an extra crew member on a flight or had seen ghosts on airfields or near the sites of crashes, but he had never counted himself one of those. And why Julie, why not Tim or one of the others from the station who had died? Mentally he shook himself and climbed into the taxi taking him to the railway station.

He had to cross London from Waterloo to Liverpool Street and, in a moment of guilt, decided to visit Highgate Cemetery. It was three and a half years since he had stood there talking to Miss Paterson. He wondered what had become of her and whether she had managed to keep the grave tidy. He bought a bunch of lilies at an exorbitant price from a flower seller at the station and took the Underground to Highgate.

The cemetery was a haven of quiet and he strolled among the gravestones and statuary, letting the peace of it wash over him. After the turbulence of the last few days and the death of his pilot, it helped him to unwind. The grave was just as he had remembered it. The garden gnome remained stood at its head, still smiling, although the broken arm had weathered, the rawness of the stump changed from white to dirty grey. It was a casualty of the war, just as Julie and George had been, just as Tim Harrison had been, just as the thousands who had died on the beaches of Normandy were. He removed his cap and, kneeling, took the faded flowers out of the vase and replaced them with the lilies he had bought and picked up the gnome and cradled it in his hands, saying a prayer for all those who had suffered and continued to suffer, for Tim and others who had died, brave men and good pals whose like he would never see again. Giving thanks for his own deliverance, he carefully replaced the gnome to stand sentinel over the grave. Then he stood up and spent a moment in quiet contemplation, remembering the girl Julie had been. He recalled that first meeting on the beach with wry amusement, and the woman she had become, so innocently naive, so loving, so anxious to please him. What would their life together have been like if she had lived, he wondered? How would they have changed, because everyone changed as they matured? Would they have continued to love each other through the years into old age? There was no sense in torturing himself with unanswerable questions; his future was with Pam and his children and in a few hours, God willing, he would be with them again.

'Ted Austen, as I live and breathe, can it be you?'

Ted swivelled round to face his sister whom he had not set eyes on since, as a twelve-year-old, he had run away from home. 'Josie, I'd never have recognised you.'

'I'm not surprised. How old was I when you left? Eight or nine. Why didn't you come home? Mum went out of her mind worrying about you. Didn't you give her a thought?'

'Yes, I did. I thought of her a lot, but I swore never to go back while the old man was alive and I meant it. How is she?'

'She's dead, died three months ago with your name on her lips. She kept saying if she could see you one more time, she'd die happy, but no one knew where you were.'

'Dead?' he repeated, shocked. 'You mean dead and buried?'

'Yes, that's exactly what I mean.'

'The bugger killed her. I knew he would.'

'Then you should have stayed around to prevent it.' She gave an empty laugh. 'As it happens, he died first. Got run over by a bus in the blackout when he was drunk. I wanted to let you know, but I couldn't find you.'

'No, I move about a lot.'

'Doing what?'

'This and that,' he said vaguely. That last batch of stolen ration books had sold like hot cakes and the nylons he bought from a certain Yank, whose ideas about trade were the same as his own, had brought in a tidy profit. He lived like a lord, dressed to kill and could afford to treat his lady friends generously, as long as they were generous to him. Otherwise he soon dumped them. He no longer worked the East End, the pickings in the west were much more lucrative; the toffee-nosed women had money to burn and he could get pretty well anything for money. His move to the north of the river had been a wise and fortuitous one.

He had been strolling past the Walkers' home in Islington when he remembered they had moved with the factory to Letchworth and the house was shut up. It had been the work of a moment to break in and make himself comfortable. A nosy neighbour wanted to know what he was doing there and he had explained that he was looking after the house for the owners. 'Too many looters about to leave the place unguarded,' he had said. It was an argument he had used again when writing to Mr Walker to suggest he could keep an eye on the house for him and make sure no one got in. Mr Walker had no reason to distrust him and had readily agreed to pay him a small fee. It tickled Ted's fancy to think he was being paid to squat in his one-time boss's home. It was from here he ran his business. He hadn't given a thought to the fact that it was only a few streets away from his childhood home.

'You seem to be doing all right on it.'

'I do OK.'

'You could have helped Mum if you were doing so well. I helped when I could, but I never earned very much and I married young. My old man's in the army, gone to France I shouldn't wonder. Good riddance to him.'

'Did Mum get a good send-off?'

'What do you think? I did what I could and the neighbours chipped in so she didn't have to rely on the parish. That would have broken her heart. She's buried in Highgate in the far corner. There's no headstone, just a wooden cross. It wouldn't hurt you to pay your respects.'

'Yes, I'll do that. And I'll order a stone.'

'Not much good to her now she's gone, is it?' she said. 'But I suppose it will look better. And then how about visiting us and making the acquaintance of your nephews and nieces?'

'Nephews and nieces?' he queried. 'How many of them are there?'

'Two of each. My name's Porson now. You know where to find us, I've taken over the tenancy of the old house.'

She turned and walked away, leaving him staring after her. She was only twenty-four but she looked a lot older. Her hair was bedraggled and her shoes down at heel, and he seemed to remember his mother wearing that black straw hat with the flopping silk rose on it. He watched her out of sight and then went to the cemetery where he found the grave after a long search. Hidden away in the corner, its simple cross was carved with his mother's name and the date, nothing more. For the first time in his life he felt remorse, but it did not last. He became angry – angry with his father for his brutality, angry with his mother for not sticking up for herself, angry with Josie for not trying harder to find him, angry with the world.

He was still angry when he spotted Harry Walker kneeling beside his wife's grave. The bugger looked so clean and smart in his uniform, his dark auburn hair sleek and shiny, he could have kicked him. He held fire, though, because he remembered the man was handy with his fists. It wouldn't do to go about with evidence of a beating. It made his customers wary, it made the police suspicious and it wouldn't look good when he went home bearing gifts.

The disappearance of Rosie Summers had set him thinking and he had come to certain conclusions, impossible to prove, but if he were right, Julie Monday was not in that grave. What use he could make of that he had no idea, but he smiled to himself imagining the horror on Walker's face when he told him. He wouldn't believe him, of course, so there would have to be telling evidence that he knew what he was talking about. A living wife, perhaps. He walked past the kneeling figure and on down the path and out of the gate. 'One day, Harry Walker, you'll pay dearly for what you did to me,' he said. 'Just you wait.'

Chapter Ten

'I thought I saw a ghost today,' Harry told Pam, as they sat together on the sofa with his arm about her shoulders and her head nestling on his chest. As soon as he arrived back, he had reported to the group captain to be debriefed, then run home to grab Pam in his arms and hold her so tightly she had pulled back laughing. 'Harry, you'll squeeze me to death. And the children want you to say hallo and goodnight. I let them stay up to see you.'

He let her go and hugged the babies, then carried Colin up to his cot while Pam followed with Louise. They went off to sleep almost at once and he and Pam crept down to sit cosily side by side to bring each other up to date on what they had been doing. It was then he mentioned the ghost. 'I was feeling really low because Tim had died, when I passed this WAAF. She was the spitting image of Julie.'

'There's no such things as ghosts. You just saw a girl who looked like her.'

'Yes, I know. I kept telling myself that, but I couldn't get her out of my head. On the way through London, I went to Highgate Cemetery just to convince myself she was dead. Silly, I know.'

'And did you? Convince yourself I mean.'

'Yes, of course. There was her grave and her name and George's carved on the stone and that silly garden gnome grinning back at me for being such a fool.'

'There you are, then.' She paused. 'You aren't wishing she was back and you weren't married to me, are you?'

'No, course not.' He hugged her and kissed the tip of her nose. 'I don't know what I'd do without you.'

'But there's always a place in your heart for your first love, is that what you're trying to say?'

'I suppose I am. Do you mind? It doesn't alter how I feel about you.'

'I can live with it,' she said. 'After all, how can a dead woman hurt me? Now can we change the subject? Shall I make some cocoa? Then we'll go to bed.' She stood up to go to the kitchen but he grabbed her arm and dragged her down again. 'I can't wait.'

She laughed and fell into his lap where he proceeded to demonstrate that ghosts had no power over his love for her.

Julie had gone back to Manston on the bicycle she had borrowed and returned to work. She was kept busy the rest of that day and the next. Going off duty the second night, she made her way to the mess, expecting Florrie to be back from London. Her friend wasn't there. 'Anyone seen Sergeant Cotton?' she asked.

'I saw her drive through the gates half an hour ago,' the mess servant said. 'Perhaps she's gone to her billet.'

Julie went off to find her. She was going to tell her about

the three airmen, who had been so stoically cheerful and talking about getting back into the air, as if it were some game they were playing. She knew it was all show, a way of covering up their fear and hurt.

She found Florrie sprawled face down across her bed, her shoulders heaving. She ran to her at once, sat on the bed and put her hand on her shoulder. 'Florrie,' she said softly. 'What's up?'

Florrie turned a tear-stained face towards her. 'He's missing, Eve, missing believed killed.'

'Matt?'

'No, not Matt. Alec.'

'Alec?' Julie recoiled. It was like a blow to the stomach and for a moment she felt winded. She didn't want to believe it. It couldn't be, not Alec, not the fun-loving man who had captured her heart. 'No. It can't be true.'

'It is. I rang Mum from a call box while I was hanging about waiting for the CO outside Adastral House. She'd only just heard. She was in a terrible state, crying all the time. She had to hand the phone to Dad and he wasn't much better.' Her words came out in jerks. 'He said he'd had a call from someone at Brize Norton, who said the Dakota he was flying in never returned to base and they think it was shot down somewhere over the Channel.' She suddenly noticed the stricken look on Julie's face. 'Oh, Eve, I'm so sorry. You're hurting too.'

Julie couldn't cry. She was numb. All their love, all their hopes and plans, all gone. No, she could not, would not believe it. '"Missing believed dead" doesn't mean he's definitely dead,' she said, with a strange kind of fury which made her snap it out, but the anger soon abated and left her clinging on to the only thing that gave her hope. 'He might be picked up. There's still time.'

'Yes, you're right.' Florrie sat up and scrubbed at her eyes. 'We'll just have to go on hoping.'

'What about Matt?'

'He's all right. I spoke to him first. He told me it was pandemonium over in France. The weather was so bad half the troops didn't land where they were supposed to. He got his glider as near as he could to the right spot to release the tow, but he had no idea whether it had got down all right. And the ground troops were having a tough time of it. He was getting ready to go again with reinforcements. We didn't have time to talk any longer.'

'Then we will go to church and pray for them both, pray for them all and all those left behind to wait and worry.' She was determined not to give way to misery, but it was oh, so hard.

'I'm ruddy starving,' Trooper Langford muttered. They had only been issued with rations for twenty-four hours and some of those needed mixing with water and heating up. Alec would not let them light a fire and they had eaten everything else

'So am I,' came from Corporal Glover, a sentiment echoed by the rest of the stick. 'Can't we knock up one of these Frenchies and ask for food?'

As Alec had anticipated, they had been well scattered on landing, some coming down in trees, some on one side of a river, some on the other, and it had taken until dawn to get them all together again. They were way off the map as far as the invasion was concerned and had no idea where they were, nor the name of the river, nor, come to that, if there were any enemy troops nearby. For all they knew their parachutes had been seen coming down and they were already being hunted. And would the French inhabitants be too frightened to help them? They might even hand them in. He had ordered the men to bury their parachutes and lie low and they had spent the whole of the following day hiding in woods.

Alec had ventured out into the open at dusk to try and work out where they were. He thought they ought to strike out in a northerly direction but he'd lost his compass and the cloud cover was too thick to see the stars. He could see a village a little way off and ventured up the road towards it. He heard the sound of a motorcycle and dived into a ditch. It roared past him, a helmeted German riding it. He emerged from the ditch and went back to his men. 'There's Jerries about; we'll wait until dark and cut across country.'

Cutting across country was more difficult than he imagined. The area was heavily wooded in places and where there were no trees it was criss-crossed with waterways, some merely ditches, but others several feet from bank to bank, which engendered some debate whether they should try to wade or swim across or whether to try and find a bridge. Bridges, he felt sure, would be guarded. After he had insisted on wading across, holding their weapons above their heads, they emerged wet, cold and too fed up to carry on walking, only to come across a bend in the selfsame river, which meant they had to wade through it again.

'I don't reckon you know where we're going, Sarge,' Langford said, after they had spent three days hiding and three nights walking.

'We're going to find our own lines.'

'Are you sure you know which direction they're in? I

haven't heard a single shot in anger, so we must be a long way from where we should be.'

'We knew that when we jumped.'

'Yes, but the Frogs are supposed to be our allies, so I don't see why we can't ask them. They might give us something to eat too.'

'Shut up moaning, Langford,' the corporal told him. 'And be quiet. D'you want the whole German army down on us?'

They stumbled on in the darkness unable to see where they were putting their feet. Sometimes the ground was firm, sometimes it was marshy. The wind was strong and rain spattered on their heads. June it might be, but they had never felt so wet, cold and hungry.

'I can't believe we're so far from the action, we can't even hear it,' Corporal Glover said quietly so that the rest of the stick could not hear. 'Are you sure we're going in the right direction, Sarge?'

'No, I'm not sure, but it's best to keep moving. Sitting on our arses waiting to be taken prisoner is not an option.'

'D'you think they know at home what's happened?'

'The invasion? No doubt there'll have been some sort of announcement. I don't suppose they'll give away many details.'

'No, I meant what's happened to us, being missing an' all.'

'The pilot will have reported dropping us, won't he? Perhaps in hindsight he might be able to pinpoint where. In any case, the sooner we find the rest of the battalion the better.'

'Yes, but where are they all? You can usually hear Colonel Luard's hunting horn for miles.'

'He won't be blowing that now, he'll be stuck into the job he was given.'

'And doing it without us.'

'I don't suppose we were the only ones dropped off course.'

They had come out on a country road and looked up and down for signs of traffic, but it appeared empty. 'There's a farmhouse up ahead,' the corporal said. 'Couldn't one of us knock on the door while the rest cover him?'

'OK.' Alec stopped and turned to gather the men about him. 'We'll keep on the road and recce that farmhouse. Corporal, you take half the men and go round the back. If there's any sign of a Hun, give a whistle to warn us and then make yourselves scarce. The rest of you follow me and cover me. I'm going to knock on the door.'

Their caution was in vain, because as soon at they entered the farmyard a couple of dogs set up a ferocious barking. Alec swore as the door of the house was opened and a middle-aged man stood in its frame. 'Who's there?' he called in French, squinting into the darkness.

Alec gave up trying to hide and walked boldly forward. '*Je suis anglais,*' he said, holding out his open hands to show he meant no harm.

'*Anglais, mon Dieu!*' This was followed by a stream of questions at such speed Alec's schoolboy French could not keep up with them.

'Germans?' Alec interrupted this. 'Where are the Germans?'

The man shrugged and pointed up the road in the direction they were going.

'Good job we didn't keep going,' Langford said.

Alec ignored him and continued to address the farmer.

'We are hungry and thirsty.' He pointed to his mouth. 'Have you food and drink?'

By this time the rest of the men had come up behind him. The man came out of the house and beckoned them to follow him. They did so cautiously as he led them round to the back of the house, where those Alec had sent there emerged from their hiding places among the outbuildings, rifles pointing, startling the Frenchman who thought the whole British army must be on his doorstep.

Reassured by Alec, he led them into a barn, lit a hurricane lamp and pointed to a heap of straw. '*Attendez,*' he said, turned on his heel and went back into the house by a back door.

'You reckon he's gone to alert the Jerries?' Corporal Glover asked.

'Could be, though he didn't seem antagonistic. We'll post a guard where he can see anyone coming along the road. Corporal, take Smith with you. Any sign of Jerry, you double back and we'll make for that group of trees over there. If you can't get back, make your own way there.'

Some of the men flopped onto the straw, others, too nervous to relax, paced up and down. Several minutes later the farmer came back with a young woman; both were carrying trays of food which they set down on the floor. There was a tureen of soup, some mugs, bread, cheese and pickled onions. 'Eat,' she said in English. She was, he decided, about nineteen or twenty, dark-haired and tall, but thinner than girls of her age back home. It made him wonder what life was like under the occupation. Did they have enough to eat?

'You speak English?' he queried, as the others, needing no second bidding, dipped mugs into the soup and set to filling their stomachs.

'A little. My father has no English and you frightened him.'

'Tell him he has nothing to fear from us. We are here to liberate France.'

She turned to translate and the man seized Alec by the hand and shook it vigorously, then went round and shook everyone else by the hand, speaking volubly as he did so.

'Has the invasion begun?' the girl asked Alec. 'We heard rumours that the Americans and British had tried to land but they had been driven back into the sea.'

'God help us if they have,' Langford said.

She turned to look at him, but did not comment and continued to address Alec. 'You are a long way from the sea.'

'Yes. We are part of the advance and parachuted in four nights ago but we were blown off course. We are trying to find our way back to our own lines. Are there Germans about here?'

'In the village. If they find you here, there will be reprisals.'

'I understand. We are keeping watch and will go if there is any sign of Germans coming.'

She nodded towards the fast-dwindling food. 'Eat, Sergeant, before your men finish it all.'

'Langford, if you have finished, take Martin and relieve Corporal Glover,' he said, helping himself to a mug of soup. 'Tell them there's food.' Langford and Martin disappeared and he turned back to the girl. 'Have you a map I can look at?'

She turned and spoke to the farmer and he went off and came back with a map. They spread it out on the floor and knelt down to look at it with the aid of the lamp. 'We are here,' she said pointing.

'Good Lord, we're thirty miles adrift,' Alec said. He studied it more closely. 'I remember crossing the river just there. And again there. And we went into that wood.' He laughed. 'Twice. I reckon we've been going round in circles.' He looked at the girl beside him. 'Where are the Germans?'

'All around.' She pointed at places on the map. 'They were here and here and here. They may have been moved to go and fight.'

'It's nearly daylight,' Alec said, folding the map and returning it to her. 'We'll have to wait for dark again. May we stay here?'

She spoke to her father, then turned back to Alec. 'He says yes, but if anyone comes you must go quickly.'

'We will, I promise.' He spoke to the man. '*Merci. Merci.*'

The couple took the trays and disappeared and Alec's men spread the straw out and settled down to sleep. Most were so exhausted they were soon snoring. Alec took a little longer to settle. His responsibility towards the men weighed heavily. His first duty was to see them safely back to their own lines, but if they ran into the enemy, he was not sure whether they ought to put up a fight or surrender. He supposed it would depend on the strength of the enemy and whether they were not too exhausted by their trekking about to give a good account of themselves. He didn't want to put their lives at risk if he could help it. He certainly did not want to die himself. He had too much to live for.

Eve would be waiting, knowing he must be involved in the operation – 'Overlord' they called it – and she would be anxious, as would Florrie and his parents. He had probably been posted missing, which would be worrying for them, but the pilot of the Dakota would have reported that he had dropped the stick successfully, so it was just a question of getting back to the battalion. If, on the other hand, he were taken prisoner, then they would eventually learn that too, but it would take longer and he had no intention of letting it happen if he could help it.

He lay back on the straw, knowing he, like the rest of them, was stinking of river water and sweat and Eve would certainly not like to be near him in that state. He shut his eyes, attempted to ignore the sound of the others snoring and tried to picture Eve getting up, putting on her uniform and going to work, probably knowing more about how the invasion was going than he did. He went over again all that they had done while on that leave in the Lake District, walking in the hills, talking and laughing and planning, but most of all the feel of her soft body in his arms as they lay together in a big double bed, the sweet smell of her shampoo as her head nestled in his shoulder, the warmth of her as she flung a leg over his, her kisses on his body as she explored it with her mouth. He felt himself harden at the memory and turned on his side, away from the others. 'Wait for me, Eve,' he murmured to himself. 'I'm coming back.'

Just before dusk, the farmer came again with more food, and by the time they had consumed it, it was dark enough to set off again. The girl handed him the map and a small torch. 'You will need these, Sergeant. Good luck to you.'

They thanked their host and hostess and set off again, avoiding the village and striking out across the fields. With full stomachs and a map, they were much more cheerful and made good progress, chatting in undertones as they went. Once they ventured onto a road but were forced to scatter into a ditch when they heard the sound of vehicles behind them. A long convoy of lorries, a gun carrier and several motorcyclists, headed by a staff car, went past them at speed.

'I bet they're off to the front.' Langford was the first to emerge from hiding. He was also the driest. Everyone else had hurled themselves into the ditch without checking whether it contained water. They were wet and miserable again.

'Proves we're going in the right direction,' Corporal Glover said as they set off again.

As the light strengthened they looked for somewhere to lay up for the day, and encouraged by their previous experience, decided to try another farmhouse. Here they found only a middle-aged woman who spoke no English. She was clearly terrified and refused to help them. Alec begged her pardon and made a swift retreat.

The light was strengthening; finding shelter was a matter of urgency. 'She'll tell the Jerries about us,' Alec said. 'We'd better keep going.'

They struck out across the field, knowing they could be seen by anyone looking from the windows of the farmhouse. The knowledge lent wings to their feet and they did not stop until they had covered several miles. 'We'd better lie up,' Alec said. 'Any stray plane flying over will spot us, and you never know, they may be on the lookout for us.'

There was a rough wooden shelter for animals in the corner of a field and they tumbled inside and stretched themselves out to wait out the day. A couple of black and white cows came to stand in the entrance, as if wondering who it was that had invaded their home. Trooper Smith laughed. 'They make good sentries.'

Langford decided to milk one of them, catching the liquid in his mess tin. He drank deeply and offered the tin to the others. When it was empty he refilled it. 'The owner of that beast is going to wonder why his cow isn't giving any milk this morning,' Corporal Glover said.

'You mean he'll be here soon?'

'Well, the cows haven't been milked, have they? Stands to reason.'

He was right. A man in his fifties plodded across the field, calling to his animals. Langford gave one of them a thump on its rear. 'Go on, Daisy, old girl, go when you're called.'

Daisy didn't see why she should. She stood defying him, swishing her tail. The cowman drew nearer. The men tried squeezing themselves further back but there was no room. Alec drew his pistol and waited. As the man spotted them, he stood up. The terrified man turned and ran, the cows lolloping behind him. 'Now we're in trouble,' Langford said.

There was nothing for it but to leave. They crossed a field which was bounded by a hedge and a ditch. Scrambling down into it, they waded along it until they came to a village. They dared not move and stayed there the rest of the day. When it grew dark, Alec left them there while he went to reconnoitre. The place was alive with German troops. Hastily he retraced his steps and they set off again, away from what they had hoped might provide them with food and shelter.

Everyone was miserable and irritable and some of the less resilient of them were flagging. Alec chivvied them along with a mixture of encouragement and forcefulness. He swore he could hear gunfire, which surely meant they were nearing the battle lines. Alec was not sure how many miles they had covered when, in the early hours, they came to a wood. He paused, wondering whether to go through it or round it. He stopped the men to rest, while he studied the map. The wood was extensive, going round it would take much longer. On the other hand, it would be easy to lose one's bearings if the canopy were dense. 'What do you think?' he asked Corporal Glover, as his number two studied the map with him.

'We'll take all night going round it.'

'Just what I thought. There's a clearing just there.' He pointed to a gap in the green on the map. 'If the clouds clear we might be able to see a star or two to give us a bearing.'

He folded the map and put it back in his pocket before rousing the men and setting off again, plunging into the wood. The undergrowth had been cleared near the edge but the further in they went the more overgrown it was and they had to hack their way through. Alec was beginning to think he had made a wrong decision, but it was too late to change his mind now. They struggled on and suddenly came to a well-used path which seemed to be going in the direction they wanted, so they marched briskly along it.

Alec, who was a few paces in front of his men, suddenly heard voices speaking German. He held up his hand and turned to signal the men to take cover. They scrambled back into the thicket beside the path. Alec crept forward to investigate. The trees thinned out and there was the clearing they had been aiming for, but right in the middle of it was a gun emplacement, surrounded by tents. Men in German uniform were walking about, their rifles over their shoulders, or sitting round a campfire eating. Some electrical wiring held a few bulbs which provided light for them, but beyond the circle of light, the forest was dark as pitch. They were completely at ease and unaware that their enemy was so close. He turned and crept back to the men.

'Jerry has a big gun up there,' he told them in a whisper.

'How many of them?' Corporal Glover wanted to know. 'Could we take them on?'

'That was what I was wondering, but we'd be outnumbered three to one and we haven't much ammunition. If we tried and failed, we'd take casualties and the rest would be taken prisoner. We wouldn't be much help to the war effort then, so I think we'll try to get by them unheard and unseen.'

'That won't be easy if we have to go back into the wood,' the corporal said. 'We'll make a devil of a noise crashing about.'

'Quite,' Alec said. 'I propose simply to walk past them and hope they don't look at us too closely in the dark.'

Trooper Smith gave a low chuckle. 'You reckon we'll get away with it, Sarge?'

'Yes, as long as we look as though we belong with them and know where we're going. And for goodness' sake, don't speak.'

'I can speak a little German,' one of the other men said. He had only joined the stick a day or two before they took off to replace someone who had gone sick and Alec did not know him as well as the others. 'If they start looking curious, I could pretend to be talking to you.'

'Right,' Alec said. 'Shoulder your rifles and get into double file and follow me. Don't crouch and don't hurry.'

They very nearly made it. They were on the far edge of the clearing and about to pick up the path again, when Langford tripped over a log and in trying to save himself grabbed the branch of a bush which snapped in his hand, going off like a gunshot. The next moment there was a shout behind them and then gunshots, which had them flinging themselves to the ground and wriggling towards the shelter of the forest.

Two Germans came running along the path, guns pointing. Alec's crew, now under the canopy of trees, froze. The Germans went up and down poking the undergrowth, talking to each other. Everyone tucked their faces down and held their breath, not daring to move a muscle. And then a miracle happened. A pig appeared from behind them and trotted out onto the path, snorting in anger at having its sleep disturbed. The Germans laughed and went back to their camp, chasing the pig in front of them, obviously intending to slaughter and eat it.

It was a long time before anyone dared to move and then they crept silently away, giving thanks for their deliverance. By now Alec was beginning to think they were living a charmed life, but it would not do to be complacent. He would have to be even more careful; it had become a matter of pride to get his whole stick back to their own lines in one piece.

'I saw one of those buzz bomb things today,' Florrie told Julie one evening, ten days after D-Day. They were eating their evening meal in the canteen, which is where they usually met after the day's work was done. Around them, others were eating, chattering to friends and exchanging gossip and opinion, to the accompaniment of the clatter of cutlery. 'I was driving the group captain to London and it flew over our heads. We stopped the car to look at it.'

The girls functioned because they had to. Each day

they hoped for news of Alec and each day they were disappointed. After a week passed with no news, they had begun to fear the worst, though they tried to comfort each other by pretending there was still hope. Published reports from the front were buoyant, but it seemed all had not gone to plan and the Allies had not been able to take Caen, which had been one of their early objectives. Resistance had been fierce and there had been casualties. Exactly how many was not divulged but the girls guessed they must be in the thousands. It didn't bear thinking about.

The Germans, far from being beaten, were hitting back, not only in France but in the air over London and the Home Counties. There had been several incidents of strange explosions, with loss of life and terrible damage to property, which were not the usual kind of air raid and had everyone speculating. Only the day before it had been admitted officially that the enemy were using flying bombs, which had no pilots and simply ran out of fuel and came down indiscriminately to explode with devastating force on impact. They were aimed at London, but many came down prematurely in Kent. This was the secret weapon Hitler had been boasting about for years and it struck terror into the population. Hundreds of barrage balloons were put up to stop them and fighter planes sent up to intercept them but far too many of them got through.

'Did you see it come down?'

'No. It flew on. It was like a little aeroplane, a bomb with wings and an engine. It makes a kind of loud droning noise. You can't mistake it. We watched it for ages. Then a Hurricane arrived and started shooting at it. It exploded and there were bits of it flying everywhere and coming down in flames. Some of the debris hit the Hurricane and I thought that would go down too, but it wobbled a bit, straightened itself and flew off. Group told me that some of our planes had been brought down by flying debris and the latest thing was to fly close enough to tip their wings and make the bombs fly off course, but they still can't control where they come down.'

'That must take some very precise flying.'

'Yes. It's worse than the Blitz, it's so indiscriminate.'

'I wish it could end, Florrie. All this hate and slaughter. I'm desperately tired of it all. I wish I could lie down and sleep and sleep.'

'Aren't you sleeping?'

'No, I keep having nightmares and wake up in a sweat. I'm running along a beach and it's covered with dead bodies, all swirling about as the tide moves them, and I'm searching for someone and getting more and more desperate . . .'

'Alec?'

'I don't know. I suppose it must be. I wish we could hear some positive news. This not knowing is getting me down.'

'Me too. There's only a little over a year between us and we were always close, Alec and I. It's as if half of me is missing too. But I am convinced he's alive somewhere, or half of me would feel dead. D'you know what I mean?'

'Yes, I feel like that sometimes, not just about Alec, but about my loss of memory. It's missing, but not dead. One day, perhaps, I'll admit to myself it's gone for good.'

'Do you still have those pictures of the past?'

'Now and again, when something triggers one off, but I still can't make any sense of them, like running along a beach searching for someone. Why would it be Alec? I know I'm worried about him, but he didn't go in with the seaborne troops, did he? And I've never been on a beach with him; they've been mined and off-limits ever since I've known him.'

'I don't know. The mind can play funny tricks sometimes. Maybe we'll hear soon, but then I keep thinking, if the plane came down in the sea, we may never know for sure. Maybe that's why you dream of searching a beach, expecting him to be washed up.'

Julie shuddered. 'It could be, I suppose. One of the pilots told me the beaches in Normandy were awash with bodies.'

'There you are, then. That's what stuck in your mind and gave you nightmares.'

'You could be right.'

'I dread to think what all this waiting is doing to Mum and Dad. I've asked for leave to go and see them, but no luck so far.'

Julie was not Alec's next of kin and so no official news would come to her and she would have to rely on Florrie being told by her parents. 'I wish I could come too.'

'Then ask. They can only say no.'

Florrie was granted seven days leave the following day and she went off telling Julie she would let her know the minute she heard anything. Julie put in her own request and continued her routine job, doing it almost automatically, while her mind was at Hillside Farm with Florrie and Maggie and Walter, and worrying about Alec. She had been reluctant to commit herself to him because of her loss of memory and the feeling that there was something in her past that could hinder their happiness, but he had overcome that with his love for her and good solid argument. He was her rock, the one stable thing in her life that kept her feet on the ground and gave her a future, if not a past. She had to believe he was alive, but the waiting to hear was unbearable.

Julie's hands were shaking as she picked up the telephone in the office and asked for the Kilbys' number. The number of Hillside Farm and a message to ring Sergeant Cotton urgently had been left on her desk. That was all. Good news or bad, she had no way of knowing and she was a mass of nerves. The lines were all busy and she had to wait for what seemed an eternity before she heard Florrie's voice at the other end of the line.

'He's safe, Eve. Alec is safe. We heard this morning.'

'Oh, thank God. What a relief. But what happened to him? Was he shot down in the sea? Is he wounded? Is he coming home?' The questions followed rapidly, one after the other.

'He's not hurt. He was dropped a long way behind enemy lines and has taken all this time to get back to his unit. Apparently he acted with commendable initiative and brought his whole stick safely back. He's being mentioned in dispatches.'

'That's typical of Alec. Are they sending him home?'

'We don't know. Probably not immediately but you never know. He's back with his unit, still in the thick of it and I don't know whether to laugh or cry.'

'Nor me. I'm doing both. At least now we know he's OK.'

'Yes. Mum and Dad are over the moon. Dad was down on the long meadow cutting hay when Mum got the news, and she shrieked loud enough to wake the dead and then tore out of the house to tell him. I've been trying to get a message through to you all day.'

'There's been no one in the billet to answer the phone.'

'We're celebrating with champagne. Any chance of you getting leave to join us? You never know, we might hear from Alec himself.'

'I put in for it the day you left. I'll try chasing it up. Oh, Florrie, you don't know how relieved I am.'

'Yes, I do. It's been the same for me. But I knew he wasn't dead. I just knew it.'

Julie could hardly sleep that night. Alec was safe, but he wasn't out of danger. She wanted him home, to touch him, to reassure herself he was in one piece. The waiting had been agonising, but it wasn't over. It wouldn't be over until Germany was finally defeated.

Section Officer Murray was not as hard-hearted as she liked to pretend and, on being told the good news, granted Julie seventy-two-hours leave. Seventy-two hours was not long, but better than nothing. Throwing a few things in a rucksack, Julie caught a train to London where she would have to change to a West Country train for Andover. It was a clear day, warm and sunny, peaceful even. There was no hint of what was happening on the other side of the Channel, nor of the menace from the skies. The train was packed but Julie found a seat in a window of one of the rear carriages and settled down to read the *Daily Sketch*. Details of the invasion had been trickling through and were being recounted in front page articles. The early reports that all had gone according to plan were being amended, and some of the problems that had been encountered were being made public, though heavily censored. Most were tales of heroism and the successful taking of town and villages, and the stories of the many wounded who had been repatriated. But the reports did not belittle the difficulties ahead. The invasion was not going to bring a quick end to the war as many had hoped.

She became aware that other passengers were peering out of the window in some excitement and she laid aside her paper to look too. Above their heads and a little to the left a flying bomb was keeping pace with them. It looked just like Florrie had described it, flying along on a steady course towards London. They could hear its steady drone above the noise of the train.

'Keep going,' someone said. 'Please God don't let its engine stop now.'

'Someone will cop it, wherever it lands up,' another said.

'In an open field would be best.'

'How does it know where to go?'

'Dunno.'

The engine driver could not have been unaware of it and he accelerated to get ahead of it, but that did not seem to work, so he tried to slow down, but still the menace was above them.

'My God, the engine's stopped,' the sailor sitting opposite Julie shouted. 'It's going to come down on top of us!'

There was a mad scramble as everyone flung themselves on the floor and put their arms over their heads. The train sped on. The next moment was chaos as train and bomb collided. The noise was deafening as the blast tore through the carriages, shattering the windows and buckling the metal like matchwood. Those in Julie's carriage who had breath enough screamed as the front reared up and came off the rails and turned over, flinging them on top of one another in a tangle of legs and arms, suitcases, rucksacks, sandwich boxes, broken glass and splintered metal. It was followed by an eerie silence broken only by the hissing of steam from the overturned engine.

Chapter Eleven

How long she was unconscious Julie did not know, but she came to her senses to find herself pinned down by a man's heavy body. He was clearly dead. Controlling her rising panic with a huge effort, she heaved him off her and tried to extricate herself. Beside her others were moaning, some screaming. She had no time to scream. She had no breath for it, and being trapped and not able to get out was like being shut in a dark cupboard. Her heart was pounding and all she could think of was getting out. There was a tiny patch of daylight. She managed to drag herself towards it. The hole was too small to crawl through. She put her arm out and waved her hand about in the hope that someone would see it and come to her rescue.

'All right, miss, we can see you,' a male voice said. 'Don't move or you'll have everything down on top of you. We'll soon have you out of there. What's your name?'

'Julie. Julie Walker.'

'Right, Sergeant Walker, keep still until I come back or you might do more damage.'

Sergeant Walker? That didn't sound right. She withdrew her arm and looked at herself. Beneath the thick dust and black smuts, she was wearing a blue uniform jacket and there were three stripes on her arm. What had happened to her? She had gone into the air-raid shelter in a cotton dress and cardigan, but this was no dress and this was no shelter; it was the remains of a train. Had she died? It was a funny version of heaven if she had. Or perhaps she was in hell? She was still puzzling over that when the man came back.

'Right, Sergeant,' he said. 'We've got some cutting equipment here, so move back as far as you can. Are there others in there with you?'

'Yes. There's one man dead that I know of, perhaps more. I don't know. The carriage was full.' She remembered that, so she must have been travelling. But why and where to? Was George with her? No, she had left him with Rosie. She had to get back to them; her friend would be worried what had happened to her.

'Right, we're going to start cutting now. If anything starts to shift, you yell out.'

'OK, but hurry. Hurry.'

The noise of the cutting equipment battered her ears as the hole was enlarged, and she was thankful when it stopped and she was carefully pulled from the wreckage and laid on the grass beside the track. Her rescuers went to extricate the others in the carriage, leaving her to take great gulps of air until her racing heart slowed. Above her the sky was blue, with one or two cotton wool clouds and no sign of the menace that had caused such devastation.

Turning her head, she could see the extent of it. An

engine lying head down beside the track, still hissing steam, the mangled first two carriages piled up on top of it, others lying like dead whales. Bits of wood, metal, glass and luggage strewn everywhere, and there were little pockets of fire in the grass caused by hot cinders. Worst of all were the bodies, some laid out in rows, others lying where they had been flung. There were wounded too, some unconscious, some stoically silent, others moaning, children crying. They were being cared for by Red Cross nurses and members of the Women's Voluntary Service. A doctor was moving from one to the next. How had a street shelter turned into a train? It was a nightmare and she wished she could wake up. She sat up and tried ineffectually to brush the black smuts off her uniform jacket. It was a uniform, there was no doubt of that. Something very strange had happened to her.

The doctor reached her and squatted down beside her. 'Are you hurt, Sergeant?'

The title still sounded strange. 'A few cuts and bruises, nothing more. Where are we?'

'Not far from Gillingham.'

'Gillingham? How did I get here?'

'You were on the train.'

'Yes, but why was I on the train? I don't remember getting on it. I don't know why I'm dressed like this? I'm not in the air force.'

'Aren't you? Look in your pockets, Sergeant.'

Julie unbuttoned her breast pocket and extracted a pay book and travel warrant. 'They belong to someone called Eve Seaton,' she said. 'I've never heard of her.'

'I think we'd better get you to hospital,' he said. 'You've obviously suffered a blow to the head.'

'No.' She struggled to sit up. 'I have to go home.'

'Where's home?'

'Bermondsey. I left my baby with a friend.'

'When?'

'Today.'

'Do you know the date?'

Julie racked her brains. 'It's the seventh of September.'

'What year?'

'Year?' she queried, wondering why he needed to ask that. 'It's 1940.'

Many of the passengers, like Julie, had been reading newspapers when the bomb struck and the pages were drifting about along with all the other debris. He reached out and grabbed one. 'Look at the date.'

'June nineteenth 1944,' she read aloud.

'That's right. That's today.'

'But I don't understand. How can it be?'

'I think you must have lost your memory. Now, are you going to let us take you to hospital to try and sort this out?'

'No, I have to go to George. He's my baby. I left him—'

'In 1940,' he said firmly. 'Nearly four years ago.'

'Oh, my God.' She couldn't take it in, she really couldn't. The world had gone mad. But more important than trying to make sense of it was the desperate need to get home to George.

He beckoned to one of the Red Cross nurses and spoke to her in an undertone, obviously telling her this patient was as mad as a hatter and must be transported to Bedlam. She waited until the nurse and doctor had moved on to other casualties, then scrambled to her feet and searched among the wreckage until she found a rucksack with the name Sgt E Seaton stencilled inside the flap, which she assumed was

267

hers. It was torn but the contents were intact. A further search brought to light an air force blue shoulder bag which contained a diary for 1944 and a temporary ration card in the name of Eve Seaton. None of that mattered in her anxiety to go home to Bermondsey. Still dazed, she set off up the track in what she believed was the direction of London.

'I'm being posted back to Cosford.'

Pam stared at her husband in dismay. They had just finished their evening meal and he was helping her wash up. He had been trying to find a way of breaking the news ever since he came home and in the end had just blurted it out.

'Oh, Harry, you can't be. You're needed here.'

'I'm needed there too. They want me to take on the training of new wireless operators.'

'Other people can do that.'

'So they can, but I've been grounded again because of the number of missions I've flown. According to the CO I need a rest from flying ops.'

'I'll certainly go along with that, but can't they find you a job here?'

'Apparently not.'

'What am I to do?'

'What you always do, sweetheart. Stay here and look after the house and the little ones. You've got plenty to keep you busy and I'll come home as often as I can get leave. It's not that far to travel.'

She was standing with her hands in the washing-up water, but was making no attempt to continue with the task. 'Didn't you tell Group you couldn't possibly leave me and the children?'

He smiled. 'Darling, you should know better than that. You don't argue with the group captain. He says I'm going and I go, that's it.'

'When?'

'Tomorrow.'

'Tomorrow! But that doesn't give us any time at all.'

'What time do you need to stuff a few things in a kitbag? This is wartime, Pam, and we've been extraordinarily lucky up to now. Let's be thankful for that.'

'I am. I've always known how lucky I am, I just didn't think of it ending.'

'The war can't last for ever. When it's over we'll settle down and never be parted again.'

She laughed suddenly. 'I'll hold you to that, Harry Walker.'

She was remarkably resilient, he told himself. He didn't know why he expected tantrums – it was not her way and she had been living close to the airfield for years and knew the rules as well as anyone.

They finished the washing-up and he put away the crockery while she took the bowl of water out of the back door and threw it on the garden in a wide arc. He watched her come back and grabbed her to kiss her.

'I'm going to miss you and the children like hell,' he said. 'But I'll write often, I promise.'

She put a soapy finger on the end of his nose. 'I know you will.'

He brushed the bubbles off and kissed her again. 'I'm a lucky man,' he said. 'Let's go and listen to the news.'

The news, read by Alvar Lidell, was mostly about the situation in Normandy where Caen had still not been taken. The Germans were determined not to give an inch if they could help it and were resisting fiercely. There was also a report of more flying bombs getting through and the frightening casualties, including one that had landed on a crowded train. 'The Government is considering a new evacuation of children and mothers with babies,' the newsreader said.

'I'm glad we don't live in London,' Pam said, snuggling up to him on the sofa. 'It must be awful.'

'Is Sergeant Seaton with you?'

'No,' Florrie said, puzzled that Section Officer Murray should telephone her while on leave. 'Isn't she on the station?'

'She was given seventy-two-hours leave.'

'Then she'll be on her way.'

'I hope so. She left here yesterday morning.'

'Yesterday? She should have been here by now. Where can she have got to? She's not in trouble, is she?'

'I don't know. She was involved in an incident when the train she was travelling in was hit by a flying bomb. She had a few cuts and bruises but was otherwise physically unhurt, but she was very confused and the doctor who treated her at the scene suspected a brain injury. He was making arrangements for her to go to hospital, but she disappeared before he could do so. He saw her pay book and guessed she might have come from here. He rang to see if she had returned, otherwise we would never have known she was missing. I thought she might be with you. She told me that was where she was going.'

'No, ma'am, we haven't seen her.'

'She's not absent without leave yet, but if she doesn't report back by tomorrow midnight, she could be in trouble.'

270

'I think I know where she's gone,' Florrie said. 'I'll find her.'

'Good. Report back the minute you have news. She must be got to hospital.'

Florrie rang off and turned to her mother. 'Eve's gone missing,' she said and explained what had happened. 'My guess is that her memory has come back and she's gone back to where she lost it.'

'Where's that?' her father asked. He had just come in from supervising the land girls turning the hay on the far meadow, and was sitting in his rocking chair by the empty hearth, pulling off his boots.

'Southwark. At least, that's where she told us she'd been pulled from the shelter way back in 1940. Mum, do you mind if I cut my leave short? I must find her.'

'No, of course not. It's all this worry about Alec at the bottom of it, I shouldn't wonder.'

Florrie did not comment, but she was concerned on Alec's behalf. Just suppose Eve had forgotten him . . . he would be devastated. Not only that, but supposing her past turned up an encumbrance, like the child she was supposed to have had? A husband even? While these things were forgotten and Eve was the Eve they knew and loved, they could be ignored. But if she had remembered . . .

Julie stood in the street where her home had been and stared at the empty space. There was nothing of it left. The shared wall which had attached it to the Goldings' house had been shored up with huge buttresses of wood. The rest of the neighbouring house had been repaired. There were clean curtains at its windows. She was shaking, not only with delayed shock from the train derailment but the thought

271

that four years had passed since she had last seen George. And what about Harry, the husband she had adored? Had he made no effort to find her? Had no one missed her?

As she stood there, it began coming back to her: pawning her wedding ring, leaving George with Rosie while she went to see Miss Paterson, hurrying home when the air-raid siren went and being conducted to the shelter. It was all a bit hazy after that. She remembered being trapped in a tiny space surrounded by rubble and choking on dust, and a voice saying, 'All right, miss, we can see you. Don't move or you'll have everything down on top of you. We'll soon have you out of there.' They were the exact words used by the man who spoke to her after the train crash. That's what had triggered her returning memory, she decided: the words, combined with the situation in which she found herself. It was as if there had been no time in between the two events, as if they were one and the same. But there had been nearly four years! Four years! What had she been doing in all that time? And where were Harry and George? That small square of flattened earth and the shored-up house were frightening; it was as if all she had been and known had been swept off the face of the earth, been deliberately obliterated and forgotten.

She turned when she saw Mrs Golding coming out of her house with a shopping basket on her arm. The woman stopped and stared at her, her mouth half open.

Julie gave her a brave smile. 'Mrs Golding, how are you?'

'Mrs Walker, it is you. I couldn't believe my eyes. They told me you had been killed, and your little boy too. When the bomb fell.'

'Dead? George is dead?' She was already so traumatised

this extra shock set her senses reeling. Nothing made sense anymore, and yet, and yet . . . Her brain ticked over. If it was assumed she had died too, it might explain why no one had been looking for her.

'So they said.' Mrs Golding's voice broke in on her thoughts. 'I came home last year, that's when I heard. Of course, I may have got it wrong. What happened to you? You look as if you've been in the wars.'

Julie looked down at herself. She had tried to clean the smuts from her jacket in the toilets at Waterloo Station, some had been hot enough to scorch it. One or two had burnt her face and hands and there were tiny red blisters on her cheeks. She had not at first felt any pain, but now they were beginning to sting. 'You could say that. A doodlebug came down on the train I was travelling in.'

'I heard about that. It was on the news. Were you hurt?'

'Only a few scrapes and bruises. I was lucky I was in a rear compartment.'

'Come in and I'll make a cup of tea. You could do with one, I expect.'

'Yes, that would be lovely, thank you. But you were just going out.'

'It can wait, it was only a few bits of shopping. I can do that later.' She turned and went back into the house, holding the door for Julie.

It was the first time Julie had been in the house. It was a mirror image of her own, but the repairs to the bomb damage and the new paint had made it brighter and more modern. She was soon sitting at the kitchen table while Mrs Golding busied herself making tea. 'We were interned on the Isle of Man,' she told Julie. 'My husband died there. Last year I was allowed to come home. The council made

273

the place habitable for me and I've found a part-time job sewing buttons on new uniforms, which keeps the wolf from the door. The neighbours don't speak to me, but that doesn't bother me. It's ignorance, that's what it is.'

'I'm sorry about your husband.'

'He just pined away. He couldn't understand why he was being treated like an enemy when he was a victim of the Nazi terror and loyal to this country.' She put a cup of tea in front of Julie and pushed a sugar bowl towards her. Julie declined the sugar but accepted a biscuit. 'Thank you. You are very kind.'

'You were kind to me, I remember. Now, tell me what has been happening to you. I won't breathe a word to anyone if you don't want me to.'

As Julie attempted to try and put her thoughts in order, things started to make more sense and she began to piece together what had happened to her as Julie Walker and what had happened as Eve Seaton. At first she had been inclined to deny her identity as Eve, but she had had time to think since that train derailment. She had walked for miles, earning some strange looks from others she passed, but no one had spoken to her, or if they had, she had not heard them; she had been in another world, a world of returning memories, all swirling about in her head. Eventually, too tired to continue, she had fallen asleep under a haystack in the corner of a field. Setting off again next morning, she had come to a railway station and boarded a train to Waterloo. From there it was only one stop on the Underground to the Elephant and Castle. She had walked from there to her old home. There was still a lot of bomb damage and open craters along the way, but an attempt had been made to clear most of the rubble away, and some repairs had been made to those houses not badly damaged. It was strangely alien and yet achingly familiar.

She recounted all this to an astonished Mrs Golding. 'I couldn't understand why no one came looking for me,' she told her. 'Now I realise it was because everyone thought I had died. But I left George with Rosie. You remember my friend, Rosie, don't you?'

'Yes, I do. She was a lot like you. Do you think she could have been mistaken for you?'

'But surely my husband would have known the difference. Did he come back from Canada?'

'I don't know. I wasn't here.'

'No, of course you weren't. I'll have to go and see his parents. They will know where he is.' She gave a mirthless chuckle. 'I'm afraid I'm going to be a terrible shock to them. And to Harry, if he's still alive.'

'Surely you didn't forget everything?'

'I did. I really did. Until yesterday. Now I can hardly remember what I did last week. It's so confusing. I don't know whether I'm coming or going, what's real and what's fantasy.'

'I can't begin to imagine what that must be like. But you are in uniform; surely the authorities will know all about you.'

'Yes, I expect they will. The medics at the train wanted to take me to hospital, but it was more important for me to find my son.'

'I understand. I'm sorry I can't tell you any more. You could ask around.'

Julie didn't feel inclined to let the whole world know her troubles; they would assume she was mad. Besides, how many of the people living in the street had been there four years before? 'If George really did die, there must be a record of it somewhere. I'll go to the council offices when I've drunk this tea.'

Mrs Golding watched Julie drain her cup. 'Would you like a bath while you're here? I can soon heat the water. The council put a new gas geyser in when they did the repairs. It's so much better than lighting a fire and waiting for the water to get hot. If you've got a change of clothes . . .'

'I've underwear and a clean shirt in my rucksack. There's a pair of trousers too, but no jacket.'

'I'll see what I can do with that while you have your bath.'

An hour later, feeling clean and fresh and wearing trousers, shirt and an air force pullover, and with some ointment on her burns, she thanked Mrs Golding and set off once again, her damaged clothes in her rucksack. She was still in a kind of limbo between two lives which seemed to have no connection with each other, and she could not summon the courage or energy to explain it to other people. In any case, it would make her look foolish, if not devious. Instead she asked at the council offices if she could look at the casualty records for 7th September 1940, saying she was trying to trace a friend who had disappeared. There were pages and pages of them. She scanned them all, recognising some names she had known, until at last she found what she was looking for: Julie Walker, wife of Harry Walker, aged twenty-two, and George Walker, aged one year and nine months, casualties of war. She was officially dead!

She shut the book and stumbled from the office. Standing outside in the warm June sunshine, she wondered what to do, where to go, who to tell. George, the baby she had idolised, had died without her even knowing it.

Had he been frightened? Had he been crying for her? Had Rosie been looking after him properly? Had they both still been in the garden playing with the water in the pool when the bomb dropped? He had been so happy, smacking at the water with his hands, his plump pink limbs working away, making the water slop over the edge of the bath, splashing her and laughing at her pretended outrage. Until now she had been numb, almost unfeeling, but that image of George as she had last seen him opened the floodgates. She collapsed onto a low wall and burst into tears.

Several people paused as they passed her, some moved on without speaking, others asked, 'Are you all right, miss?'

She nodded, but could not answer for the sobs that racked her. They stood a moment, undecided, then moved on.

At last the sobs faded to a watery hiccough and then stopped. She fumbled in her rucksack for another handkerchief to replace the sodden one she had been using, blew her nose and stood up, surprised to find the sun still shining, people still going about their business, traffic still moving up and down the street. Life went on around her and she must think what to do, where to go next.

It was important to find Harry, though what he would make of her sudden reappearance she could not begin to imagine. His parents would know where he was. She remembered Chalfont's factory had been due to move to Letchworth, but she had no idea if her in-laws had gone, or if they had come back to Islington when the Blitz ended. If she had accepted the offer to go with them, instead of stubbornly refusing to leave her home, her life would have been very different. George would still be alive and she would never have become Eve Seaton, joined the WAAF and met Florrie and Alec. Alec. The name flew into her head, followed by a mental picture of a cheerful young man with crinkly fair hair and laughing hazel eyes, a man to whom she had willingly given herself. Memories of him jumbled with memories of Harry until she felt as if her head would burst open and spill them all on the pavement. She could not face going to Islington, not today, not until she had calmed down and sorted out her thoughts. Instead she went to Shoreditch to throw herself on the mercy of Miss Paterson.

Grace had just finished making herself some scrambled egg with reconstituted dried egg for her lunch and was on the point of sitting down to eat it when there was a knock at the door. 'Now who can that be?' she asked aloud, getting up to answer it. She must be getting old, talking to herself, she really must stop doing it or everyone would call her mad. She thought she might truly be mad when she opened the door to see an apparition on the doorstep. It was enough to send her reeling against the wall.

Julie stepped into the hall and took her elbow. 'Don't faint on me, Grace, please. I've got so much to tell you.'

'Julie. God in heaven, you're alive.'

'I'm glad you think so. I have been wondering myself whether I might be in some kind of limbo, not good enough for heaven and not bad enough for hell. Can we sit down somewhere, you look as though you are about to fall down.'

'Do you wonder at it?'

Julie, who had made her home in the flat before she married Harry, knew her way around it and guided her friend to the kitchen, where the uneaten plate of scrambled egg, garishly yellow, was growing cold. 'You were in the middle of your lunch.'

Grace sank into a chair. 'Never mind that. I couldn't eat it now anyway. Tell me what happened. Where have you sprung from? Who is in that grave? There's a stone with your name and the date and everything.'

'Gravestone? There's a stone on my grave?' That there must be physical evidence of her death in the form of a grave and a stone was something she had not stopped to consider.

'Yes. Your husband had it put there. And I take flowers. But if it wasn't you, who was it?'

Julie set about making tea because Grace was still shaky. 'I think it must be my friend Rosie Summers. I left her looking after George.'

'Yes, I remember. And when the siren went you insisted on going home, even though I said you should go in the shelter. I assumed you'd arrived home only to be killed by a direct hit. I remember saying, at least you were with him at the end.'

'I wasn't.' Her hands were busy while she talked, making tea, fetching cups and saucers from the cupboard and a jug of milk which was standing on the cool floor of the larder, covered with a little cap of beaded gauze. 'An air-raid warden insisted on taking me to the Linsey Street shelter. It was jam-packed and I was stuck beside a pillar. It got a direct hit, but all I remember is being pulled out by the ARP and being taken to hospital.'

'I don't understand. Why didn't you come back? Why stay away? Harry was broken-hearted when he got back from Canada and found you already dead and buried. I met him once at the cemetery. He was standing looking down at the grave with a garden gnome in his hand. He didn't seem to know what to do with it.'

She would not allow herself to be deflected by imagining

279

Harry's grief or asking about the gnome. She could do that later. Now she had to concentrate on staying calm and telling her story as coherently as she could, which was difficult, considering how muddle-headed she was. 'I couldn't come back because I lost my memory. "Amnesia", they call it. I didn't know who I was or anything about myself. I was given a new identity.'

'You mean you couldn't even remember your own name?'

She put a cup of tea in front of Grace, poured one for herself and sat down opposite her. 'Strange as it may seem, that's exactly what happened. I forgot everything: my name, Harry, George, the Coram. It was all gone, except little snatches like you have when you first wake up from a dream and it's still with you. You don't know what's real and what's not.'

'But you do now.'

'I think so. You see, the same thing happened again, being bombed and being pulled out. I didn't know so much time had passed – I thought it was the same day and I was worried about leaving George with Rosie.'

'What have you been doing all this time?'

They sat sipping tea while Julie tried to remember enlisting and the different stations she had been on, the jobs she had had and the people she met. To start with her memory was hazy, but as she talked and corrected herself, it began to clear and with it came the realisation that her troubles were far from over.

'This Alec,' Grace said, after they had drunk three cups of tea each and consumed half a packet of digestive biscuits without even realising it. 'You agreed to marry him?'

'Yes.'

'You can't. You're married already.'

'I know.' It was said with a heavy sigh.

'You belong with your husband.'

'I know that too.'

'You do remember him?'

'Yes. I remember he was handsome, with dark auburn hair and soft brown eyes. He was virile and caring and so loving. He made a woman of me.' Even as she spoke she remembered another man who had had a hand in making a woman of her. She loved him too.

'You must go to him and you must tell this new man in your life the truth.'

Grace was only saying what Julie knew in her heart was right, but she knew both tasks were going to be very difficult. 'And there are others who will have to know – the Air Force, though whether they will discharge me when they've been told, or whether they will simply change the name on my records, I have no idea. And then there's Rosie's parents. You don't suppose they know the truth, do you?'

'I doubt it. They came to see me. Poor things were searching all over London for her. I felt sorry I couldn't tell them anything.'

'But if I was dead and buried when Harry came back from Canada, who arranged the funeral?'

'Mr Walker, your father-in-law.'

'He would surely have been asked to identify me. How can he have made such a mistake?'

'I don't know. Perhaps the body was too badly injured to tell. It happens, you know.'

'I know.' Julie shuddered. It was all getting too complicated. 'I could simply forget I had remembered and carry on being Eve Seaton.'

'And marry your Alec?'

'Well, no. That would be bigamy, wouldn't it?'

'It most certainly would.'

'He'll wonder why I've suddenly changed my mind. After being parachuted behind enemy lines and struggling to get back, it would be a cruel blow.'

'No more cruel than going through with a bigamous marriage. Not only cruel, but illegal.'

Julie fell silent. There was too much to think of and her head was aching abominably. She put her elbows on the table and her head in her hands, shutting her eyes.

'You're exhausted,' Grace said. 'I'll make a bed up for you. We'll talk some more tomorrow. Should you let your commanding officer know where you are?'

'Not tonight. I'm on leave.' She gave a grunt that passed for a laugh. 'At least, Eve Seaton is. I don't know about Julie Walker. If Eve Seaton disappeared, would anyone be able to find her, considering she never existed?'

'You're suffering from shock,' Grace said. 'I'm going to give you one of my sleeping pills, otherwise you'll be tossing and turning all night.'

Sleeping pills might stop her running off, Grace decided, because denying what had happened would help no one. It had to be sorted out. It was strange that one fictitious identity should be replaced by another, equally fictitious. No one had known who Julie Monday was either. Grace considered herself the nearest thing to a relative Julie had and she felt responsible for her. She wondered whether to try and contact Harry's parents herself while Julie slept, but decided that would be underhand, like ratting on her. All she could do was support the girl as well as she could and offer to go with her.

* * *

Finding someone who did not want to be found in a busy place like Southwark, right on the river with its shipping, warehouses and factories, was next to impossible, Florrie realised. She could not ask questions, simply because she did not know what questions to ask. All she had was a grainy snapshot of Eve taken on the farm on one leave. Showing that to anyone who cared to look at it produced nothing but a shaking head and a mumbled 'Sorry'. By evening, she realised she would have to give up for the time being. She telephoned Manston and spoke to Section Officer Murray. 'I don't want to give up yet and there's a day of my leave still to go, so I'll stay here tomorrow and go on with the search. Please don't post Sergeant Seaton AWOL. I'm sure she's not deliberately hiding.'

'Very well. An extra twenty-four hours and then you must return from your own leave and you can brief me about what's been going on.'

'Yes, ma'am. I'll do that.'

She found a boarding house advertising bed and breakfast and booked in there, but she had no sooner been shown to her room than the siren wailed. If it was a doodlebug, she had no time to find a shelter because the warning the authorities were able to give was so short. It was one of the reasons why the bombs struck so much terror. Night or day made no difference, except that during the day there were more people on the streets. As soon as one was spotted, everyone rushed for cover and flung themselves down, praying the engine would not stop. Florrie squeezed herself under the bed and covered her face with her arms. She had no sooner done so than the whole building shook and the windows rattled and pictures fell off the walls. And then the shaking stopped and there was silence. She emerged from under the bed just as her landlady called up the stairs. 'Are you all right, Sergeant?'

'Yes, I'm fine.' She went out onto the landing to see her hostess peering up the stairs. 'One of your pictures has been smashed.'

'Is that all? Pictures can be replaced. I'm making tea. Would you like a cup?'

'Yes, please.' Florrie went downstairs to join her. 'Where do you reckon it came down?'

'Can't say. It seemed to be over Bermondsey way. There's far too many of them and it's just not fair. We don't get enough warning.'

Florrie followed her to the kitchen. 'Is anything fair in war?'

'No, I suppose not, but at least in the Blitz we had time to take shelter. Sit down. I'll soon have the kettle boiled.'

Florrie watched her moving about the kitchen and wondered how she could be so calm. 'Were you here during the Blitz?'

'Yes. I lost a few windows and the door blew in once, but I was lucky, the house stayed up.'

'I'm looking for someone who lived round here in the early part of the war. I think she was bombed out, but I lost track of her. I've got a picture of her in my bag. I'll go and get it.'

She raced upstairs and came back with Julie's picture. 'You don't by any chance recognise her, do you?'

The woman studied the picture. 'No, can't say I do. You could go to the council offices and ask to see the casualty lists. They might help you.'

Florrie agreed that might be a good idea. She did not tell her hostess that she had no idea what name to ask for and reading lists of meaningless names would be a fruitless exercise. But Eve had become Eve while in hospital. 'Where would the wounded have been taken?'

'To one or other of the hospitals, probably St Olave's.'

Florrie thanked her and, having been given directions, went to St Olave's the following morning. The hospital was very busy; dozens of casualties were being admitted from the latest flying bomb attacks and the staff had no time for her. 'Try the Edward the Seventh in Windsor,' a nursing sister said as she hurried along the ward in the wake of a stretcher being carried to a bed. 'We used to send some of our casualties there.'

Florrie was coming to the conclusion she was on a wild goose chase. She had no idea what Eve was called before she met her, was not even sure Eve had correctly remembered the circumstances of being bombed out or if, remembering, she had deliberately concealed some of the facts. 'All I've got to go on,' she told the matron at the Edward the Seventh, 'is that she lost her memory and adopted the name of Eve Seaton. And I believe she had a broken leg and arm.'

'And what is your interest in the young lady, Sergeant?'

'She's a friend and she's gone missing. She could be in trouble if I don't find her.'

'I'm afraid it will mean trawling through hundreds of records and I really haven't time to do that for you, Sergeant.'

'I could do it.'

'Certainly not. Patient records are confidential. I'm afraid you will have to pursue your enquiries elsewhere, Sergeant.'

'There is nowhere else.'

'Then I'm sorry. Perhaps she'll turn up of her own accord.'

'If her memory came back suddenly, would she forget everything that had happened since she lost it?'

'Possibly. Maybe not. It depends.'

Realising she was getting nowhere, Florrie thanked her and left. It was time she returned to Manston or she would be in trouble too. What should she – what *could* she – tell Section Officer Murray? And there was Alec. Perhaps it was a good thing he was many miles away and unaware of what was going on. Of course, her guess could have been wrong and Eve's memory had not returned. In that case, where on earth had she got to? She found a call box and rang her mother. Eve had not arrived. 'If she turns up, ring me at Manston,' she told her. 'I've got to go back there now.'

Chapter Twelve

You couldn't get anyone to do a good day's work these days, Ted told himself. He had had the devil of a job to find a stonemason to make the memorial stone he wanted. True, he had asked for a carved cherub on each side and twining ivy, as well as the words, but that shouldn't have been beyond the capabilities of a good sculptor. 'There's a war on,' he had been told, which was everybody's excuse for not doing what they did not want to do. 'It'll take too long and we haven't got the staff now.' Money had talked in the end and the monument had been erected to his satisfaction. It looked a bit too large and a bit too white compared to the weather-beaten, lichen-covered stones surrounding it, but it was done now. He stood admiring it for several minutes, then turned to leave. He would go and see Josie and tell her to come and see it. He'd better take a few presents for the kids too; they seemed to expect it whenever he visited, which wasn't very often. He had no time for kids.

He stopped suddenly and skipped behind a gravestone. That Paterson woman was standing by the Walker grave and she was not alone. Standing beside her with head bowed was a living breathing Julie Monday. He had been right all along; it was not Julie in that grave but Rosie Summers. Where the devil had Julie been all these years? She was in a WAAF uniform. A sergeant too. What a turn up for the books! There was hay to be made from this, he felt sure, though it would need some thought.

'I remember that gnome,' Julie said. 'Harry bought it in Southend when we were on our honeymoon. It made me laugh. I said it was Happy, one of Snow White's dwarves, so he bought it and carried it home on the train and put it in the garden. He said it would be a reminder of how happy we were.'

She and Grace had talked and talked over supper the previous evening, during which Julie remembered more and more detail of what she had forgotten and Grace reminded her that Harry was her husband and as far as she knew was still alive and still in the air force. It had been Grace's idea to visit the grave. 'It might remind you of just how much you loved him and how much you owed to him,' she had said at breakfast that morning. Julie hadn't slept well; there was too much swimming round in her head and questions she couldn't answer.

'Harry stood it outside our Anderson shelter. Why did he bring it here, do you think?'

'He said it was to keep you smiling in heaven.'

'Oh.' She felt the tears well in her eyes and slowly run down her cheeks. She had loved Harry beyond everything, and he her, right from that first meeting on the beach when he had befriended a skinny little orphan from a charitable home. It was why he had chosen that same seaside resort for their honeymoon. Believing her dead, he had put the gnome on the grave and said his goodbyes. That must, in his eyes, have seemed final. He would have gone on with his life without her, might even have found someone else. Had she any right to upset him by suddenly reappearing? Should Julie Walker stay dead? Her head told her one thing, her heart another.

'Let's go,' she said suddenly, and turned away. 'I've got a lot of thinking to do and I must go back to Manston before I'm posted absent without leave.'

They returned to the flat in Shoreditch where Julie picked up her rucksack.

'You will do what is right, won't you, Julie?' Grace queried as she said goodbye. 'And let me know what happens. And if you ever need help, you know where to come.'

'Yes.' Julie smiled as she hefted the rucksack onto her back. 'I've always known that.' She kissed the old lady on the cheek. 'Look after yourself.'

'And you.'

'Do what is right' echoed in her mind as she walked down the street towards the Underground station. But what was right? Go back to being Julie Walker and cause mayhem to those whose lives had moved on, or stay Eve Seaton? But even if she did that, she couldn't marry Alec. Should he be told the whole truth or should she simply say she had changed her mind about marrying him? She could not do either until he came home on leave; it was not something you could put in a letter to a man risking his life on the battle front. And she wanted to see Harry again.

She was so immersed in her thoughts that it was some

time before she realised she was being followed. She quickened her pace, but so did her follower and he was gaining on her. She stopped and twisted round to find herself face to face with Ted Austen. He was grinning, his thin lips stretched over tobacco-stained teeth. 'Well, well, well,' he said. 'If it isn't my old friend Julie Monday. Or should I say Julie Walker? What do you call yourself nowadays?'

'What do you want?' He was the last person, the very last person, she wanted to see. He had always spelt trouble and his sudden appearance had her quaking.

'Me? Well that depends. There's a café just round the corner. Come and join me for a cup of tea. I might even stretch to a bun if you're good.'

'Why should I want to spend any time at all with you, Ted Austen, never mind join you for tea?'

'Because I could do a deal with you to our mutual advantage. And I'm curious about you. Did you deliberately walk out on your husband? What a clever ruse it was pretending to be dead.'

'I didn't pretend to be dead.'

'No? Harry thought you were. So did his family. They had a funeral for you and the nipper.' He took her rucksack from her. 'Come with me and I'll tell you all about it.'

She seemed to have lost her will to resist and allowed him to guide her into the café where he pushed her into a chair and called to the waitress to bring a pot of strong tea. It was not the sort of place to use cups and saucers, nor even tablecloths. The teapot was placed on the greasy oilcloth that covered the table. Two chipped enamel mugs were put beside it, together with a jug of milk, a bowl of sugar and a plate containing two plain buns. She ignored them.

'Now,' he said, pouring the tea, because she made no move to do so. 'Let's have a little chat.'

'There's nothing to chat about.'

'Oh, but there is. You disappeared for goodness knows how long and let your husband and all your friends think you were dead. You even had Rosie's grieving parents scouring London looking for her. That's not the action of a rational person.'

Rosie's parents scouring London? Grace had already told her that, but she had no idea Rosie had known Ted and it gave her a nasty jolt. She must be careful not to let him see that; he'd make sure to add to her discomfort if he did. 'It's none of your business.'

He ignored that. 'Am I to take it you now propose to reappear and shock everyone out of their wits? What can be the reason for that, I wonder?'

'It's still none of your business.' Her tone was flat. Her mind was struggling to come to terms with the dilemma that faced her. And this horrible man wasn't helping.

'I can make it my business. Now let me guess what happened. You left your baby with Rosie Summers so that you could go to your lover. And when she conveniently died in your place – owing me money incidentally – you decided to take advantage of that and disappear. Now your lover has ditched you and you are looking for a new protector. Who better than your husband—?'

'That's absolute nonsense.'

'Nonsense you had a lover or nonsense that you intend to go back to your husband?'

She stood up, unwilling to answer that and angry with herself for listening to him. 'I've had enough of this. I'm off.'

He grabbed her arm and pulled her down again. 'I could help you, you know. If you wanted to stay dead, that is. It might be the best all round, don't you think? People have moved on; they don't want to be confronted with a ghost. A little contribution and my lips are sealed. Besides, I never did get the money Rosie owed me.'

'Blackmail.' Her voice was as scornful as she could make it, given that she was nervous of what he could do. 'I might have known. If you think I'm going to give you money, then you can think again, Ted Austen. I've nothing to hide.' She picked up her rucksack from the floor where he had dropped it and made for the door.

'You might be sorry for that decision, Mrs Walker,' he called after her.

Anger kept her going as she hurried down the street to the Underground station and took the tube back to Waterloo, anger overcame her nervousness of the Underground. It was there, while waiting for the train to Manston, that she sat on a bench and let it go. It left her limp. Ted Austen was a nasty piece of work and there was no telling what he would do. Did he know where Harry was? She really should have turned the tables and taken the initiative to find out exactly what he did know and what use he intended to make of it. It was too late now.

'Eve Seaton, where the hell have you been?' Florrie flopped down on the bench beside her. 'I've been looking high and low for you.'

Julie turned to look at her friend and the enormity of what had happened struck her again. She couldn't find the words to explain. 'Wandering about,' she said.

'But you're going back to Manston now?'

'Yes. I don't want to be posted AWOL, do I?'

'Thank God.'

'What for?'

'That you remember me and where you've come from and that you know you have to go back.'

'Of course I do. Why shouldn't I?'

'You were on that train that got hit by a buzz bomb and disappeared afterwards.'

'How do you know that?'

'Section Officer Murray rang me at home. She thought you might have come to me. Why didn't you?'

'I wasn't thinking straight.'

'You bet you weren't. She said you had sustained a brain injury and needed to go to hospital.'

'There's nothing wrong with my brain. I wasn't hurt at all except for a few cuts and bruises. I just needed to think.'

'And I can guess why.' She stood up suddenly as a train steamed into the station. 'Here's our train. You can tell me all about it while we go along.'

Julie followed her friend onto the crowded train. They couldn't find a seat and had to stand in the corridor. It was not conducive to conversation, particularly the sort of conversation that Florrie expected. 'Just where have you been?' she demanded as soon as the train jerked into motion.

'To Southwark and Bermondsey, Shoreditch and Highgate Cemetery.'

'Looking for your past?'

'You could say that.'

'And did you find it?'

'Sort of.'

'What kind of an answer is that? Am I to assume from that your memory has come back?'

293

'Florrie, don't quiz me, please. I've got to sort this out on my own.'

'Then I was right, you have remembered and by the looks of you it isn't something to celebrate.'

'It's complicated.'

'OK, so it's complicated. But I hope you'll think about Alec while you decide what to do. He's out there fighting for us and his future with you. He loves you and deserves the whole truth.'

'I know that. You don't have to rub it in.'

'Sorry. I'm concerned, that's all. We've been friends for ages, you're like a sister to me. I was expecting you to become one officially when Alec came home. You do still love him, don't you?'

'Of course I do.'

'There's no one else?'

People were passing up and down the corridor, pushing past them and their rucksacks, and their conversation was punctuated with 'Excuse me' and 'Thank you'. After it happened the fourth time, Julie, glad of the excuse, said, 'We can't talk now. I'll tell you everything later.'

Florrie had to be content with that and they lapsed into silence which lasted for the remainder of the journey; neither could think of anything to say that did not hinge on Julie's dilemma. When they arrived back at camp, she was told to report to Section Officer Murray immediately and it was late that evening before she and Florrie were able to talk properly, which they chose to do by going for a walk. On a busy station it was the only way they could be sure of not being overheard.

'What did Murray say? Did you get a wigging?'

'No, why should I? I didn't overstay my leave.'

'No, but you did disappear when you should have gone to hospital.'

'So she said and I've got to report to St Hugh's in Oxford. Apparently they have a unit there specialising in brain injuries and psychological trauma. It's a complete waste of time – I know exactly what happened and how it happened.'

'Then I wish you'd tell me.'

'I will if you give me half a chance.' With double summer time it stayed light until nearly ten o'clock, but now daylight was just beginning to fade and the air was cooling. Julie stopped to gather her thoughts. 'I'd better begin at the beginning, when I was a little girl and went to the seaside for the day.'

'I don't need your life history.'

'It's relevant and please don't interrupt.'

'Very well. I won't say another word until you give me leave.'

They started walking again, turning to walk round Pegwell Bay between the golf course and the beach, while Julie talked. Once she had started the words tumbled out and Florrie listened in astonishment, but true to her word she did not interrupt until Julie finished. 'There you have it. I always suffered from claustrophobia. I had to summon all my courage to use the Underground. That, together with a bump on the head and being trapped in that air-raid shelter, took my memory. It came back when I was stuck in the wreckage of that train and I thought it was the same day.'

'Did you forget what had happened in between? About me and Alec and the air force?'

'For a little while, yes. I was terribly confused and began to doubt my sanity. I denied being Eve Seaton; the only thought in my head as I walked away from that carnage – it was awful, Florrie, truly awful – was finding my baby. I only really accepted what had happened when I got to Bermondsey and saw the house had gone and was told George had died . . .'

'My God, what a tale! What are you going to do?'

'I don't know.'

'I can't imagine what this will do to Alec. You'll have to find your husband and divorce him.'

'On what grounds? He didn't desert me – I left him, not voluntarily, but I did. I'm the guilty party and perhaps he won't want to divorce me. People look down their noses at anyone who's divorced, and I don't know what his parents will say.'

'You won't find out unless you ask him.'

'I'm not sure I can.'

'Eve!'

'I loved Harry, Florrie. He was everything to me, my childhood sweetheart, the father of my baby. I can't just pretend that never happened. When I see him again, who knows how I'll feel? Or how he'll feel?'

'Did you tell Murray all this?'

'Yes. In any case, she knew Eve Seaton was a made-up name, it's on my medical records.'

'So? Are you Julie Walker or Eve Seaton?'

'I'm Eve Seaton. It's the name I'm registered with and it's on all my documentation. Unless I do something official, like changing it back by deed poll, that's the way it stays.'

'There you are, then. Stay Eve Seaton.'

'That doesn't change the fact that I have a husband. The section officer is going to ask the station commander if he can find out where he is.'

'And then what?'

'I don't know. Murray insists on me going to Oxford, whether I like it or not, so whatever I do will have to wait until they let me go. I don't know what they can tell me I don't already know, so I don't suppose I'll be there long.'

'What a mess!'

'I know. Please don't say anything to Alec yet.'

'I'm not likely to do that while he's in the thick of the fighting, it could make him careless and cost him his life. But the minute he gets leave he'll be home, and you had better have it sorted out by then.' It sounded like a threat.

The artillery bombardment of Caen had been going on for days and the noise was deafening as shell after shell exploded on the city, which was being defended by Rommel's panzers and, according to rumour, they had been ordered to defend it to the last man. Alec began to wonder if anything would be left standing at the end of it. The city, one of the largest in Normandy, was of strategic importance to both sides, being a centre of communications, and until it was captured the Allied armies could not move forward. It was supposed to have been taken on D-Day itself, so they heard, but here they were in July and the Germans were still holding out. No one among the planners and strategists had realised it would take so long. According to the vociferous Trooper Langford, they should have been halfway to Paris by now.

Alec and his men had arrived back at their unit ten days after being parachuted in. Coming as they had from German-occupied country, they had been subjected to fierce rifle fire from their compatriots and had been obliged to dive for cover. After all they had been through, it seemed like the last straw.

'Hey, give over, you lot,' Langford had yelled at them. 'We're not bloody Jerries.'

'How do we know that?' a voice answered. 'Identify yourselves.'

'We will if you hold your fire,' Alec had shouted. 'We're coming out now.'

They got up gingerly and walked, with hands raised, down the road towards a group of British soldiers manning a roadblock, who pointed their rifles at them, looking as if they would not need much temptation to fire. Alec had convinced them who they were, aided by a string of expletives from Langford who took their cool reception as a personal slight.

'Where can I find Colonel Luard?' Alec had asked the corporal in charge when the rifles had been lowered and they had all shaken hands.

'As far as I know he's at the brickworks.'

'Where's that?'

'At Le Mesnil. It's on the outskirts of Caen.'

'Is that in our hands?'

'No, but not for want of trying. We've had three goes at taking it and each time had to withdraw.' He had pointed up the road and given him directions, ending, 'Be careful, there's still snipers about. They creep through the lines at night and shoot anything that moves in daylight.'

Le Mesnil was a small hamlet which housed kilns making roofing tiles, but it was known among the troops as 'the brickworks'. Here they found the survivors of their battalion ensconced. The colonel's greeting on seeing the exhausted band of paratroopers had been, 'Where the hell have you been, Sergeant?'

Alec had grinned and given an account of what had happened to them, and been questioned about enemy troops – where they were, and in what numbers – which he had answered as well as he could. It was from the colonel he learnt that General Montgomery had decided trying to take Caen was costing too many lives and it would be better to outflank it and occupy Villers-Bocage, a few miles to the south-west and in the line of the American advance from the Cherbourg Peninsula. They had been driven back by SS tanks. 'I've no doubt Caen will be on the cards again before long,' he was told. 'Get your heads down for an hour or two, then report for duty. You are going to be needed.'

His stick had rejoined the rest of the company, who were tired, disgruntled and frustrated at their lack of progress. The Germans were only on the other side of a field and everyone had to be vigilant, and every night the two sides sent mortar bombs into each other's positions, which kept everyone's heads down. One night was particularly severe. They were subjected to a devastating barrage of shells and mortars which began at eleven in the evening and went on for several hours. The casualties were horrendous and the stretcher parties braved the hail to bring them in and, after preliminary treatment at the Regimental Aid Post, they were sent by road to Ranville. It was the first time Alec had seen any real action, and watching friends and comrades being maimed or killed and knowing he could be next was a terrifying experience, shared by everyone, which they all felt deeply but kept hidden with silly jokes and grim determination. Next day they had been sent back behind the lines. Their relief in the shape of the 51st Highlanders had arrived and many thought they would be going home to England. After all, they were specialist troops and were not expected to stay with the invasion force.

In that they were disappointed. They hadn't gone home, simply to the banks of the Orne, but it gave them a little respite; they were able to sleep undisturbed at night, take a shower and go to the little cinema in Luc-sur-Mer, which had been taken over by ENSA and was where Charlie Chester entertained them with the Stars in Battledress. But best of all, Alec was able to write to Eve. He said nothing of the terrible scenes he had witnessed but tried to be optimistic about their future together. It was thinking of her, so sweet and clean, that kept him from dwelling on the horrors.

Their rest ended all too soon and they returned to Le Mesnil to more of the same.

Now the Allies were going to try once again to take Caen. The RAF had been bombing the town all night and the battleship *Rodney*, out in the Channel, had bombarded it with hundreds of sixteen-inch shells. The men knew that when the bombardment stopped they would have to move out of the shelter of their foxholes and bunkers and advance. The Germans knew it too and would be ready for them.

The guns suddenly stopped and there was an eerie silence, followed by a whistle and shouted commands. In a second Alec was up and running, dodging this way and that, his heart pumping as the heavy guns were replaced by small-arms fire. He was leading his men into the city itself. It had been devastated by Allied bombing and was in ruins. Rifles at the ready, they ran down what had once been a quiet residential street, dodging into doorways, taking shelter behind broken walls to return the fire of the defenders, before running on again. They had almost reached the River Orne, which dissected the town, and Alec was charging through someone's garden when he felt something hit his shoulder hard enough to knock him backwards. The attack continued over his inert body.

*   *   *

'You remember that oily little man we met in London when we were looking for Rosie?' Stuart Summers said to his wife. Her dark hair was streaked with grey and she was too thin, but she was looking a little more like her old self since they had stopped their fruitless search and agreed that Rosie must have died. The service in the kirk had helped her to come to terms with that. Now this. He wondered whether to keep it from her but decided she had to be told.

She dropped the newspaper she had been reading, pulled her glasses down to the end of her nose and looked at him over the top of them. 'What about him?'

'He's written to say he knows what happened to her.'

'Oh, what does he say? Let me see.' She held out her hand for the missive.

It was frustratingly short. 'You will be pleased to hear that I have continued my enquiries on your behalf and have discovered why your daughter disappeared. I remember you offered a reward for information, and as the search has been prolonged and cost me dear in time and money, I would appreciate recompense. A postal order for fifty pounds sent to the address at the top of this letter will find me more than willing to tell you all I know.'

'He's having us on,' he said when she returned it to him. 'He'll cash the postal order and disappear.'

'We don't know that,' she said. 'It might be genuine.'

'Only one way to find out and that's to go and see him and get the information out of him before we part with a penny. We'll go down this weekend.'

If Ted expected to have a postal order drop through his letter box by return of post, he was disappointed. After seeing Julie, it had taken him ten days of feverish searching

301

to find the calling card Stuart Summers had given him. He had turned the house upside down, gone through all the drawers and cupboards, even those he had not touched since moving in, but the card could not be found. Of all the possible plans of action, he had decided to try the Summers first as being the most likely to cough up. He didn't know where Harry Walker was and it might be difficult to find him without going through official channels, and what reason could he give for wanting to know? He could ask the man's parents, old man Walker could be contacted at the Chalfont factory in Letchworth, but they would also want to know why he wanted to know. He could tell them, but he didn't want to lose the comfort of the Walkers' Islington house, which he had come to look on as home. He got on well with the neighbours, who had been led to believe he was a hard-working businessman who was reluctantly not fit for active service. Contacting the Walkers might put that at risk.

If he told the Summers what had happened, they would undoubtedly chase Walker up themselves and that would put the cat among the pigeons. The trouble was he hadn't been able to find that damned calling card. It had turned up in the end, just when he'd given up, caught in the lining of the jacket he'd been wearing at the time. He was much too fussy to wear clothes that had seen better days and it had hung in the wardrobe unworn. What made him feel in the pocket he didn't know, but there it was, gone through into the lining. He had pulled it out with a yell of triumph and lost no time writing his letter. And still he was frustrated because they didn't answer it.

The reason became obvious the following Saturday when they arrived on the doorstep. He was taken aback at first, but swiftly recovered himself and invited them in. 'Sorry, I'm a bit untidy,' he said, leading them into the sitting room. There were stacks of books, papers and boxes all over the floor, where he had been searching for the card and not bothered to put everything away again. He swept his jacket off the sofa and invited them to sit. 'Tea? Coffee?' he queried. 'Or something stronger?'

'Nothing, thank you,' Angela said primly, though she did sit down. Her husband did not. He stood and faced Ted squarely.

'I think you know why we are here.'

'I assume it is in response to my letter. I thought you might be pleased to know the truth, even if it is not what you want to hear.'

'Spit it out.'

'You forget, sir, that I am a freelance and earn my money by helping people in any way I can. I am afraid I cannot work for nothing, not even in such a good cause. I was fond of Rosie too, you know.'

Stuart withdrew his wallet from the inside pocket of his jacket, but he did not open it. 'Information, Mr Austen, and then we will negotiate payment depending on what you tell us.'

'I'll do more than that, I'll show you, if you care to take a walk.'

'You mean she's living close by?' Angela said, unable to keep the excitement from her voice.

'Living close by? No, I can't say that,' he said, allowing himself a faint smile. 'Come, I'll show you.'

He took them to Highgate Cemetery and pointed to a grave. 'The answer's there.'

'I don't understand,' Angela said, looking down at the grave. It was not a new one, but it was well tended and there was a vase of flowers and a damaged garden gnome on it. The name wasn't Rosie's, though. 'What has Julie Walker to do with our daughter?'

'Rosie's in that grave,' Ted said. 'She and Julie were friends. Rosie was looking after Julie's baby and was in the shelter with him when the house was bombed. They died together. Everyone thought she was Julie.'

'How can such a thing have happened?' Stuart asked, disinclined to believe the man. 'Surely someone knew she wasn't Julie?'

'Undoubtedly they did, but it was convenient to keep mum about it.'

'Why?'

'Harry was away in Canada and while the cat's away the mice will play. Julie found herself another love and jumped at the chance to disappear. And the Walkers never took to her, so they let it ride.'

'That's too fantastic to believe,' Stuart said furiously. 'If you think I'm going to pay you good money for that so-called information, then you'll have to think again.'

Ted grinned. 'No doubt you require proof. Would a living breathing Julie Walker convince you?'

'You know where she is?'

'Not precisely at this moment, but I've seen her recently and confronted her so I know what I'm saying is true. I'll find her again and bring her to see you, shall I?' He already knew what she was calling herself; the name had been stencilled in the flap of her rucksack and he had managed to open it enough to read it when he took the bag from her at the café. He had followed her from there, more cautiously this time, and seen her speaking to another WAAF at Waterloo Station. He'd hopped on the train behind them and kept an eye on them all the way to Ramsgate. He had yet to confirm that she was stationed at Manston but he'd take an even bet that she was. Whether he passed on the information depended on what he could milk out of the Summers and what other opportunities presented themselves. It really wasn't the Summers he was after, but getting revenge for the humiliation he had endured at the hands of Harry Walker. He didn't care how he did it.

'You do that,' Stuart said. 'Not a penny will you get until you do.'

'I have expenses, Mr Summers. People who furnish me with information require payment.'

Stuart gave him a grim smile. 'As you do.'

'As I do,' Ted acknowledged. 'Money talks.'

Stuart extracted two five-pound notes from his wallet and handed them to Ted, who looked at the white sheets briefly as if to check they were what they purported to be, then crumpled them into his pocket. 'I will be in touch again, Mr Summers, and if I were you, I should begin to think what you want done about the situation. You can't leave your daughter in the wrong grave, can you?' And with that he turned on his heel and left them standing.

They watched him go, then turned back to look at the grave with its simple inscription. 'Do you think it's true?' she whispered. 'Is Rosie really there?'

'Who knows?'

'What are we going to do?'

'I'm not waiting for that scallywag to find Julie Walker, if he ever intends to. If she and the baby were buried while Harry Walker was away, someone must have identified the bodies and arranged the funeral, and my guess is that it was his father. We'll go and see him tomorrow, see what he has to say.'

* * *

Donald and Hilda were walking home from church where they had prayed for all those caught up in the war: for those in France battling it out for the liberation of Caen still holding out weeks after the invasion; for the troops in Italy, making their way northwards against stiff resistance, even though the Italians had changed sides; for those in the Far East fighting the Japanese; for those risking their lives on the high seas and in the air. They had prayed for civilians caught up in the latest attack on London by flying bombs. Here, in Letchworth, they felt comparatively safe, although one of the buzz bombs had reached Ashwell, the other side of Baldock, not many miles away. They were talking about it as they walked.

Approaching the garden gate of the semi-detached villa they were renting in Norton Road, they were surprised to see Mr and Mrs Summers standing on the step.

'We're sorry to intrude on your Sunday,' Stuart said. 'But we felt we had to see you.'

'Not at all. Do come in.' Donald unlocked the door and ushered them ahead of him. The smell of slow-roasting beef came to them from the kitchen. Hilda hurried off to check on it and put the kettle on to offer them a hot drink, while Donald took them into the sitting room and bade them be seated. 'Sherry?' he queried holding up a decanter. 'I've nothing else to offer you, I'm afraid.'

'A glass of sherry will be just fine,' Stuart said. His wife sat on the end of the sofa, trying to smile, but Donald could tell she was wound up like a spring, twisting her gloved hands together, touching her hair, then opening and closing the clasp on her handbag.

'Have you come all the way down from Scotland today?' he asked.

'No, we've been in London for a few days.'

'No news of your daughter, then? I'm sorry I couldn't help you.'

'Oh, but you have,' Stuart said. 'You put us in touch with Mr Austen and he has been doing some probing on our behalf and what he has discovered is astonishing.'

'Really?' He heard his wife call him from the kitchen and excused himself to go to her. She was basting the tiny joint of brisket. 'Ought we ask them to lunch?' she whispered. 'I was going to have this hot today and finish it up cold tomorrow, but I could stretch it to four. We'd have to have something else tomorrow.'

'I'll ask them. Put that back in the oven to finish off and come and join us for a sherry.'

She followed him back into the sitting room and took her place beside Angela. Donald poured and handed round the sherry. 'Not the best, I'm afraid,' he said. 'But it's drinkable. Just about. You were saying . . .' This prompt was addressed to Stuart.

'Mr Austen showed us your daughter-in-law's grave,' Stuart said.

'Only it isn't your daughter-in-law,' Angela cried out, twisting her handkerchief into a knot. 'It's our Rosie.'

Donald stared at her, then turned to Mr Summers who was the calmer of the two. 'Ted Austen said that?'

'Yes, he did. He said Julie had left her baby in the care of Rosie, and when the house got a direct hit, everyone thought Rosie was Julie.'

'But that's impossible!' Hilda said. 'Do you think we wouldn't know our own daughter-in-law and grandson? Tell them, Don.'

Donald squirmed. 'How sure is he of that?'

'Very sure,' Stuart said. 'He told us he had seen Julie recently and she was alive and well.'

Hilda gave a gasp and spilt her sherry all down her blouse. 'He's lying,' she said, ineffectually dabbing at it with a handkerchief. 'Excuse me. I must go and change.' She hurried from the room, leaving the others facing each other.

There was silence for a time, then Stuart said, 'Do you think the man is lying, Mr Walker?'

'I don't know.'

'But unlike your wife you are prepared to concede the possibility of a mistake. Austen said you knew it was Rosie in the coffin but you chose not to say so.'

'Rubbish. Why on earth would I do that?'

'According to him, because you never felt the girl was good enough for your son and it was a way of freeing him from her.'

'That's ridiculous nonsense.'

'But you did identify the body.'

'I looked at a mangled corpse, whose features were unrecognisable. She was the same build and colouring as Julie and she was cradling George in her arms, protecting him. Perhaps I should have looked more closely at the body and questioned the circumstances, but it never occurred to me that the baby would be with anyone else.'

Angela gave a huge intake of breath, then burst into tears. 'It *is* her,' she sobbed. 'It *is* our Rosie. The man wasn't lying.'

Hilda came back into the room in a fresh blouse and looked round at the little tableau. Mrs Summers was weeping uncontrollably, Mr Summers was trying to comfort her and looking grim and her husband seemed bewildered and embarrassed.

'It seems I might have made a mistake, Hilda,' he told her. 'I might have incorrectly identified Julie.'

'How could you? You told me, told Harry too, that there wasn't a mark on her and she looked peaceful.'

'I lied to spare you both,' he said quietly.

She collapsed into the nearest chair and stared up at him. 'Then what happened to Julie?'

'According to Austen, she's alive,' Stuart put in. 'He said he'd seen her.'

'Oh, my God, what's Harry going to say about this?' Hilda asked. 'We can't tell him, we simply *can't*. There's Pam—' She stopped suddenly.

'My son has married again,' Donald told his visitors. 'They have twins, a boy and a girl.'

'Pam's a lovely girl too,' Hilda put in. 'We are all very fond of her, and the babies are adorable. I wish you had never come here. You should have left well alone.'

'And left our daughter in the wrong grave?' Angela exclaimed. 'No, I don't think so, Mrs Walker.'

'You're not thinking of having her exhumed?' Hilda was rapidly becoming as distraught as Angela. 'Our grandson is in that grave too. We can't allow it.'

'We will have to see what your son says about it,' Stuart put in. 'It affects him more than anyone.'

'I think we need to meet the person claiming to be Julie before we do anything,' Donald said. 'Certainly before we say anything to Harry. Does anyone know where she is?'

'Ted Austen said he'd find her for us.'

'And if she isn't Julie?'

'Then we will just have to accept that our daughter is still missing,' Stuart said.

'Oh my, the beef!' Hilda dashed from the room in the

direction of the kitchen, just in time to rescue the joint from becoming uneatable.

It seemed to be the signal for Mr and Mrs Summers to leave. They both stood up.

'Will you stay and have a bite of lunch with us?' Donald asked.

'No, thank you.' Stuart spoke for both of them. 'We'll go straight back to London to see Austen again. If we have anything to report, we'll come back to you.'

'Very well. You can contact me by telephone at the factory. We don't have one here.' He found a piece of paper and a pencil in the writing desk in the alcove of the fireplace and scribbled down the number. 'We'll say nothing to Harry in the meantime. No sense in upsetting him for nothing.'

He saw them to the door, then went to the kitchen where Hilda was putting some cabbage on to cook while she made the gravy. 'They've gone,' he said. 'They didn't want to stay for lunch.'

'Good. I'm glad. Quite apart from the fact that the joint has shrunk to almost nothing and the potatoes are a bit too crisp to offer guests, I wouldn't have known what to say to them. They're obviously deranged, particularly Mrs Summers. I'm sorry for them but that doesn't alter the fact that what they've been saying is too far-fetched to be true.' She looked up at her husband who was looking doubtful. 'It is, isn't it?'

'I don't know. It could be. If I made a mistake . . .'

'Don!'

'Well, it's possible.'

'Don't you dare say a word to Harry.'

'Of course not. We'll wait until we have proof.'

Chapter Thirteen

It cost Ted a box of chocolates, two pairs of nylons, a bottle of Evening in Paris and an evening at the cinema to find out where Julie was. The young WAAF at Manston had been up for a bit of fun too, so he hadn't rushed off when he had the information he needed. There was no hurry. Eve Seaton had been sent to hospital in Oxfordshire. 'She's not right in the head,' the girl had said, as they walked back to camp from Ramsgate in the dark. 'I heard she got caught in a buzz bomb raid and now she thinks she's someone else. Queen of Sheba, I shouldn't wonder.'

'What will happen to her?'

'I dunno, do I? Either she'll be discharged as unfit for service or she'll get well and come back here. Why are you interested in her anyway?'

'She's a childhood friend I lost touch with during the Blitz.'

'Oh, so you're making use of me to find a lost love.'

'No, it's not like that at all. I promised her family I'd

find her. She hasn't written home in ages. But they can wait, I'd much rather be with you.' He demonstrated that by drawing her into an empty air-raid shelter and getting inside her bloomers.

He'd seen her once more after that, but as the money Summers had given him had run out, he had stood her up and gone back to London. Julie was, for the moment, out of reach, but there was more than one way to skin a cat.

St Hugh's was an all-female college which had been taken over by the War Office as a military hospital, and its lovely lawns had been covered with brick huts used for wards. Sitting up in bed being subjected to innumerable interrogations and test after test was more than frustrating, especially when all Julie had on her mind was finding Harry. Traumatic amnesia was not uncommon, she was told, especially in wartime, but it didn't usually last so long. The doctors and specialists who came to see her were intrigued and questioned her over and over again. She wondered if they were trying to make her slip up so they could reveal her as a fraud. All that did was make her angry. 'I did have glimpses of the past,' she told them over and over again. 'But I couldn't hold onto them. They were just pictures in my brain.'

'What kind of pictures?'

So she went through it all again: a beach and the sea, a long shiny corridor, children playing in a garden, the demonstration of the bouncing bomb she had seen at the cinema, odd words that resonated.

'But you say you only had one child.'

'I think the children were my charges when I was in service before I married, or maybe children from the Coram home. I often used to look after the younger ones.'

'They were important to you?'

'Yes. I love children. I was overjoyed when I had one of my own.'

'Were you always claustrophobic?'

'Yes. I think it was because I was shut in a cupboard as a punishment when I was in the orphanage.'

'But you happily travel on the Underground.'

'Not happily. I have to grit my teeth every time I do it and I'm always glad to get above ground again. And I hated the Anderson shelter.'

'So you let someone else take your child to the shelter.'

'It wasn't like that. I've told you.'

'Tell us again.' It went on and on until, in desperation, she said, 'When are you going to let me go? There's nothing wrong with me and you have other people who need your help far more than I do.' They were bringing casualties back from Normandy in increasing numbers. Julie saw them arriving, some of them in a very bad way and it set her thinking of Alec. A letter from him had been forwarded to her soon after her arrival at the hospital. It had been written shortly after his return to his unit.

'Sorry, if I worried you,' he had written. 'I had a few adventures, but I'm back with my unit where I belong. At least for the time being. Where I really belong is in your arms, and the minute I get leave, I shall be home to claim them. I think we should be married straight away. I don't think this scrap is going to be over quickly, so there's no sense in waiting. Florrie and Matt were right to say you should grab your happiness while you can. Do you agree? The war will be over one day, and pray God that won't be too long, then we can settle down and bring our children* *up in peace. I know we will be happy together because there can never be anyone else for me but you.'*

There was more of a loving nature, but it only added to her dilemma. What would he say when he learnt she already had a husband, one she had promised to love, honour and obey until death parted them? Was it possible to love two men at the same time? She would not know the answer to that unless she came face to face with Harry again. 'Let me go,' she pleaded.

In the end one of them said he would write a paper on her case for *The Lancet* and might need to speak to her again, to which she replied, 'You know where to find me. I'm not going to run away.'

Two weeks after her arrival there, they gave her a travel warrant back to Manston and let her go. She hoped SO Murray had discovered where Harry was and was prepared to give her leave to go to him. Telling him she was alive when he thought her dead was not something she could put into a letter.

Alec arrived back at Brize Norton and was transferred to St Hugh's the day after Julie left. He had been picked up off the Caen street by stretcher-bearers braving a hail of bullets to do so and been carried to safety, then given a very bumpy ambulance ride back to the regimental aid post in the brickfields. He hadn't at first noticed any pain, but that ride along a road potholed by shellfire set his body on fire and he had to bite his lip to stop himself crying out. Even so, he couldn't prevent a moan or two escaping when the vehicle jolted into a particularly deep hole. At the forward aid post they gave him morphine, dressed his wound and sent him on again to Ranville. At the field hospital there they dug a lump of shrapnel out of his shoulder under anaesthetic, and a few days later he was shipped back to England, his war over for the time being.

He was unsure whether to be glad or sorry. He had been pulled out of the battle and spared the rest of the carnage, but he had left his men behind, left them to fight on. He wanted to be with them, to live or die alongside them, to be in at the kill when the enemy was finally defeated. But perhaps he would be; the battalion was due to be relieved and brought back to train for the next phase of the war and he might make a full recovery and rejoin them then. If they all survived. They had managed it so far, but how long before their luck ran out? He felt as if he had deserted them.

On the other hand, he was in England and that meant seeing Eve and his family and being able to sleep and eat from a plate instead of a mess tin, and then sleeping some more. He remembered asking if anyone had informed his family where he was before drifting off again. The answer must have been yes, because his mother arrived one afternoon to see him.

She brought him grapes off the vine that grew in the greenhouse on the farm garden. Fat and juicy, they brought home to him that there was life away from the noise and stench of battle and that life was waiting for him at the end of the conflict, a life to look forward to.

'How are you, Ma?' he asked, studying her face. She looked worn, there were dark rings round her eyes and her hair seemed greyer than he remembered, yet it had only been a couple of months since he had last been home on leave.

'I'm fine. How are you?'

'Coming along nicely. It's not a bad wound but it's damaged the muscle, so I'm going to need physiotherapy

315

when it's healed. It could have been much worse.'

'Yes, you could have been killed and I thank God you were not. When they told us you were missing believed killed it was terrible. We didn't know whether to hope or not. Of course, we kept telling each other you would turn up, but sometimes we got very low. We couldn't see how you could survive being shot down over the sea.'

'Shot down over the sea? Is that what they told you?'

'Yes, the plane you were in didn't make it back. We thought it had gone down on the outward journey, not the return.'

'Poor you. I'm sorry you were so worried.'

'Florrie took it badly and so did Eve.'

'Have you seen Eve?'

'Not recently. She was coming to see us but something happened . . .' She stopped, wondering how much to tell him.

'What happened?' When she did not immediately answer, he added, 'Come on, Ma, out with it.'

'She was on a train that got hit by a doodlebug . . .'

He caught his breath in shock. 'She's not . . . not dead?'

'No, she's not dead, she wasn't even hurt. She just disappeared. Florrie said . . .' Again she paused.

'What?' He pulled himself into a sitting position, ignoring the stab of pain the movement caused. 'Why are you so reluctant to tell me?'

'Because Eve ought to tell you herself, not me. In any case I don't know all the details.'

'But you'll tell me all you know, even if I have to wring it out of you. Come on, Ma, don't leave me hanging like this.'

Maggie took a deep breath and launched into a garbled account of what had happened, ending, 'She was in hospital here for a couple of weeks, then they sent her back to Manston . . .'

'Is she there now?'

'I don't know. Florrie seemed to think they would give her leave to sort things out, but I've no idea if they did. We didn't want to say anything to you while you were fighting in France in case it upset you.'

He fell back against the pillows. 'Damn this shoulder! Damn this bloody war!'

'Alec, language!'

He smiled wryly. It was typical of his mother to tick him off about his language in the middle of a conversation that had the power to ruin his life. 'I've got to get out of here, got to find her. I can't let her go—'

She put a hand over his. 'Calm down, son; you can't do anything until you've recovered and you won't do that getting all het up. I'm sure Eve will sort things out herself. Florrie said she would, but it might take time. You must be patient and concentrate on getting better.'

A bell signalled the end of visiting hours and she stood up to leave. 'I'll come again when I can. Maybe your dad will come with me.' She bent to kiss his cheek. 'When you're well they'll let you come home to convalesce, I'm sure.'

He was not as sure as she was and watched her walk down the ward and disappear through the door. The language he used when she could no longer hear him would have shocked her to the core. He tried to get out of bed and had almost succeeded when a nurse saw what he was up to and stopped him. 'Come, Sergeant, back into bed with you. If you need anything fetched, I'll fetch it.'

But she couldn't fetch Eve, could she?

* * *

317

'According to Mr Austen, Julie Walker is a sergeant in the WAAFs stationed in Kent. He went to speak to her, and though he confirmed she was based there, he did not see her because she is in hospital being treated for injuries she received in a doodlebug raid. He says he'll go back when she returns to the station and will bring her to us. He wants more money.'

'We're not going to wait for him, are we?' she said. 'We've got to go down and confront this woman, whoever she is, and settle this thing once and for all.'

'How can we if she isn't prepared to admit it?' he said. 'We've never met her. Besides, they probably won't let us see her in a military hospital.'

'Then we'll get Donald Walker to come with us. It's all his fault anyway. You'd think he'd know his own daughter-in-law, wouldn't you? I'm beginning to think that dreadful Austen man was right and he deliberately said it was her when he knew perfectly well it was not.'

'Angie, that's unfair,' he said. 'You heard what he said when we talked to him about it. The features were unrecognisable, and if she was the same colouring and build as our Rosie, it's understandable.'

'Well, are we going down or not?' she demanded.

He sighed. She had become bitter and short-tempered since that last meeting with Ted Austen. He wished the horrible man had never reappeared. She had been so much better since she had come to accept that Rosie was dead, and this didn't make their daughter any more or any less dead. It would be better to let matters rest. Unfortunately, it was not her way, and he knew he would have to take her down to London yet again, doodlebugs or no doodlebugs. 'I'll write to Mr Walker and ask him to suggest somewhere for us to meet,' he said. 'We don't need to involve Mr Austen.'

Unfortunately Ted could not be excluded, because the meeting place Donald Walker suggested was his home in Islington.

The minute he unlocked the door and stepped inside Donald knew that someone had been squatting there. Afraid he might still be in the house, he made Hilda wait outside while he searched all the rooms. He was furious when he saw the state of the sitting room: there was an unwashed glass mug making a ring on the polished table, a dirty plate on the floor and scattered newspapers over the sofa. He was even angrier when he saw his unmade bed and a wardrobe full of strange clothes, but there was no one there. He went back to Hilda. 'Whoever it was, they're not here now. We'll have to report it to the police.'

As he spoke, Ted came whistling up the path. He came to an abrupt halt and the whistle died on his lips when he saw his one-time employer. 'Mr Walker,' he said, recovering himself quickly. 'Why didn't you let me know you were coming, I'd have made sure the house was aired.'

'It's aired all right,' Donald said grimly. 'I thought you were supposed to be keeping an eye on the place. Someone's been in and made themselves at home.'

'Really? But I was here a few days ago and I didn't see anyone. It must be a tramp, or perhaps someone who's been bombed out. They do that sometimes when they're desperate. I'll sort him out, never fear.'

'You can start by gathering up all that stuff in the bedroom and throwing it out. Better still, take it to the WVS, they can no doubt make use of it.' He turned to his wife. 'Come, Hilda, we'd better clear up the mess in the sitting room before the Summers get here.'

'Did you say the Summers?' Ted put in. 'You mean Mr and Mrs Summers, Rosie's parents?'

'Yes. You'd better stick around, considering you seem to know more about Julie than any of us.'

Ted followed them into the sitting room, had a quick look round to see if there was anything that could identify him as the intruder, and then hastened to the bedroom to gather his clothes and toiletries into a couple of suitcases. He took them down and stood them in the hall before rejoining Donald and his wife in the sitting room. He would put them back after everyone had gone. 'Would you like me to make you both a cup of tea?' he asked. 'I'm sure you could do with it.'

'Is there anything to make tea with?' Hilda asked.

Ted knew he had slipped up but as usual he quickly recovered. 'If someone's been squatting here, ten to one they brought tea and milk with them,' he said. 'I'll go and look, shall I?'

While he was in the kitchen, Mr and Mrs Summers arrived and the conference began with Ted serving tea. It was perfectly clear to all of them that there was a difference of opinion about what should be done. Donald and Hilda wanted everything left as it was. 'If I see Julie, and I'm yet to be convinced it is Julie,' Donald said, 'I'll tell her to take herself off and stay dead. Harry can do without the upheaval in his life. He's happy with Pam and they have two beautiful children. I reckon we should leave well alone.'

Stuart was inclined to agree with him, but not so Angela. 'We can't leave our daughter in a grave with the wrong name on it,' she said. 'I want her exhumed and buried again in our own kirkyard.'

'And what about our grandson?' Hilda snapped. 'What you are proposing will mean digging him up too. It will break Harry's heart.'

'You are assuming it *is* your daughter in that grave,' Donald said. 'We only have Mr Austen's word for it.'

They all looked at Ted, who was standing with the teapot poised over Hilda's cup. 'I am ninety-nine per cent sure,' he said, carefully pouring tea. 'I know it isn't Julie because I've seen her recently.'

'It's a pity you didn't keep that information to yourself,' Donald said.

'I couldn't do that,' Ted defended himself. 'Not with Mr and Mrs Summers searching all over for their daughter and asking me to keep an eye out for her. It was my bounden duty to tell what I knew.'

'Not to mention seeing a way to make money,' Stuart put in.

'I haven't made any money out if it.' Ted pretended to be aggrieved. 'If anything, it has *cost* me money, what with travel and board and lodging down in Kent and having to pay other people for information. I am well out of pocket.'

'That's as maybe,' Donald said. 'We can't decide on anything until we've spoken to Julie. So where is she?'

'In hospital in Oxford,' Ted said. 'When she's discharged, she'll have to report back to Manston. I've got someone there who'll tell me when she arrives and I'll bring her to you.' He wished he hadn't been so offhand with that WAAF at Manston. He needed to know when Julie returned from hospital so he could take her to her husband and watch them tearing each other apart. And if she wouldn't come

321

willingly, he'd kidnap her. The idea of that appealed to him. 'If she'll come.'

'Oh, I have ways of persuading her.'

'Then what?' Hilda demanded.

'If she confirms that it is Rosie in that grave, then we can't put off telling Harry,' Donald said. 'And then there's Pam. How's she going to take it? I think we should warn Mr and Mrs Godwin so they can break the news to her when the time comes.'

'Who are Mr and Mrs Godwin?' Angela asked.

'Pam's parents. They live at Swanton Morley in Norfolk. Our son was stationed there until recently.'

'Then that's where we'll go,' Angela said. 'We can see them all together.'

'Flight Lieutenant, there is someone to see you,' the station commander told Harry. 'I've put her in my office, you can talk to her there.'

Harry had settled down at Cosford, living in barracks, working with new intakes and enjoying pandering to their youthful enthusiasm, but he missed Pam and the children more than he could say. He wrote every day and had loving letters in return, some with small smudged fingermarks or crayon squiggles, purporting to come from the twins, which made him smile and long to hug them both. They had talked of Pam bringing them up to Cosford on a visit, but he had been so tied up with work, nothing had, as yet, been arranged. Had she decided to pre-empt him and come up to surprise him? His face wore a broad smile as he hurried from the outer office where he had been talking to the group captain and went into the inner sanctum.

But it was not Pam who stood with her back to him

looking out of the window, it was someone in a WAAF uniform with a sergeant's stripes on her arm. She turned when she heard the door open and he was confronted with the ghost he had seen at Canterbury Hospital. Except this time he knew she was not a ghost. This was Julie. This was the girl he had loved and married and mourned. He stared, his mouth half open, unable to frame the hundreds of questions that battered his brain.

The silence between them went on and on until at last she spoke. 'Hallo, Harry.' It was her voice too, soft and appealing, just as he remembered it.

'Julie.' It was a croak. 'I thought . . . I thought—'

'You thought I was dead, yes I know. I've seen my own grave.' She gave a cracked laugh. 'How many people can say that, I wonder? "In memory of a beloved wife, Julie Walker, and son, George Harold, twenty-one months, who died as a result of an air raid, September the 7th 1940. May they rest in peace until we meet again in heaven."' The laughter stopped as she stumbled over the words.

'Oh, my God, Julie!' He opened his arms.

She ran into them.

He pulled her close, smelt the once familiar scent of her hair, felt the heart of her thumping under her uniform jacket and all his old feelings for her rushed back. This was his Julie, his childhood sweetheart, whom he had loved. 'I can't believe it's you.'

'It is. I was afraid you might have forgotten me.'

'I couldn't forget you, Julie. We meant too much to each other for that ever to happen.' There was an old horsehair sofa against the wall, which the CO used when he had to stay on call overnight, and he pulled her down onto that to sit beside him, keeping his arm about her shoulders, as if holding her helped him to believe she was real. 'Tell me what happened. Why did you let me believe you were dead? That was a cruel thing to do, Julie.'

'I didn't let you believe anything, Harry. I couldn't tell you where I was because I'd been injured in an air raid and lost my memory. I didn't know who I was or anything about myself.'

'It's hard to believe.'

'I'm not lying, Harry.'

'No, of course not. I meant I find it hard to believe you're alive,' he said, shaking his head as if to shake his tumbling thoughts into some sort of order. 'We buried you. At least we buried someone, or rather my parents did. Dad said there wasn't a mark on you. He must have known . . .'

'I don't know about that. Perhaps he was trying to spare you. I was pulled out of the shelter alive, but I had a broken leg and a broken arm and my face was a mess. It was ages before I could look at myself in the mirror and not shudder.'

'And George?'

'I'm sure George is in the grave, alongside my friend, Rosie. You remember Rosie Summers, don't you?'

'I remember you speaking of her but I never met her. Her parents were looking for her. They went to Dad and he contacted me, but I couldn't tell them anything. I never dreamt . . . I still can't take it in.'

'I can understand that, I had problems believing it myself, but if you listen a minute, I'll tell you the whole story.'

It took some time to tell, especially as he kept interrupting, and once someone came into the room, apologised, and made a quick exit, but she got it out in the end. She said nothing about Alec; it didn't seem appropriate. 'Grace Paterson took me to see the grave,' she finished, 'otherwise I might have thought I was having a nightmare and would wake up and find everything as it was before the war started.'

'It can't be like that again.'

'I know.'

'How did you find me?'

'It was easy enough. My section officer made enquiries through the RAF and gave me a week's leave to come and see you.'

'God, this has taken the wind out of my sails.'

'I expect it'll take a little while to get used to the idea.'

'You can say that again.' He was silent a moment or two, trying to digest all she had said. 'I could talk to you the rest of the day, but I think the Group wants his office back and I've got to go back on duty, but I'll be off tonight. Have you got somewhere to stay?'

'I've booked into the Park House Hotel.'

'Shall I come and see you there? Talk some more?'

'Yes. No doubt you've lots to tell me. And to tell you the truth, I'm exhausted.'

They rose together and he accompanied her to the outer office, where he arranged for a taxi to come and take her back to her hotel. They had little to say while they waited for it to arrive. Harry's head was still full of questions but there were other people working in the office and he couldn't voice them. He was glad when the cab arrived. He saw her into it, bent to kiss her briefly, and watched as she was driven away, then he took a huge breath and turned to go back to the workshop where he had been taking a class when summoned to the office. He had been gone a long time and the men had dispersed. He sat at one of the benches, cluttered with earphones and wireless parts, and tried to sort out what Julie's reappearance really meant to him.

It was not an easy task. She was sturdier and more mature than the half-grown woman he had married – he supposed that was down to being in the services; in wartime you grew up quickly – but underneath she was still Julie, still the lovely girl he had married, still vulnerable, for all her sergeant's stripes. God help him, still his wife. The fact that he was a bigamist suddenly struck him and he put his head into his hands and groaned. 'Pam, oh Pam, what have I done to you?'

The note was short. It was put together with words cut from a newspaper and stuck on a sheet of white paper. 'Your husband is a bigamist.' Pam dismissed it as the work of a crank, but she couldn't get it out of her head. All day, while she went about her usual chores, bathing and dressing the twins, giving them their breakfast and putting them in the garden in their pram to enjoy the sunshine, washing and ironing their little garments and cleaning the house, she worried about it. Of course it couldn't be true. Harry was a widower, everyone knew that. But then she remembered him telling her he thought he had seen Julie's ghost. It couldn't have been Julie, could it? Julie was dead and buried. But supposing she was alive after all? No, that couldn't be. She had a grave with a headstone. But Harry had never seen her dead. Could his family have made a mistake? But why wait until now to come back to life? Perhaps whoever had sent that nasty missive had seen the woman Harry had called a ghost and jumped to the wrong conclusion. Or had it been sent by Julie herself to cause trouble?

It all went round and round in her head, from sheer disbelief to doubting and then to thinking it might be true, until she thought it would drive her mad. Harry had loved Julie and made no secret of it. She remembered telling him a dead woman could not harm her. But was she dead? Would Harry abandon his new family for an old love? Jealousy swept through her and made her irritable. She took the rag rug from the kitchen hearth, flung it over the clothes line and thumped it with a cane carpet beater until her arm ached.

'Pam, whatever's the matter?' Her mother's voice penetrated the red heat of her anger. 'You'll knock that rug to bits – it can't be that grubby.'

Pam dropped the carpet beater and burst into tears. The astonished Jane took her into her arms and let her sob for a few moments, then led her indoors and sat her at the kitchen table. 'Now what's this all about? Is it Harry?'

Pam nodded without speaking.

'Oh, my God. And we thought he'd be safe at Cosford away from the action.'

'He's not dead,' Pam cried. 'He's not dead.'

'What, then?'

Pam bent and picked the screwed-up letter out of the log basket where she had hurled it and handed it to her mother.

Jane smoothed it out to read it. 'Good Lord, where did this come from?'

'It was in this morning's post.'

'It can't be true. His first wife's dead and buried. It's someone with a grudge trying to cause trouble.'

'Who?'

'I don't know.' She paused and searched her daughter's tear-streaked face. 'You surely don't believe it?'

'I wouldn't, except that a few weeks ago Harry said he thought he'd seen a ghost, someone the spitting image of Julie. It shook him up so much he had to go to see her grave to convince himself she was dead.'

'Everyone has a double, they say.'

'Yes, I'm being silly.'

'Tell you what, I'll look after the twins; you take yourself off to Cosford and see Harry, set your mind at rest.'

'Do you think I should?'

'Why not? Give him a nice surprise.'

Pam managed a lopsided smile. 'Or a dreadful shock.'

'You married again?' Julie queried, wondering why that surprised her. After all, she had been telling herself ever since her memory returned that he might have found someone else, had even wondered if she might welcome it, considering she had found Alec. Instead it hit her like a blow to the stomach. The sight of him in the station commander's office, tall and handsome in his uniform, just as he had been when she waved him goodbye at the door when he went to Canada, had flung her back to that day and how miserable she had felt then, and she had run into his arms. She hadn't intended to do that; her plan had been to remain cool and practical, to discover how he felt about her sudden appearance. Instead she had been overcome with emotion.

She changed into a civilian frock to meet him again that evening, a printed floral cotton with white collar and cuffs and a white belt, and brushed her fair hair out of the severe style she wore in uniform. Then she had ordered a meal and a bottle of wine to be served in her room. 'I'm on leave and spending precious time with my husband,' she had told the proprietor.

He grinned. 'I understand. Seven o'clock do you?'

'Yes, perfectly. Will you send him up when he arrives?'

She had returned to her room to wait for him with growing trepidation. Their earlier meeting had been unsatisfactory in so many ways. The surroundings had hardly been conducive to loving reunions and he had been too shocked to take in everything she said or to talk about himself. She had known she would have to repeat it all when he arrived, which is exactly what had happened, and this time he had many more questions for her. While they ate and drank the wine, she told him everything all over again, and it was not until after they had finished and sat over the remnants of the meal, drinking the last of the wine, that she began to question him about himself. It was then he told her he had remarried.

'Yes. I met her when I was stationed at Swanton Morley. We hit it off right from the start. You were gone and I was lonely and needed someone to keep me going, someone to come back to after an op. We married in March 1943 and have two children, twins, a boy and a girl.' It sounded flat said like that, but he couldn't tell her how he had fallen in love with Pam, how she was a steadying influence when he felt like going off half-cocked, how they laughed at the same things, how good they were together in bed, how much he adored the twins, who were fast-developing characters of their own and whose wide grins when they saw him coming made his spirits soar. He couldn't say any of that.

'But you can't be married to her, can you? You're still married to me.'

'I know that now. I didn't at the time.'

'What are you going to do about it?'

'I can't leave her, Julie, if that's what you think. She's the mother of my children.'

'Do you love her?'

'Of course I love her. I wouldn't have married her if I didn't.'

'But you loved me. You said you did, and I adored you, right from the beginning when we met on the beach. Do you remember saying we were fated to meet again when you rescued me from Ted Austen?'

'Of course I do. I remember everything about our life together – your funny little ways, how you learnt to cook and how well you looked after George, which is why I find it difficult to understand why you left him with your friend that day.'

'It was one of the things I found hard to understand myself when my memory came back, but Grace reminded me. I owed her some money and I needed to pay it back. I knew you wouldn't like me getting into debt.'

'So you went to see Miss Paterson in the middle of an air raid and left our son to be looked after by someone you hardly knew because you were afraid I would be cross with you.'

Stated baldly like that, it didn't sound like the actions of a loving mother and she hastened to explain. 'The raid hadn't started when I left, and it was such a hot day I didn't want to drag him across London with me.'

'Why did you owe Miss Paterson money?'

'I borrowed some from her to pay Rosie. Rosie had been providing me with stuff that was hard to get: extra rations, bits and pieces for George.'

'Black market.'

'Yes, I suppose it was. I didn't think of it like that. It was simply stuff I needed for George.'

'And you couldn't pay for it. Oh, Julie, we talked about how you could manage your housekeeping before I went away, remember?'

'Yes, and I tried, I really did, but having a few extras was so tempting and Rosie didn't charge much, not at first.'

'That's how those things usually start, and then it grows from there. You get into someone's clutches and you can't get out of them. Where was Rosie getting the stuff?'

'I think it was from Ted Austen.'

'That creep who tried to rape you?' he asked in astonishment.

'Yes. I didn't know it was him. I didn't even know he knew Rosie, not until I saw him again just over a fortnight ago, and then the penny dropped. I would have stopped it sooner if I had known.'

'How did that come about? Seeing him again, I mean.'

The meeting wasn't going at all as she had expected it to. Instead of talking about how they felt for each other, their joy at being together again, he was quizzing her about Ted Austen. 'He saw me when I visited the cemetery. He seemed to get a great deal of pleasure out of it. He tried to blackmail me – said if I didn't want you to know I was alive, he'd keep mum for a consideration.'

'So you decided it would be better to come clean?'

'No, Harry, that's not fair. I wanted to see you again, it was the first thing I thought of when my memory came back, after worrying about leaving George. He got hold of the wrong end of the stick there. Why are we talking about him? He's a reptile and I loathe him.'

'Where did you get the money to pay Miss Paterson back?'

'I pawned my wedding ring. I was going to redeem it, truly I was, but I didn't get the chance.'

'I've been wondering about that,' he said looking down at her bare fingers.

'When I came round in the hospital after they pulled me out of the shelter, I couldn't remember being married, and as I wasn't wearing a ring everyone assumed I was single. I was given the surname Seaton and chose Eve for a Christian name and was issued with a new identity card and ration book in that name. I had nowhere to go when I came out of hospital and took a job in Southwark for a time hoping someone might recognise me, but no one ever did, so I joined up.' She paused, searching his face. 'Perhaps I shouldn't have come back. There have been times in the past couple of weeks, while they were doing all sorts of tests on me in hospital, that I wondered if it would have been better if I'd never remembered. I even thought of pretending I hadn't and carrying on as Eve Seaton to the end of my days.'

'Why didn't you?'

'Because I loved you, Harry, and we are husband and wife, until death us do part—' She stopped suddenly.

'I know. I dread to think what this is going to do to Pam.'

'You have to tell her.'

'I suppose I must, but it's going to be difficult.'

She watched him struggling with his inner turmoil and understood only too well. Why she didn't tell him about Alec she didn't know, although it had been the last thing Florrie had said to her before she left Manston. 'Don't forget Alec is waiting for you.' In the emotion of her reunion with Harry, she almost had.

She drained the last of the wine in her glass and stood up, only to discover her legs were decidedly wobbly. 'Oh dear,' she said, stumbling against the table.

Laughing, he jumped up to guide her to the bed. 'You never could hold your drink, could you, my love?' He sat her down, took off her shoes and stockings and her dress, then pushed her back onto the pillows and lifted her feet onto the bed, before pulling the eiderdown over her. She was only half aware of what he was doing. 'Harry,' she mumbled. 'I'm sorry . . .'

'You're exhausted,' he murmured. 'And small wonder. I'm shattered myself. I'll try and see you again tomorrow.' He dropped a kiss on her forehead and left her to sleep.

Chapter Fourteen

After a sleepless night which was plagued with visions of Pam and the twins and his cosy home, Harry applied for a pass to spend some time with his wife. He was given twenty-four hours, which did not give him time to do anything to sort out the muddle he was in. How could he turn his back on Pam and his children for an old love? He had loved Julie, still did in a way, but it wasn't the same, or he didn't think it was. Whichever way he went, he was going to break someone's heart. And he dreaded to think what Pam's parents would have to say about it, or his own parents, come to that. Divorce was unheard of in their circles; it carried a stigma not easily overcome. But if he didn't go down that road, he would make bastards of his lovely babies, not to mention ruin Pam's life. And he loved her.

He had to make Julie see that, so he called for her at the hotel and suggested a day out in the countryside. 'Shropshire is a particularly lovely county,' he told her. She was dressed in the floral cotton again, topped with a rose-coloured cardigan. Her fair hair was held back by a blue Alice band. Anyone less like a servicewoman and more like the girl he had married was hard to imagine.

She laughed. 'I know. I was stationed at Bridgnorth.'

There was so much he didn't know about her life since they parted, it was like getting to know a stranger. They took a bus into the hills and set off to walk and talk, catching up on the last four years as old school pals might do at a reunion. It was difficult for him to refrain from mentioning Pam because she was in his thoughts, and difficult for her not to speak of Alec because he had been such a large part of those years, but neither wanted to introduce a jarring note, though both knew they would have to face up to the implications.

They returned in the late afternoon with nothing decided, only to find a furious Pam waiting in the lobby for them. She had evidently been there some time. An ashtray overflowing with lipstick-tinted dog ends and a half-empty wine glass bore witness to that. Seeing the two of them come in, laughing together, inflamed her even further. She stood up. 'So it *is* true! Harry Walker, you two-timing low-down skunk. You bastard! Not content with one wife, you have to be greedy and have two . . .' She looked Julie up and down, a flushed but decidedly attractive Julie. 'As for you . . .' Words failed her and, picking up the wine glass, she dashed the remaining contents in Julie's face. 'Or perhaps you didn't know. Perhaps he kept you in the dark just as he did me.'

'Pam' he said, taking the glass from her hand and setting it back on the table before it followed the wine. 'Calm down, for goodness' sake, everyone is looking at you. I can explain.'

'Are you going to tell me she isn't your wife?' She jerked her head towards Julie who had wiped the wine from her face and was dabbing at the stain on the front of her dress

335

with a handkerchief. 'Because I won't believe you.'

'No, I'm not saying that.' He took her arm. 'Let's go somewhere where we can talk in private.'

'There's nothing to talk about. I've finished with you. I'm going back home to my children. They need me more than you do.' She picked up her handbag and rushed from the room.

He gave Julie a despairing glance and followed Pam out to the street. She walked a few yards, then stopped and turned towards him. She was calmer now, the high colour of anger drained from her face, leaving it pale and drawn. 'That is Julie, isn't it?'

'Yes.'

'How long?'

'How long have I known she wasn't dead?'

'Yes.'

'Only since yesterday.'

'You saw her in Canterbury.'

'I thought I was seeing a ghost, I told you that at the time. I can't tell you how shocked I was when she turned up here.'

'I went to the airfield. They said you'd been given leave. Leave! I don't suppose it occurred to you to come home to me. Instead of that you booked in here.'

'I did not.'

'According to the manager you were. He told me your wife had come to spend her leave with you.'

'I don't know where he got that from. I only went to her room to talk to her.'

'I'm supposed to believe that?'

'Yes. It's the truth.'

'Where have you been today, if not spending your leave

with your wife?' The venom she put into the last word made him shudder.

'Out walking. Talking mostly.' He forced himself to stay calm. Becoming angry would not help. 'She had an extraordinary tale to tell.'

'I bet she did.'

'How did you know she was here?'

'I didn't know. I booked into the hotel and saw her name in the register. Mrs Julie Walker. It confirmed it.'

'Confirmed what?'

'This.' She opened her bag and delved in it for the anonymous letter and thrust it at him.

'Oh, Pam,' he said forlornly, studying the crumpled missive. 'I'd have done anything for you not to have found out this way.'

'Any way would have been bad. You've made a whore of me and bastards of our children.'

He winced. 'Not intentionally, and it can be put right. I'll get a divorce and marry you again.'

'I'm not sure I want to be married to you, Harry Walker.'

'You can't mean that.'

'You never made any secret of how much you loved your first wife. And now she's here and you can go on loving her . . .'

'But I love *you* and you love me and we both love our children. Surely you don't want to throw all that away?'

'I don't know what I want. I don't know anything anymore. I'm going home. Just leave me alone.' She turned on her heel and left him standing. He took a couple of steps to follow her, but changed his mind and went back to the hotel. A confrontation with Julie about the future could not be put off any longer.

* * *

Julie had gone to her room, where she sat at the dressing table and contemplated the wine stain on the front of her dress. It wouldn't come out and the garment was ruined, though that was the least of her worries. She felt desperately sorry for Pam, who hadn't given either of them time to explain what had really happened. She hoped Harry would be able to calm her down; the last thing she wanted was to come between them. She wanted to get out of their lives, but simply disappearing again was not an option because there would have to be a divorce, and something had to be decided about Rosie and that grave. And that meant involving Mr and Mrs Summers and her parents-in-law. She was dreading that.

She stripped off the dress and put her uniform on again. In that she could be Sergeant Eve Seaton which, she realised, was what she wanted to be, and it helped her to be more sensible. She was a mature woman, not the child bride she had once been. Both she and Harry had moved on; the past could not be recaptured.

She turned when she heard a knock at her door and Harry's voice saying, 'May I come in?'

'Yes, of course.'

He came in, almost shamefaced. 'I'm sorry about that outburst, Julie.'

'It was understandable. How did she find out?'

'An anonymous letter.'

'How awful for her. Someone really wanted to cause trouble – and I can guess who.'

'Who?'

'Ted Austen. He's wicked, that man. I can't understand how good people are being killed every day in raids and he seems to survive without a scratch. I hope you managed to

338

persuade Pam I'm no threat to her or your life together.'

'Aren't you?'

'No, of course not. I shouldn't have come up here; I should have left it to a lawyer to sort out the legal side and been content with that. It was silly of me, but I just wanted to see your face when you saw me again and realised I was alive.'

He sat on the bed, his hands dangling between his knees. 'Did you expect us to carry on where we left off?'

'No, Harry. Silly I might be, but I'm also a realist. I couldn't expect you to mourn me for ever, much as it would have boosted my ego.' She sat on the dressing table stool and faced him squarely, putting on a smile to cheer him because he looked so miserable. 'Even before I knew you had married again, I knew it could never happen. We aren't the same people we were. We've grown up a bit, don't you think? You have a life with Pam. She is the mother of your children and you love her. Besides, you are not the only one to find someone else.'

'You mean you married again?'

'No. I didn't dare commit myself that far while I couldn't remember who I was or whether I was already married.'

'But you want to?'

'Yes,' she said firmly. 'I want to. I loved you, Harry. The naive girl I was will always love you for what you once meant to me, for the good times we had together, but I am no longer that naive girl, no longer Julie Monday. We have both changed.'

'Bless you,' he said, reaching out to take her hands in his. 'I'll have to try and make Pam understand that. At the moment she says she doesn't want to be married to me and has told me to leave her alone.'

'She doesn't mean it. Go to her, Harry.'

He raised her hands to his lips in a gentle kiss, then stood up, took a long look at her and left.

Everyone was crammed into the sitting room behind the bakery in Swanton Morley – everyone except the main protagonists. Pam's father was sitting in his rocking chair gripping his pipe, though there was no tobacco in it and he wasn't attempting to smoke it. Jane was dispensing tea to Mr and Mrs Walker and Mr and Mrs Summers. The men were sitting on upright chairs brought in from the dining room, the women sat together on the sofa. It was, so they had decided, a council of war.

'Pam is in a right pickle, poor dear,' Jane said. 'She came back late last night. I gave her one of my sleeping pills and put her to bed.'

'So it's true, then. Julie is alive,' Hilda said.

'Yes. Pam saw them together.'

'So, it must be our Rosie in that grave,' Angela said. She was not concerned with how Pam was feeling or what Harry and Julie would do about their marriage; her only concern was that her daughter should be exhumed and reburied in Scotland.

'It looks like it,' Donald said. 'I can't tell you how sorry I am. It's my fault. I didn't look closely enough before confirming the body was that of my daughter-in-law, but it never occurred to me it wasn't Julie.'

'I want the grave opened,' Angela said. 'Who would be responsible for authorising that?'

'The coroner, I reckon,' Bert said. 'But I don't see what you'd gain by that. Beggin' your pardon, Mrs Summers, but you wouldn't be able to tell it were your daughter, not after all this time. All we can be sure of is that it i'n't Julie.'

'Where's she been all these years, I should like to know?' Jane said. 'Has Harry known all along she wasn't dead?'

'Of course he hasn't,' Hilda said in defence of her son. 'When he came back from Canada, we told him we had buried his wife and he believed us. He had no reason not to.'

'Well, he'll have to divorce her and marry Pam properly,' Jane said. 'Goodness knows I don't hold with divorce; marriage is for life in my book, but I can't see any other way out. We have to think of the children.'

'I agree,' Hilda said. 'I was all for sending Julie packing and saying nothing, but too many people know she's alive now.'

'Not least that creep Austen,' Stuart said with feeling. 'He'll not let it drop if he thinks there's money to be made out of the situation.'

'Seems Julie herself scuppered that by going to see Harry,' Donald said. 'Do you think Austen knows that?'

Stuart shrugged. 'Couldn't say, but it makes no difference, does it? We've got to get everyone out of this mess before the papers get hold of it.'

'You think it will get in the papers?' Jane asked, horrified at the thought.

'I wouldn't put it past Austen to sell them the story.'

'Who's going to be the guilty party in a divorce?' Jane asked, having no interest in Ted Austen's antics.

'Not Harry,' Hilda said. 'He's done nothing wrong.'

'Neither has Pam.'

'I think we're jumpin' the gun,' Bert put in, fiddling with his pipe. 'It's up to Harry and Pam and Julie how this is resolved, not us.'

'That doesn't alter the fact that our daughter needs to be

buried properly.' Angela was determined to have her say.

'She was buried properly,' Donald protested. 'It was a very moving service. The only thing that's wrong is the name on the stone. I suggest we simply have that changed.'

'And the baby?' Hilda asked.

'George is at peace. He is with someone who tried to protect him. Let's leave it like that, shall we?' He turned to Stuart. 'I'll undertake to have the headstone changed if you tell me what you want put on a new one.'

'That seems to be a sensible solution all round,' Stuart said slowly. 'We could have another short service when it's put in place. You'll agree to that, Angie, won't you?'

She sighed. 'I suppose I must.'

'If Harry agrees,' Hilda said.

There was no one there who cared whether Julie agreed or not.

Not a quarter of a mile away, in Honeysuckle Cottage, Harry had arrived and persuaded Pam to talk to him. He had been summoned to the Station Commander's office when he went back to the station after leaving Julie. Two wives turning up to see him in the space of two days was not to be tolerated, he had been told. He was to take a week's compassionate leave and sort himself out and then get back on duty, which was no more than he wanted to do anyway.

'Say what you've got to say, I'm listening,' she said tonelessly. She had arrived home very late the night before after an uncomfortable journey on two crowded trains. Physically tired and emotionally drained, she had few words to say to her mother before she had been packed off to bed with a mug of cocoa and a sleeping tablet. Unused to it, it had felled her like a log and she was still not properly awake.

'There is only one thing I need to say,' he said quietly. 'I love you. There is no one else . . .'

'That's two things,' she said, managing a smile.

'So it is, but they can't be separated.' He reached across the table and took both her hands in his. 'I love you. I want to spend the rest of my life with you. Nothing and no one can alter that.'

'Not even your wife?'

'Not even Julie. Please say you believe me.'

'I want to, but—'

'There are no "buts". Do you love me?'

'Harry, you know I do. Would I be so upset if I didn't?'

'Thank heaven for that.'

'That doesn't mean I'm not angry. I thought I was married, but I'm not, am I? I am what is called an "unmarried mother".' She shuddered. 'Horrible phrase.'

'You are married to me. In the sight of God and in my heart we are man and wife. Nothing can alter that. All we have to do is make it legal.'

'How?'

'Divorce, and after that a quiet marriage ceremony, and we'll be back to how we were.'

'But Julie was dead and now she's alive. I can't help thinking that you loved her once and if it hadn't been for that air raid you'd be with her still.'

'Perhaps. Perhaps not. Who knows? I wouldn't have met you. But it happened and I *did* meet you and I *did* fall in love with you. We have a future together. You must believe that.'

'Oh, Harry.'

He stood up, went round the table to her and drew her to her feet. He put his finger under her chin and tipped her face to his. 'OK?'

'Yes.'

He bent to kiss her, a gentle kiss of reconciliation, but that led to another and another and to each she responded with growing passion. 'Let's go to bed,' he said, making for the stairs.

'But the twins . . . I left them with Mum. I'll have to go and fetch them soon.'

'The twins are in good hands. We need this time together.'

It was not until some time later that she was willing to listen to Julie's extraordinary story. The twins had been fetched and put to bed and their parents were in their favourite position, cuddled up on the sofa. 'Fancy Mum and Dad having to play pig in the middle to that lot,' she said, referring to his parents and Rosie's. 'Do you agree with what they decided?'

'Yes, if Julie does. I can't see her objecting.'

The little twinge of jealousy she felt at the mention of her rival's name was dismissed. After all, Harry had assured her Julie herself had a new love. If that was the case, she wished her well. As far as Pam was concerned she had the best of the bargain.

Julie seemed to have spent an awful lot of time on trains in the last few weeks, most of them crowded. There were mothers, babies and young children coming away from London and the flying bombs, service personnel, British and American, spending their leave looking for a good time in the capital, and others moving from one posting to another. The trains were often shunted into sidings while troop trains or ammunition trains hurtled past them. Sometimes they were diverted because the track had been damaged by bombs. And at night they went at the pace of a snail with a tiny blue light in each carriage, certainly not enough to read by. Taking a journey by train required patience. Julie had plenty of time to think while she journeyed southwards.

The emotion of the last two days had drained her. Finding an identity and then deliberately discarding it had taken all her inner strength, but she was convinced it had been the right thing to do. Harry had a family he loved and she had seen how confused he had been when she turned up, torn by conflicting loyalties. Telling him about Alec had been her way to convince him he was not breaking her heart by choosing to stay with Pam. But what about Alec?

Squashed between a mother nursing a baby and a thin-faced man in a shabby jacket, she went over all the good times she had spent with him, recalled his sense of fun, his infectious laugh, and found herself smiling. He could always make her smile. Hearing he was missing believed killed had been a harrowing time and made her realise just how much she loved him. That had somehow been overlooked in the confusion of regaining her memory and her determination to find Harry. Would Alec still want her when he knew the truth? Would he be prepared to wait while she and Harry divorced or would he reject her? If only she could see him face to face, then she might find out, but that would have to wait until he came back to England.

She left the train at Liverpool Street Station and debated whether to take the Underground or go by bus to Waterloo. She decided she was strong enough now to take the Underground. Being shut in cupboards was a thing of the past and she was a new woman. She arrived back at Manston very late and tumbled straight into her bed. She didn't hear the string of buzz bombs that droned overhead towards the capital.

She was woken early the next morning by Florrie who

had heard she was back. 'Wake up, Eve. I want to know what happened and I'm on duty at eight. Did you see him?'

Julie rubbed sleep from her eyes and sat up. 'Harry? Yes, I saw him.'

'And?'

'We're getting a divorce. He's got a new wife and a couple of babies.'

'Oh. Do you mind?'

'Not at all. What's past is past.'

'You sure?'

'I'm sure.'

'Thank heaven for that. I was afraid you'd want to go back to him. I've got some news for you. Alec's back in England. He's been wounded.'

'Wounded? When? How? How bad is he?'

'He's in hospital at St Hugh's. He caught some shrapnel in the shoulder but it's on the mend.'

Julie scrambled from her bed and began stuffing her things back into her rucksack. 'I've still got three days of my leave left. I'm going to see him.'

'Good idea.' Florrie paused. 'He knows you've remembered. I wasn't going to tell him, but Mum blurted it out, so be prepared for a lot of questions.'

'Do you think he'll still want me?'

'He'll be a fool if he doesn't.' She paused. 'I've got to pick up some bigwig from Adastral House today. I'll take you as far as London, if you like.'

'Thanks, that'll be a help.'

'Hurry and dress, then – I've got to leave in half an hour. You'll have to get some breakfast in London.'

'OK.'

Julie spent the journey telling Florrie about her reunion

with Harry in minute detail. 'He's still incredibly good-looking,' she said. 'When I first saw him, my heart turned over. It was almost as if we'd never been parted, but that didn't last beyond that first meeting. I soon realised we were strangers, and the more we talked the more I knew it had gone, that love we once had. It's a memory, Florrie, a pleasant memory, that's all.'

'And Alec?'

'I love him, Florrie, more than ever.'

'Good.' Florrie negotiated the traffic in Kingsway and drew up at the kerb outside Adastral House. The wall which had been built to protect the windows had been destroyed by a doodlebug and there was nothing left of it. 'You'll be all right from here?'

'Yes, of course. See you later.' She got out, fetched her rucksack from the boot and set off up the road, looking for a bus stop. Everywhere was evidence of new bomb damage. The flying bombs didn't make craters like conventional bombs but the blast from the explosion as they reached the ground was far-reaching and terrifying. If one of those dreadful things could do that much damage, how much more could a whole lot of them do? It didn't bear thinking about.

Before she caught the train to take her away from her youthful past for good, she had one more thing to do. She went to Highgate Cemetery. She wanted to kneel at the grave and say a little prayer for her son, and for Rosie who had died looking after him, and to say goodbye to Julie Walker who was no more. It was Eve Seaton who would finish her service as a WAAF, Eve Seaton who would marry Alec Kilby, if he would have her. Julie Walker would be among those who had disappeared during this dreadful war, never to be seen again.

She had left the cemetery and was strolling down Highgate Hill to the Underground station, at peace within herself, when she found herself walking towards the hated figure of Ted Austen. He had his hands in his pockets and was whistling tunelessly. He was some distance away when he saw her, but then he stopped whistling and hurried forward, grinning in delight. She hesitated, but realising he had lost the power to harm her, strode on, prepared to walk right past him.

She wasn't given the chance. Above her the drone that Londoners had come to know and dread grew louder. People in the street looked up and, as the engine cut out, screamed and ran for cover, including Julie, who dived into the front garden of a villa she was passing and threw herself under a bush, curling herself up into a ball with her arms over her head.

The blast from the explosion sucked the breath from her body and left her gasping for air, her mouth full of dust. Her eyes burnt and felt as if they were being pulled out of their sockets, her ears hummed painfully, filled with the sound of falling walls, breaking glass, shrieks and moans. The bush which had afforded her shelter had been completely stripped of its leaves. She lay there, covered in leaves and broken glass from the windows of the house, too winded to move, convinced that every bone in her body had been crushed. It was worse than the experience in the train because that had taken the force of the blast. It took several huge breaths to fill her lungs with air again and then she tentatively moved her head and then her arms and legs and realised she was unhurt.

It was several minutes before she was able to get to her feet and by then three ambulances, an ARP Warden and two policemen had arrived on the scene. They set to work with commendable efficiency, helping the injured and laying out the dead for removal. Julie walked down to see what she could do to help.

'You all right, miss?' one of the policemen asked her.

She caught sight of the body the man was dragging to the side of the road and shuddered. It belonged to Ted Austen. 'Yes,' she said, suppressing a shudder. 'I'm fine. Can I help?'

It was some time later, when all the injured had been taken to hospital and those who had died had been removed to the mortuary, that she recovered her rucksack from the garden of the villa and was directed to a casualty centre and offered tea and sandwiches and, more to the point, a towel and soap and somewhere to clean herself up and change. After that, assuring everyone she was fine, she was ready to continue her journey to Oxford. She had had another lucky escape, but Ted Austen's luck had run out. Was that God's justice, she wondered? She didn't wish anyone dead, but it seemed to be the final closing of the door on her past life.

Alec saw her walking down the ward towards him and his heart did a quick flip. She was in a civilian skirt, a pale green-and-white-striped cotton. It was topped with a white blouse, the outfit cinched in at the waist with a wide leather belt. Her hair curled in her neck, a little longer than he remembered it. She walked quickly towards him, a tentative smile on her lips as if unsure of her welcome.

He reached his good arm out towards her. 'Eve. You're back.'

She took his hand and bent to kiss his cheek. 'I'm back.' She meant more than just her physical presence, she meant all of her, heart and soul as well. 'All present and correct.'

She paused to study his face. 'How are you?'

'All present and correct.' He echoed her words. 'Or I will be when they let me out of here. Never mind me. What about you? Mum said your memory had returned and you'd disappeared.'

'I didn't disappear exactly. I went to sort things out.'

'And did you?'

'Yes. I can tell you the whole story now from beginning to end. No gaps – or only a few. That's if you want to hear it.'

'Of course I do.'

She pulled up a chair and sat close to his bed, her hand in his while she told him everything, from her first meeting with Harry right up to their last goodbye. 'I was in such a muddle when I first remembered,' she finished. 'But I knew I had to find Harry. I couldn't come to terms with it until I had.'

His grip on her hand tightened. 'And?'

'And we decided the past has gone, dead and buried, along with our son. There is no Julie Walker, only Eve Seaton. There are practicalities, of course. Getting a divorce for one thing . . .' She paused. 'I don't know how you feel about that.'

'If it means you are free to marry me, then I'd welcome it.'

'You still want me? After all that?'

'Of course I do, you goose. Come here.' He pulled on her hand so that she fell across him, and gathering her in his good arm kissed her good and long to the accompaniment of wolf whistles from some of the other patients and their visitors.

'Alec!' She extricated herself at last and sat up.

He grinned at her. 'You wait until I get out of here,

there'll be more of the same. How long do you think the divorce will take?'

'I don't know. Not long, I hope. No one is going to contest it.'

'Then you had better be making plans for a wedding. We'll get married in Harston Church, if that's all right with you.'

'Of course it is. I look upon Hillside Farm as home and your parents as the mum and dad I never had.'

'Oh, Eve,' he said. It was inadequate for what he felt, but he couldn't put it into words. The uncertainty of the last few days had been unbearable: not hearing from her, wondering if her old love would claim her, and being intensely jealous of the unknown man. He needn't have worried; she had come back to him and all was well. He felt a lump in his throat and an unaccustomed wetness in his eyes. This would never do. 'I've got to have some intensive physiotherapy but I'll get leave at the end of it. With luck we should be able to get married before I return to duty.'

'You're going back, then?'

'Got to, haven't I? There's a war to be won.'

A bell clanged loudly and the visitors stood up to leave, including Julie, who knew how strict the staff were about visiting times. 'I'm not due back at Manston until the day after tomorrow, so I've booked in at a bed and breakfast. I'll come and see you again tomorrow. We'll talk some more, make plans.' She bent to kiss him and trooped out with all the other visitors, treading on air. She wouldn't forget Harry again, nor George, but the memories would be happy, not regretful. Alec was right; there was a war to be won, but they would win it and there would be peace – peace to love Alec, have his children and grow old with him.